KIMBERLY AMATO

Cover Art by Deranged Doctor Design

LITES.WBBK1.5252024

Contents

Dedication

For my beautiful wife, Sheila:
You are my North Star,
You are my rock,
You are my dive buddy,
But more importantly -
You are the love of my life.
Thank you for being the other half of my soul, Meine Liebe.

Chapter One

Reilly stayed silent in the car ride to the high school, but once she and Helen were outside of the building, the tension forced her to speak.

"You okay? I know this isn't the typical thing we do on a Friday night, but it means a lot to Jenna." She hoped for a positive response, but when the line didn't have the desired effect, she added, "It means a lot to me too."

Helen's tall, lanky frame sagged a bit as her short hair fell in front of her face. "I know that. I'm just thinking about the premiere we could be attending right now. You understand how important those are to my career."

"And mine." Reilly's hushed tone left a nasty taste in her mouth. If there was one thing she was aware of, it was the demands of Helen's job. Who knew working for a major public relations firm could be so demanding? According to her fiancée, her hours were worse than an emergency room doctors, and more important. The reason was always the same: to lose the client meant she'd lose her job. Reilly hated the comparison. In what world would saving a life being considered on par with spinning the latest faux pas of Helen's wealthy clientele?

"Did you say something?" Helen sneered at the crowd bumping their way through the three sets of auditorium doors. "You think they'd be more organized at this level."

"It's high school, not Broadway, love." Reilly slipped her arm around her fiancée's as they squeezed their way into the open space.

The sound of creaking chairs as they folded down caused Helen's arm to tense. Reilly led them to the last row in the center section. Helen dropped into the aisle chair as Reilly slid her jacket off her shoulders and folded it over the back of her seat.

"If I knew you liked sitting all the way back here, we could save a ton of money on Broadway tickets."

"It's tradition. Trust me, I'd rather sit closer to actually see what's going on." Reilly couldn't stop the smile forming on her face. Her best friend Jenna, the one responsible for the craziness on stage, asked her to sit in the back of the auditorium the first year she took over the drama department. Reilly watched the audience, taking in all the comments uttered during intermission and at the end of the performance to report back to her friend. The first year was a success, and Jenna, being as superstitious as she was, begged for Reilly to sit there every year until she was fired or retired.

That was five years ago, and every year she'd sit alone in the center back row, taking in the reactions of those in front of her. This time was different, and it made Reilly's heart swell with pride. Helen had ensured she had this day off on their shared calendar. It might have been for that other event, but Reilly took it as a win. Helen lived and breathed her work life in Manhattan, but giving Reilly the evening meant more to Reilly than she could ever express in words. Of course, when they got back to the city, she'd make sure to show her in all the right ways.

"I've been thinking . . ." Reilly trailed off. She knew it wasn't smart to bring the conversation to light now, but if it veered off course, the show would be a good distraction.

"About what?" Helen stared at her cell phone, right leg bouncing in what Reilly could only assume was nerves.

"When we got engaged, we never talked about where we'd live."

"Rei." Helen's sighed heavily. They'd started this talk so many times before, and Reilly knew this was her fiancée's way of shutting it down.

"Wait, just hear me out. You're right. It's asking a lot for you to commute all the time into the city. We can live in your place, and I can always visit Mom on the weekends. She seems to be doing better now, so maybe Harrison can make sure she's taking all her meds and getting regular exercise." Reilly hoped saying it out loud would increase her confidence in the decision. It didn't, but Reilly believed marriage was about compromise.

"Yeah, maybe." Helen's dismissive response as her thumbs typed out a message made Reilly's chest tighten.

"Forget I said anything." Reilly watched Helen stare at her device with more intrigue than when Reilly lay nude in bed waiting. "Is everything all right?"

Helen's expression didn't change. The phone went back into her purse as uneasiness rolled off her in waves.

"Helen, talk to me. What's going on?" The lights dimmed to cheers from the audience, but Reilly was solely focused on her fiancée. Reilly took both of Helen's hands in hers, forcing the woman to face her. Helen's hands were clammy, something that only happened in extreme situations.

"We can wait outside in the lobby and come back in when you're ready. No one will notice a thing with an easy escape from the aisle. Okay?" Her soft tone should have calmed Helen by now as it had done many times before during an episode. Yet, Helen's eyes remained glazed over, unfocused, and fear crawled up Reilly's spine as the seconds ticked by.

"I can't do this." The words fell like an anvil between them.

Couldn't do what?

"We'll go—" Reilly's words cut off at the feeling of Helen gripping her engagement ring. "What are . . . Helen, no." Reilly bent her finger, preventing its removal. "Just wait one second." Her hand trembled as she covered Helen's once more. "Please . . ."

"I thought it would be different, but it's not. It's always what you want and never about us. Even moving in together after we're married . . . " Helen shook her head as the crowd laughed at the performance. "I can't even get a word in edgewise with you. Why should I expect tonight to be any different?"

"Helen, that's not fair. Mom was sick. I was her medical proxy—"

"It's always your family, your mom, your fears . . . Did you ever think what all those events were to me? How they helped me get a stable footing at work? No, because your family's needs come before mine." Reilly felt a strong tug on the ring as Helen slipped it from her finger. "I loved you, but I can't be second to them. I need to leave. Please don't follow me." The tears slipping down Helen's cheeks looked so out of place to Reilly. Helen was confident, powerful . . . crying was so unlike her.

Without saying another word, Helen left. Reilly sat back in her chair, her fists clenched as she fought the sobs threatening to erupt. Silently, the tears fell, and her body shook as the laughter continued around her.

As quickly as the pain overtook her body, walls popped into place. If there was one thing Reilly was good at, it was protecting herself. She'd quickly lock herself inside a shell as the bullies tormented her to the verge of tears. Her defense mechanism was strong. As each brick fell into place, Reilly's heart and emotions would slink away to a trunk for safety. Right now, that was all she had to hold on to; that lockbox would keep her from breaking down.

She'd stay until the end for her best friend and sister-in-law. She'd regale her about all the wonders this year's show presented and add comments from the audience. When the time was right, Reilly would tell her about the breakup.

Helen was right; she put her family before her now ex-girlfriend. If Reilly was being honest, she put her privacy first too, but Helen was always considered in that equation. Reilly's rational mind screamed at her to stop the irrational knee-jerk reactions. But she'd been broken once before, and the walls she put up protected her for years. Until Helen broke them down. Reilly was sure this time, no one would get past the barriers anymore. It wasn't worth this pain.

Chapter Two

Five years later....

Reilly jumped up in bed as her phone blared the most annoying sound she could find for her alarm. Her clothes were damp from the previous night's terror-filled dreams. She flipped open the cover of her journal and made a new entry for today's thoughts. One of her closest friends, Lily, also happened to be a licensed therapist. Following Lily's advice, Reilly had begun logging her night terrors in recent years. Like all the nightmares before, this one preyed on her darkest insecurities.

She wrote what she could remember: being on a red carpet, Helen pointing at her and laughing with a stunning beauty on her arm, and the sneering, faceless people, the ones screaming she was a liar or criticizing her books as contrite and trope-ish.

Right now, she was fighting to focus on her breathing as her hand shakily finished the day's entry, using the coping mechanisms Lily had given her to slow the anxiety from becoming all-encompassing. The dreams weren't about Helen or their tumultuous end specifically, but the woman was always prominent in them. She was the manifestation of all the worries that swarmed through Reilly's mind daily. At some point, she knew she'd need to find a new replacement image. Helen's smiling face was not helping her in any capacity.

After such a horrible night, Reilly knew the negative emotions of guilt would remain, regardless of how she fought them. Instead, she leaned into it, put on her oversized sweatshirt, and went to face the morning with a plastered-on smile. The house was quiet as usual this early in the morning. Her mother was still in bed, but the creak of the walls was calming. The howling of the wind outside pushed away some of her discomfort. But if the walls could talk, they'd tell the story of a young woman with aspirations of fame and fortune. They'd entertain you with a tale of woe as Reilly moved into a small studio barely big enough to breathe in, let alone live in, and how her dreams shattered into a million pieces with her debut novel.

Even after her rebirth as someone new in the writing world, they might detail what Reilly deemed her pitiful return home after her father's passing. Helen fought her on all of it, but being the only girl in the family came with certain responsibilities. She'd needed to take care of her mother, the same independent woman who thought her major heart surgery was a minor procedure. The same woman who mistakenly took her dog's medication while regaling Reilly about an RV trip she wanted to plan with Aunt Amy. But her mother never argued when Reilly carried her suitcase upstairs. She never made any attempt to push Reilly back out into the world.

In fact, her mother welcomed her back with open arms, and they fell into a calming routine. Wendy never ventured upstairs, which Reilly called her home office. Reilly never touched the basement tool room or the rooms on the main floor. Reilly laughed at the idea of the walls tellin her life's history. Hopefully, the bedroom walls could be paid off, Reilly thought. They knew her darkest secrets, both good and bad. Not to mention some people she'd rather forget.

Seven years, she mused. At this point, she knew she'd never leave the place. The walls were steadfast in their loyalty to her, spilling nothing beyond the creak or groan of the wind or an old pipe. She was safe here.

Even after the success of her new self-publishing career, fear of failure burned through her veins. The security of these walls gave her the confidence to ignore calls from literary agents or publishing houses who found her old resume online. Her first Manhattan apartment was smaller than a closet and funded by her low-level entry position for an agent, which gave her insight into the business side of being an author, and she hated every moment. If she was being honest with herself, there were only two things she cared to hold on to from her experience.

The first was advice from her original boss in Manhattan. He informed her emotions were weapons to be used to manipulate the masses. A literary agent's feelings should be locked away unless convincing someone to sign a contract or selling their client's manuscripts. She'd adapted it to her life in her hometown.

She was cordial to anyone and everyone. Only her family, chosen and by blood, were privy to the full gamut of her emotions.

The second was Otto Henrich, her former agent. Even though her debut novel he'd published was so poorly received, she'd wanted to quit, Reilly stayed on and found some new clients. He'd helped others find a successful path in the industry, just not Reilly. He'd closed up shop some years ago and became a confidant and, more importantly, a friend.

She trudged down the stairs, flipped on the coffee machine, and waited for the aroma to wake her up. Her shaky body latched onto the morning beverage like a lifeline as these negative thoughts invaded her mind. Knowing the smell would reach her mother as well, Reilly grabbed two mugs from the cupboard.

The soft breathing and delicate scratches on the hardwood floor alerted Reilly to her senior dog making her way to the kitchen. Bubba, a French Bulldog, snorted as she shuffled her way between Reilly's legs to the back door. Like a trained seal, Reilly opened it, revealing a fresh dusting of snow that fell overnight. Bubba huffed and dropped her butt on the tiled kitchen floor.

"It's okay, Bubba. The sun will melt it by mid-afternoon." Reilly motions outside, but the dog didn't budge. "Honey, it's cold. Either go out, or I'm closing the door." A gust of frigid wind blasted them back a few steps. Bubba looked up at her owner with the most pathetic-looking eyes that always worked on. "Okay. Okay."

"No, don't fall for that. Bubba, get your bum outside and go to the bathroom or no breakfast." Her mother's words echoed in the kitchen as the pup rushed outside for fear of losing her treats.

"I got her." Reilly closed the door behind her and waved her mother away. "I saw we were out of the food the vet approved. I can pass by and pick it up if you'd like."

"She doesn't like that. It's all filler foods. Have you read those labels?" Her mother shivered in disgust. "I went to the butcher and got some chicken jerky. She loves it."

"Ma! You know the vet says she needs to eat better. That stuff's too salty for her."

"She's old, like me. Let us enjoy the little things before we're worm food." Reilly knew her mother was struggling with life after surgery. The doctors wanted her to lose weight, but Wendy's short, plump frame never changed. Her smile was halfhearted most of the time as time had left its mark on her face. But not her hair, and for that Reilly was jealous. She took after her father and grayed in her early twenties, and she spent one day every month in the salon to cover it up. Her mother's dark hair with slivers of silver shot through it was dashing, but her mother disliked that too. It was as if her mother thought every part of her was dreadful, topped off with a scar down her chest.

"What? Ma, come on. Yes, you're both old, but I'd prefer if you were both around for a really long time." Reilly held up two mugs, one with a Disney reference and the other a cartoon of a farting dog. "Disney or doggie?" It was little decisions like this that gave her mother pause. Ask her about her plans to remove Helen from the world, and Wendy was on top of it. Ask about a mug, and it might require a full hour or two discussing the merits of each.

"I'm not in a miracles kind of mood." The quickness of her decision both surprised and worried Reilly.

"You okay?" Reilly's concern washed away whatever residual fears remained from her dreams. Mindlessly, she grabbed a seven-day pill container and popped the current days' worth of medications into her hand.

"Just not in the mood for drama today." Reilly immediately knew the reason behind her mother's response. She'd seen it many times in her life, and it broke her heart every single instance it happened.

"I told you not to answer the phone when he calls. I can block him on everything so he can't get through." Reilly felt the anger boil up to the surface faster than she liked. If she had her way, her uncle would have a one-way ticket to Mars.

"He's my brother, not a spam political call." Wendy's raw emotions spilled out, laced with anguish more than anger. "He's having a rough go of it lately." As the youngest child, Reilly couldn't understand the oldest sibling protectiveness of her older brother. Maybe it was an inherited trait from her mother, another eldest child. But as the baby of the family, she knew how to undercut and slice anyone down with an innocent smile. She would rip the man her mother was related to a new one in broad daylight to prove a point. It was another reason she refused to call him uncle. In her mind the man never earned the right to the title. In the end, he was the epitome of evil.

"You had bypass surgery and the man never called to check up on you." Reilly's skin blazed with fury.

"He called . . ." Wendy tried to dismiss the concern, but Reilly was having none of it.

"When Grandma died, he cheered about getting an inheritance. When Dad died, he never showed up to the funeral. In fact, he called from Italy, bragging about his newest business venture! What kind of man—"

Reilly watched her mother fold into herself as she organized her morning pills. "He's family, Reilly."

"No, he's a leech and user. We can't choose what family we're born into, Mom. But I promise you, the friends you've made along the way—Harrison's and my friends that call you mom with the respect and love you deserve—they're your family. That man? He's the epitome of everything wrong in this world."

"You might think that, but he's still my brother. No matter how vile a human being he is . . . he's still . . . I don't know." Wendy crossed her arms as she stared at the pills in front of her.

The ache in Reilly's chest was so strong she could feel it in her toes. Wendy always made the world safer for her, but Reilly couldn't return the favor. Not with this. Not now. Not ever. "Take the blue one first with water only. Thirty minutes later—"

"I know. If he calls again, just let me handle it." Reilly heard the defeat in her mother's voice. There was no changing her mind.

"I'll respect your wishes, but I can't promise how I'll react to him in person. The man is a cancer to our happiness and doesn't deserve the time of day from us. Let him have his new friends, life, or whatever. If not for Grandma he'd be destitute, divorced for the tenth time, or dead. Besides, we both know his actions just sucked life out of her. If he treated her like a mother and not a bank, maybe she'd have had a few more years with us. And watching how he hurts you . . . history is repeating itself. Just promise me you'll put yourself first. Whatever that means."

Wendy stood without saying another word and swung open a lower cabinet door. Bubba bounced back and forth as Reilly shook her head. Avoidance was her mother's favorite action. If Reilly was honest with herself, it was hers as well. "You want your breakfast, my love?"

"Ma . . ."

"It's too early for this, Reilly."

The conversation was over. So, Reilly continued her morning routine, making her mom oatmeal and some cereal for herself. Maybe she'd revisit the point later if her mother was receptive. She turned around in time to watch Wendy down the rest of her pills with one gulp of coffee. "Ma! What did I just say? The doc told you to take the blue one and wait thirty minutes before the rest of them. Come on, it's not that hard."

"I heard you. I heard them too. I waited a few minutes, but you have to stop being such a stick in the mud. They all go to the same place." Her mother's nonchalance was something Reilly regularly fought against daily. Her mother didn't understand what Reilly saw during Wendy's recovery. The once strong woman that carried her around, was weak, attached to wires and tubes. She wanted to trust the woman to take care of herself, but her mother continued to procrastinate her health away. How could Reilly explain that level of fear to her mother? Instead, she held it inside and put those emotions into her characters.

"The medication won't be as effective if you don't follow instructions."

"Reilly, I'm in my seventies. Give me and the dog a break. Just be happy I'm downing this pharmacy worth of pills every morning." Her mother reached down with a spoon full of apple cinnamon oatmeal to share with Bubba. "We do this every morning, Rei, and it always remains the same. Just let it go, love. I'm too old to start doing things over for you."

"Fine." Reilly gave up. She just needed the conversation to be over. "But next time we see the doc, I'm telling her the truth."

"Narc." Her mother's laugh lightened the mood in the kitchen, but that was how Wendy changed topics.

Reilly flopped into the chair across from her mother, wanting breakfast to be over already. Once she knew her mother had her meal, she could get to work.

Everything from her nightmare to the events of the previous evening begged to come out in a new chapter.

"I didn't hear you come in last night. I assume your date went well?" The suggestive tone made Reilly fidget in her seat. Her mother's wiggling eyebrows added to the discomfort.

"I doubt you could hear me with your tablet blaring. What were you watching anyway?"

"Some action flick with half-dressed men. Now talk."

Reilly didn't want to. She wanted to forget the week of discomfort leading up to a forgettable date and the subsequent lack of sleep. She didn't need to date anyone at this point in her life, or ever. Lily would tell her all about the trauma response and how in time she'd be ready to open herself up again. Reilly usually replied there were toys for what she needed. Nothing else was worth it. After that, their online calls would devolve into silence or random sexual references.

"You going to answer me?" her mother prodded.

"It went how they all go, Mom. Can we talk about something else?" Reilly really didn't want to relive the mortification.

"That's it? You going to see her again? Betty says—"

"I don't really want to hear what Betty says, Mom. The girl was pretty. She had a good job. You and your online friends were nice to set me up." The nerves crept in again and Reilly wanted to run. Maybe her mom would take the short version to her friends and they'd stop trying to set her up. "She took me to the city, we had a nice dinner, and then she took me to see *Chicago*."

Reilly knew her mother wouldn't like that part of the conversation. Reilly hadn't been back in any theater since Helen broke off their engagement. It was a triggering environment.

"You made it through the performance! That's a good thing, right?" Wendy seemed hopeful, and she was right that Reilly made it through. But barely.

"Yeah, no. The minute we sat down, she wouldn't stop whispering . . . you know . . . things in my ear. I couldn't enjoy the show at all."

"Ahh, well, you're a beautiful woman who deserves to enjoy some . . . things." Her mother's smirk caused Reilly's cheeks to flush. "Did you?"

"Mom!" Reilly was no prude, and she wasn't averse to having sex on the first date if she wanted to. In this case, Reilly was definitely not interested, but Wendy's bouncing eyebrows certainly were. "No, I did not indulge. I mean she was hot, but I swear some of the things she wanted to do sounded physically impossible."

"That's why you need to do yoga. Get some flexibility in those hips. Aunt Amy swears by it!"

"Oh my God, I did not need that image in my head." Reilly downed the rest of her coffee to cover the embarrassment scorching her skin. "I'm going to get to work." Reilly filled her coffee mug with a second cup.

"Reilly, we're both old, not dead. Sex has no age limit!"

Reilly wanted to bleach her brain after her mother forced more images into her head. It was moments like this that another closet apartment in Manhattan sounded like a dream. "Mom, please stop. I want more than just sex, okay? So, please, no more blind dates or visuals that will haunt me until I die."

"Fine. I got you." Wendy's words felt off as far as Reilly was concerned. Her mother never gave up that easily. "Just remember, good ones don't come with batteries. They take work to keep going."

"Oh, dear goddess. Bubba, please save me." Reilly had adopted the dog years ago in a shelter. It took one week before the dog ditched her for Wendy. She didn't blame her one bit, considering her mother treated her like a princess. Though right now, Reilly begged for her help changing subjects.

"Fine, I'll stop. You're too easy to fluster, Rei. You need to lighten up and get out from behind your computer screen. Maybe you'll meet a nice girl out there in the great wide open!"

"Mom, I'm a writer. Sitting in front of my laptop screen is part of the job description. Besides, I do leave the house."

"Ahh yes, visiting Jenna, getting coffee with Jenna, or hanging out with Harrison and/or Jenna and maybe the kids. None of that counts. Consider a dating app or an online group for sexy, middle-aged, queer women."

"Yeah, no thanks."

"Rei, you've got to get out and live a little. You've been here for me since I got sick, and I know me lying technically dead on the table during heart surgery scared the bejesus out of you, but that's life, sweetheart. One day you're going to bury me next to your father, and then what? I don't want you alone in this house forever." Her mother gripped her hand tightly. The thought of Wendy leaving her made her stomach lurch. Being alone was one of her worst anxieties, but she wasn't about to express that to anyone.

"I'll adopt some old dogs and write about a great love lost in my books. Ma, I'll be fine." Reilly leaned into her sarcasm to push her emotions to the backburner.

"You're not listening, but fine. As for being buried, I better be in the plot next to your father. I don't want to be on top of that man for all eternity."

Reilly cringed at the image her mother's words created in her mind. "What are your plans for today?" Reilly was desperate to change the conversation.

"Working on the van before your Aunt Amy screams we're not taking it anywhere. Then book club at the library in the afternoon. We're picking a new series to start soon. Want me to toss M. E. Kline's name into the suggestion box?"

"No, they might connect the dots and start digging into . . . I can't handle the backlash. Just let it go, for me?"

"Rei, recommending a book is not the same as me saying my daughter writes under the name of M. E. Kline, let's read her stuff. Speaking of which, when is the next book coming out? I need to know what happens."

"Maybe not, but you know I don't want . . . I just like the anonymity. As for the next in the series, it'll come out when I'm inspired to finish it. Right now, I feel like I need a break from it all. I've got the entire thing outlined, it's just the execution feels off." Reilly sipped her coffee once again, hiding behind it like a shield. "I better go sit in front of my screen and hope the words can pulse out of my fingers and into the void—"

Wendy coughed on her sip of coffee. "Reilly Vail! Warn me before you say something like that!"

"You dirty old lady, you were talking about vibrators not too long ago." The slight laughter was something Reilly cherished when she found it. Her mom meant well, but overall, she was just a mom being a mom. Reilly was clear. She needed to maintain a distance from her pen name, M. E. Kline, and Reilly Vail. She had her reasons, and hopefully people would understand them.

Chapter Three

Papers riddled with red ink covered Breanna's desk. She'd come into the office with the sunrise, hoping the numbers were better this week. But they weren't. *Why would they be? They've been teetering on the cliff for months.* Breanna's mind raced around the pages, looking for anything to give her hope. Her leg bounced, her heart rate increased, and Breanna felt an anxiety attack taking hold. She grabbed her tablet, flipped through several screens, and started reading. She slipped into a fantasy world where money wasn't an issue and she didn't feel like a failure.

She rested her sneakers on the edge of her desk as her eyes scanned the book she was engrossed in. She dug her right hand into a bag of chocolates and popped one in her mouth, the sweetness calming the emotions she was trying to forget. A notification of a new email popped up on the screen, followed by Breanna's deep sigh. Once she finished the book, Breanna would decipher a plan to turn the company around. But not until she learned what happened—

"No! Come on!" Breanna yelled, her feet slamming onto the ground. She swiped her hand across the screen a few times. "Where's the link to the next book?"

"Should I be worried?" The sound of her business partner's voice caused Breanna to drop the tablet.

Kai unbuttoned their suit jacket, cracked their neck, and slid into a chair across from Breanna. "If you're screaming at your tablet, I assume things aren't going well with the latest acquisition? Have you called the agent back? Offered a better deal? What's the status?"

Breanna hated facing the reality of her recent emails and preferred hiding in her own little world. It was safer, but not realistic. Switching to her email app confirmed her fear as her anxiety returned with a vengeance. It was moments like this she regretted going into production. "Her agent's refusing to pass along our proposal. She wants . . . Are you kidding? She wants us to double the offer. That's ridiculous. We can't afford that." She rubbed her eyes, trying to push the frustration to the back of her brain. Breanna felt a glimmer of rage as she thought more about it. The agent was playing games with her future, and she hated it.

"Dammit." Kai's lithe frame visibly tensed. Breanna knew her partner was holding back their anger. "Did you offer a percentage of the profits?"

"Already in the contract. We gave them everything they asked for and then some. I'm sure her agent read the industry reports and knows we're in an awkward position." The previous conversations Breanna had with the agent still pissed her off beyond measure. She'd been hoping to find some common ground with the latest proposal, but it was clear she hadn't.

Her anger swelled at the long hours and days she wasted working through the new offer. She cut back on several things to ensure the offer met the demands, just to find out via email they wanted double. Word was out K.B. Studios was desperate, and people could smell the blood in the water.

"If we don't guarantee by the end of business today, they're accepting a different deal."

"What? No one knew these books existed until K.B. Studios wanted to secure the rights. You're telling me we were just used for a bidding war among the bigger conglomerates?" Kai was angry, an emotion they rarely showed within the walls of their company. Breanna felt responsible for it all. *I need a better solution so no one ends up in a critical situation.* Negative images from her youth filtered into her mind. Breanna wasn't above working a crappy job, but she couldn't go back to the roach infested apartment.

"Did they even read the series?"

"Doubtful."

"Any suggestions?" Kai's tone threw Breanna back into the terrifying reality of unemployment and possible debts they could never overcome. "We need something, Bre."

"We have *Nightmare on the Island*—"

"While that might be a compelling documentary, that's not going to keep our doors open. We need distribution deals for projects that have the possibility of sequels and maybe spin-offs. *Nightmare on the Island* is literally a one and done film. I don't see that creating an income stream strong enough to counter our debts."

"I know that, Kai!" Her fear-laced scream filled the room. Breanna was aware of the financial constraints K.B. Studios was facing. The concerns kept her up late at night, but Kai was being realistic. There might not be a lot of options left, but Breanna believed there had to be another way. She owed it to her staff to find something.

She'd secured the sale of international rights of their film catalog months ago to cover their production costs and basic payroll. While their product was now streaming across the globe, there wasn't a lot of money left in their accounts. Breanna could use her savings to cover a month at most, but then she'd be unable to *cover her own bills.*

To make matters worse, some of the smaller companies Breanna and Kai had fostered relationships with were drying up. Breanna's cynical mind wondered if the other companies were holding off, waiting for them to die out. Like vultures, they'd swoop in and buy off the result of all her hard work for peanuts on the dollar.

Part of her wanted to turn back the clock and go back to the beginning. Sure, when Kai and she started this company, things were rough. They had to overcome numerous obstacles, some they created and others that were put in front of them by others. But no matter what they faced, Breanna always felt in control of the situation. Right now, regardless of her positive thoughts, she felt like the captain of a sinking ship. Beyond the money, having their production partners taking credit for most of their work was depressing. Kai simply referred to it as survival of the fittest in the cutthroat industry.

Breanna screamed a few four-letter words in her head each time their company was a footnote. Kai would pour themselves a glass of whiskey and sip it silently. *I'd love a glass right now. It has to be happy hour somewhere. Stop it, Bre. You can't risk someone with a cell phone recording you and creating a half-baked story of the crazy lesbian CEO.*

"I know you have a desk full of manuscripts. Something good has to be in there." Breanna knew what Kai was doing. This was their way of methodically going through things in order to find a pattern or solution. It's why they'd worked so well together over the years. While Breanna was tangential and might forget where she started, Kai was systematic in their approach.

"I do, and I guarantee you the authors would sign in a heartbeat." Breanna felt her body slump in defeat.

"So, why aren't we going that route?"

"Cookie-cutter scripts with the usual tropes. No new take or execution."

"Bre, people love those types of stories. It's something they're accustomed to. We get a good cast, it could work."

"Kai, it might keep us afloat for a bit, but we need more than one project to survive this. We need a series of solid films to move us out of this . . . hole." Breanna waved her hands over the papers riddled with red ink as if to explain her words. "We make one mistake and we'll be right back where we started. Hell, we don't even know if we could get funding for these films."

"So, we buy it, gut it, and rebuilt it to suit our needs."

"Do we have the time, let alone the budget for that kind of work?" Breanna wasn't playing around. She knew Kai was trying to help, but they couldn't waste money on a project that couldn't guarantee a significant return. The companies that answered their calls did not want romantic comedies or horror films, which made up the pile in her drawer.

"We could fund it, then sell all the rights to the film and recoup what we could."

"You know how long it takes for that to happen. I'm not trying to be negative here, but we know people aren't going to buy a film before it's shot from a company that might go under before it's finished." It hurt to say those words. Breanna visibly shivered at the thought.

"Seacliff Studios wants to know what we're presenting and what our schedule might look like going forward. If we don't have something, they'll break our contract. There's no coming back from that, Bre. If they walk, we really have no options left."

"I know." When they'd added the clause to their agreement, Breanna was riding high. Her slate was full of interesting projects that kept investors happy. Now she had one contractually obligated company waiting on a project to knock their socks off. Nothing in her drawer of drivel would sate that. "I can't pull the next Sundance surprise out of thin air, Kai. We can only work with what's in front of us." The frustration burned through her body. She stood and left her office to gain some clarity.

A migraine threatened from the tightness in her neck. Breanna had lofty dreams, and this unyielding stress was never part of them. When they started the company, they promised to swing for the fences with every project they developed. Somewhere along the line, they strayed from that premise and played it safe. They'd lost their identity, and it showed in the product they produced.

"Maybe we need to take one colossal risk and jump into the deep end. We signed the unsignable, filmed the unadaptable . . . We need to remind people of who we are."

Breanna knew they needed a plan. She had a wild one that swam behind her eyes as she slept for the last two weeks. If it failed, she wouldn't work in the industry ever again, as her decision-making would be called into question. But if it worked, K.B. Studios would be out of the danger zone for quite some time. It was a risky move and would put her in a terrifying position, but what was worse than what she was facing now?

Breanna needed Kai to take that leap of faith with her. She stormed back into her office on a mission. "I have an idea, but it's a long shot."

"Breanna, I'm on a—"

Breanna waved off her partner's concerns. She needed to get this out before she lost her nerve. "M. E. Kline's Shadows Rise series is just screaming for film adaptation."

"You got Kline to sign? Studios have been clamoring for the rights for years! Consider us on board with whatever you need. Let's set up a meeting in the future to discuss details." The voice on speakerphone sent ice running through Breanna's veins. The distinct sound of the call disconnecting forced bile to rush up her throat.

"What the hell was that? You called Seacliff? Why didn't you tell me?"

"You were outside, so I called Michaela to ask for more time. I didn't expect you to say anything. But then you just threw out this outrageous idea, which she apparently loves!"

"We don't have the rights to the books, Kai." Now Breanna wanted to scream. Kline was considered a lucrative white whale. People kept chasing the author down, but no one landed the deal. Breanna had just walked into a steaming pile without a shovel. Worse yet, she dragged Kai with her.

"Then we better get them," Kai said with a confidence Breanna wished she had.

"Kai, no one even knows who Kline is. It was a wild shot in the dark. I have no idea how to even start—"

"I'll do some digging. I better read the books too so I know what we're producing."

Breanna slumped into her seat as Kai stormed out of her office on a mission. Breanna scanned the internet for information on the author, finding links to her website and various social media profiles. Breanna knew the website host information was probably private, but she searched the WHOIS database anyway and only found the hosting company's information. *Why would it be that easy?*

A quick click on each social media account left Breanna groaning again. Direct messaging was turned off.

Great. How the hell am I going to find you?

Without a direct way to contact the author, how could they negotiate a book deal? They needed to find her agent, social media team . . . anything that could help them find the elusive writer.

The faces of their office employees as well as the crew she loved to work with flashed before her eyes in a blur. The weight of responsibility pressed into her chest like a boulder. Then there was Kai.

Kai would be hired in a minute. The thought calmed her for a moment. *But where would that job be?* Her stomach twisted in knots. Kai was her best friend in this busy city. *What would life be like without them for the first time in years?* Bre sat back in her chair as fear overwhelmed her.

***

"You're not seriously forcing that, are you? Reilly, come on. Alexi betrayed Katya in book two. He has to earn her forgiveness, not buy it. I don't care if he has money or whatever. It just feels wrong." The voice screeched from the speaker system. *Leave it to Lily to be the overly dramatic one.*

Reilly's weekly online call with her friends was a hassle today. She was stuck with one particular section of her book, and Reilly trusted her close group of friends to help her sort it out. Right now, the response wasn't what she expected.

"I can just disconnect the call, you know!" Reilly ran her hands through her hair. She had written herself into a corner, but a rewrite would set her back several months. "It's the only way to make the plot move forward."

"Yeah, but Lily has a point," Gina smirked. "Even if she had to be all over the top about it."

"You're my friends and I love you all, but why do you have to be so nitpicky about everything I do? No one will notice, Gina. And if they do, maybe the books are just not for them." Reilly knew her frustration wasn't their fault, but she needed to write, not edit. "I shouldn't have even mentioned it to you all. I don't have time to . . ." She stalled, feeling the pressure. "Look, I have a deadline with my editor."

"Rei, we might be friends, but we're also invested in your writing. You can't just do that to Katrina. It would cheapen the arc you gave her. Plus, why would she just willingly allow her twin back in her world after what he'd done?" Vera's voice cut above all the other arguments.

"Because blood is thicker than water." Reilly didn't want to admit the truth—the plot needed it. *Why the hell did I publish a release date on my website?* If she hadn't done that, this writer's block she was struggling with wouldn't be an issue.

"Just stop for one second, okay? Look at us."

Reilly reluctantly stopped writing and spun her chair to face her online friends. "I love that you all care, but this really isn't the point—"

"No, it isn't, but if you give him instant forgiveness without proving he's changed, the rabid fans will feel cheated. In the previous two books, you've given Katrina a deeper character arc. She's not alone, and she's finding connections with her small group of people. Spoiler alert, because Lily is still on book one, but her brother crosses a serious line. If mine did that to me, I wouldn't just allow him back into my world anytime soon." Natalie leaned back in her chair, having said her piece.

She knew they were right, but Reilly needed suggestions, not more problems. At the worst point in her life, these individuals had connected with her through her books. They would constantly post on her social media with accolades and quotes that struck a chord. With her sister-in-law's support, Reilly slowly started replying, each day a little bit more than the last one, chipping away at those walls she was so proud of.

Jenna insisted she host an online event to answer questions from her readers. At first, Reilly was against it. She'd have to show her face and talk to strangers about her characters when she used a pen name to stay relatively hidden. Surprisingly, Helen had been the one to suggest a way to compromise and protect her anonymity. They hired the book cover artist to create a profile image from the upcoming second book. That way she could leave her camera off and promote the book but still answer with her authentic voice.

While some people were upset they couldn't unmask M. E. Kline and signed off, most stayed. It turned out better than expected. As her fans spoke about how the series affected them, warmth spread through her entire being. Some would speculate what would happen in future installments, and others obsessed about small tidbits in her books she forgot about. She'd even taken notes to revisit those parts to close some loopholes she didn't know she'd created.

"I'll take it under advisement." That was her canned response when she wanted the conversation to end. While her friends' points of view were valid, Reilly knew the bigger picture, and the reconciliation needed to happen. She would have to adjust the execution and hope readers would accept it. Reilly really needed this book to be finished already. *Maybe even give M. E. Kline a rest after this one? But then you lose fans, lose money, lose everything all over again.* The fear always won out.

"Excellent! Now, tell us about your date," Vera piped in. "Apologies for the sound. Taking lunch at the site today." They'd discussed her friend's job at the construction company being busier than usual. Vera blamed it on the change of seasons, but Lily argued that New Mexico had no such thing. Until there was snow, there was no real delineation between the times of year. The group often broke into random disagreements about the weather that ended up with drinks and laughter.

Reilly wished for such a distraction right now. "Did you get to the city? How did you feel about it?" Sadly, Camila's follow-up question prevented that escape route.

"I did." She'd already given her mother the short version of the disaster of her date. There was a lot more to it, but she wasn't in the mood to share with her friends or anyone beyond her tearstained pillow. "It sucked, but I managed. Overall, the date was a bust. Just not my type." If she mentioned all the dirty talk, the group would have descended into a downward spiral of obscene jokes and sexual references, and Reilly didn't feel like being the reason for the humor. She'd have to play along and not deal with the emotions playing ping-pong in her chest.

"Sorry, Reilly. But hey, silver lining, you finally went back to the city again." Lily deflected the other questions that remained on the tips of her friends' tongues. Out of everyone, Reilly and Lily understood each other the best. Both had experienced horrible relationships that tore them down to their core. It's why she was Reilly's shoulder to cry on when Reilly needed it.

"I'll take it, Lily. Let's just hope the next one doesn't slurp her coffee." Vera's laughter meant the comment landed wrong. "That's not . . . no. Do not go there, V. Please."

"But I mean—"

"V, isn't lunch almost over?" Camila cut her girlfriend off. "Did you have a proper one, or did you have a soda and a muffin again?"

"Would you look at the time! Love you all. Gotta run." Before anyone could even say goodbye, Vera's square disappeared from the screen.

The call only lasted for another ten minutes before everyone's break times ended. Reilly's mind slipped back to when Jenna hosted random meetups online to promote Kline's books. She'd benefited from it, but never want to run another event. It worsened when the world caved in on her. Reilly allowed herself to slip into oblivion and avoided events completely. That's when Lily reached out to her to touch base.

It was a kindness Reilly needed to get out of her funk. She'd replied, and that led to them forming a small group to chat. Lily, Vera, Natalie, Camila, and Gina were there without judgement. Reilly didn't have to connect with them at all, but she made a counteroffer.

Once a month, they would all join a virtual meeting, and she would read the latest chapters to gauge their interest. Once the signed nondisclosure agreements were in place, the meetings began. Other authors told her she was crazy for allowing people into her process this way. Her biggest concern was listeners claiming they created the chapter, character, or situation within the pages. It's why she had a lawyer come up with the NDA with clauses protecting Reilly from everything she could think of and more.

In the end, the meetings became less about the books and more of a girls' night. Sure, they lived all over the United States, but spending the hour together was therapeutic. Whether it was Lily's love life, Gina's kids running amok, Vera and Camila randomly showing up in a shared square, or Natalie filling them in on the latest romantic celebrity gossip, the meetings were lifelines for them all. Especially for Reilly, who even now struggled to open up to anyone.

Maybe they're right. Could I push the deadline?

Her phone buzzed on the desk. The face of her social media manager, Ellen, appeared on the screen.

"Hey, Ellen, I assume you calling instead of texting me is not a good thing. What's going on?"

"Good afternoon, Ms. Vail. I apologize for the call, but I'm in the car. We received an email from a Breanna Blaine regarding contacting you. I verified the name corresponds to a legit company, K.B. Studios, in New York City. I can forward it to you if you'd like?"

"First, I keep telling you to call me Reilly. Ms. Vail makes me feel old and decrepit. I appreciate you verifying the name and directory. I'm sure it's nothing, but you forward it to me. Did they give any indication they knew my whereabouts or real name?" Anxiety crawled up her spine with the last sentence. If this Breanna person could find out her identity, it meant anyone could. That might lead to cross-referenced links and images popping up. The last thing Reilly needed was her past history with her ex-girlfriend becoming social media fodder. Then again,

Helen could be behind all of this. She hadn't thrown Reilly under the bus yet, but Reilly felt like it was only a matter of time.

"Not at all, Ms.— Reilly. Just seemed like a generic inquiry about your book rights."

"Okay, thank you, Ellen. How's your sister doing?"

"Nelle is doing well. Excelling in high school, despite her uncool sister hanging around more often. She complains to me about your third book taking so long. She has no idea that I work with you." The laughter on the other end of the line calmed Reilly's fears. Even as a business associate, Ellen was part of her small core circle. She wasn't sure if Nelle knowing her identity would be a problem, but it wasn't something she felt comfortable with.

"Maybe I can send her a signed copy of the third one before it's readily available. If I can ever finish it, that is." The weight of the truth hung in the air like lead. Books one and two flew out of her mind like water from a faucet. Sure, there were minor bumps in the flow of her creativity, but she always sorted through it. This time, nothing seemed to work. The third installment felt forced, rushed, and as if nothing within the pages felt right. The outline flowed well, but the words were slow to appear.

"That'd be amazing. Thank you."

"Always. Have a great day!" Ellen returned their farewell before the line disconnected. Within seconds, Reilly's phone beeped with a new email. The forwarded message was simple enough. They wanted to know how to contact M. E. Kline regarding their book series Shadows Rise. It went further, asking for information or to send the original correspondence to the author directly.

Reilly was at a loss. The email was polite but felt urgent, like time was of the essence. Yet the tone made her feel oddly comfortable. All the previous companies who contacted her promised her fame, fortune, and all the things she had no desire to own. One company even offered to fix her lead character to a proper straight and powerful male. Reilly laughed at that one before saving the correspondence in a *never work with* folder. This was the first time she had the desire to reply, and that raised concerns within her.

They want a series, Rei! Not two books with the hopes of a third. Imagine what they would say if you don't write the next book? Reilly's mind was in overdrive. She had other things to focus on right now, and emailing Ms. Blaine back would have to wait.

So she focused . . . on the blank screen on her computer where her story should be.

Chapter Four

Chapter Four

Breanna emailed M. E. Kline a week ago with hopes of some acknowledgment. Yet, her inbox was filled with everything but the email she wanted. Breanna had been searching nonstop for the elusive author, only to come up empty-handed. Websites, social media, and all domain registrations led to dead ends. She was running on empty.

"How the hell are you so well hidden?" Her sleep-slurred words betrayed her put together exterior. The stress was getting to her, and no amount of espresso would fix it.

"People do not just disappear in today's world. Someone has to know something."

"Hey." Kai slipped into the office, dark circles under their red-rimmed eyes. The guilt Breanna felt was palpable. "I found something that . . . well, it's a long shot."

"I'll take anything at this point."

"Otto Henrich, owner of the now defunct Henrich Literary Agency, touted M. E. Kline as the next up-and-coming author before book one even launched."

"Wait, as I understand it, Kline is a self-published author. That leads me to believe they handle everything from writing, editing to marketing and whatever else they need. It also means they pocket the profits. Why would they pay a literary agent when you're already doing all the work? It's not like they're actively shopping the rights to their books, so it seems pointless."

"They are, but back in the day they traditionally published through their agent Henrich. Kline's debut novel, some crime drama, launched and tanked. Initial reviews from outlets were good, but once the book was in the hands of the public, it didn't bode well. Reviews went from 'this is an okay first entry' to 'this person should never write again.'"

"Let me guess, the publishing house ended the deal and Henrich dropped Kline." That would explain why the author hid underground. Breanna knew what it was like having to rebuild your reputation after an unpleasant situation. K.B. Studios were smack-dab in the middle of one such episode. "But why stay under the same name? Like any entity, they could have closed up shop and started fresh. Why stick with that name?"

"Maybe it has some significance to them? Would you want to change K.B. Studios' name? It's our initials, and we're proud of it. Changing it would feel wrong, like we cheated the system to try something new. I think it's admirable that they stuck it through. Besides, according to a friend of mine, Kline had another book that Henrich was pitching. No one picked it up. Since no one was biting on the offering, they parted ways amicably. Not sure if that new book was part of the Shadows Rise series or something else. What I do know is Henrich continued to sing Kline's praise even after they went solo."

"That doesn't sound like a long shot, Kai. It feels like the best lead we've had all week. They must have something we can work with." The day seemed to pick up with this new information. The agents K.B. Studios dealt with in the past were all about their current clients. If one was still promoting someone without financial gain, maybe there was a more personal connection. If Henrich could see the benefit in adapting Kline's books to the screen, his words could carry more weight than just a monetary contract.

Maybe there was something more to their relationship?

Breanna's thoughts were interrupted by Kai dropping a piece of paper with a phone number in front of her. "There's a bit more to it." Kai mumbled.

Her stomach rolled as Kai fell into the chair opposite her desk. What more could there be to this situation? A book was launched, it failed, everyone moved on. It seemed rather simple.

"If this is about the bad reviews, every author gets them now and again. Just like us, they're entitled to a dud." She didn't want to dwell on the negatives of the situation. Regardless of the exhaustion rumbling in her veins, she needed to call this agent and find Kline now. "Have you called this number already?"

"No." Breanna was at a loss with her business partner. Kai was always forthcoming with information, almost giddy when they had new leads. This calm, almost depressed look was freaking her out. "Look, from an industry standpoint, it wasn't that horrible. But the readers, man they were vicious. They went after Kline on a personal level, and then they attacked Henrich and his agency. No one ever found out or shared where Kline lived, but they brutally went after them on social media. Even the first book of the Shadows Rise series has some one-star reviews mentioning the previous books. Some comments asked if they hired a ghostwriter since the book was so much better than their first. Why subject themselves to this? Why not write under a different moniker?"

"When we find them, we can ask why they continued writing under M. E. Kline. Until then . . ."

"Right." Kai's gaze burned into Breanna's chest. She could tell her business partner had second thoughts about finding Kline. She could understand it. The anonymity of the internet bred a new version of human excrement that Breanna wished she could flush into oblivion. The cruelty, mob obsession, and destructive nature of it all made her sick. If this had come up earlier in their business, they'd leave the author alone. But they couldn't afford to do that. Not this time.

"So, we assume the online abuse forced them into hiding and proceed accordingly."

"It would be a safe bet. It also means we need to tread lightly." Kai slipped forward and dialed the number on Breanna's desk phone. Normally, the invasion of her personal space would be enough to force Breanna to get up, but today she was too tired to care.

"Hello?" A woman's voice came through the speaker.

"Hi, my name is Breanna Blaine. We were given this number as a contact for Otto Henrich. Is he available?"

The woman didn't answer. Breanna listened as muffled sounds filled the room. She closed her eyes and focused on the tones of the people talking on the other end. One was lighter, like the voice of the woman who answered. The second seemed deeper, and Breanna wished she could discern what they were saying. Breanna scribbled a note to Kai, hoping their mind was clearer than hers.

If this fails, next move? it read.

The other end of the phone went silent.

"I have another lead, but it's in a holding pattern right now. If nothing comes of this, maybe we reach out to our social followers for help? Someone must know something." Kai's hushed voice calmed her a bit.

Breanna's mind went to what they could offer in exchange for information. It felt dirty and wrong, but it's how the business worked. Maybe they could bring someone on set, give them a role as an extra if the lead was viable. Of course, this all depended on Kline signing on the dotted line of a contract.

Would they even trust us after all this? The question worried Breanna. How far was too far?

"Hello? Is someone there?"

Breanna's voice failed her as the man came on the line. Her leg bounced, her hands clammy as her mind went completely blank.

"Yes, sir. Is this Otto Henrich?" Kai took over the conversation, allowing thoughts to flow back into her brain.

"My granddaughter said you wanted to speak to me, so go ahead."

"Sir, my name is Kai Vincent. My business partner, Breanna, who is also on the line, and I run K.B. Studios. We've been trying to find M. E. Kline's agency to discuss the production of her most recent series. Considering they were a former client of yours, we were wondering if you could send us in the right direction."

The laughter from the other end of the line chilled Breanna to the core. They were used to the sound when discussing a first offer. It was how they played the negotiating game. Kai played the bad cop, making a serious offer lower than expected or requested. The agent would snicker before intimating their client would never sign off on that. That's when Breanna slipped into good cop mode and made a counteroffer that seemed higher but was more in line with market value without agent inflation. By the time the negotiations were done, all parties agreed on a reasonable deal everyone seemed content with.

This was not the response of someone willing to play ball.

This is the end of everything. A cold, clammy chill rolled over her skin forcing her to shiver.

"With all due respect, Ms. Kline won't be interested. If she's not signing with the bigger companies, she won't have any interest in handing over the rights to a studio my daughter had to Google to find. I'm sorry."

Breanna heard the words, but the alternative made her more nauseous. This was not going as well as she'd hoped. "Mr. Henrich, unlike the conglomerates, my partner and I actually read the books and are committed to bringing a proper adaptation to the big screen. Of course, Ms. Kline would be influential in that translation."

She never enjoyed having the creators on set or working on screenplays from original material. More often than not, Kai would end up spending days explaining what the budget could and couldn't do, and Breanna would spend days editing out things that didn't translate well to the medium. But it was a concession she was willing to make to secure a deal.

They were met with silence. Both Kai and Breanna leaned close to the phone, willing the man to talk to them. Kai waved at the receiver as if it would make words fly out of it faster, but the silence dragged on.

It must have been a minute or two, but her clammy palms said it was a lifetime to wait.

"I appreciate the sentiment, but ultimately those are all meaningless words. How can you protect the author from the same people online who forced Ms. Kline into life away from the spotlight? If this project is made, it will force her out before she's ready. I don't feel comfortable—"

"She would never have to show her face. She could avoid every event, premiere, production days, and whatnot. If she wished to be present, she could hide behind an avatar during a video call. Whatever Ms. Kline needs, we'll find a way to provide it." Breanna was thankful Kai stepped in at that moment to speak. Their determined tone could be exactly what they needed to cut through the red tape to get to the author herself.

"After the issues with her first release, the second one was impossible to sell. I had to let her go. My agency closed not long after that. Too many risks, you know? So, as you can see, I don't think Ms. Kline would be receptive to my advice. I wish I could help you folks. I'm sorry."

Breanna watched her partner sink into their chair, resigned. Nothing seemed to change his mind, but she had to try one more time.

"She's an amazing writer though. The way she discusses pain . . . grieving over loss . . . It transcends the page." Breanna wasn't sure why she added that, but the most recent book hit her hard.

"Yes, well, Kline knew she wasn't a brilliant writer. Unlike some new authors, she held such refreshing modesty about her talent and sales projections. Her willingness to learn and hone her craft by attending workshops, finding new editors, and writing daily . . . it was impressive. It's the other reason I signed her. I truly felt success was right there for the taking. She just wanted to have enough to survive. Damn smart kid . . ." The silence deepened the emotional connection Breanna felt forming in her chest. This writer, this elusive person felt more in tune to Breanna than any one she'd ever met before. The focus on bettering yourself, hiding from the naysayers, wanting a simple life . . . it was all Breanna ever wanted.

Breanna, stop putting people on a pedestal. They're still human and capable of screwing you over. Breanna shook away the thought of the author being some sort of super sexy heroine. *Wait, what? When did sexy enter the equation?* Breanna needed to finish this call and find a release for her energy.

"Sir?" Kai asked, ensuring the man was still on the other line.

"You must understand. People were relentless in their dismantling of Ms. Kline. You can't imagine the damage those kinds of personal attacks can do. The disdain for the character's sexualities and what some called demonic imagery. One can't fault her for not wishing to be found."

Character's sexualities? Demonic imagery? That didn't sound like the author behind her favorite series. Breanna made quick work of adding the original book to her to-be-read list. Maybe she'd find something between the lines to help her get this deal done.

"It was a crime story . . ." Kai's words brought Breanna back to the conversation.

"Yes, but the case was darker and dove deep into the political divide. Hate and fear are powerful things. I doubt you can change that with one phone call or film production. I'm sorry, but I don't feel comfortable putting her in harm's way. I appreciate the call and the trip down memory lane. Please consider backing off this trail. I don't want to see anyone hurt. There's enough of that in the world already."

"What if—" Kai tried before the phone beeped twice, signaling the call had been disconnected. "Okay, then."

Breanna rested her head in her hands. She'd never been one to give up on something, but this task was feeling increasingly difficult. They needed a new plan to handle the fallout.

"You said there was another option?" Breanna's fingers punched the screen of her cell phone to add a reply to a message thread. She needed to release this negative ball of energy parked in her chest. *This is not how you handle stress, Breanna! Call your therapist, not a random hookup.* Her mind begged for her to make a different choice, but the text was already sent.

"Yeah, but like I said, holding pattern. Once I know something, I'll share it with you. What about hiring a private investigator? Maybe they can find a different lead?"

That might be a step too far. Breanna wavered as she thought about the situation. Kline lived away from the limelight. How would she feel being thrust into it because of K.B. Studios? That could backfire horribly.

"I don't know, Kai." The worry hung in the air, but neither of them acknowledged it.

"Michaela expects a signed contract like yesterday." Kai spoke the truth. There was no alternative. Breanna would deal with the consequences later.

A knock on the door brought her back to the present. A tall woman with long, wavy, brown hair covering a red, satin, button-down shirt straining against her voluptuous breasts stood in the doorway. The pencil skirt clung to her hips as Breanna's eyes traveled down her legs to the stiletto heels.

"Hi, Bre." The velvet tone forced all of Breanna's stress to migrate south, increasing the heat between her legs.

"Really?" Kai's disapproving tone did nothing to stop Breanna from focusing on the woman leaning against her office doorframe. "Yeah, right. Okay, I'll leave you to it then. I'll call Michaela and ask if they have a specific deadline or if it's flexible. Then I'll call the cleaning crew and ask for a complete disinfection of your office."

"Focus on the desk." The woman waltzed across the room, stopping directly in front of Breanna. "Trust me." She shimmied her skirt higher before sitting on the wood furniture.

"I'll call Henrich later in the week. In the meantime, think about this before you do it again. Not cool." The door slamming didn't deter Breanna's hands from sliding up the woman's thighs.

"That was fast." Breanna's lips grazed over the exposed skin, the heat from her breath causing the other woman to moan.

"The elevator was right on time. Besides, being the boss of an office two floors up helps expedite my travel." She slipped her hand into Breanna's hair and pulled her up for a kiss.

Breanna knew this was wrong. These random hookups with a woman she referred to as *Biz Babe* in her phone who worked in the same building was never a good idea. But sometimes she just needed this release. No strings attached. Just helping each other reach their peak before slipping back into work mode.

As the button of her pants opened and the zipper moved down, Breanna's mind was clear. Kline could wait. K.B. Studios could wait. The world could wait.

***

Writing couldn't wait. Reilly knew this, but the blank computer screen staring back at her missed the memo. After her weekly call with her friends, her plan for the rest of the day involved writing the next chapter, and the rest of the book if things went very well. Yet, every time she tried to change some aspect to handle her friends' concerns, the arc lost some of the punch she loved.

Maybe it's time to go back to the drawing board and start this entire book over.

The thought was enticing but impossible. While Reilly might have a stable bank account right now, she still had bills associated with all aspects of her business. If she stopped writing and never finished the series, her income would shrivel up, and she might need financial support from her mother. Not to mention her reputation with her editor and fans would be destroyed. She had deadlines and preorders from her website to fulfill. Not finishing wasn't an option.

"Dammit." Reilly harshly pushed herself away from her desk, hating everything swirling in her mind. "Reilly, you should know better than to release rough drafts to your friends! They're trying to be helpful, but you see the big picture. It's just a bunch of suggestions, but you have to write it. So just stop!" She stormed out of the room, the door's hinges screaming in protest at her anger. Maybe some coffee and more chocolate would help her focus.

Each step groaned as Reilly slammed her feet down the stairs to the main floor. Nothing was safe from her negative exertion of energy. The cabinet doors hit so hard against the food, they bounced. The Keurig clanged, snapped, and bubbled to life as she threw her mug underneath it.

Reilly knew she had to find a way to process her emotions better than with caffeine and dark chocolate. She'd walked around town talking to herself, figuring out storylines in the beginning. But once the temperature dropped, her walks became workout sessions in the shed. The small, battery-operated heater kept her warm as she grunted, lifting and squatting.

But nothing helped like a good piece of dark chocolate. She dug through the cabinet and found her childhood lunchbox. The dented image of The Care Bears hid her most precious bounty. Flipping open the top, Reilly wasted no time in grabbing a truffle and popping it in her mouth.

She moaned in pleasure as the flavor excited her taste buds. The machine beeped as her mug filled with freshly brewed coffee. Without a second thought, Reilly slipped on her mother's baggy flannel from the chair. With the coffee in one hand and the lunchbox in the other, Reilly walked outside into the brisk air.

She felt her energy level even out when her body felt the cold frame of the outside swing. Reilly would take the cushions out later in the spring, but right now, this was exactly what she needed. She blew on her coffee and took a sip. Home was her heaven, the only place she felt truly safe, where her mind could calm. Wendy normally joined her outside for iced tea in the summer, but not in this weather.

Once again you're alone.

The statement rattled her soul, but it was true. Throughout her life, Reilly was the expendable friend, girlfriend and now fiancée. The thought of dying and decomposing before someone found her body chilled her more than the icy wind.

She shoved another piece of chocolate in her mouth and focused on the hint of peppermint as a way to calm her racing heart.

Why was this all so hard?

Writing had been her dream. The first failure did nothing to diminish that goal. In fact, it spurred her to be better, to prove the naysayers wrong. She wanted the validation her current books received. She thrived on it, as if her self-worth was wrapped up in a star or a word from a review.

Sometimes she wondered if the quiet was the problem. In Manhattan, there was a school directly behind her apartment. She couldn't sleep late as the bells and laughter would wake her up promptly each morning. They'd quiet down for a few hours before recess and then again before dismissal. The aroma of her neighbor's delicious cooking reminded her of dinner, and then her day was complete.

There was a schedule with minimal distractions back then. Now she could barely get through one chapter before the random power surge, or her mother calling her cell phone from the kitchen would disrupt her day. Reilly didn't regret the change. She had a responsibility to take care of her mother, but she needed to write.

That requires figuring out what's stopping you from writing.

That's what Lilly mentioned. Something was blocking her, and she had no idea what. After several minutes of gorging on sweets, washing them down with the dark roast, Reilly realized words wouldn't come to her today.

But she needed to do something. With a renewed determination, she decided to attack her mental to-do list of minor items she always pushed to the backburner. The first one was organizing her mother's medication. Flipping open the notes application, Reilly went about updating names and dosages, as well as verifying Wendy wasn't due for a refill. Before she could click save, Otto's face popped up on the screen of her phone.

"Hello, my former knight in shining armor." The sarcasm-laden line ended with a slight laugh.

"Only former because you really wanted my assistant in that outfit." Otto's laughter recharged her soul. He always knew how to do that with a hug or a smile.

"Can you blame me? Greta was smart—an infectious laugh and legs for days!" The memory of her office crush and their harmless flirting warmed her heart. "It's been forever. How are you and the family doing?"

"Everyone's good, but you'd know that if you came to visit us in the city once in a while. You missed the agency reunion dinner and everything."

"I had no idea. When was it?" The pit of her stomach sank. Otto never shared her author identity with any of the staff, but she'd left that life behind. It was hard to think of it in happy terms. Sure, the event would have been the perfect excuse to try to overcome her feeling about the city. It would have been more entertaining than listening to her date describe swinging from the ceiling and being bent in half. It still would have required more confidence than Reilly had currently.

"A few months ago, but that's not important. Helen came. I thought you'd be with her."

"Yeah, no." She fought back the urge to ask why Helen was invited, but she didn't. Reilly hadn't made it public knowledge they weren't together anymore. She let it fade away so she could avoid answering questions. "That ended a long time ago. I'm sorry I've been so out of touch. It's been rough."

"Reilly, I'm so sorry. I had no idea."

"Why would you? I was busy hiding under a rock, and we just lost touch. It happens, Otto. But it's fine. I know you'd have been here if I called. I just sort of wanted to disconnect from everyone. I shouldn't have cut you out like that. You've always been good to me and . . . I'm sorry." She never wanted to hurt those close to her, but when Reilly cut off her old life, there was collateral damage. Hearing Otto's voice again, she regretted it immediately.

"Well, let's not do that again. Now, while I wish that was the only reason I reached out, I received an interesting phone call today."

Shit, what did Helen do now? The thought worried her. If Helen used her name or tried to promote her career under Kline's name, what could Reilly do? Her lawyer had some contingencies in place, but Reilly never wanted to use them. Could she even remain anonymous if she had to sue her ex? She shivered, unsure if it was due to the wind or her fear. Her knees came to her chest for comfort as she sipped her drink again.

"I got a call from K.B. Studios. A Breanna Blaine and Kai Vincent. They were hoping to contact you. Now, my daughter did some digging and they're legit, but I know you prefer your privacy. I didn't give them anything to go off of, but they seem determined to get in touch with you."

The email Ellen forwarded to her flashed to the front of her mind. She'd thought nothing of it after reading the correspondence. In fact, she planned on ignoring it completely. But if they were contacting people who knew her, it was only a matter of time before Helen came across their radar. If there was a way to profit off her name, her ex would find a way to do it. Maybe she couldn't capitalize off her books, but if there was an exposé to be written or gossip to sell, Helen would do it. People might pay handsomely to have Reilly's real name and photo.

"I'll handle it. No worries."

"You know how I feel about these things, but if the offer is good, maybe you should consider it. This could help you retire without all those fears of yours. They mentioned never having to show your face in public or even meetings. Not sure how that would work, but if you want to do it . . ."

If she was being honest, she always wanted see her creations on the screen. But Reilly was leery of the press, social media, and her previous experiences with them all. Add to that Helen as her marketing manager made deals on Reilly's behalf that she couldn't deliver. Reilly hated confrontation and facing the consequences of her past was not in her to do list. She just wanted them to go away.

"Thanks, Otto, but I'm not sure. There's more to it than showing my face, you know? Shadows Rise's my baby. I don't know if it would work as a film or even a television series." Reilly wondered how much Otto knew of her and Helen's relationship. Specifically, if he was aware she attended events with Helen under the guise of Kline attending. It seemed her ex and Otto were still in touch and she was leery of what, if anything, the woman shared with him.

Would he think of me differently if he knew? The thought soured her stomach. Otto was a friend and mentor to her. The last thing she wanted to do was embarrass him or place him between herself and this company. If nothing else, Reilly needed to stop this company from getting any closer. Maybe if she spoke to them directly, they would leave her be. "Did you grab the number off caller ID?"

"Yes, I can text it to you once we're off the phone."

"Thanks."

"I better go. Grandkid's setting up the computer for me and I have to make sure he doesn't lock me out of Facebook. Don't be a stranger, kiddo."

And just like that, he was gone. No goodbye. Reilly was used to it, but it brought back memories of smoothing things over for others in the office.

The silence of the house enveloped her again. K.B. Studios was going to be a problem she had to deal with, regardless of her desire to avoid confrontation. In that moment, Reilly decided to email Breanna Blaine directly. She would initiate polite conversation, state she was uninterested in their endeavors, and move on. Maybe the company would press a bit, but she would hold firm in her decision.

"Dear Ms. Blaine . . . No, that doesn't work well. To whom it may concern would be worse than using dear . . . Hello is bad too. Dammit to hell. An email should not be this difficult." Reilly dropped her head to the desk. If she couldn't write a simple email, how was she going to finish her book?

Chapter Five

·♥·♥·♥·♥·♥·

Chapter Five

The ride back to her apartment did nothing to brighten her day. Breanna thought of contingency plans for her future. She had other options, including working for a rival company. *They'd probably remind me of my failure daily.* But she'd worked in horrible situations before.

Concerns for her small staff and best friend loomed large over her head. Maybe she should start making calls and see what openings were available. If any of her team members were interested in a new position, she'd offer a recommendation to anyone who required it. She huffed at the thought. Her staff's resumes spoke for themselves, anyone would be lucky to have them on board.

And then there was Kai. They'd shown her emails from varying headhunters. Breanna knew they'd get a new job quickly, but she'd never stop worrying about her chosen sibling. She was selfish and wanted Kai to stay in the city. But the bigger production companies were mostly in Los Angeles. Breanna hated that her failure as a businessperson was the reason her best friend would be three thousand miles away. It wasn't something she wanted at all.

That just meant Breanna had to work harder to find the elusive author or face the inevitable. When she left the office, Kai was still plugging away on two computers and two phones. Breanna chuckled to herself at the image, as Kai seamlessly balanced everything like the younger generation seemed to do. They agreed to ask Sea Cliff for a clearer picture of their deadline. While she didn't really want a firm date, Breanna knew she needed it. Not just for the business side of things, but also to ensure she stayed on track.

But for now, even after her earlier escapade in her office, she needed a mental break. Her mind swam with varying outcomes and ideas, but as she stripped out of her work clothes, the stress went with it. Her bedroom was her sanctuary. If K.B. Studios were going to survive, the solution would come to her within these walls.

Five minutes later, she was clad in sweatpants and an old, worn concert shirt. Breanna took a nice gulp from her second glass of Moscato, allowing the stresses of the day become fuzzy and distant. She knew drinking on an empty stomach wasn't a good idea, but she had no desire to eat. Looking over her laptop screen, she locked eyes with Max. She swore that cat could see into her soul.

Security mentioned the feline wandering into their building during an early nor'easter that dumped over two feet of snow. They complained about him meowing at doors, avoiding capture until Breanna opened hers. He darted inside, and she waved off the out of breath, burly man. Her allergies flared, and she sneezed horribly until she could trek down to the local pharmacy for some over-the-counter medication. She'd taken one a day until her allergist recommended monthly injections.

She could have given him up, but just like her, he was lost. So, they kept each other company. They yelled back and forth over food being served late or the corners of the new couch resembling a waterfall of torn fabric. But they also snuggled, which surprised her. Breanna enjoyed watching bad horror films regularly with Max. He'd meow or hiss at the antics of the characters. If he was tired, he'd hide in the little shelter she bought for him.

If Breanna was being honest, beyond her two college best friends, he was the only other love in her life. The oddball family she'd built from scraps and broken pieces was what held her up each day. Sure, she loved work, but it was still business. She looked forward to coming home to Max. She made sure her vacations plans included him, and a leash hung by the front door. In her mind, he was originally an outdoor cat. Who was she to deny him the fresh air?

She finally caved and moved to grab her glass of white wine, breaking the stalemate. Max meowed in victory before strutting across the coffee table and onto the couch next to her.

"You're not getting a treat for that."

He hissed in displeasure and plopped himself on her keyboard.

"I don't care. Blocking the screen doesn't help." She finished off her glass, waiting for the cat to move. "Fine, you win." Her body ached as she went to the kitchen to grab some cat treats and the wine bottle before plopping back down on the couch.

A few steps and gulps later, Max was snuggled into her side, and the warmth of alcohol was swimming through her body. Clicking the mousepad on her laptop, Breanna brought up a random drama on a streaming service.

"Might as well watch it before we can't afford it anymore? Right, Max?"

The cat's head popped up, his eyes round and wide.

"Don't worry. I'll stop eating before you do."

Max slumped his head back onto her thigh, waiting for attention.

Before she could indulge in the opening sequence of the show, her phone buzzed with a notification. Scanning it quickly, her heart flew into her throat on a wave of intoxication. Breanna made a silent prayer as her thumb slid over the screen, opening it.

Good morning, Ms. Blaine,

I understand you've been trying to reach me regarding the Shadows Rise series. I appreciate K.B. Studios' interest in developing film adaptations of my novels. However, at this point in time, this is not something I wish to pursue. Thank you for your inquiry, and good luck on your future endeavors.

Sincerely,

M. E. Kline

Before she could think, her thumb was sliding across the screen in a frantic response. Her words flew together.

"You can't hide behind an email forever." Her mind swirled under the influence of the wine as she attempted a coherent message. "You just need to talk to me in person. Or Kai, 'cause I don't think I can talk so good now."

Max meowed in reply as she hit the send button.

"Don't worry, buddy. She'll talk to us, and then we'll be right as rain."

A notification popped back on screen.

Mailer-daemon reply.

Breanna's alcohol-induced confidence sank through her toes into the floor. The author had used a temporary email address with no reply feature. Between this and the social media management team's regurgitated generic response, Breanna was done. She dropped her phone on the coffee table before filling her glass to the brim. Tomorrow she'd face her hangover; tonight she'd just drown her sorrows. Three large gulps of wine pushed the lump of inadequacy down her throat.

As she fought to stay awake, her phone taunted her again. Breanna was quite sure another email would destroy her, but when her phone vibrated repeatedly, it was obvious someone was calling. Could it be the author's people telling her to give up? Maybe a lawyer asking if there were plans to liquidate all of K.B. Studios assets? No matter what, Breanna knew she shouldn't answer the phone in her inebriated state. But her brain didn't get the message through to her hand before her thumb slid across the screen to connect the call.

"Hello?" She barely got the word out. It sounded normal in her head, but her mouth felt numb, and the sound didn't quite fit what she meant to say.

"Damn, woman. How much have you had?" Kai's concern brought a smile to her face. They always made her feel better no matter how down she got.

"Max insisted we open the Moscato and enjoy some family time. Come over. I think I have another bottle or at least one glass left of this one."

"Don't blame the poor cat for bad decisions. I thought you wanted to save those bottles to celebrate a new milestone."

"I'm celebrating my demise." Her words barely made sense to her ears. "Kline gave an emphatic no with a bogus email address." A knock at her apartment door pierced her intoxicated brain. Breanna slipped and stumbled to the entryway. She ignored the peephole and fumbled with the chain lock. On the third try, it slid free. The bolts flipped open with a little difficulty.

She swung open the door. Breanna stumbled to the side as Kai moved into her space and locked the entryway. She was sure they were human, but Kai seemed to move with superhero speed. The world spun as her back hit the wall and gravity dragged her to the floor. The cat hissed and Breanna knew he was judging her.

"I agree, Max. She's a mess." The traitorous cat rubbed up against Kai's leg. "Come on, Bre. Let's go sit down."

"I am sitting." The slurred words made her giggle.

"Properly."

Breanna crawled to the couch and climbed up, struggling like a toddler. Once situated, she watched her business partner put the wine bottle away and out of reach. Max was constantly between Kai's feet but it didn't seem to bother her friend.

"You want something to eat?" Breanna's eyes tried to focus on which blurry image was Kai and the glass of water placed on the coffee table. It took all of her strength not to fall over onto the cushions. She felt Kai's hands hold her in place. Breanna knew getting drunk was idiotic. If they were going to get through this, they both needed to be clearheaded. "I could order in or scour your fridge."

"Oreos in the cabinet," Breanna said through sips of water. Kai wandered through the kitchen as Breanna blinked rapidly hoping for visual clarity. Why did she ingest so much so quickly?

"Don't eat them all at once." Kai slid onto the couch as Breanna ripped open the package like a starved animal. "Bre—"

"She replied. Refused to even talk about the rights." Crumbs hit the worn concert logo as she shoved another one into her mouth. "Who does that? Maybe those people were right."

"Hey, don't be like that." Kai's soothing voice did nothing to lift Breanna's mood. "We both know there are reviewers and then there are reviewers."

"That makes no sense without more wine."

"You're cut off, and you know what I mean." Of course, Breanna did. Their movies had critical success but that didn't stop trolls from bashing everything they touched because the company was run by a woman and a non-binary individual. *Get woke, go broke* was the usual line hurled her way. She never understood how simply existing and creating quality projects with diverse casts was woke, but the world needed therapy and chocolate. Neither of which she could provide.

"Maybe we call every number in our contacts and get a bigger name on board with our ideas. Maybe we grovel and beg to be part of another company's projects. Worst case, we could sell our souls to the banks for a loan." She finished her glass of water and grabbed more cookies.

Before Breanna knew what happened, her glass was refilled. Her friend's compassion warmed the cold depths of her chest. "I can make some calls, see if anyone else wants to jump on board. Maybe more names will get Kline to listen and negotiate with us. I'm not about to give up on this yet."

A deep sigh left Breanna's lips as she tried to sort through the remaining options they had. How could Kai keep fighting when it felt like there was nothing left they could do? *It feels like fielding an entire football team without a quarterback to throw the ball.* "Kai, maybe we gotta let it go."

"Stop that! We've never played this 'poor pitiful me' crap. Sure, we're in a horrible situation, but we've faced worse. You've looked A-list actors in the face and denied them frivolous wants because it would remove funding from the crew. I've seen you fight for the last penny to ensure the lowest on the totem pole got a fair paycheck. Why are you giving in now? As far as I'm concerned, if there's enough money in the bank to cover payroll, we keep fighting. We find a way. Full stop."

The rousing speech sobered Breanna up a little. "If this fails, where would you go?"

"I don't know. I'll cross that bridge if I get to it. Right now, I don't need to."

"I'll do my best to—"

"You'll do nothing. Look, I know this is a massive longshot, but Kline sent out their newsletter this afternoon."

"Cool, so now we know all about their upcoming work? Events?" She jumped forward as possibility filled her soul. "Please tell me they're doing an actual signing, convention, public burning of their first book? I don't care, just something!"

"No, nothing that simple. But the address at the bottom lists a P.O. box located in Plensglade."

"So, we have the location of a town that her wall of team members might be in?" Her words dripped with venom, something Breanna knew she'd regret in the morning.

"Look, it's something. From what I found, the social media management team's office is in Manhattan. If they're located in the big city, why is there an address leading to a sleepy town slightly north of here? That doesn't seem right."

"And if there's no connection? Maybe the box is owned by one of the team working for her and she's nowhere in sight. Then what?"

"Then you get a breather from the stress at the office while I handle things here. We divide and conquer. Plus, my favorite Etsy shop is up there. Maybe you can stop by their storefront and pick up some of my orders." Breanna groaned into her pillow. Traveling up to some small town to get the rights to a book was one thing, but now it felt like an in-store pickup from Walmart. Not what she, nor her pounding head, wanted to think about.

"You're incorrigible."

"You're drunk, and you'll be hungover on the drive." Kai dropped a key fob into her hand. Max tried to grab the offending object. "I'll take care of Maximous Caticus."

"He's just Max. Not some gladiator kitty."

"You've never seen him knock over every glass on the table with one swoosh of his arm. Now, you go find out whatever you can. And above everything else, be nice to my baby."

That thought alone made Breanna stop chewing the last of her cookie. She lived in the city. There was no need to drive anywhere. The last time she'd been behind the wheel, the vehicle had more duct tape than a freshly stocked shelf at the hardware store. Now she had to drive her friend's prized possession through the throngs of eighteen-wheelers, cabs, and lord knows what else. She'd always wanted adventure, but she meant traveling, not driving during rush hour.

Breanna found herself sobering up very quickly.

***

Plensglade was nothing like what Breanna was expecting. In her mind, she thought there would be one main street with nothing but grass or trees beyond it. Instead, she found her rental place with a small property within walking distance from the heart of town. It felt like the old stomping grounds of her youth. She admonished herself internally as she dumped her luggage inside the small one-bedroom home.

"Dial Kai," she muttered, digging through her bag for a warmer jacket. The phone barely rang before her business partner answered.

"Please tell me you did not crash Speed Demon."

"What?"

"My car. How is my baby?"

"If you cared about the car, you shouldn't have let me borrow it. Thanks for worrying about me, by the way. We're safe in . . . whatever this place could be considered."

"You're in a compact version of suburbia, not some Podunk town with no cellular service. Grow up."

"I know where I am. You forget I grew up in a place like this where every lawn is perfectly manicured and gossip travels faster than light." She could see her younger self running along the street, playing tag or getting coffee with friends from high school. But for all the good times, the bad ones crept in as well. The less time she spent here, the better.

"No, I didn't. It's why you traveled up there, and I am meeting with Michaela in a few minutes. We both have our strengths." The dinging sound of an elevator came through the receiver. "Have you been to the post yet? Talk to anyone local? See if anyone knows anything?"

"Kai, I just got here."

"Dude, let me break it down for you. There's one long main street where the magic happens. Then you have box stores and one large supermarket for the entire community. It's not hard to tell where the locals spend their time. The travel reviews alone make it clear. Main Street is where the people are."

"Yeah, yeah, walk down Main Street and see if I can tap into the gossip food chain. I hate this. You have any idea how to get the information from the post office? Technically, they'd be breaking the law if they share the owner's information with us."

"Not a clue, ergo the shot in the dark comments from yesterday. Besides, but you didn't have a better idea. I can't have you hovering around me while I try to salvage our careers."

"I'm not that bad with— "

"Bre, you babble when you're uncomfortable, and it's worse when you're nervous. Last time you spent forty-five minutes talking about your shellfish allergy at a steakhouse. Seriously, this is not your forte. You're the convincer. I'm the fixer.

We both handle production. It's how we work. So, go get coffee and get to work. I found you a place close to town so you could get your steps in."

"And not damage your car."

"That was just a bonus. A very welcome one. Now, get moving. Introduce yourself to people and go all Clarice Starling or something. I don't care. I'll take the train up when I'm done with all these meetings. I might get that agent to come down in price. We're meeting for dinner to discuss the future of their client's wealth. I went through our finances."

"Kai—"

"I know you hate firm dates, but we have one month to turn this around. That's it. Goodbye."

The line disconnected before Breanna could muster up a snarky reply. She knew Kai was right, but this was not her strong suit. It reminded her of her first job as a teenager, calling people to pick up their orders. Needless to say, she was fired after three weeks of poor attempts to shift her calls to someone else. She'd tried convincing her boss she was delegating like a proper manager until he reminded her that HE was, in fact, the manager. She didn't think it through, but it was clear Breanna would not do well working for someone else. She'd suffer through it if she had to, but it was not ideal.

But that was then, and this was now. One thing Breanna knew for sure; she didn't have any time to waste. Where would she begin? Her reflection of a New York City executive taunted her. *Start with making myself look more approachable*, she mused.

If she was going to meander about town, she'd do it as comfortably as possible. That meant ditching the designer boots for her beat-up Columbia ones. Her suit with low-rise jeans and an old concert T-shirt. Her leather jacket stayed behind as she grabbed a sherpa-lined flannel Kai gave her as a holiday gift.

"If this doesn't scream 'I'm normal, come say hi,' I don't know what will."

Before she could overthink it, Breanna grabbed her keys and was out of the house. Her cell phone bellowed directions to the local coffee shop she passed on the way in. If she had to put on a fake smile to schmooze the locals, caffeination was sorely needed.

I'll figure out the rest once I get there. Her mind wandered. Her body wanted nothing more than to lie down and sleep for a week. Her hungover head begged for the same, but her feet kept moving . . . off the curb and into the street.

The screeching of tires and loud horn jolted Breanna out of her reverie. The figure in the red compact SUV waved in the direction of the blinking red crosswalk sign. Breanna waved in understanding as she jogged across the street. She didn't have to, but the fear-fueled adrenaline needed an outlet. She berated herself for being so preoccupied. She swallowed the bile in her throat as the SUV parked behind a strip of stores.

"Great first impression, Breanna. Mom would be so proud of you almost becoming one with a moving vehicle. Kai'd be laughing their ass off at the irony. Getting run over crossing the damn street before you could even talk to one person. Talk about shirking your responsibilities."

This day was not going well. Her phone barked the location of the coffee shop. A few more steps to the right and she'd be able to hide in a corner to collect herself. Maybe she could dispel the negative energy swirling around her mind and smile at a few people in the shop. Who knows, maybe she'd find someone willing to help.

The one main street cutting through the small town with two streetlights did nothing to help her mood. Breanna thought about home, her childhood, and the bigger than average town with more bad memories than she'd care to remember. Her vision swirled, and she blinked to shut it all down. She had a job to do, and dammit, she was going to get it done.

Amy's Coffee Haven—the dark wood sign swung from the metal post connecting it to the wall. The intimate setting was just what Breanna needed to get started. Her body tingled in anticipation of her three-shot latte with fresh cinnamon sprinkled on top. Her mouth salivated at the thought of a chocolate pastry to go with it.

Peering inside the windows of the coffee shop, Breanna noticed the cozy setting and a beautiful woman at the counter. The way her jeans hugged her frame was enticing. Maybe this trip wouldn't be so bad after all.

Breanna shook the sexy thoughts from her mind. She was here to work. *But there's always time for play.* The devil in her spoke loud and clear.

Chapter Six

Chapter Six

Reilly grabbed her coffee and her chocolate croissant as her sister-in-law continued to babble about something her nieces were up to. She loved hearing about the kids, but right now her nerves were shot. After she sent the email to K.B. Studios, her stomach rolled with waves of nervous energy. She desperately wanted a reply, a final closure to the discussion, but ensure there wouldn't be one. *How could they reply when you sent it from a temporary email address??* Reilly's mind yelled at her. She hated feeling this way. Like the shoe was about to drop, but she had no idea where or when it would.

It didn't help that her aunt's coffee shop was busier than normal. Reilly recommended this time of day so they'd have easy access to a table and less noise. But between the book not flowing, the email about the film rights, and almost running over a beautiful woman outside, Reilly was all out of calmness.

"Sorry, our normal table's occupied." Jenna's voice drifted into Reilly's consciousness.

"It's fine." Reilly slid into her chair, hating that there were people sitting behind her. She always preferred to keep her back to the wall with the entire room in her purview. She preferred to be prepared for a quick escape should something happen at any time. Sitting in the center of the room was not ideal, not at all.

"You okay? I can always ask them to move if you'd like. I can make something up." Jenna was always thoughtful like that, but Reilly didn't want to make a scene.

"No, it's okay," she lied. *It's what you do best*, Reilly thought negatively.

The front door opened, ringing the bell attached to it. On any other day, the sound blended into part of the ambiance. Today, it was jarring. When her eyes slammed over to the offending person who dared enter, she choked on her coffee.

The woman stood tall with her shoulders back, with an air of confidence around her that Reilly envied. Her hands were tucked deep into the front pockets of her jeans as she moved to the counter. Reilly couldn't hear what the woman ordered, but when the woman flipped her dark hair over her shoulder, Reilly thought she'd have a heart attack.

Before Reilly knew what was happening, her coffee cup crashed to the floor, shattering into little pieces.

Just like in her nightmares, time stood still as patrons spun to focus on the offending sound. The woman at the counter stared with her bright eyes and a sly smirk that melted Reilly's embarrassment away. Until she recognized the woman as the person she almost ran over. Then her face flushed as she slipped to the floor, desperate to hide and clean up the broken pieces.

"Dammit! Just great. I can't believe this. Of all the days in the world, Reilly, this is the day you're having. Karma . . . she hates you. That's what this is." The words tumbled out of her mouth.

"Stop your worrying, child. It's just a cup. Accidents happen." Amy, her beloved aunt and owner of the coffee shop, pushed Reilly gently to the side. Reilly watched as her aunt used a small broom to sweep up the remaining pieces. Once done, Amy dumped that in the trash before grabbing a mop. Reilly just stood there, frozen in her embarrassment. *How could that woman fluster me so much?*

"I'm really sorry." Reilly's cheeks felt hot, and she was sure the other woman was still watching her. But Reilly stayed focused on her aunt. Anything to keep her eyes off the other woman. She was a distraction Reilly struggled to control at the moment. There were too many moving pieces around her, and a woman with that level of confidence was well out of her league.

"Look, but don't engage." Her mumbled words came out like a mantra. "I'm really sorry, Aunt Amy. I'll pay for it."

"Stop it, child. The girls are making you a new one when they've got a moment. I told them to put it in a to-go cup just in case." The deep belly laughter was infectious and even caused Reilly to chuckle . . . a little.

"Let me clean up. It's my fault. You shouldn't be doing this."

"I'm old, not dead. Besides, I'm almost done."

"You sound just like Mom."

"Well, my best friend is a rather smart woman. I mean, she's friends with me, ain't she? Right there, smart as a whip." Her aunt provided a wonderful, stable relationship in Reilly's world. In a family where people died because they were stubborn or left their family members, devoting their lives to the almighty dollar, Amy was just herself. She lived as she wanted, unashamed by her personal choices, with no judgments against anyone else. She just loved purely and fully.

"You okay, kid?"

How should she answer that? There were so many options, but the lie was on the tip of her tongue as usual.

"I'm good, just jumpy." It wasn't exactly a lie.

"You're a good kid, but you were never good at fibbing. Even if you try to stay as close to the truth as possible. Just know the door's always open, not just to this place, but to the apartment upstairs. I even got a fancy new smartphone. Your mom's teaching me how to use it. You'd be proud."

"You know she asks me all your questions before helping you, right?"

"Shush, you. Let your mom have the spotlight for a bit. There's plenty of time for you later." Amy slid away from Reilly's table. "I'm gonna send you all those GIF things. Maybe some pictures of my cat too. Everyone loves cat photos!"

The smile formed on Reilly's lips as she imagined her aunt sending her those random texts. Reilly disliked being their tech support when anything went wrong, which was quite often, but she wouldn't trade their connection for anything.

"I don't know if her having a smartphone is a good thing." Jenna's infectious laughter brought out some giggles from Reilly's chest.

Of course, right behind Jenna's chair was the woman who caught Reilly's eye. She was at the counter, waiting or still ordering. Reilly had no idea. Just seeing the woman had her stomach bouncing on a trampoline of nerves. Reilly knew the woman would be out of the store soon, and whatever this reaction was would be over. That thought calmed but also upset her.

"Seriously, pick your jaw up off the floor and sit down!" Jenna said loud enough for the table next to her to laugh.

Embarrassed, Reilly slid onto the bench of the larger corner table suitable for four people. Without saying a word, she bit into her croissant. The melted chocolate hit her tongue, and her eyes closed. If there was one thing that could calm her down instantly, it was the luxury of her favorite treat.

"Okay, now you're just being gross. Do you always moan for chocolate?" Jenna continued to tease her as Reilly smirked.

"You just don't understand the finer things in life."

"Oh, yes, I do. Like that woman you were staring at. She is fine." Jenna waved her hands around for emphasis. "I have to ask about those boots. They look so comfy."

"No, you don't." She tried to stop the butterflies from taking control. "You have two kids. All your boots have zippers. You have time for laces like that?"

"You're probably right." Reilly sipped her coffee and watched Jenna's eyes flick over to the counter and back to her. "You should introduce yourself."

Reilly's elbow missed the edge of the table in response. Sure, she could say hello, but then what? She wasn't known for communication outside of writing her books. Would she even be able to form a sentence? When she met Helen, she looked like a bobblehead, just accepting whatever was said. She couldn't approach her. It was impossible.

"No, I can't. I'm not going there again. Swore off romantic relationships for good."

"Yeah, I said that about men, and then I married your brother and popped out his spawn. Seriously, life has its own plan."

But you were lucky. The sarcastic comment floated across Reilly's mind, but the words remained unspoken. She'd watched Jenna and Harrison's relationship develop into something larger than life. The way they moved as one unit through tough times and good ones without ever missing a beat. It felt like watching a fairytale in reality.

"Not everyone has that kind of connection, Jenna." In Reilly's experience, any connection that involved compromise and work, she failed miserably at.

"Maybe, but how do you know if you don't actually go over there and open your mouth—"

"And stumble out idiotic phrases that make no sense as I fumble for words like a fool? No, thank you."

"Reilly, you're a writer. Words should be easy," Jenna said softly.

"What do I say when she asks what I do for a living? I mean, that's small talk, right? Do I lie? Do I say nothing? You heard Aunt Amy. I am a terrible liar."

"Keep it close to the truth. Like you don't write novels, but you write fan fiction . . ."

"I don't do that. Have you seen some of those writers' stories? They write better than I do!"

"Reilly, it's not rocket science. You just need something close enough to the truth so you can partake in some enjoyable activities with that woman before she leaves town."

"How do you know she's leaving?" Did she even want that kind of connection? Reilly was a serial monogamist. It was in her DNA to have relationships, not just hookups. No matter how strong a pull she felt to the woman at the counter, she didn't need meaningless sex. She had a private drawer for that.

"That woman is a city girl. Boots barely have any dirt on them. Jeans are perfect. Nails, clean and trimmed. She looks like she bought brand-new clothes prepping for a magazine cover shoot."

"Or she just takes care of what she owns. Looks can be deceiving."

"Fine, then tell her you study sharks and take care of your mom when you're on land."

Reilly's boisterous laughter stopped once a shadow fell upon the table.

"I apologize for interrupting." Reilly followed the woman's body and fell upon a set of brown eyes that held the world in them. There was an innocent nervousness reflected back that pulled at her heart. A heart that had begun to race at the woman's closeness. "I saw you drop your coffee and thought you could use another one. The barista said it was a large latte. I hope that's right."

"Yeah, it is." The words tumbled out of Reilly's mouth in a rushed heap. "Thank you."

"Right."

"Huh?" There was a disconnect between Reilly's brain and her body. She knew Jenna was watching them closely, but her body stayed rooted in the stranger's direction.

"Why don't you join us? There's plenty of room." Jenna's words snapped Reilly to attention. Her jaw locked into a nervous smile as her hand gripped her cup until her knuckles went white.

"Oh, only if you're sure I'm not intruding."

"You're not. My sis and I usually meet up when I get the rugrats off to school. Which was a chore this morning, let me tell you." Jenna extended her hand. "I'm Jenna Vail, and the silent wonder over there is my sister-in-law, Reilly."

"Breanna Blaine," the other woman said, lifting her elbow to tap the inside of Jenna's hand. "Sorry." She held up the two steaming cups.

Jenna moved her chair forward so Breanna could slip into the chair next to her. "So, why are you in our little town?"

"Slight break from the city." Reilly watched with rapt attention as Breanna sipped her drink. Her jealousy of a porcelain cup embarrassed her. "I apologize for eavesdropping, but you work with sharks? That's cool."

She swallowed as her eyes rolled down the woman's neck as her reply stuck in her throat. A sudden shock of pain in her shin forced her gaze to land on Jenna.

"Are you okay?" Breanna's voice brought her back to their conversation.

"Yeah, I'm good. But, um, no I don't work with sharks. I've gone diving with them though. To see them just living their lives and swimming on by. It's the most majestic thing I've ever experienced. We're killing them all, of course, because that's what we humans do. Destroy all that's good—"

"I'm gonna head out. Tons of errands to run." Jenna abruptly cut off Reilly's nervous babbling.

"What? You just got here. I thought you cleared . . . I mean . . ." Reilly stumbled over her words, begging for Jenna to stay. Reilly was not prepared to be alone with this woman. *She could be a serial killer, but what a way to go.* She shook the absurd thought from her brain. "Okay, yeah, sure. Give the kids my love." Once Jenna was out of the coffee shop, Reilly would spiral and make a fool of herself. It was her MO.

"It was a pleasure meeting you, Jenna."

"Same. Maybe we'll see you around town again?"

"I hope so." Reilly didn't look up for fear of looking goofy in front of Breanna. So she ripped her croissant apart to eat it. "Good pastry?"

"What?" Reilly popped her head up. Breanna pointed to the treat. "Oh, yeah. I get one every time we come here. Just a pleasant treat, ya know?"

"You have a little in the corner of your mouth."

Horrified, Reilly grabbed a napkin and wiped her mouth. The dabs of chocolate and pastry pushed her deeper into embarrassment. "Thank you." The words softly fell from her lips.

"So, based on what you said earlier, you do not work with sharks." Breanna's tone was lighthearted and made Reilly's mind race for an answer.

"Yeah, no. I donate some money to a place that works with lemon sharks. Keeps their pupping grounds protected from expansion." This was normally the point where people usually lost interest and walked away. Yet, Breanna leaned forward toward her, as if Reilly's words held value.

"Sounds commendable."

"Nah, just what I believe in." Reilly sipped her coffee and enjoyed the explosion of caffeine hitting her body. "You really didn't have to do this. Thank you."

"Well, it was my fault you dropped it. If you hadn't been looking my way, I might not have spooked you. Felt appropriate to replace it." Breanna's flirtatious tone had the desired effect.

Reilly wanted to die. She wanted to fade away into the bench and disappear.

"I'm sorry. I'm not a creep or something."

"Famous last words." Breanna's laughter hit Reilly in the chest like a sledgehammer. She curled her fingers tighter around the cup and tried to calm her raging body. "Seriously though, I'm from the city, so words like that are usually a red flag."

"No red flags here. The bisexual flag, sure . . ." Reilly internally screamed at herself for sharing that bit of information. She could write the most intricate stories in the world, but right now, she was a bumbling idiot. "Yeah, I'm sorry for being so weird. I don't do well with new people."

"It's all good." Another phrase that Reilly often heard in a negative light. Yet, in this moment, it felt positive. As if Breanna was really okay with her nervous babbling and awkwardness. "I deal with meeting new people all the time. You get used to it."

"What do you do?"

"I run a production company with my partner, Kai."

No, no, no. Reilly's mind went into overdrive. "K.B. Studios?" she whispered.

"You've heard of us?" Breanna sat a little taller with pride. "Not many people pay attention to the smaller companies in the credits."

"Yes, well, when you have friends with serious film obsessions, you hear the names of all the companies." The lie flowed out of her with an ease she'd never felt before. Her heart hammered for a different reason now. The fear burning through her was bringing up every wall she could erect for defensive posturing.

"Here's your coffee, kiddo. But I see you have one already." Aunt Amy looked over at the other woman at the table. "I'm Amy. Haven't seen you around here."

"Breanna, and I'm just visiting."

"Breanna bought me a coffee, Aunt Amy," Reilly blurted out as her mind continued to try to find a way out of the situation. She needed time and space to plan a response. Reilly knew herself well enough to understand Breanna's eyes were going to be a problem. She'd inadvertently tell the woman everything just because of the pure, honest emotions coming from Breanna's eyeballs. *Damn this woman and her genetics!*

"Well, that was awfully kind of you." Reilly looked up at her aunt, pleading for help. Instead, she found a teasing smirk. "Let me repay you for it. My niece is a klutz. You shouldn't have to pay for her inability to carry a cup."

"Can we not, Aunt Amy? Please?" Reilly's cheeks felt flushed, and her right leg bounced uncontrollably. Her aunt's words were not helping the situation.

"I appreciate that, but it's unnecessary. I could use some help though."

"Of course. What can we do for ya?"

"I'm looking for someone, but I only have their initials."

Reilly clenched her jaw as a stab of pain pierced Reilly's chest. She was waiting for the inevitable to happen.

"It's not a huge town, but not too small either. I might be able to help, but I can't promise anything."

"Of course, I understand. The name's M. E. Kline."

And there it was. Everything Reilly was terrified of was no longer far away but sitting in her aunt's shop, flirting with her. Teasing her with the joys she could have, as if the devil were testing her. *Give in,* the demon would whisper, but she'd fight it back.

"I have to go." She quickly stood up and chugged her somewhat hot coffee. "I just remembered mom needed help."

"Okay, kiddo." Her aunt's powerful hug calmed her raging fears, but only a bit. Her secret was still safe for a little while longer.

"It was a pleasure meeting you, Breanna," she said as she broke from the embrace.

"Maybe we could see one another again?" Breanna stood, her eyes pleading for an affirmative answer. "If you'd like to, that is. I'm in town for little while and would love to see everything it has to offer."

If it had been any other person in the world, Reilly would have caved in immediately. But this woman, the reason her body hummed in two different wavelengths all at once, could break her beyond repair. "Maybe," was all she could say.

"I'll take it," Breanna answered as Reilly kissed her aunt on the cheek, grabbed her coffee, and walked out of the building.

Her back hit the stone façade on the outside of the shop as she hid. She could walk the short way in front of the glass windows, see Breanna, and probably trip on the sidewalk. Or she could take the long way in the opposite direction around the avenue of shops.

She peered inside to see if Breanna had left. That would decide which way she went. Instead, she saw her aunt laughing at something the flannel clad woman said.. "Aunt Amy, what are you doing?" The confusion laced words fell from her lips. Part of her wanted to rush back in and pull her aunt into the back room. But seeing the older woman enjoying the animated conversation gave her pause. She couldn't embarrass her aunt because of her insecurity.

So, she shoved her hands into her pockets and trudged the long way back to her car. The cold air nipping at her skin would do her some good. The rational side of her had faith the situation would blow over soon. The pang in her chest wasn't so optimistic.

Chapter Seven

Reilly's fingers flew across the keyboard, plotting out a new idea that took center stage after she left the coffee shop. She'd loved working on her other series, but right now, she was stuck. Her friend's comments pounded her mind into submission. *Was the plot fixable? Would she alienate everyone if she published something just to finish it?* The concern rattled her to the core more than those red marks on her wall calendar warning of deadlines ahead. Reilly hoped this break would clear her mind and allow the story to unfold as it needed behind her mind's eye.

She set an alarm on her computer to bring her back to her other series. She couldn't abandon it completely, but her creative muse needed out. Her brain screamed as she continued plugging in small plot points to ensure this new story stayed on track. It raged as she exported it to her writing program.

But her heart stayed calm. She blamed it on the chance meeting in the café. She tried to ignore the tingles overtaking her body but failed. Her stomach hadn't been so flip-floppy since Helen. Reilly shook the thought from her head. She didn't want those negative memories to spill into her work. Right now, she focused on the eruption of butterflies throughout her body when Breanna smiled at her. God, she was a pathetic mess. *I can't worry about that now.*

The novel was taking shape faster than anything she'd written before. These new characters would run into one another in a coffee shop. It seemed fitting. But unlike her reality, the story would have a happy ending, with a grand gesture to prove the love they felt was real.

She forced herself to take a moment to sip her tea. The fluid warmed her as the chill outside kept her room colder this time of year. She chuckled for a moment, remembering Helen and Wendy arguing about the temperature during the evening hours. Her mother insisted on lowering the heat to sleep better.

Helen had complained that Reilly was always cold, and she couldn't handle her ice-cold feet. Reilly had watched that disagreement with such endearment. Her two favorite people in the world were having a heated discussion over her. It felt natural. Until it wasn't.

"Jenna's coming over with the kids." Reilly could feel her mother's closeness before her arms wrapped around her torso. "Wait, you labeled a chapter 'sex scene to be added later'? Are you writing a romance?"

"You know I hate it when you read over my shoulder, Mom. Yes, that is a chapter, and this book just came to me. You know how it is. When the muse speaks, you listen."

"If you're referring to my RV and my tool room, then yes, I do. If you're talking about writing, no, honey, I don't."

"I can't explain it, but something just . . . It's like the excitement before a big trip." Reilly removed her mother's arms and spun around in her chair to see her mother's confused expression.

"Sweetheart, you pack a week or two early, stress out about flight details, and don't sleep the night before you leave. Most times you end up with a cold. If that's what you're feeling, I beg you to walk away from the computer before you give it a virus." Wendy laughed, placing her hand on her daughter's shoulder. "If you're talking about how *I* feel about hopping in my RV and traveling . . . then yes, I do follow you. It's usually followed by disappointment when I don't get on the road though."

Reilly grabbed her mother's hands and held them tightly. She didn't like these conversations, but the slight tremble in her voice reminded her why they were important. "Mom, you know the doc said—"

"To live my life fully and get healthy. I've lost weight, cholesterol is in check, and my ticker is doing much better since I decided to take care of myself. I'd like to be out on the road this summer."

Reilly leaned back and absorbed her mother's words. Wendy hadn't taken her RV on a long trip for three or four years. In fact, she couldn't remember the last time the vehicle had left the state line. Normally, Wendy just drove it around town to the places with a big enough parking lot to keep it running well. She planned to hit some local state parks but never actually left the house.

Reilly saw the meticulous planning for various trips hanging on her mom's corkboard in the smaller office. She'd ensure her mom and Aunt Amy ate during their animated discussions over a new adventure. It usually involved a bottle or two of Merlot and infectious laughter. It wasn't unusual if they crashed on the living room pull out later in the evening. They were impossible to wake in the morning, but Reilly wouldn't trade those two for anything else in the world.

While her mother lay in a hospital bed with wires attached to her skin and a tube down her throat, Reilly realized her happiness was wrapped up in her mom's. The moments of joy the two older women experienced gave her hope. Not just that there was life after fifty, but that they were both still here. Her mom was still with her, alive.

"Now, I know I told the doc you're a dragon lady and I listen to what you say to do. So, when are you going to let me travel?" Wendy's words cut through Reilly's ribs and pierced her heart. She hated hearing the anguish in her mother's voice. But fear clung to Reilly like spandex. If Wendy fell ill on the road, how would Reilly get to her? What if Wendy had no cell signal to call for help? Could a small hospital even handle a cardiac patient? The thoughts were never ending, and those were just the ones she acknowledged. Being left behind . . . that was something she wouldn't discuss.

"I'm not stopping you, Mom. I just think you'd need to prepare and have all your ducks in a row. You'd need enough meds to get you through the time you're away. Maybe an emergency kit with numbers, extra supplies, alarms on that smart watch of yours to ensure you remember to take everything at the right time. And I'd like to have a detailed itinerary of when I should expect you to be there."

"Right." Wendy shuffled to the doorway, turned, and leaned on the frame. "You know, the best laid plans change. People do too. I just never thought you'd lock yourself away from life. I did that. Don't be like me, sweetheart. I keep telling you there's more to life than these four walls. Don't ignore the world while you're holed up inside."

"Really?" Reilly's hackles went up. "I'm an author. Our very existence requires us being locked up in an office for however many hours a day."

"You could write from anywhere, Reilly. You choose to stay home."

"Yes, I came home, but you needed me. So, I stayed." Reilly responded with more conviction than she really had. She came home because her mom almost died. She only meant to stay until Wendy was back on her feet again. But she couldn't shake the fear that haunted her on the train ride to the hospital the night they called about her mom. It ate away at her core and left a void she couldn't escape. She allowed it to shape her current situation and indirectly hid her from the pain of her past life. What would happen if her mother left and she was alone?

"I needed you, and you were there for me when no one else was, but I wish . . ." Reilly knew that look—guilt. She knew Wendy was mortified about how much she leaned on her daughter regularly. Reilly had tried and failed to convince her mom moving back home was necessary multiple times.

"I enjoy being here, Ma. It's quiet. I get work done. I have friends I talk to regularly. I have my two nieces a stone's throw away. More importantly, I get to help you out whenever you need me. I'm where I belong." Reilly's tone was harsher than she intended, but she needed the conversation to end. They'd rehashed this squabble whenever Reilly went into a funk. She didn't have the capacity to handle it today.

"Whatever you say, Reilly. Like I said, Jenna and the kids will be over in a few minutes. It would be nice if you could join us." Wendy's motherly timbre left no room for discussion. Regardless of where she was in her current work, Reily was expected downstairs. Call it responsibility or her inability to say no, but she'd comply.

"I'll be right down."

Her mother didn't reply. She just moved away from the doorframe and out of the room. The silence was deafening, and Reilly was well aware she had to apologize to her mother. For what, she hadn't quite worked out, but she needed to take responsibility for whatever it was.

She jumped right back into the story and wrote until she heard the telltale sign of two tiny humans running through the house. Reilly quickly typed out notes about the next sequence and saved her file. Clicking her monitor off, she grabbed her mug and headed downstairs to make a fresh cup of tea before joining everyone.

Millie and Edie were already outside with Bubba. The little terrier was desperately trying to catch one of the two speedy youngsters. Jenna and Wendy sat on the patio laughing. This was why Reilly had no desire to leave. She knew how lucky she was to have a loving family nearby. The same family that accepted her sexuality with a smile and a glass of wine. When Reilly came out to her brother Harrison, his response made her laugh. *So, I have a new wing . . . uh woman.* He'd pulled her into a hug right after.

"Aunt Reilly!" Edie screamed from the lawn. "Bubba's gonna eat me!"

Reilly walked onto the adjoining patio and placed her mug on the table. Before Edie could react, her aunt lifted her up over her shoulder and ran around the yard like a crazy person. Millie and Bubba gave chase as Edie laughingly begged for help. This was what Reilly lived for. Moments like this, where the world faded away into nothing.

Reilly placed Edie on her feet and fell to the ground as if the child had knocked her over. In seconds, both girls were jumping on her. Bubba was cleaning her face of any trace of lotion she'd put on this morning. She rolled on the grass as if there was no way to get up while the two girls tried to tickle her and get her to admit defeat.

"Your tea's gonna get cold." Jenna's voice pierced their laughter.

"You win!" Reilly wiggled her way out of her nieces' grasp and bowed down to them both. "Dear nieces, you have slain the evil auntie monster, and now I must have a beverage to regain my strength. For I shall be back to challenge thee again." She lowered her head as she backed away from the trio.

"You're so silly, Aunt Reilly," Millie replied.

"We'll be ready for you, evil auntie. You will never defeat us, cause good always wins!" Edie had her hands on her hips, looking every bit of a superhero.

Jenna offered Reilly her mug as she sat down in an empty chair next to them. "The more I watch them grow up, the more they remind me of you and Harrison. Don't get me wrong, I see a lot of myself in them too. But sometimes, that sibling stuff . . . it's just so the two of you. Oh, and Edie's protectiveness is all Reilly."

"You should have seen her as a kid. She once walked her friend into kindergarten because he was too scared. They were five."

"Ma, come on. I didn't do that." Reilly didn't remember much of her childhood. She blamed the aging process and stress of being an adult.

"Yes, you did. You always protected your brother too. Jenna, did he ever tell you about the bullies in eighth grade?"

"No." Jenna leaned forward on the table, eyes wide and lips curved upward. "He always tells me school was horrid, but no big deal."

"Mom, please." Warmth flooded Reilly's face and she feared it would be completely red if her mother continued.

"Harrison was the kind of kid that if he saw something wrong, he'd jump in the middle to stop it. He was such a politician, trying to talk through any argument on the playground or in the classroom. One day, the principle calls telling me to pick both my kids up early. When I get there, Harrison has a black eye and Reilly doesn't have a scratch on her. But she's in a corner, her ears a dark red, arms folded, and man is she heated. The principal immediately tells me three boys jumped my son during recess. He refused to fight back, even though we taught him to defend himself. Reilly, on the other hand, decided she'd seen enough. She stormed over there, tapped one boy on the shoulder, and decked him. All three boys ended up on the ground, nursing their egos and bruises. She led Harrison to the nurse's office while the bullies tattled on Reilly. He brought them to the office, but the other kids were nowhere to be found."

"Did she get suspended?"

"Oh, they didn't dare. She had to apologize and talk to the guidance counselor about violence not being the answer. The other parents were fuming, of course. Their little angels would do nothing like that, but several kids and security cameras painted an accurate picture. So, Reilly was a hero, and the bullies got a three-day vacation."

"Wait, you actually apologized?" Jenna turned her attention back to Reilly, who slid down the chair, trying to blend in with the paver stones.

"Yes, I told all the adults I was sorry for doing their jobs. I'd told the principle about the bullies and how bad it was getting. He didn't do anything."

"You didn't!"

"She did. My little Reilly was a spitfire then."

"Where's that confidence now? You didn't say one word to Breanna that didn't involve babbling nonsensically."

"Breanna? What am I missing?" Wendy leaned forward on the table with a smirk etched on her face.

"Nothing to get excited over, Ma. Just a woman we met at Aunt Amy's coffee shop. No big deal." She hoped the cold hid the flush in her cheeks from embarrassment. She didn't want to think about something that would never happen.

"She's gorgeous, and Reilly couldn't stop staring. What happened after I left?"

"Nothing. She runs a production company in the city and she's looking for the elusive author, M. E. Kline. Nothing is or will ever happen. Full stop." This was not something Reilly wanted to think about or even entertain. She hoped her firm words would have the desired effect.

"Maybe she's worth spending time with? You never know she's worth the risk until you try," Wendy prodded.

Apparently not.

"There's a reason I like anonymity. I don't want people around me all the time, praising me and blowing smoke up my bum. What if they blab it all over? What if it connects me back to the people Helen lied to about Kline to bolster her career? Then what? I can't risk that backlash on social media channels saying I'm a cheat or a liar. I've watched careers crash and burn without context. I'd rather not go down that road if I can avoid it."

"You sure that's all it is?" Jenna placed her hand over Reilly's. "If it is, then we've got your back. If it's not . . ."

Reilly knew she should finish that hanging sentence, but she couldn't. She didn't know which it truly was. She'd buried both fears so deep down that she was unaware if she could ever free them again. Instead, Reilly did what she was good at. She gulped her tea down, ran to play with the kids, and ignored the fear and shame coursing through her veins.

***

Alarm bells kept ringing in Breanna's head when she walked to Amy's Coffee Shop to get her morning drink. She tried to convince herself that she just preferred professionally brewed coffee to the instant delivered with her groceries, but it fell flat. She'd hoped to run into Reilly again. She even talked to Amy for twenty minutes, trying to pry more information from the woman. The only thing she managed to get across was her phone number with the hope of a call.

Breanna ordered another drink with a pastry and left. Sitting here at the breakfast bar at the house, the desire to know more about this mysterious woman overtook her. *It was only natural to Google someone you just met, right?* Breanna reasoned as she scanned the results.

There wasn't much available, truthfully. Reilly had no website. She had a Facebook account with the most recent post being months ago. Worse yet, it was private so she could scan the woman's timeline to learn more. Reilly seemed to be more a ghost than the author she was desperate to find.

The notification of Kai's call covered the screen with their name and image of two crossing swords. With a swipe of her finger, Breanna answered the phone and tapped the speaker phone icon.

"Please tell me you have some good news." The low, sensual tone of her voice took Breanna by surprise. She stretched and yawned from the lack of sleep and caffeine her body desired.

"Damn, girl. At least we know you could do voiceover work for . . . fun things. Hell, you do that and we'd be in the black within a week."

"Funny, Kai. I didn't sleep last night."

"Yeah, several reviews said headlights lit up the main bedroom all night. Switch rooms, see if it helps."

"It's not that." If it had just been the room, Breanna's entire body wouldn't be this on edge. After her conversation with Amy yesterday, her concern for finding the elusive author grew. The woman seemed tight lipped and changed the conversation to her niece whenever Breanna asked about Kline. Then there was the guilt weighing on her shoulders since she really didn't mind talking about Reilly. Those blue eyes and the woman's smile as she laughed overwhelmed her senses creating a desire beyond the physical. She couldn't deny the arousal those cerulean depths elicited within her, but there was something more. It was a no-win situation for resting, no matter how many cold showers she subjected herself to.

"Bre, what's got you so worked up?" She could hear the concern in her friend's voice, but she had more important things to focus on. Like the company.

"Kai, please tell me you found something."

"I joined the main Facebook group for Kline's fans. I've been politely commenting and asking questions, seeing if anyone takes the bait. They said she hosts chats every now and again, without video of course. At least we have that connection to work with now. It's a small step in the right direction!"

"Good, keep digging. See if her fans will give us anything. But beyond that, I assume I'm staying here until we find her. This might get expensive, Kai."

"It's off season, and I got a deal for a certain time frame. Truthfully, we're desperate, Bre." The solemn sound of Kai's voice increased her anxiety tenfold. They'd discussed their situation ad nauseam. It wasn't going away just because the words were unspoken at the moment.

"Well, if push comes to shove, I can sleep in the car. We've been there, done that." Breanna sipped her coffee and thought about Reilly again. Her insecurity slipped in. *You're a failing producer with nothing to offer.* She shook her head, swallowed hard, and forced herself to focus. "What happened at the meeting yesterday?"

"They were more receptive than I thought they would be. Nothing signed yet, but we have more meetings scheduled soon."

"It's a lifeline. I'll take it."

"Now that I've laid out my cards, your turn. Anything up there?"

"Nothing. I'm sorry. I thought people would chomp at the bit to tell me about a famous resident. No one I spoke to thus far will spill anything. I'm headed to the post office today, though I doubt they'll break the law and tell us who owns the box. Unless you have some magical way to get more information . . . I'm sorry, Kai. Thought this would be easier."

"Hey, it's been one day. Give yourself a break. Now, I don't know magic, but I know the P.O. Box is rented under Blessed Favor, LLC. It's not the same company running the social media accounts, so I have a friend digging into the state's records to find the filing information. Could be something."

"Are you sure? Sounds like a religious organization or some kind of porn connection."

Kai's laughter lifted through the phone, easing Breanna's stress. "I doubt Kline would be attached to something like that. From what I've read, the books question the fabric of religion as we know it, and the relationships read authentically. Biggest complaint I've found is the lack of sex, so . . ."

"Lack of sex? It's a young adult series. Why is the world obsessed with sex?" The thought just reiterated Breanna's theory that the world needed tons of chocolate and therapy.

"The same reason producers argue we need to add more scantily clad women in our films. It sells."

"But we fight against that stupidity, Kai." Memories of past altercations flew to the forefront. They verbally lambasted producers who belittled female leads, demanding scraps of leather instead of armor. Every time a company backed out of a project because of outlandish demands, it fueled the fire behind each of their successes. K.B. Studios wasn't perfect, but it would never cower to idiocy.

"And we're facing closure while the other companies continue to thrive. It's not fair, but it's the bottom line. Maybe they were right."

"I don't agree with that. We both know films that don't require denigrating people for pleasure." If those other companies were right, then Breanna should just close shop now. She shook the negative thoughts away.

"Yea, we do. I'm just the messenger for all that stuff, Bre. You know we're on the same page here." The sound of brewing coffee came through the phone as Breanna chomped the last bit of her breakfast pastry. It was so good, she moaned as she chewed. She'd have to buy another when she went back out. "Okay, what was that?"

"Amy's Coffee Shop makes some pastries on the premises. The barista recommended it. It's chocolate, buttery goodness, and oh, man, it's heavenly."

"At least you found the coffee shop." Kai laughed as the brewing stopped on their end of the phone. "Have you met any of the locals? Mingled a bit? Asked if they know anything?"

Breanna's stomach swirled with nerves. "Yeah. I met Amy, who runs the coffee place. She's nice. I asked her about Kline. She said she didn't know who she was, but I got that answer from everyone. Then again, Amy was keener on helping me with her niece, so . . ." *There, now it's out in the open.* Breanna felt relieved.

"Wait, her niece? Did you meet someone? When did that happen? Why didn't you call me last night?"

"Because I was digging into things around here, trying to find a pathway to our salvation. I gave her my number but—"

"You did what? You never give out your number. I've watched women vault across a room to say hi, but you're gone by morning with their digits. Breanna Blaine remains an enigma just out of reach unless she chooses to contact you."

"I'm not that bad, Kai." She was though. "And I dated a few of those women. They just didn't last. They saw a woman who looked like her life was together, and once they got to know the fallible me, they fled. Not the other way around."

"Bre, you deliberately chose women who were so shallow they live in a perpetual drought. What makes this one different?"

"I don't know. Reilly's eyes . . . and her smile . . . just made me feel like the rest of the world didn't matter. I mean it does, obviously, but I felt calm around her. And she was adorably nervous. Like I wanted to hug her each time she fidgeted around me, which was most of the conversation. Kai, I went to the coffee shop this morning hoping to see her. I don't know if her aunt gave her my phone number yet, but she hasn't reached out, so . . ."

"Reilly, huh? Look, Bre, you're going through some serious stress right now. Maybe this trip is a blessing in disguise. Sure, you have a job to do, but maybe enjoy what the place has to offer. Maybe it will help you sort out your head. Hell, this woman could be the one to get you over the past."

"I don't know about that, Kai. Max has a better chance of learning to talk before that happens. Seriously though, I've never experienced anything like this before. The moment I saw her smile, I wanted to say hi. Then she dropped her coffee, and I wanted to replace it. But let's be honest, my connections are all about power and sex."

"You got her a new one because you're a good person, Bre."

"Maybe, but it also allowed me to say hello. Everything about her was so inviting. And the worst part is she almost ran me over when I crossed the street! Oh my God, I can't believe I didn't apologize for that!"

"Hold up, what? How did you piss her off so quickly? I thought you bought her coffee."

"Sorry, let me start at the beginning. I crossed the street without looking, and she stopped short and honked at me. When I walk into the coffee shop, she was already there. I don't know how she got there before me. Maybe speed walking, teleporter or—"

"She walked in the back door? I mean the parking lot is right behind the shop, it would make sense. Anyway, we've officially reached the nauseating stage. I'll be up there when I can to help you out. I'll keep you posted on everything around here."

"I'll do the same."

Without saying another word, they disconnected the call. Kai's words still hung in the air. Breanna was there for however long it took to get an answer. Maybe she could use that time to get to know Reilly better. Maybe there was more to that woman than just her gay panic-filled lemon shark babble. The memory warmed her heart, but she couldn't focus on it now. She turned her attention back to the notes on her phone. Breanna figured out various ways to approach different people at the post office. Until she bumped into Reilly, or the woman texted her, there was nothing she could do but wait.

Chapter Eight

Reilly sat in front of her computer, editing the previous chapter she'd written. Other authors would tell her it was a maddening feat, but she would write her quota for the day and then go back. It allowed her to verify things were moving in the proper direction and continuity was maintained. Rereading her chapters also allowed her to fantasize about a certain woman in a flannel shirt.

The online video chat popped to life. Her friends taking up small boxes across her secondary monitor screen. She'd called an emergency meeting with them to get some advice on everything that had happened within the last twenty-four hours. Her aunt's text message lingered unanswered, but the message forced her breath to quicken as her blood pressure rose. Her aunt had her best interest at heart when she obtained Breanna's number. Reilly should be upset for the woman meddling in her love life. The slight smile and flushed cheeks pushed any anger away.

And because of that physical response, she sent an SOS out immediately.

"Okay." Natalie yawned in her scrubs. "What's so important that it couldn't wait and required an immediate response?"

"Don't hate me, but I put Shadows Rise on the backburner for now. Not forever, just right now. I started writing this . . . romance that I can't get out of my head." Reilly wondered how crazed she looked on screen. She glanced toward her image and then back to her phone's messages.

"As a reader of the series, sure it makes me unhappy to hear this. But we've waited this long, what's a bit more time? The bigger question I have is . . . romance? When have you even thought about that?" Vera asked from a temporary office on a construction site.

"I hadn't, truthfully. I love to read them, but how could someone who's been so unlucky . . . How could I write it?" Reminders of her relationship failures screamed in the back of her mind with every key press of the new novel. Could she even write something with such adoration when she'd never experienced that depth before?

"I doubt Stan Lee knew anything about radioactive spiders or alien planets. It was in his imagination, Reilly. You can write anything you want," Gina answered from her studio. Paint smudges on her shirt and left cheek highlighted her newest endeavor. "Seriously, Rei. You just create whatever is in that noggin of yours. If our creations don't work, consumers let us know with their wallets. But we owe it to ourselves to try. Plus, it removes that idea and allows others to flow in. Yes, I say that from experience."

"Reilly, we know you well enough to understand that writing takes time, and switching gears is always a possibility." Lily's words chilled Reilly's body back down to normal levels. Regardless of the words spoken, the tone was more motherly and understanding, cracking the firm façade Reilly put on. "But you wouldn't call a meeting like this for something so trivial. What's really going on?"

"She's here!" Reilly blurted out, her arms waving in the air as if to pull Breanna from the ether to show her friends. "The woman who keeps emailing me about my books. The one who won't take no for an answer." Reilly bounced up as the weird energy filled her to capacity. She needed to burn it off to think clearly, and that meant moving about the room as the full story tumbled out of her mouth. "The one who wears flannel like a second skin, whose jeans hug her body in all the right ways, whose smile pulled me in and made me want to get to know her better. God, don't get me started on her eyes or the fact that she bought me coffee."

"She bought you coffee!" The voices of all her friends at various points in the same sentence brought her back to reality.

"Yeah, let's just say I couldn't take my eyes off of her and she noticed. Me being me, I was my normal uncoordinated self and promptly dropped my cup on the floor. Pieces flew everywhere, and it was so damn loud! So, the woman in question—Breanna is her name—she bought me a replacement since it was her fault for . . . you know, just being there." Reilly flopped back in her chair, her hands pressed into her face trying to wipe away the embarrassment. "Even after all that, she left her number with my aunt for me. So of course, now I'm staring at it, wondering if I should call, text, or delete it from my memory banks forever."

Her hand shook over the phone as her throat constricted. She could always get the number back if this was a mistake. She'd just have to ask her aunt again, right? But then she'd have to explain why she lost it. Especially when she'd already seen it and her aunt knew it. *Damn phones and their read status notification.*

"Well, you know deletion is never forever, right?" The tech side of Camila creeped up, making them all laugh. "Seriously, it isn't."

"Reilly, Faye said she'd help you. If you want a scathing, legalese-filled letter, she'd do it for nothing. Also, my wife is really sexy when she gets protective. Just saying." Gina waved around her paint brush for emphasis as Reilly's tension eased with the act of kindness.

"Thank you, but I'm not sure if a letter would help at this point. She's already in town asking questions. I wish I listened to Ellen when she recommended the team handle my P.O. Box. They could have forwarded all pertinent things my way. But no, I wanted control over something. Why did I think I could get away with having it in my hometown? I'm sure that led her right to me. It's the only thing I can think of."

"Because, legally, you needed to do that when you formed the LLC. Remember, Faye handled everything, but they required your information. They can petition the state for your filing forms. You knew this was always a possibility, love." Faye's voice echoed through the call from beyond the screen.

"I never thought— Ahh, it doesn't matter what I thought. Doesn't seem like they accessed the state information. Breanna was asking questions about Kline, not me. So, for now, I am still anonymous."

"It can take time to find you, so maybe now's the time for a letter from your lawyer saying thanks but no thanks."

"Or you could just get to know Breanna better and see if she's trustworthy?" Natalie's eyes brightened with her suggestion. Reilly could practically taste the sugary sweetness of the hopeless romantic oozing through the monitor. She'd expected her teeth to tingle with pain, but instead she found herself mulling over Natalie's words. "Maybe she turns out to be something you weren't expecting.

If you can trust her, tell her the truth. Do some big romantic gesture explaining everything and why you hid it all."

"Nat, this isn't a rom-com with a happy ending. Breanna's here for the rights to Reilly's books. If I were you, Rei, I'd be careful what I texted or posted or whatever. In today's age, anyone could use anything against you in any way they can imagine."

"Why are you always so cynical, Camila?" Natalie piped in.

"Hey, she's just being truthful!" Vera's defense of Camila was stronger than necessary, but not unexpected. Reilly knew Vera's harshness was fed by her insecurities. Especially since she purchased an engagement ring for Camila but was too terrified about her response to ask the question. Instead, its remained in her office safe, buried under the responsibilities of her adult life.

"Can you all just stop, please? This isn't helping. I already Googled Breanna and her partner, Kai. It was the first thing I did when they emailed. All positive things. Beyond their company profiles, I found articles praising their work ethic, some critical reviews for films they worked on, their socials post normal stuff. The only thing I get is they are good to those they work with." In fact, they were a company she would pitch her books to if she wanted them adapted to film. But she didn't want that, right? Reilly swatted the thoughts away as her stomach rolled with the pain associated with her panic attacks. The air entered her lungs, and she pressed it out slowly. The ritual stopped the discomfort from escalating beyond her control. *Thank goodness for years of experience.*

"Can I ask a silly question?" Lily joined the conversation. Her eyes looked directly at the camera as Reilly looked anywhere but the screen. She couldn't handle the intensity from a woman trained to see through smokescreens. "Why not just talk to her about your books? Have Faye set up a nondisclosure agreement and go from there. I know you prefer to stay anonymous, but you've never truly explained why you can't just entertain the conversation."

"Because . . ." The words faded from all rational explanations. Why wasn't Reilly willing to discuss everything with the proper safeguards and documentation in place to ensure her anonymity? It would give her the protection she desired and the ability to expand her reach as an author. When did her fears from an abusive relationship in her past really control her future? *Since I can remember.*

"They're not ironclad," Camila said before Reilly could answer her own questions. "People blow through them every day. Some end up in lawsuits, and others get away with it. All it takes is one comment on social media, and Reilly's anonymity is gone. Remember, Faye had that case a few years ago? Person went on a tirade online, blew through their NDA. Company sued, but the misinformation is still out there. Can't unring a bell, you know."

The discomfort in Reilly's stomach returned. She couldn't afford lawyers to sue a company. Reilly had no idea what K.B. Studio's financial situation was. They could drag it out until the very last penny was spent. Or they could settle with a crappy contract and the rights to her books. Regardless, it was uncharted waters Reilly had no intention of swimming in.

"While I posed the question, I can see your point, Camila. The internet is rife with people hiding behind weird names, twisting narratives to further their fame, but it also exposes who they really are. If they threaten someone or twist things to suit their own case, they should be prosecuted. The rule is simple, if someone shows you who they are, believe them," Lily added.

"Still can't prosecute or stop someone who hides behind a keyboard. And Rei, you're a best-selling author who no one has ever met. If I was an internet sleuth, I would take that morsel of information and run with it. It wouldn't take long to connect the dots to your name, your history, and even Helen," Camila continued. "I know this is all doom and gloom, and it might be the worst-case scenario, but still one that needs to be addressed."

"And that's why I hide in my office for days at a time. I don't need my failure at love splattered all over the place, let alone have Helen portraying our relationship failure however she wants in the tabloids. I just want to write, make a living, and be left alone. When I'm dead, the vultures can swarm over the carcass of my career."

"You are so morbid sometimes." Natalie yawned again. "Honey, you need to do what's best for you, but this isn't going away. If you want the company to back down, focus on making that happen."

"Right now all I want is to send her a text and . . ." Reilly stopped herself from adding the desire to kiss Breanna until her lips were swollen. The warmth spread from her chest up her neck and settled at the tips of her ears. There was no way to hide how her thoughts manifested on her skin. "Forget it. I can't. It's just too complicated to think about all of this." Reilly dropped her head to her desk and moaned in frustration.

"I'll say to you what I tell my kids regularly. Part of being a human being is facing things we don't want to do every day. You're an adult, Reilly. You can't hide from the train speeding in your direction. You either get off the tracks or go along for the ride. Either way, you need to decide. We'll support you to the end. But let's be honest, the past will come out. No matter how much we don't want it to." Gina words settled her.

Holding up her phone, Reilly swallowed the lump in her throat and clicked on her aunt's message. After a quick copy and paste, Breanna Blaine was in her contacts list. Before she could overthink it further, Reilly typed out a simple message.

Coffee six tonight at Amy's? It's Reilly, in case you're wondering.

Her hand trembled as she dropped the phone on her desk. She berated herself for not using an app that allowed message deletion after sending in case she changed her mind. She had no recourse but to see it through.

If she replies at all.

Her breath quickened as the idea of rejection filled her mind.

***

Breanna stood waiting for the manager as the second hand on her watch ticked by. There was a short line in the post office, but nothing that would warrant waiting as long as she had. Questions about her approach were swirling in her mind, and the longer she paced in the lobby, the more she overanalyzed it all.

"Ms. Blaine?" an elderly woman called out from the top part of a split "staff only" door. "I apologize for the wait, but sorting needs to be done timely regardless of one's station."

"I'm sorry to bother you, ma'am. I was just curious about the owner of a PO box here. I was wondering if you could share any information about box five thirty-one?"

"I'm sorry, honey, but legally we can't share any details about our clients." The older woman was kind about it, but the firm admonishment her tone let Breanna know there was no room for discussion.

"Could you tell me when Blessed Favor, LLC opened it or if M. E. Kline comes in here to check it?" Breanna hedged her bets and pressed on.

"All I can say is I have no idea who checks the box or when. I've been working here for three years, and I don't remember it being rented during that time. So it predates me." The woman crossed her arms and leaned on the ledge of the door. "I don't know why you're interested in the box, but no employee will give you more than I already have. If you're with the authorities, I need proper paperwork to give you more. Otherwise, have a wonderful day, Ms. Blaine."

"Thank you for your help." Breanna smiled as she walked away, but her disappointment was evident. She expected this response, but it didn't make the sting hurt any less. Now she had to call Kai and to figure out their next course of action. Maybe she'd risk a ticket or, worse, an arrest by staking out the post office to see who came to the box. But she had no idea when the box was checked. All Breanna had in her arsenal was its location by the window. She could sit and wait it out . . . possibly. They needed another plan.

"Anything?" Kai answered before her phone even rang.

"Like we expected. All I got was it's been open longer than three years and gets emptied. Timetable and who does it, unknown. I don't know what I'm doing here, Kai. I could stay in the parking lot and see what happens, but this just feels impossible. It's crazy, Kai."

"I know, but you just keep digging things up there while we find more stuff. My friend is working on getting the state filing paperwork for the LLC, but it's registered there. I'm thinking Kline uses the company as a layer of protection from the masses. Smart thing to do, if you ask me."

Breanna's phone beeped with Reilly's message. A warmth spread throughout her chest with a mix of joy and fear.

"Okay, I'll keep looking around, but I have a bigger problem. Reilly wants to meet up for coffee."

"And why is that a problem?"

"No. I mean I left my number for . . . I feel . . ." Words failed her. How could she describe something she hadn't experienced before?

"What? Are you nervous like a sexually active girl missing her period?" The comment flew out of the phone and instantly stopped the feeling from festering within her.

"Please stop," Breanna begged through her laughter. "How do I handle this, Kai?"

"Here's a novel idea. Text her back and say yes. Then you meet, sip some of that coffee you brag about. Talk to the girl and see where things go. Just be yourself, Bre. I expect updates on all of that, and I'll keep you posted about things here. Deal?"

"Yeah, love you, Kai. Thanks for having my back on all this." It seemed simple enough. Just take the woman out for coffee, converse, and see where the evening led her. The air returned to her lungs as her concerns faded away.

"You're my family. It's what we do. Now, off with you. Go get the girl!"

The call disconnected, leaving Breanna staring at her phone. How should she reply to Reilly? Like Kai said, she was horrible at this. She was the best wing person for everyone else, but when she needed to come up with some perfect reply, she faltered. Before she could think about it any further, she replied, in the most pathetic way possible.

Love to.

Chapter Nine

Reilly rubbed her hands on her bare legs for the millionth time. The clammy feeling added to her discomfort as she paced around her room. She'd tried on almost every outfit in her closet, but nothing lifted her confidence or made her feel desirable. Her bare feet trounced over old concert shirts, various jeans in different styles, and her non-sexy underwear. Her entire wardrobe was built for around her comfort zone or jeans and basic tops. It was perfect for most days, but not this one. It wasn't good enough for her coffee date.

Is it even a date? She shook the question out of her mind. Reilly could only handle one crisis at a time.

"Why don't I have sexy underwear? I mean, I love hipster comfy undies, but seriously, I'm an adult. I mean, I should have stuff that matches, right?"

"Yes, as a single woman you should always have some 'take me to bed' undergarments," Gina commented as one of her children ran across the square naked, with Faye chasing them holding a diaper over her head.

"Look, I've never been like that. I just feel so not myself."

"No lingerie at all?" Natalie retorted as her nails continued to click away at the keyboard.

"No. Even when I found something I could wear, Helen insisted it stay in a drawer. Something about wandering eyes, but it wasn't like I'd ever let anyone else see it!" *God, why does everything in my life always go back to her?* Reilly squashed the thought immediately. This was her life now. She lived in comfort and never thought of herself as a sexual being. *Neither did Helen.*

"Yeah, sweetheart, that was your natural beauty. Your ex was just a jealous, oppressive, and evil wench. You can't help people looking at you."

"But I could have—" Reilly stopped. She knew her past relationship wasn't perfect, but she never thought it was that bad. Her mother taught her it took two people to make it work and two people to tank a connection. How could she blame Helen for everything? It was easier, but was it accurate?

A new window popped up, stopping Reilly from defending Helen's controlling actions. The noise of construction and a sweaty Vera in a hard hat slid into the frame. "Hey, all. What's the emergency?" The others pointed in different directions. "What are you all—"

Reilly took one look at the screen and screamed into her hands. She didn't want to explain this all again. Going through it the first time was embarrassing enough.

"Oh, boy." Vera smirked from her square on the screen. "Rei, if we could hug you and help calm you down, we would, but you need to stop pacing and mumbling and lower that shade of red you got going on. Love the Cookie Monster underwear, by the way."

Reilly stopped and grabbed her little webcam. "Do you have any idea what I've done? I asked a woman out for coffee, it might be a date. At least I think it is. Doesn't matter. It's the same woman who wants to—"

"Buy the rights to your books." All of her friends answered in unison, and why wouldn't they? Reilly couldn't talk about anything else this entire time.

"Yes! I'm a fool. What if this goes south? What if she figures out who I am? What if . . ." She ran her hands over her unshaved legs. "What if she wants to have sex on the first date?" It was one thing to feel sexy with lingerie, but actually acting on it was another story. Reilly hadn't been intimate in years. Would she even remember how to? Bumps formed on her skin as her fear tracked all over her body.

"Jesus, woman, calm the hell down!" Lily's raised voice sliced through Reilly's ramblings as she fell into her desk chair. "Sorry for raising my voice, but you need someone to put things into perspective for you. First, it's just coffee. You're going to a public place, so if you're uncomfortable, you can leave. In fact, we can text you two hours in and see how things are going. If you give us a thumbs-up emoji, we'll text again in another two. You give us a thumbs-down, one of us will call you and give you an excuse to leave."

"What if she doesn't want the date to end and we're bugging her too much?" Camila sheepishly asked.

"Give us a smiley face with heart eyes and we'll leave you be for the evening. But we got you, okay?" Lily answered.

Reilly hung her head, pressing the air between her lips as she counted to ten. She could do this. Lily was right. Reilly had friends behind her this time. She wasn't trapped in a theater or in a relationship. This was a situation she could handle.

"And don't shave your legs. That way you won't be tempted by that sexy body of hers," Gina chimed in.

"That's your go-to?" Reilly's voice cracked with a slight laugh. "What am I going to do with y'all?"

"She said it!" Vera laughed. "Okay, now if you're good, I need to get back to work. If one more guy tries to mansplain the architectural designs I drew, I swear I'm going to make them part of the cement foundation."

"Honey, please don't do that," Camila soothed through the phone. "I'll see you this weekend, right?"

"Yeah, babe. Love you." Vera's feed cut out with her yelling at someone.

"What if she talks about Kline?" The worry crept back into Reilly's bones.

"Then you change the topic," Gina tossed out.

"Or you tell her the truth," Natalie answered. "It's a novel idea, I know. But really, Rei, what are you afraid of? If Vera was here, she'd say you can't build something on a shoddy foundation. Be honest. If she can't handle it, then she wasn't the person you thought she was. If she goes crazy with the information, you have Ellen and her team to handle the fallout."

Reilly wanted to give Breanna the benefit of the doubt, but her experience with people like her was purely negative. The industry and the masses who ingested celebrity entertainment were a fickle bunch. Some weeks her PR team had a wonderful time sharing and promoting her pen name with no worries about the response. Other weeks someone found a snippet of an interview done years ago, posted it online, and found offense to it, and BAM, PR was in a frenzy fixing things.

The most recent example was in reference to Reilly commenting on a post asking if she liked Italian food. She did, but mentioned she wasn't a fan of tomatoes. That led to a random parental organization going on a tirade about Kline being a horrible role model for young children because she hated the healthy red vegetable. It was nonsensical and pointless, but it gained traction. So much so that her PR firm had to release a statement saying that Kline had nothing against tomatoes but was highly allergic. Reilly hated that her team needed to make a professional announcement when a simple Google search would have proven the organization's falsehood. But no one was willing to do that. They simply jumped on the bandwagon, spreading it across social media channels.

"I don't need a PR nightmare. If she asks, I'll change topics." Reilly was good at giving non-answers and redirecting conversations. It worked for years when she denied she was a lesbian to her parents in high school and college. She just had to channel that energy once again.

"I don't think that's—"

Reilly ended the chat before her friends could offer a rebuttal. Fear coursed through her body as time ticked by. She sent off a quick text apologizing and reminding them where she would be and when. Why had she chosen the evening for a coffee date? If it was earlier, they could stay at the shop all day. If she was having a wonderful time tonight, they'd have to leave when the shop closed at nine.

"Reilly?" Wendy soothed through the door. "I'm coming in." She swung the door open and took in the mess around her. "Oh, sweetheart."

"This is a mistake, Mom. I don't know what I'm doing." Reilly moved quickly, grabbing shirts and haphazardly folding them. "I went on a date already, and it was a pathetic failure. Why did I think I could do this properly? Maybe I'm not ready to really date. Worse yet, I chose the one woman who could destroy everything I've built! What the hell was I thinking?"

"You were thinking she was pretty, and you were attracted to her."

"Not the point!"

Before Reilly could say anymore, Wendy's arms enveloped her with the warmth and calm she truly needed. "Honey, you want to get to know her better. There's nothing wrong with that."

"But what if she doesn't like me?" Reilly mumbled into Wendy's shoulder. "What if she finds out and sees me as nothing more than a contract?"

"Then she isn't worth a damn." Wendy pulled back from the hug. "And we deal with the ramifications as a family. We'll hop in my RV and leave for a while. You can write from anywhere, and maybe we meet those friends of yours in person. Whatever you want to do. By the time we come back, your team will have everything settled. It'll be okay, love."

Wendy kissed Reilly on the forehead. "Now clean up this mess before you leave. And do not wear your Cookie Monster underwear. Not on the first date." She laughed, taking all the tension out of the room before she left.

***

By the time Reilly finished cleaning her office and getting ready, she was late. If she wasn't a minimum of five minutes early, her anxiety would let her know its displeasure. Her palms were clammy and her face hot with embarrassment as she walked into Amy's coffee shop. Her eyes scanned the sitting area until they fell upon their target.

Breanna sat in the back, staring down at her coffee clutched between her hands. Her left leg bounced on its own, the black laces of her boots flopping up and down. A sense of calm rolled down Reilly's entire frame as she took in Breanna's state. In that moment, the façade of writer and producer fell away. She only saw Breanna, a woman with a lovely smile who thought sharks were cool. The person who politely bought her a drink without anticipation of what it would get her in return.

Reilly took her in from a safe distance. Breanna's hair was pulled into a ponytail, showing off her long neck and sharp jawline. She could just imagine the woman walking through New York City wearing sunglasses and a leather jacket, owning the street. Her physical appearance was intoxicating, Reilly couldn't deny that. But there were more layers beneath she desperately wanted to uncover. It was both inviting and terrifying.

"Excuse me." A loud voice pushed her to the side. The noise brought attention to her in the doorway, but she was only concerned about the pair of eyes smiling at her from the back corner. Reilly caught Breanna's stare as butterflies flew around in her chest. There was also an unfamiliar warmth expanding beyond the tingles. She was smitten before she even sat down, and it scared her to death.

Before another person pushed her away from the entrance, Reilly went over to the table and shed her jacket.

"Sorry I'm late."

"You're fine. No worries. I mean, unless something happened, in which case, I totally understand if you need to . . ." Breanna stopped mid-sentence and took a breath. "Sorry. I just got my coffee, so it's all good. I ordered you a latte but requested they wait until you arrived to make it. Just have to ask for it."

If she wasn't already taken by the kindness Breanna showed when they first met, this would do it. *Is this woman Jekyll and Hyde? Thoughtful on one hand but a producer who won't take no for an answer on the other?*

"That's so nice of you. Would you like a snack? My aunt always makes these dark chocolate graham crackers that are to die for."

"Sure, I'll take one."

She felt Breanna's eyes on her retreating form. When she was growing up, Reilly would comment to her friends about ogling a woman's body. She could hear her youthful words repeating in her head: "They're people, not objects for your desire." And yet, here she was letting another woman take in her form. Peeking over her shoulder, Reilly caught the other woman focused solely on her rear end.

Breanna's face flushed when her blown pupils met Reilly's. A sultry side smirk, and the writer was smashing out of her comfort zone. Her step was lighter, her voice confident, and she was curious how far she could push it. Reilly leaned on the counter, accentuating her butt as she ordered the treats.

A chuckle erupted from her table. She spun around and watched Breanna use some napkins to clean up her spilled drink.

"Can I have another of whatever she ordered, please?" It amused her to see the other woman flounder about and try to calm herself down. There was an innocence in her motions that tugged at her chest like a tractor beam. The desire to spend time together, and enjoy the other woman's company was stronger than she thought possible.

Reilly had been down this road before, falling deeply into a relationship with someone who captivated her entire being. It ended poorly. Was she willing to try it again? *I did almost run her over with my car.* The soft giggle came out before she could stop it. Maybe her body knew before her mind caught up?

There were so many questions clouding her thoughts as she paid for everything. Did she want to just enjoy the woman's body and shed the commitment before it became too serious? She couldn't deny the fantasies she'd slipped into her newest novel that raised the level of spiciness, but could she do that in real life? Was Reilly made of the material necessary to have a casual sexual relationship? With every step back to the table, Reilly accepted that the journey would give her the answers she needed in time. She hoped she was willing and capable of accepting them.

"Here you go. One coffee and two chocolate masterpieces." She slipped the huge graham crackers on the table. The cashier followed with the beverages.

"I'm sorry about that. I didn't . . . I'm not normally that much of a klutz." Breanna stumbled.

"It happens to the best of us." Reilly slipped into her chair and broke off a corner of her cookie. "Before you think they're massive, trust me, they're not. My Aunt Amy always makes the crackers from scratch on Sundays. I used to roll them out super thin, and then she'd bake them."

She watched her date break a small piece of cookie off and pop in into her mouth. The small moan hit her ears, and Reilly closed her legs tightly. Breanna sipped some coffee and released another sound that made Reilly curl her toes.

"This is so unfair. How could anything taste this good?"

"It's like having a mocha latte." Reilly took a bite of hers with a sip of coffee as she tried to center herself. "My aunt introduced it to me eons ago. It was our little secret part of the recipe, but yeah . . ." Reilly hadn't shared that with anyone, not even her mom. "Anyway, it's dense in calories, but so worth it."

"Your aunt makes these? From scratch?" The fact that Breanna didn't press further about the family's formula for the drink surprised Reilly. She was used to people's desire to know hidden information. To her, it was human nature to grab gossip wherever you can. But the expression on her date's face was more wonder of the treat than that of power-hungry people she'd met before.

"Yeah. She and my mom talk about their hidden book of treasures, but I can't cook, so they leave me out of it."

"How does that work? Sharing it." Breanna leaned onto the table, one hand on the mug and the other holding the sweet treat. Her authentic interest in Reilly's life was foreign to her, but she continued the conversation before her insecurity crept in.

"Well, it's interesting, to say the least. My grandma told me her great-grandmother started it. It would go to the eldest girl in the group, and they would share as needed. If the eldest didn't have girls, it went to the next in line who did. Grandma was the baby of the family, but everyone else had boys. Grandma had one girl. I mean, of all the luck in the world, my mom is the only female out of fifteen grandkids."

"Your mom was meant to have it. What about Amy, though? She wasn't allowed access?"

"Oh, she's not related by blood. Mom and Aunt Amy grew up together, so they became sisters from another mister." Reilly took in Breanna's nod and a look she couldn't quite place. Reilly was raised to believe family was blood and chosen, with no difference between. There was something more to Breanna's reaction, but she'd let it go for now. "So, Mom gave her the book to use as needed. Aunt Amy has added a ton of her family recipes as well."

"Can you still read the pages from your great grandma?"

"It's faded, and some of it's in German. But yes. I've made it a bit of a mission to protect it after all these years. I sealed all the old pages, digitized them, and printed them out on laminated sheets. Boring, but it keeps the original safe."

"I'm sure your mom appreciates it. Would you inherit it next?"

"Well, she did in time, but she wasn't a fan at first. As for who gets it, I hold on to it for my daughter or for whichever niece can cook." Reilly knew one of Harrison's girls would hold the book in the future. She wanted her own kids, but Helen never did. Now it seemed time and lack of a partner had other plans for her.

"You really can't cook?"

"I ran out of the house carrying a tray of burning garlic bread. I tossed the baking tray into the snow so fast to put it out. When the recipe says put it on the top shelf, make sure it isn't on the super top of the oven underneath the burner."

Breanna's laugh connected with Reilly's soul. The woman seemed honestly interested in who she was. No judgment on her inability to cook or mention of a potential child in the future. It was a normal conversation. One filled with awkwardness, newness, and frankly everything she needed.

"Reilly?"

"Sorry, yes?"

"I lost you for a second. It was the mention of desserts, wasn't it? I swear I can bake with the best of them. My chocolate cupcakes are delicious, if I say so myself." Breanna's playful tone made Reilly smile.

"Just thinking of all the meals I'll have to order in if we continue . . . this." Reilly knew the words were meant to stay in her head, but she needed to give them life. She needed to hear what Breanna wanted.

"Well . . ." Breanna paused. Reilly watched her eyes flash from desire to fear and finally settle on a soft, inviting gaze. "If we were to continue this, I think you'd enjoy the kitchen with me. I follow recipes like a champ, and I love cooking. There might be an accident or two, but I haven't burned my place down, and I don't intend to."

"That's good to know." She hoped her meaning wasn't lost on Breanna. The hopefulness of a tomorrow was something she wanted more now than before. Just to talk to her, watch her cook dinner, and laugh together was appealing to Reilly. It also made her head hurt with the implications of their future and how it would all end.

"So . . ." Her date shifted in her chair as if the conversation was too serious for the moment. "I know you love sharks, but what else do you enjoy? Corny question, I know, but my friend Kai sent it to me as a *how to break the ice when you're nervous*. And I just admitted that out loud, didn't I?"

"If it helps, I feel the same way." Reilly sipped her coffee but found it impossible to break eye contact with Breanna. There was something about her eyes that held her there, like an invisible force. "Umm, but I love sports. My teams are all loveable losers. The New York Islanders, New York Mets—"

"If you say you're a Jets fan, we won't work." Breanna laughed.

"No. Surprisingly, a San Francisco 49ers fan."

"How did that happen?"

"My ex was a bandwagon fan. But for me, it just stuck. Mom and I would watch the game on Sunday's using a VPN. She'd comment on the men. I'd scream at the bad penalties."

"I have no real allegiance to any team."

"Then why—"

"Because even I know the Jets are horrible and have the worst luck every year. Truthfully, I'm too busy at work to pay attention to sports much. Bills and all that."

"Ah yes, adulting. It's like technology. The more we have it, the more it needs a sledgehammer when it doesn't work properly."

Reilly enjoyed the silence. She thought back to her freak-out earlier in the day and smiled at how silly it all seemed now. The conversation flowed easily between them. She found herself responding with no barriers or concerns over what was a taboo topic. She didn't have to fill in the silence with babbling or nonsensical things she didn't care about. Reilly was just the person across the small table, nothing more and nothing less.

Above all, she felt safe with Breanna. The coffee shop closed in two hours, and Reilly knew she wanted the date to continue. She was catching feelings and quickly.

Chapter Ten

Chapter Ten

Reilly's eyes followed the employees moving around the shop, cleaning things up to close for the evening. She had no desire to end the conversation and leave just yet, but they couldn't stay here. It was only a matter of moments before one of the newer employees her aunt hired stood by their table.

"I'm sorry to bother you, Ms. Vail, but we're closing in fifteen minutes." The employee fumbled with her fingers as Reilly looked up at her. She wondered if others had rudely replied after being given such information."

"Thank you." Reilly smiled and turned her attention back to the woman across from her. "It's only nine. Would you consider a walk in the park near here?"

"You really don't know how horror films play out, do you?" Breanna chuckled, grabbing her cup to toss away in the recycling bin.

"Maybe I do." Reilly looked up through her eyelashes at a stunned Breanna before laughing at herself.

"I'm scared and also a little intrigued." Breanna shoveled her hands in her jeans pocket. "I guess this is where I should run away and say don't hurt me?" Breanna leaned on the door, holding it open for Reilly to leave the coffee shop.

"That depends, but personally I think you like it." The flirtatious tone felt foreign coming out of Reilly's mouth. She'd never openly flirted with anyone, including her ex. Yet, there was no anxiety creeping in. No doubt crawling across her skin screaming at her to stop. Instead, she found herself captivated by the way she interacted with the other woman.

Breanna mumbled a curse behind Reilly. She turned to find the woman stumbling out of the doorway to follow her. It was endearing. "You okay there?"

"Yeah, umm..." Breanna cleared her throat and nodded to the employees inside. "Thanks again."

Reilly enjoyed the silence as they walked to the park. If she was writing a scene in her book, this would be where the tension became too much for one of them to handle. Their hands would brush, and one would pull away as their cheeks blushed red from embarrassment.

Reilly let her pinky reach out and grab Breanna's. Hooked together by one finger, she led the other woman through the entrance gate.

"I haven't been here in years." Reilly swallowed hard as Breanna's fingers secured their hands together. She shivered at the simple action, the connection being more than she could hope for.

"Even with your nieces?"

The crunch of cedar chips in front of the swings helped slow her racing heart. "They prefer the park by their school. It has one of those spinners that they ask me or another adult to make go as fast as possible."

"I remember those. I was more of a swing person myself. I'd lean back and stare at the sky." Breanna pressed her lips to Reilly's knuckles before letting them go and slipping onto the swing.

"Hmm, I did that until I saw the ground coming back at me." Reilly wasn't sure if she was shuddering at the memory or the tingling the kiss left behind. She sat on the swing next to Breanna and launched herself into the air. "My dad always brought Harrison and me here. He'd push me, and it felt like I could reach the sun and accomplish anything I wanted to."

"Did you?"

Reilly wasn't sure how to answer that question. "I don't know. Maybe I'm more like Icarus, flying too close to the sun and melting my wings. Smashing back to Earth in a heap." She hadn't meant to share her darkness with Breanna, but the woman made it so easy to be vulnerable.

"From where I'm sitting, you're not a pile of mush on the planet's surface. I can't say figuratively, but literally, you are in fine shape." Breanna's snort and laughter caused Reilly to chuckle. "So, why not come here with your dad for old time's sake?"

"He died." Reilly hated the way the words sounded. It was years ago, but the thought of her father being in the ground still seemed wrong. "It took me months to even drive past the park, let alone come here."

"We can go somewhere else. I don't have a clue what's nearby, but I don't mind leaving if you'd like." Breanna slowed her motion as Reilly kicked for more speed.

"No, it's okay. When my mom got sick, I came here to talk to him. It gave me a connection and, oddly enough, some support, you know? God, I am such a downer here. I'm sorry." Reilly's mind screamed to switch gears and stop talking. "What about you? You told me about some of your likes and the fact that we will never agree on a baseball or football team but tell me more about the infamous Breanna Blaine."

"Infamous . . . I don't know about that. What's there to say?" Breanna kicked her legs higher in the air, but Reilly kept pace as their swings moved in tandem. "I'm boring compared to what search engines tell you. That's all business, with parties, premieres, and whatnot. But I'm not all about that life. I love reading, watching movies and TV shows. When I was a kid, my mom got me into crime dramas. We'd usually figure it out before the big reveal. It was the one thing we did well together." Her tone softened, a deeper sadness taking hole. "Yeah. . . Oh, and my net worth is not accurate on any website. I don't know where they get that many zeroes next to my name."

"Shucks, there goes my nefarious plan to plunder your bank account!" Reilly cringed at herself. Who the hell says things like that? "Umm . . . Do you and your mom enjoy crime documentaries? Kind of wondering what snacks work with binging murder shows."

"Popcorn and M&M's, but we never binged anything." Breanna slowed her pace on the swing. "We don't talk much anymore." Breanna dragged her feet in the chips to stop her movement. Reilly slowed down as the other woman stared up at the moon. "I wish I could say things were different, but my parents weren't too fond of my aspirations in life or who I wanted to do them with."

"They didn't like your business partner?" Reilly was blessed to have parents so willing to accept her sexuality easily. She couldn't imagine life without that kind of support.

"Kai? Nah, they were the final straw. They couldn't understand my desire to date women. They'd ignore me, so I tried to be their version of normal for most of my life. I couldn't really be myself around them."

"That must have been hard." Reilly had read about horror stories like this in the past, but it was different hearing it and the depth of pain Reilly could see in the way Breanna's muscles tensed or how she fidgeted as her body rocked to expel the negative energy.

"It was one of the many reasons Kai and I continue to fight for representation in media. I was luckier than most when it came to my upbringing. But I know my childhood would have been so very different if I saw more queer people like me on screen. Kai and I've spoken to fans, and most lean on entertainment as their only source for connection to their true selves. Politicians and lawmakers spread lies about us or wipe out the history of so many, and for what? To calm fear that isn't there to begin with?"

The words hung in the air around Reilly's head like storm clouds. She avoided all politics for this very reason. Breanna looked lost, broken, and in some ways hopeless. Reilly ran her fingers across Breanna's as she wondered how a world so full of choices could breed such darkness. How could life take goodness and contort it to such a horrible degree?

Reilly thought about how her childhood was relatively calm. Sure, she was a misfit and an outcast among her classmates. Bullies tormented her every year for reasons that still eluded her. But through it all, she had her family. Her brother stood beside her, flew home from college when her heart shattered with the loss of a friend. Her mom, the free spirit she was, pulled her away from the cruelty of the world with laughter, minor home improvement projects, or whatever else her mind could create. Her father, while not as vocal or even that communicative with Reilly, never left her side. That was enough. They'd protected her so well; she never thought cruelty would find her as an adult.

But evil is like water, it knows no boundaries.

She'd learned that the hard way.

"Sorry, bit of a soap box there." Reilly could feel Breanna stiffen and move her fingers away. The chill on Reilly's skin made her miss the other woman's warmth.

"No, it's fine. I've been blessed beyond measure to have an accepting family . . . to live in a state that accepts me." Before Breanna pulled further away, Reilly changed the conversation to a safer topic. "So, when did you and Kai decide to start K.B. Studios?"

"Truthfully, we sort of fell into it. We met in college and started making these short films. We always cast Kai's roommate as the lead. Out of nowhere, she submitted one of those shorts to a film festival. It did well enough that we formed the company a few months later. We started small and continued making short films, small documentaries, and whatnot. Everything hit the festival circuit before we streamed them online. The *Rainbow Coalition* was the first project that really got us noticed." The pride in Breanna's voice was such a change from the pain a few moments ago.

"That was you? Millie and Edie loved that kids show. They'd watch it with sock puppets since they didn't have the official ones. Those girls made me suffer through every episode multiple times. I guess I have you to thank for all the wine Jenna and I drank to get those songs out of our heads." Reilly playfully kicked Breanna in the shin and grunted for effect.

"Yeah, I guess so. But you have to admit, the show had its purpose . . . and a really annoying earworm of a theme song."

Reilly's chest constricted when Breanna focused on her. A slow burn swelled between her legs, and she swore she could hear her heart hammering in her chest. It would only take Reilly a moment to lean forward. Her breath quickened as she toyed with her next step.

Breanna made it for her when she turned back to the sky. "It started out well, but we were so ambitious. Thought we knew what the market could handle. Ignorance of youth, ya know? We took on so much in those early years, and some projects paid the price for our aspirations. At one point, there were all these companies willing to work with us. Now, not so many. We thought we were building a company that would open the horizons of people worldwide, and in the process forgot we needed to keep the doors open. It's such a screwy fine line that neither Kai nor I wanted to deal with. Which is why Shadows Rise is so important now. Yeah, other production teams have been clamoring for the rights for years, but they only see it as a moneymaker. I see it as a message of hope."

The cold splash of reality slammed Reilly back to Earth. She shivered at the sudden change within her. "And to save your company."

Reilly hated how she sounded. She wanted to enjoy this moment, learn more about Breanna and not have guilt swell in her stomach.

But you can't hide from a lie, Reilly. Her mother's words echoed around her head as she stared at the stars, praying they would swallow her whole.

"Yeah, I'd be lying if I said I didn't hope for that outcome." Breanna's soft touch caused Reilly's heart to hitch. The literal shock from static electricity made her smirk at the bluntness of the universe. Reilly allowed herself to face the other woman again. She could tell Breanna wanted to say more, but she wasn't sure she wanted to hear it.

"People depend on K.B. Studios for their livelihoods. If I can't get us out of the situation, I'm letting them all down, and their future will be uncertain. Kai and I know we've got a loyal team, and they deserve bosses who fight for them until there's nothing left."

The impassioned speech almost made Reilly admit the truth. Almost. Her former agent was the closest thing to a boss like Breanna. The relationship they still had was proof of his kindness and support. Even if she rarely picked up the phone, she knew he was always there to support her. *I wish it was someone else's stories they wanted.*

"You know I didn't even want to read the series? A fan sent me the first one, and I couldn't put it down. I just kept reading into the morning hours. Hell, I'm still waiting for the next book to be released. It's been a hot minute." Breanna's continued heartfelt words brought a smile back to Reilly's face.

She leaned back, holding onto the chains of her swing for dear life as Breanna jumped up to stand in front of her. The woman leaned into toward Reilly as her ab muscles yelled at being called to action without any preparation.

"Writing takes time." Reilly husked out. "I'm sure the writer isn't intentionally not publishing the next book. Maybe they just need a break."

Her body screamed to be closer, so she pulled herself up into Breanna's space. The woman's shampoo, a subtle hint of strawberries, set her senses ablaze. Each inhale brought her closer to losing control. When Breanna closed the gap between them, the kiss ignited a desire that coursed through Reilly's entire body. Her hands left the security of the swings to take purchase in Breanna's hair. But slipped and promptly fell backwards breaking the kiss.

"Oh, crap. Are you okay? I'm so sorry!" Reilly groaned, before a light chuckle left her chest. The small cedar chips gripped her hair as she struggled to get off the ground.

Her stomach ached as her giggles continued. Reilly barely felt the woman lie down next to her on the ground, but once she did, her breathing quickened. Breanna had an intensity in her eyes that she fell into. Reilly's hand finally found its way to the woman's hair and felt the soft locks between her fingers.

"Just to be clear, I'm going to kiss you again. Considering we're both already on the ground, I don't expect further injuries." The velvety tone forced Reilly to nod since she didn't trust her voice. "Good."

Her past experiences of kissing were sloppy and lifeless. Reilly's first kiss had so much pressure, the girl's teeth left an imprint on her lips. Helen used to swallow her mouth as if giving lifesaving breaths. This was nothing like that. It was gentle and delicious.

She felt Breanna trace her tongue along her lip and allowed her entry. Their tongues danced in tandem, causing a soft moan to bubble up from her throat. She pulled Breanna to her and deepened the kiss. It was intoxicating, and Reilly wanted more.

Too soon, their lips broke apart, and Reilly tried to catch her breath. She stared into Breanna's eyes and knew instantly she'd give her the world if she could. Her heart was so invested it made her speak before her mind could filter the words.

"I might have a way to contact Kline. No promises, but I'll try to help you."

If she wasn't so lust drunk, she would have understood the ramifications of what she uttered. But she couldn't. Reilly hoped she could change the trajectory of Breanna's future and the company she adored. She just needed time to organize a plan. The rational side of her brain screamed to take it back and run as far away as possible. But her heart betrayed her, and Reilly wasn't sure she wanted to fight it anymore.

She pulled a shocked Breanna down for another kiss, preventing her mind from thinking any further.

***

Kai hadn't walked into a small town since they left home years ago. After the call with Breanna, they knew coming to her rescue was the only option. Granted, the surprise would have worked out better had they informed Breanna of their arrival. Even with all these people milling about, the ride share app was terribly silent.

Opening the map app on their phone, Kai found Breanna sitting in a park near town. They knew Breanna was out on a date, and hoped it was going well. But they worried their best friend would end up with a broken heart. They'd watched Breanna dive headfirst into new relationships quickly that ended poorly. Regardless of the outcome, Kai would be there.

In the meantime, they were wandering around a sleepy town alone. Kai sent off a quick text to Breanna but wondered what to do in a town closing up shop for the evening. With each step toward the park, Kai hoped they would get an answer to their message. The last thing they needed to interrupt was Breanna flirting. She sucked at it, and Kai didn't want to embarrass her by laughing.

A familiar tune hit Kai's ears, and they sang along. They spun around and used their ears to gauge where the song came from. Their eyes landed on a square cinderblock building that instantly brought back horrible memories of their youth, but they had nothing else to do. *This is how horror films start.* As the song shifted into another one Kai enjoyed, their steps lightened. Maybe there wasn't a killer behind the music, just a janitor or some other person willing to talk.

Kai just wanted to waste some time until Breanna replied. This was normal behavior in the city. Out here in the suburbs . . . not so much. Kai pulled on the doors until they found one that was open. Music blasted through the desolate hallways. Posters for various clubs and a play hung on the walls with sticky tack. The sound of a floor polisher gave Kai goose bumps. Would the janitor here be as kind as theirs back in the day?

Instead of finding out, Kai followed the music. The auditorium smelled musty with age. The place was empty, with only a few scant folding chairs strewn about. A shorter woman bounced on the stage at the end of the room. Her body swaying back and forth between set pieces brought a smile to Kai's face. Maybe this town wasn't as bad as they thought.

But it wasn't the woman's dance moves that grabbed Kai's attention and silenced them. It was the exquisite design and execution of the sets that stopped Kai in their tracks.

The music cut off. "Umm, can I help you?"

"Students did this? I would love to meet them."

"Look, I don't mean to sound harsh, but I don't know you. What makes you think I'd introduced you to any students? And the kids around here focus on graphic novels and computer animation. These works of art are all me, but no one will ever know. Beyond present company of course."

The woman stood tall and waved her paint brush around like a wand, making magic appear, and Kai found it endearing. There was an innocence about her many lost as they progressed in the creative field. Kai knew it firsthand, but seeing the woman enjoy the process made them jealous. They wanted to bottle up whatever it was and take it back home.

"Are you the art or drama teacher? Forgive me, I don't know which title handles what tasks anymore. It's been a while since I was in school." Kai waved their hands about with each step closer to the woman.

"Fair. Budget cuts being what they are, there is no drama or art teacher anymore. I run everything as an after-school program." The woman placed the brushes down on her tray and wiped her hands off on a rag. "I'm Jenna Vail. And you are?"

"Kai Vincent."

"Nice to meet you, Kai. What brings you our way?"

"Just trying to locate someone, but I found myself alone and wandering through a shutdown town. The music led me here." Kai waited to see how Jenna interpreted the first part of their statement. If the woman pressed further, they'd ask about Kline. Time might be a factor, but having the townspeople close ranks would kill any chance.

"Your person needs one of those tag things. You'd find them in a heartbeat."

"Sadly, it wouldn't work in this case. The author has worked rather hard to remain hidden." Kai waved the comment off. They watched Jenna's eyes flash with something before turning back to her radio.

That's an odd response. Does Jenna know something?

The gears spun on hyperdrive within their mind. Bumps prickled their skin as their defensive nature popped into place.

"You a fan of eighties freestyle?" Jenna asked.

"One could call me an eighties music connoisseur." Kai's voice cracked as they attempted an upper-class British accent.

Jenna's laughter radiated through the theater. "You want some cookies? Before you ask, they're double chocolate, gluten-free. My kids have sensitivities."

Most small towns Kai visited preferred they proceed through as quickly as possible. Jenna didn't worry about their appearance or how they carried themselves. She just offered cookies and conversation. What was this woman's motive? "You're being awfully kind to a stranger."

"Are you though?"

"I . . . you seem to have me at a disadvantage." Kai's firm, professional tone reared its head.

"Sorry, that sounded overly ominous. I've seen your picture before on the K.B. Studios website. Breanna Blaine, your partner, is currently on a date with my sister-in-law." Jenna sat on the edge of the stage with her map app open on her phone, facing Kai. "Hopefully she's at the park with your partner and not hiding from me."

"No, Breanna's there too." Her previous concerns faded to the background at the information. *That was what they were hiding.* "So, you Googled my friend, didn't you?" Kai climbed onto the stage and sat down on the edge, facing Jenna.

"Big shot producer coming to town, not so normal. Just did my due diligence before allowing her to go. Happy to know they're still together. Trust me, Reilly needs to get out more. Well, besides babysitting my girls and our coffee shop dates. She's great with my kids, but she needs adult conversation, you know?"

"I don't, honestly. No tiny humans around me."

"You want a cookie, or no?" Jenna held the container out for Kai.

"Did you do everything here?" Their fingers grabbed a smaller sized cookie with more chips.

"Oh, yeah. Set design, costumes, and if they want an original script, that's me and Reilly."

"You two write as well?" Kai watched Jenna instantly tense up and avoid eye contact. "Are you all right?"

"Yes, sorry. Just thinking about the amount of work still ahead of me. But no, Reilly edits. I write. She's smart that way. Always knows where a comma should be. Except the Oxford one. We fight about that a lot."

Kai sensed there was more there but didn't want to press the issue. For all they knew, Jenna couldn't have Reilly contributing more than the school permitted. Kai just entered this woman's world. They needed to tread carefully if they hoped to garner anything from them.

"You should work on film sets, not school programs. With your talent, you'd be in high demand."

"Maybe, but I've got kids and a husband who acts like one most days. This"—Jenna paused to look at the work surrounding them—"is enough for me. One day I'd love to have this turn into a full-blown theater class, you know? Let kids learn the entire process from idea to budgeting to building to performance to the cleanup. I always thought it would help them understand the real world better."

"That would be an excellent idea. Beyond the obvious, any financial experience would help them in adulthood." Kai wished they had that knowledge back then. Understanding the art world was one thing, but money was always their downfall. Without Breanna, Kai wasn't sure they'd ever gotten to where they were. It was an ambition they could understand.

"That's very true, but I'm hoping for a bigger picture sort of lesson as well. One of the major things I learned doing this is that sometimes things just don't line up, you know? I can sketch, paint, and clamp it properly, but it might not come out the way I need it to. It happens. You've got to start over. Hell, even if it does work well, once the shows are over you have to tear it all down and start again. Like life. It never stops moving . . . changing. You have no choice but to go with the flow and start again when needed."

"Rather interesting comparison." Kai paused and took the last bite of the cookie. They allowed their mind time to absorb Jenna's description. It was spot-on but phrased in a way that they hadn't considered before. A perfectionist themselves, Kai thought about wasted materials, not philosophical ideas. In an instant, they saw their work differently. "I'm not sure many high school students would make that connection."

"Maybe not, but maybe they will." Jenna chomped down on a cookie and handed Kai the last one. "Why do you want Kline's books so badly? Small town, people talk."

Regardless of how good the cookies were, Kai was taken off guard by the direct question. Jenna opened the door, but they had to tread lightly. "Truth?"

"Always the best policy."

"We need a compelling production to present to our partners. If we don't, K.B. Studios will fold, and our former partners will pick away at our corpse like vultures." Kai shuddered as their mouth went dry. They didn't want to focus on losing everything. Not yet.

"That's rather morbid."

"That's life."

"I'm sure there are millions of stories or scripts just begging for an adaptation. Why Kline? What makes them so important?"

"I just started reading it, so I can't speak from personal experience. But the fanbase is immense and rather passionate about the characters. It could be a success at the box office . . . for the first few films at least. Not sure if Kline's releasing another one or if we'd have to bring in writers to complete it." Kai kept their answer truthful. The other woman smirked, nodded, and stood up in front of them. Kai jumped to their feet in response, concerned the conversation was already dead without them gaining any insight.

"If that's your sales pitch, it's no wonder you're here. It's all about your company and possibly creating your own ending. I wouldn't buy into that deal. No real connection, you know?"

"How about because my business partner stupidly mentioned the series during a call without thinking?" Kai tossed out, their arms flailing around for emphasis.

"See, now that is interesting." Jenna looked like a cat ready to pounce on a juicy bit of gossip.

"Is this whole town protective of Kline?" Kai hoped Jenna would answer, but her side-eye gave them pause. "Like I said, I just started reading them. But Breanna loves them."

"But people can already read it or listen to it on an audiobook. Why a film? Why should we change the image of imaginations worldwide for the possibility of a feature that may or may not live up to expectations?"

It was a fair question that Kai often asked when watching an adaptation that missed the mark. Breanna used those kinds of failures as learning tools, but their company was different.

"Why are you so meticulous with your set pieces?"

"Let the record show I hate having questions answered with questions. As for my answer, I wish I knew. It's just in my DNA."

"Production is in mine, and films have an expansive reach. Sometimes a good movie gets a new audience to buy the books. Plus, if Kline works on the script with our staff, it will stay as true to the source material as possible. That's the goal, anyway."

"Maybe. But what if they say no?"

Kai wasn't sure if Jenna was agreeing or if they were pushing the conversation to a quicker end. "I'd like to think our record speaks for itself. If not, we'd share our desire to bring a diverse story to the screen that gives generations around the world a place to feel included and safe."

"That is rather insightful if your company actually means it. But we all know dollar signs have the last say in any decision." The shift in Jenna's tone let Kai know the conversation had come to a natural conclusion. "I guess the date's over." Jenna shared her phone screen with Kai. The park was empty with Reilly's icon in a different location. "Maybe I'll see you around."

"Or it just moved somewhere else?" Kai shared their map app, showing Breanna in the same spot as Reilly.

"Well then . . . if you want, I could use a ton of help. How are you with a paintbrush?"

Kai's interest peaked. They hadn't used one in years, but their desire to paint never waned.

"Just tell me where to start." Maybe this was exactly what they needed to center themselves. They'd taken a call from another company earlier in the day. Before they accepted any offers, they needed to talk to Breanna.

Chapter Eleven

The sounds of morning outside her window pulled Reilly back from her wonderful dreams. Her date with Breanna went so well, the woman invaded her sleeping hours. Two empty wine glasses and a bottle sat on the window seat across from her bed. In Reilly's dream, Breanna's warm arms snuggled her from behind, and she breathed softly on her shoulder. It was a perfect fantasy, and she held onto the last wisps of sleep.

Until she felt someone tighten their grip around her midriff. Reilly slid her right hand lower and found the forearm of the woman from her dreams. Everything she imagined was real. Her breathing quickened as her hand trembled. She ran through the Cliffs Notes version of the evening, trying to pinpoint how they ended here. She flashed through moments—coffee, the park, cedar chips in her hair, laughing on the couch, and finishing two bottles of wine between passionate kisses. Her head throbbed.

At least her mother had a girl's night with Aunt Amy last night. They usually drank Bailey's Irish Cream and played board games into the early hours of the morning. Thankfully, that usually meant Wendy spent the night at her aunt's house, so Breanna could slip out unnoticed. Knowing she could avoid her mother's questions calmed Reilly's head just a bit.

Glancing down at her clothing, Reilly felt relief at seeing her sweats and baggy shirt under Breanna's fingers. Kissing was one thing, but she hadn't been intimate with anyone since her breakup. Her friends had tried to set her up with willing participants or just a fun hookup, but Reilly had continuously refused. She'd done all that when she was younger and felt worse after each encounter. It wasn't in her nature to have a fling. She was a hopeless romantic at heart and wanted to give that side of herself only to a person she truly loved. Lying beside Breanna, feeling the warmth spread lower, the struggle to maintain that ideal was proving difficult.

The woman in question moaned in her sleep as she rolled over, releasing Reilly from her tight grip. Reilly slid out of bed and rushed to the privacy of the bathroom, cell phone in hand. Turning the fan on as background noise, she dialed Jenna, praying the other woman would answer this early in the morning.

"Hey, you! Getting the kids ready for a Friday is like herding wild sharks during a feeding frenzy." Muffled screams and banging came through the receiver as Reilly sat on the toilet, bouncing her leg. "So, your date went well."

Shock riddled Reilly's body. "What?" Memories of Jenna and Harrison sitting in his classic mustang, following her through the streets of their hometown on her dates, sprang into her mind. "You didn't follow me again!"

"Nope. But Kai and I may have followed you via our map apps. Breanna's business partner is fun. Did you know they had experience in set design? They helped me finish the harder pieces for the show."

Reilly's leg stopped moving. Kai was in town. Did Breanna know? She leaned on the sink for added support as her vision blurred. She could distract one of them; the two working in tandem would be too much.

"Rei? You still there?"

"Following me on an app is still following me." Her voice wavered, betraying her concerns. "You're only supposed to use that for emergencies."

"Pfft, I'm your best friend. Deal with it. Seriously, it must have gone well for you to end up at your place."

"We talked. That's it. We drank a lot of wine, and I couldn't drive her home. She crashed here, and I woke up with her arm around me. God, Jenna, it was perfect. Everything about it felt right." Reilly exhaled as the warmth returned to her chest. She enjoyed waking up in Breanna's arms, but she hadn't planned on a sleepover or the morning after. Instead of facing it head-on, she fled to the bathroom. "But I already screwed everything up."

"How is that possible? You said you talked all night. I know you, Reilly. You don't let people into your little circle if they haven't made an impression. The fact that you enjoyed waking up in her arms means you need to go on a second date. I don't see a screwup anywhere in this equation."

"She was telling me all about her business and what Shadows Rise meant to her. It broke my heart, and you know me—" The clammy cold started at her feet and crawled up her legs like ants covering their prey. Her breath hitched and stuck in her throat thinking about what she offered.

"Yeah, you always overextend yourself to help someone. Did you tell her the truth? Like, I like you so much, so I'm coming clean before we make sweet love?"

"Jenna, I'm serious. I slightly fibbed and told her I knew Kline. I literally told her I'd try to help her make a deal when I have no desire to make one!" Reilly dropped her head in her hands as she forced herself to take slow, deep breaths. "I'm all gooey inside for this woman, and I want her to desire me for me. Not for the book series or what I bring to the table. I need her to see me as a goofy human who loves her family and a good evening with a movie or video game, you know?" She wasn't sure when the tears had started, but she was struggling to keep them in check now.

"Oh, Rei," Jenna soothed. "I know it seems like you messed up, but it could be a blessing in disguise. Maybe you get to know Breanna enough to feel comfortable telling her the truth. When you're ready, don't go on tangents or talk in circles. Be straightforward with your reasons and accept that you'll be vulnerable to her hurting you."

Am I ready for that? Would it even work?

"I don't know if I can handle that. I know I don't just want a physical connection, regardless of how she makes my body feel. God, it felt like I was on fire when she kissed me. J, it was so different from every other kiss I've ever had."

"Rei, you're overthinking things. Just take it one step at a time. There's no right or wrong way to handle the beginning of a relationship. Don't overanalyze every reaction or thought. Lean on those you trust and trust your instincts. You're not alone in this, okay?"

A knock on the bathroom door pulled Reilly's focus instantly. Her head pounded, and her stomach rolled in protest. She didn't want to face her guest like this.

"Reilly, you in there?" Breanna's sleep-riddled voice hit Reilly in her core.

"I have to go," she whispered before disconnecting the call. "I'll be out in a minute." Reilly calmed herself, washed her face, and opened the door.

Breanna was even more beautiful now than she was last night. The slight crease in her cheek from being pressed against Reilly's shirt all night warmed her soul. Everything about the sleepy businesswoman was extremely enticing and tantalizing. "It's all yours" were the only words Reilly could utter as she stepped out of the way.

"I was wondering if maybe you were free today?" Breanna leaned on the doorframe with such a sultry look that Reilly stumbled backwards into her end table. "I figured I'd go back to the house, freshen up, down some painkillers . . . But if you're free, I'd love to spend some time with you today."

Breanna looked at the ground, and Reilly wondered what was going on in her mind. She watched as the woman tried to make herself smaller to blend in with the framework of the house.

"Do you like pseudo-hiking? There's a paved path nearby that leads to my favorite spot in this town." They could get to know one another better, but Reilly could also ask about Kai. "If you trust me to drag you into the woods."

"That sounds like the beginning of a horror film, but I'm in." Breanna slipped into the bathroom as Reilly threw herself face first into the mattress.

The smell of fresh coffee brewing wafted in the air. Reilly groaned. Her mother was awake.

***

They barely spoke on the way back to Breanna's rental home. Much to Reilly's dismay, Wendy was home. After some playful teasing, she made them a simple breakfast and food for their hike. At Breanna's house, Kai greeted them with a smirk from the kitchen bar. They stalked right up to Reilly, forcing her to take two steps backwards. Kai's eyes scanned her tight-fitting jeans, boots, and thick, baggy sweatshirt. Reilly wrapped her arms around her body, hating the intense scrutiny.

"I see the appeal." They held their hand out for Reilly to accept. "Kai Vincent, this one's partner in crime, but I'm sure you know that already."

"What are you doing here, Kai?" Breanna pulled Kai away from Reilly, giving her back some personal space.

"I told you I was coming up once the meetings were complete."

"I don't remember that."

"Well, you were too preoccupied to process that tidbit of information. Can I ask you a question?"

Breanna rolled her eyes. "I'm afraid to say yes."

"Did your calves hurt last night? I mean, standing on your tippy-toes for that long must have caused a Charlie horse." Reilly's face flushed a deep red at the implication of the shorter woman kissing her senseless. That led to thoughts of Breanna's swollen lips on hers, forcing her to look away.

"What are you doing, Kai?"

"Just teasing you, my friend."

"Right." Reilly felt Breanna's hand on her chin but kept her eyes toward the wall. Her embarrassment was too much. "I'm going to shower and get ready. Don't worry about this one, okay? They're harmless. Bark is bigger than their bite and all that." Breanna pressed her lips to Reilly's cheek. "Be nice!" she instructed Kai.

Then Reilly was left alone in the room with Breanna's business partner.

"So, you and Bre . . . long night?"

"Nothing happened." Reilly blurted out. She needed Kai to understand this was not her normal behavior.

"Yeah, I know. Bre drunk texted last night. Said she was too drunk to go home, as if she needed my permission to be safe."

If Breanna sent messages last night, what else did she say?

"It was the adult thing to do."

"It was." Kai slipped onto a barstool, but the burning sensation on her skin let Reilly know Kai's eyes remained locked on them. "Bre mentioned you could help us with our Kline situation."

There it is. Crap.

"Like I said to Breanna, I can't make any promises."

"I appreciate the help. So, here's the deal. Bre is one of my best friends, my family, if you will." They patted a stool next to them. Reilly hesitated, unsure of where the conversation was going. She sat on the edge, rationalizing it was easier to flee from that position. "Breanna's fragile and deserves to be treated with the utmost respect. If you aren't willing to at least try to do that, walk out the door now and morph it into a business association. Otherwise, you hurt her—"

"And no one will find the body. Got it," Reilly stuttered. She hated confrontations, even if done in jest. Standing up for herself was never a strong trait of hers.

"What? No. I'm not a killer. Trust me, I pass out at the sight of blood. But guilt, oh that is my superpower. Hurt Bre and prepare to wilt under the might of my guilt trips." Kai's smirk left nothing to the imagination.

Reilly could handle that kind of punishment. Her family were professionals at guilt trips. Even though she caved to the pressure every time, it was something her brain could process better than anger.

The smell of strawberries announced Breanna's presence before Reilly physically saw her.

"I'm ready!" Reilly stood, thankful for Breanna breaking the tension. "You okay on your own today?" She asked Kai.

"Yeah. I met your sister-in-law, Reilly. She's really talented. Think you could convince her to moonlight and work with us on set design?"

The shift from protector to professional was odd for Reilly to witness. "Umm, I don't know. Maybe? If you're not doing anything today, I'm sure Jenna could use your help at the school. She's got a ton more things to do for the show and you were invaluable to her last night. I could give you her number."

"Invaluable huh? See Bre, some people appreciate my amazing abilities." Another eye roll from Breanna at Kai's silly banter brought a smile to Reilly's face. "She gave it to me last night, and sure, I think I will. Have fun, you crazy kids." Kai's tone reminded Reilly of Harrison when he teased her.

"Text me if you need anything." She tossed back to Kai as she led Reilly to the door.

Breanna's fingers blazed a trail along Reilly's lower back as she led her out of the house. How was she going to handle an entire day with this woman? Beyond the physical desire, there was a deeper connection growing she wanted to explore. It was going to be a very long hike.

Chapter Twelve

Chapter Twelve

Reilly marveled at the comfortable silence she and Breanna fell into during the drive. She'd always been one to fill the void with mindless banter. Breanna was right next to her, helping unload the hydration packs and snacks Wendy sorted before they left. While not high humidity like summer, the temperature this morning was unseasonably warm, and Reilly thought of sweat beads rolling down Breanna's skin.

What is wrong with you? Reilly shook her head as she closed the trunk.

"You okay? We can go somewhere else if you'd like."

Reilly turned her attention back to her date. Helen's voice raged in her mind, berating her for being lost in her thoughts.

"No, I'm fine. Just focusing on the hike. The path is up there by the signs. I figured a paved trail would be the best option today. Wasn't sure about the overgrowth on the others." Reilly babbled on as she stashed her keys deep into her jeans pocket and led the way to the woods. Her hands trembled slightly as she tried to regain control of herself. This was her place of calm in the noise of the world. She hoped bringing Breanna here wasn't a mistake.

"You come here often?" Breanna's laugh broke Reilly out of her tangent. "Sorry, it was the first thing that came into my head."

Reilly smiled. It was a horrible line but seemed just perfect in the moment. "I get it. If we're being honest, I would have said the same thing."

"Yet you didn't."

"No, I held back." The ding of a bell in rapid succession forced Reilly to pull Breanna to her side of the path. "Fair warning, this trail has a lot of traffic, so we can't walk like a tourist in Times Square. I'll protect you from the occasional rogue bicycle, though. I promise."

"Good to know. I wouldn't want to be on the evening news. 'Tourist run over by mountain bike. Body devoured by wildlife. News at eleven.'"

"Wow, that escalated quickly."

"I'm a city girl. Trees and wildlife are my enemy." As if to prove her point, Breanna sneezed hard, followed by two more, just as violent sneezes. "Oh man, I forgot how much I love and hate the woods. When I was a kid, I needed twenty-four-hour allergy meds."

Breanna sneezed several more times into her elbow. "Sorry, I don't have many issues in the city. Well, I'm allergic to people that walk slow, but there's no medicine for that." Breanna tried to lighten the mood, but it didn't calm Reilly's concern.

This is my fault. I should have asked before we left. Reilly berated herself for ignoring such a simple task. She asked her nieces about their allergies before going anywhere. She kneeled on the side of the path, dug into her backpack, and pulled out a small emergency kit. It was something she always had on her, but she wasn't sure if she had refilled it in the last month or so. Thankfully, subconscious Reilly kept her kit up to date as she pulled out a small bottle of allergy pills. With a swift pop, she grabbed one and handed it to Breanna.

"It's a generic over the counter, full day pill that works for me. I had to take one this morning, but I always carry extra for the kids."

Breanna downed it with a little water as Reilly packed her kit back up. "You carry a first aid kit with you everywhere? I don't know if I should be worried you get hurt a lot or terrified you are going to kill me out here.""

"Okay, first, if I wanted to kill you, this kit is not going to help you survive. Although, if you're shot, I can plug the hole with a tampon. Though technically that is not a good solution, it sounds cool. Second, my nieces always get into trouble. Got it from their father. Plus, I'm allergic to . . . well, a lot of things. Safer to be prepared and get to a hospital than die on the way. Besides, I invited you here, and I'd like the date to continue." Reilly slipped her bag back on her shoulders.

"Right, well . . ." Breanna looked down, hiding her flushed cheeks. "I bet your nieces are perfect angels."

Laughter erupted from Reilly. "That's a good one." Reilly squeezed Breanna's hand and held it longer than necessary as the two women continued their journey. "If you need to stop, let me know."

The agreement hung in the air along with the pollen. They hiked in silence for most of the trail until Reilly stopped at an old, wooden bridge. She turned right and followed along the side of the small waterway for another mile.

Breanna was huffing but tried not to show it. She prided herself on working out and hitting her step goal in Manhattan daily, but this was different. Sure, it was a paved trail, but Reilly jutted in and out of the tree line, pointing to obstructions on the ground. The upward angle of the walk didn't help either.

After what felt like a lifetime, the path opened to a beautiful lake with a small clearing around its circumference. The sun peeked through the clouds, hitting the water and almost blinding Reilly. In the past, she'd come here when she needed to think or work through a story idea. The squirrels ran up trees, rustling the leaves above them. It was quiet, peaceful. She watched Breanna take it in for the first time. The woman stood, mouth open slightly, eyes wide, arms outstretched as if she could hug it all. That was how Reilly felt every time she was here. It was worth the discomfort of a hike that always left her sore later in the day.

"Not something you expect to see, right? It's not that large, or even that deep, but it's our little hidden gem." Reilly pulled a small blanket from her bag and spread it out on the dirt embankment. "A company bought the land eons ago for mining. They got to forty feet, but it flooded overnight. They drained it and kept going. But the water kept coming. Eventually, it cost more to clear daily than the actual mining operation brought in. The state bought it and converted the entire area to a park. Now we've got a beautiful lake full of fish, forest animals that love to hang out along the water's edge, and divers that sneak out here to see . . . I don't know what they see, actually. Fish? The bottom?"

"Or maybe they're trying to figure out where the water came from," Breanna added with honest curiosity.

"Oh, yeah, I don't know about that. Earth science was my worst class in school. Hell, any science was not high school achievable." Reilly plopped down on the blanket and pulled her bag between her legs. The other woman stared at her and rocked back and forth on her heels as if waiting for an invitation. "Forgive the cliché line, but I don't bite."

Breanna smiled and lowered herself to the edge of the mat, leaving as much room as possible between their bodies. Reilly didn't mind. She knew they were both still wading through the nerves of the newness between them. She focused on pulling out the food for their picnic and let Mother Nature set the mood as they ate.

"Do you come here often?" Breanna asked before tossing a barbecue potato chip in her mouth. "And I mean that honestly."

"Not recently. I came here when my dad died to clear my head. When Mom got sick, I couldn't come as much because I was her primary caregiver."

"Makes sense."

"So, why Kline's books?" Reilly hated her bluntness. "There are so many other queer storylines deserving of film treatment. Why go after the one author who seems uninterested?" Reilly took a few sips of water and leaned back on the towel, sinking deeper into the soil.

"Of all the questions you could ask about me, you choose the books I like." Breanna laughed as Reilly shook her head. Maybe she should have asked her favorite color first. "It's the ideas, the themes . . . it's such a rich series."

"Okay, but why Kline, though? There are many authors out there willing to work with you. You and Kai are following breadcrumbs, hoping to find a connection. It doesn't make sense to me."

"Have you read the books?" Breanna questioned Reilly, who felt compelled to nod in response. How could she explain she'd read them several times while editing?

"Okay. Have you seen the comments and interaction of the series' massive fanbase?"

"Oh God, no. It's something I actively avoid." Reilly quickly shoved chips into her mouth. She was trying to dig her way out of the hole she jumped into last night. She watched Breanna mull over her reply. The producer gave her an answer most people would love, the evidence of a lucrative possibility. Reilly didn't care about that. She'd heard the spiel before about the heaps of money that would increase her account upon release of each film. But none of them promised her anonymity, protection of her identity, or a heartfelt reason the books needed adaptation.

"This might sound odd, but I really connected to the series. I know it's meant for the young adult audience, but it helped me understand my childhood better and accept where I came from and who I am now." Breanna stood. Reilly watched her pick up some stones and skipped them along the surface of the water. "I don't talk much about growing up. I never wanted to use it as an excuse for where I am, mistakes I've made . . . whatever. Point is, it never defined me. Sure, some experiences have influenced my adult self's decision-making, but that's life. Who I truly am was decided long before I understood what that meant. Does that make any kind of sense?"

"Sort of? I've always believed family helps mold who you are. Like their version of love could comfort with no physical touch, or the opposite in teaching a child to hate in the name of righteousness. A child's psyche is like Silly Putty. You place the words you say upon it, and the tiny humans keep it verbatim." Reilly paused, drank some more water, and listened as Breanna tossed the last rock into the lake. The other woman slipped back down to the blanket and leaned back on her hands, and Reilly's heart sped up. Her left-hand slithered across the blanket, behind the bag of chips, to find purchase on top of Breanna's.

"If we're being technical, my aunt raised me. I grew up in a place like this, and my parents worked in the city. Their commute required them to leave while I was sleeping and come home when I was already in bed. My Aunt Fi would take me to school, read to me . . . all the things my parents couldn't do." Breanna kept her view on the lake, away from Reilly. Reilly watched the other woman's face, looking for any signs of discomfort. "I came out to her first. I must have been ten or eleven."

Reilly ran her thumb along Breanna's hand. She envied Breanna knowing who she was so early on in life. Reilly was so unsure of everything until she met Helen.

"You had that kind of clarity so young. That must have been a lot to handle."

"Well, I didn't know what it was exactly, but I knew I was different. I was best friends with a boy down the street. He was super shy, and I was not capable of shutting up back then. His mom used to joke that we'd get married one day. It really upset me, and I never knew why. He was great, and I liked him, but it didn't feel right. We had another friend, a girl, and I was always afraid she would feel left out. I always put her wants before mine. I told my aunt that I needed to get her a ring pop in her favorite flavor. I ended up telling her people who like each other get married, so I had to give her a ring. Aunt Fi hugged me, wiped my tears, and said love was something to be shared. It didn't matter what the person on the other end of my love looked like. All that mattered was they loved me in return." Reilly watched as Breanna blinked away the tears threatening to fall.

"Your Aunt Fi sounds like a wonderful woman."

"She was. She tried to help my parents see reason, but like I told you, they just couldn't see beyond what they learned growing up. Eventually, they divorced, and my dad walked away. My mom bottled everything up inside for years. When Aunt Fi died, Mom became a shell of herself. I went to college and never looked back."

"Have you ever visited since?"

"Once. My dad died, and my mom requested my presence. At twenty-five, I returned home with my girlfriend. She wouldn't look Quinn in the eye at all. Refused to see the woman standing beside me. Why extend an invite if you can't accept who I am? Her entire side of the family just referred to us as the girls. They stripped us of everything that made us human. That's why the book series hit home for me. The main character lost her family, not because they didn't love her, but because they didn't know how to process who she was becoming. It's not a queer story; it's a human one."

"Even though the lead character is bisexual?"

"Yeah, it's about the journey. Her relationships were just part of who she was as a person. The rest felt like the actual story. But if you read the comments, you'd know. Readers appreciated how the love she had was real, accepted, and just normal. Most people don't get that kind of understanding where they are, for whatever reason."

"I didn't know people felt that way." Reilly wanted to say so much more, but the fear bristled just below the surface of her skin, preventing her from doing it. When she originally formed the story, she pantsed the hell out of it. There was no outline, no massive plot breakdown telling her where to go. Reilly just wrote from the heart. She put so much of herself in the lead character, she worried people would miss the story and focus on her sexuality. But hearing Breanna talk about the series took her off guard. Her chest puffed out, but she had to hide her pride and the tears that threatened to fall.

"Kline isn't just interested in money, though," Reilly said, bringing herself back to reality. "Knowing the little I do about her, she'd want her choice of charities to get a percentage of all royalties. Not to mention, she might demand control over scripts and production details. If it has that much impact on the fanbase, then they'd want to ensure the essence of her words isn't lost."

"I'm sure we could find the best screenwriters available to work on the project. As for financial considerations, we could negotiate all of that. She just needs to reach out. I appreciate your help, but I don't want our time together to be hijacked by Kline."

She sees me.

Breanna didn't want to continue the conversation about her work or the books. She wanted to spend time with Reilly, enjoying their day like a normal couple. Maybe everyone was right. Maybe this could be something special.

Reilly took the hint and rolled over on top of Breanna. She stopped, waiting for permission from the other woman. It came as a fist in her shirt, pulling her downwards. Their lips met in a slow, deliberate exploration of each other's mouths, causing a heat to rise deep within Reilly's belly. A chill bounced up every vertebra in her spine. She wasn't sure if it was from the kiss or the change in temperature outside. She leaned forward to recapture Breanna's swollen lips, but the sky had other plans. Reilly jumped at the deluge of rain pouring down on them. With Breanna's help, she packed up the blanket and fixings.

Reilly had never felt her emotions war with one another before. Anger, fear, and rejection pounded the back of her brain while attraction, want, need, and a budding love forced her heart to beat. Thankfully, her tears mixed with the rain, so Breanna had no knowledge of their presence.

***

Reilly sat at her desk, looking at the blank email window. She had to send something but had no idea what to say. Her mind rolled back to her boots hitting puddles, she and Breanna laughing like teenagers as they ran to her car. The rain came down so fast Reilly's wipers couldn't clear her windshield fast enough. So, they waited out the storm, enjoying stolen kisses.

Reilly ran her fingers across her lips now, reliving the moment in her mind. Her body hummed when the other woman was around. Even after a long, cold shower, every inch of her still tingled at the mere thought of Breanna. She'd contemplated taking a nap to clear her head, but the smell of Breanna clung to her sheets. It was intoxicating, and Reilly felt herself fall further into the emotions rolling over her body. It felt like Breanna was burrowing into her soul and finding purchase there. Reilly wasn't sure of much in her life right now, but she knew she wanted more of Breanna Blaine.

Was this the feeling she read about in books, or was it just lust and pent-up sexual energy? Reilly wasn't sure, but everything seemed different with Breanna. The way her brain locked in when she spoke, or how she felt giddy when they held hands. When she started dating Helen, it was all systematic, mechanical, and on schedule. This was raw, new . . . exciting. Should she be worried? She didn't know, nor did she care. She was writing a new romance novel and living one at the same time. *How many people can say that?* Reilly hummed to herself.

These feelings were what she was writing about. The ones where human beings navigate the land mines of idiosyncrasies to land firmly on solid ground beside one another. Sure, there was the lock surrounding her heart with security alarms and cameras looking for intruders. *I don't want to be broken like that again.* Reilly shivered at the thought of her ex-girlfriend.

The memory sobered her up. She'd let Breanna walk through half of her protections like a mastermind without stopping her. No wailing of alarms to warn Reilly to slow down. It begged the question: Did she want it to stop? Could Reilly allow this to be a fling with a significant chance she'd crash and burn when the truth came out?

"Or will she be just like the last one?" The words settled in her stomach like lead. "Or maybe she's different. She didn't want to discuss my books when we were at the lake. It might end up okay." Reilly wanted to believe that, but what happened when Breanna learned the truth? Would she forgive Reilly for keeping things a secret? Reilly wasn't sure. But the thought of Kline's name being used to further a business or career reeked of her ex-girlfriend's behavior.

"Wait, what if I helped without helping?" The thought raced through her mind, like a hamster running on a wheel. That was the answer. Her fingers slipped from key to key as she typed her email to Breanna as M. E. Kline.

Her mother walked into the room, and Reilly raised one finger, stopping Wendy from interrupting her train of thought. Helen used to reply to press invitations all the time. Reilly was unaware of the deception until much later, when the coordinator of an event reached out to confirm her appearance. She'd confronted Helen, but after a long argument, Reilly felt guilty for not helping her fiancée. The words thrown her way were how Reilly wasn't supportive, she was a taker and a dark soul with her greedy need to hold these opportunities at arm's length.

It pressed the buttons that instantly made Reilly shrink into herself for protection. She couldn't handle confrontations with anyone, let alone the person she thought the world revolved around. It was always easier to accept responsibility than stand her ground. But Helen took her meekness as a reason to overextend the author's commitments. When Kline didn't show, organizers were understandably livid. It painted her pen name in a negative light. That etched guilt so deeply on her soul that she still struggled underneath the weight of it all.

But she wasn't allowing anyone else to speak for her this time. She was Reilly and Kline, so an email to K.B. Studios was honest. This could work. It had to. She hoped this would help Breanna and Kai but also free her from the obligation. Then, if or when the truth came out, Breanna would forgive her . . . should forgive her.

"I don't like it," Wendy said, reading over her daughter's shoulder. "You should tell her the truth. Not this . . . whatever this is."

"I can't, Mom."

"Honey, this is going to end badly."

"You think I don't know that? Hell, I've written this sort of ending before." Reilly bounced to her full height, her arms flailing about as she paced as nervous energy released with each step. "She'll find out who I really am. Then Breanna will feel betrayed and refuse to let me explain. She might want to walk from the whole deal. Sure, Kai will probably step in and try to fix it. What best friend and smart businessperson wouldn't, right? If they walked, K.B. Studios would have to pay the penalty we negotiated earlier. Not like the company can afford it, and then they'd scramble to salvage the company in another way. I'll do some grand gesture, and it won't land as I intend. Full stop."

"That's too dramatic for me. How about you just cut to the chase and handle your business now?" Wendy meant well, but Reilly could tell her mother was putting her proverbial foot down. She raised Reilly to put her best foot forward with her decisions. Wendy wasn't happy with what her daughter was doing. Her tone alone made Reilly aware of this. *But how do I fix it?*

Reilly flopped down on the couch in her office and pulled her knees to her chest. Tears silently fell. "I don't know how."

Wendy sat down across from Reilly. She rubbed her daughter's knee with her hand while her eyes shown with the love and comfort Reilly needed at this moment. "Reilly." She paused, and Reilly worried if her mother was disappointed in her. That was all she needed on top of her internal battle. "Harrison was easier, you know? His problems were pretty black-and-white. This or that. Left or right. But you? There is always so much gray, unknown space surrounding you. As a little girl, you would bring extra snacks to school to give to those who didn't have one. You'd offer to go above and beyond to help any person at any job you ever held. Your father and I thought you were some kind of unicorn, able to relate to any human being you came across. Along the way, those who took advantage of you hurt you. Your father and I thought you'd put up walls, but you just kept plugging along. No one destroyed your integrity or whatever made you, you."

Reilly scoffed. In her mind, she was a broken, imposter of a human being, simply riding the wave of life until it was over. Sure, there had been wonderful moments along the way that she'd cherish forever, but they were few these days.

"Stop that." Wendy's tone was firm, and Reilly hung her head, waiting for the rest of the lecture. "When you came home from the play that day alone, I saw a broken young woman. I couldn't . . ." Her mother sniffed. Reilly reached out and took her mother's hand. "You used to see the bigger picture in all directions. Now, it just seems so dark all the time. Talk to me, Reilly. Tell me what's bothering you. Maybe together we can see—"

"There's nothing to talk about. I'm being stupid and breaking my own rules. In the end, she's leaving. She'll see me as a lying fool and go back to her life in the city."

"Can we not—"

"Her home's in Manhattan, mom, not here. I've been down this road, got the T-shirt. Maybe I'm just not meant to have this kind of thing. Maybe Helen was right. I'm just a dark angel devouring the lives of those around me."

"Or she's an evil witch who lived off her girlfriend's notoriety without truly loving her." Wendy pulled Reilly into a hug and slowly rubbed small circles on her back. "I don't know the full story of your breakup, but I know it was bad. Reilly, forgive yourself for whatever it is. You can't keep living in Helen's shadow. If you're not ready to talk to Breanna, then don't. Back away from the lies and focus on the truth. No matter what happens, I'll always be here for you."

"I don't want to have feelings for her, Mom," Reilly mumbled from her perch against her mother's chest.

"Do you remember what I told you when you first came out?" Wendy leaned back and lifted Reilly's chin to face her. "We can't help who we love, but we're blessed with whatever form it comes in. It's so precious, sweetheart. Not just the capability to love, but to accept it in return. It's vulnerable. It's scary. It's worth the risk."

"And if it breaks me again?"

"If it does, I'll be here. I've got your back until my heart stops beating."

"I already lived through that once. Let's not have a repeat performance for many years. Please."

"I'll do my best, honey."

Reilly leaned back into her mother's embrace. Wendy always calmed her with a tight embrace and her devil's advocate comments. She'd sent another email as Kline, but from the address she'd created for the author. It wasn't known beyond her business circles, but maybe using it now would help remove Reilly from the communication. Rationally, it made no logical sense to use it.

But Reilly wasn't thinking clearly. She just needed to give herself time to sort out how to come clean. She just hoped it was before Breanna found out on her own.

Chapter Thirteen

The last few days flew by for Reilly, filled with smiles from every call or text message from Breanna. Her work in progress was also coming to life faster than any other book she'd written in the past. She'd plotted a romantic story with a depth she never thought she was capable of. Death, despair, and dystopian, that she could do. Romance? Never.

Write what you know! her English professor said before every class. Even when discussing the *Canterbury Tales*, he would yell about what she did or didn't know. Reilly had an answer, though. She knew they weren't finished, so why should her paper be? It was the only time she got an A.

When her friends reminisced about their college days, they entertained her with stories of wild nights and crazy experiences. For Reilly, higher education was so boringly vanilla she avoided discussing it. She struggled to find her voice amid her relationship with Helen. Sure, she was in love and happy, but the idea of who Reilly was? It was daunting. That's why the lead character's backstory rivaled her own, with some embellishments of course. She was lonely, heartbroken, and unable to face the empty world. Her love interest was powerful and cold, her heart locked away due to a painful past relationship.

"Writing more fantasy?" her mother called from the office doorway.

"Who needs that when love is just such a thing in itself?" Reilly finished the last line in a chapter and felt pride surge through her chest. Her work on the new book allowed her to see the mistakes in her fantasy series. She ignored the deadlines, pushed the pre-order date back, and emailed her editor to delay things. It would require a press release, but now she had a bit more time. She'd already figured out the plot hole fixes and character flaws she hadn't intended to rear their head in the third book of the series. Her new connection with Brenna and this new book were moving faster than she thought possible. Back in the day, she'd be hiding behind her self-depreciating humor as failure loomed around the corner. Yet these new developments created an excitement that washed over her at the very thought of their possibilities.

"Shakespeare or Reilly the cynic? I don't know who said it best."

"Funny. I thought about what you said and you're right. It's terrifying, and I've decided I'm not ready." *It's not that simple!* her mind barked back at her.

"Right." Wendy's sarcastic tone hit its mark, but Reilly didn't engage. She knew you could make plans for grand gestures, but the universe would use them to wipe away a hurricane's tears. The one thing she longed to have was the one thing Mother Nature would never relinquish—control. "Take a shower and get dressed. I've pulled something out for you to wear. Don't ask me questions. Just listen to your mother for once."

"I always listen to you. It's you who never listens."

"Keep telling yourself that, kid." Reilly ignored her mother and continued writing. "I'm giving you thirty minutes to wrap up whatever you're doing before getting into that shower. Otherwise, I'm using the hose!"

"I hate surprises, so unless you're going to tell me what's going on, I'm not going." Reilly's thumb hit the spacebar hard for emphasis.

"The hose, Reilly. Don't tempt me." The door to her office clicked shut as a shudder rolled through her body. Wendy was many things, but she wasn't a liar. Sure, she omitted things over the course of her life, but if her mother said she was doing something, she did it. Reilly could envision Wendy wrestling their ridiculously long hose from the patio, up the stairs, and into her office. Reilly wondered if her mother would open fire while she was still working. The electronics in the room were pricey, but her mother was never one to care about such things. Taking all probabilities into account, Reilly saved her work and shut down her computer.

It wasn't long before the hot water hit her skin, the steam rising to fog up the mirror. The small bathroom was a dream she designed and, with her family's help, built. The deep soaker tub let her stretch out and indulge in relaxation, which was a rare occurrence. The simple white tile with red glass accents were classic and modern at the same time. But her mind kept switching back to the hot water. Specifically, the idea of water droplets rolling down Breanna's naked form.

Her body reacted immediately. The warmth blended with the soapy water from her shampoo. Her desire ran so deep, she moaned and coughed on vanilla smelling soap suds. The fantasies faded away with every gasp of air.

"That woman is going to be the death of me," Reilly whispered between coughs as she finished up her shower. "I can set boundaries. Maybe we can form an understanding. We could explore releasing the pressure we might feel without indulging in the romantic connection side of things." She added lotion to her legs, vigorously rubbing it in as if that would wash away the confusing thoughts.

"Hey, Breanna, I know things feel great right now, but I'm not ready for commitment. I mean, you're great and all, but maybe we should just be friends. If you want to have sex, that'd be great." She pressed her face into her hands as blood rushed to her cheeks. "You're an idiot."

She slipped into her form-fitting black jeans and red button-down top. The combination surprised her. Reilly often fought with her mother over style and appearance. Wendy preferred classic slacks, button-downs and dress heels too high for her to handle. Even more surprising were the heeled boots that Reilly referred to as her sex boots because of Helen's reaction when she put them on. But she was never allowed to wear them out of their apartment. Whatever her mother was planning, she prayed it didn't involve speed dating or some random setup. Surely she'd understood Reilly's comments about Breanna. They'd discussed it before. She'd affirmed it today, so she hoped this wasn't her mother's way of helping her move on.

Reilly's reflection bolstered her confidence. Her mother had chosen something that accentuated her figure in all the right places. Maybe Wendy wanted her to be her wing woman at a local bar or restaurant. The thought of her mother dating gave her mixed feelings. She deserved to be happy, but it also made Reilly cringe.

"Reilly, stop thinking about your mother . . ." And there it was. The image of her mother having sex. She sighed into her own hands. Her brain did this when she felt overwhelmed. "What is wrong with you?"

"Reilly, are you ready?" Wendy yelled up the stairs. "You're going to be late!"

"That's amusing considering corralling you is like herding cats!" she yelled back.

With her boots on, Reilly took each step with care. Her black leather jacket hung on her frame, and her mother smiled upon seeing her.

Wendy stood in the kitchen still in her sweats and baggy, Disney-themed T-shirt from earlier. "Why aren't you dressed? You said we'd be late."

"No, she said you would be."

Reilly spun around to see Breanna standing tall in a dark pinstripe suit, and her knees wobbled. "Warn a girl before you sneak up on her."

"Sorry." Breanna's voice was soft, and Reilly barely heard her. "You look beautiful." The confident tone was back, forcing the heat to Reilly's cheeks once more.

"And a bit underdressed, apparently." Reilly tried to deflect from her embarrassment. Helen rarely gave her verbal compliments, and this change would take some getting used to.

"No, I told your mom comfy business casual."

Reilly waved her hand at Breanna's outfit. "I think we have different definitions of that phrase."

"Maybe. If you'd like, you can change, but we really are tight on time."

"If I look okay . . ." Reilly didn't own anything close to what Breanna was wearing. She purged most of her business attire after she left her city job. She did have a wonderful collection of sweats, yoga pants, and baggy shirts though. None of which would work in this case.

"Trust me, you do."

The heat returned to her face again. "Then I guess we're good to go. Are you going to share where we're headed?"

"Wendy said you were working. Did you save everything? We'll be gone all day."

Reilly's thoughts were running wild. Where could they travel, dressed like this, and be gone all day? Maybe a fancy dinner, but anything beyond that felt odd.

"I'm good."

"Excellent." Breanna walked past Reilly and gave Wendy a hug. "Thank you for your help. I gave you access to my location on maps."

"I already track Reilly but thank you."

"Wait, you what? Mom how did you even—"

"Have a good time, dear." Wendy pulled Reilly into a hug to cut off the inquiry. "Don't deny yourself happiness out of fear." The words were whispered for only her daughter to hear.

Breanna held out her hand. Reilly entwined her fingers with Breanna's and marveled at how seamlessly they fit together. Everything she told herself in the bathroom flew out the window. It was as if Breanna knew the combination to every lock Reilly had painstakingly secured around herself. Part of her didn't care. The other part could barely breathe.

***

As Breanna drove towards the city, the lights of Manhattan burned on the horizon. The place Reilly once called home. The small island beat in her veins as a pulsing creativity. From the moment she walked into the small studio apartment with her future within her grasp to the instant collapse of her foundation, New York City was infused within Reilly's being.

The buildings grew, as did the traffic, the closer they got. The recent memories of her past date flooded her mind. This would be different. It had to be. Otherwise, Reilly would mark the city off-limits for dating.

"Are you going to enlighten me about this evening's activities?"

"I planned on showing you the office so you can watch me work for a bit. Then we'll grab some dirty water hot dogs, because you just need to have one of those in the city. I'll talk about all the nasty things I have to offer you before dragging you to all the tourist spots to complain about people," Breanna deadpanned.

Oh God, please tell me she's joking. Reilly's internal panic threatened to take hold. "You're not going to tell me, are you?"

Breanna reached across the console and slid her hand into Reilly's. A connection so simple, but one that took Reilly off guard. The little touches or glances, even the brush of Breanna's lips against her own, were more erotic to her than a striptease. This language of subtly was a difficult one to master, let alone communicate, as everyone had their own interpretations of execution. Breanna spoke volumes with silence.

"You're thinking too much. Just trust me."

"The last woman I trusted to plan a date wanted to see if hoop earrings could hold my ankles."

"Wow, really?" Reilly watched Breanna's face as she mulled over her comment. "I haven't heard that expression since high school, and it wasn't meant literally. She really said that?"

"She didn't say it exactly, but trust me, she inferred that and so much more."

"Maybe your clown porn fan fiction mind ran wild with it." Breanna struggled to keep her laughter in check.

Reilly squeezed Breanna's hand tighter. "What was that?"

"I'm sorry. Jenna said it was an inside joke. I promise to never mention your clown obsession again!" Reilly watched as her date struggled to hide a smile.

She released Breanna's hand and allowed the heat to settle between them. "Remind me to talk to my sister-in-law when we get back. As for clowns, I'm terrified of them. For Halloween one year, my ex Helen thought it'd be funny to tie a red balloon to our bathroom drain."

"Wow." Breanna chuckled a bit. "That's creative, but also a rather shitty thing to do."

"Yeah, she hid a clown doll in my closet on my birthday with a small present. Thought it was hysterical." Reilly regretted the anger dripping from her lips. "What is love if you can't torment the one you're with, am I right?"

"You should put that on a Valentine's card."

The crowd on the sidewalk parted just enough to let Breanna pull into the parking garage. After getting their ticket and giving the clerk an estimated pickup time, Reilly followed Breanna out of the depths of the underground into the bright lights of Times Square. Reilly marveled at the bodies twisting and turning around barricades like a flock of birds migrating south. You could always tell the true New Yorkers in the throngs. They'd avoid this place like the plague or navigate effortlessly around human obstacles.

"I used to work here," Breanna said, the nostalgia clear in her voice. "The Viacom building. Kai and I were just starting and had to pay rent. I was a grunt, helping make sure things ran smoothly and getting the occasional coffee."

"That sounds awful. How did you deal with this madness every day? Just walking through here stresses me out. So many people not understanding you can't just stop in the middle for photos."

"It wasn't bad. People don't mean to be inconsiderate; they just forget the city isn't only for tourists. That was before they closed off the area. Safer for pedestrians and more space to walk."

"That, and other nefarious things." Reilly's cynicism crept back to the surface as people dressed in character costumes came into view.

"True, but it was fun working here. Watching people all day, seeing the joy I'd long forgotten the area held. After you work a few New Year's Eve events, they get old fast. The pushing, complaining, trash left behind—that crowd I want no part of. But this—watching kids looking up in awe, people excited about the show they're seeing—just makes me smile."

"You lost me at New Year's Eve. How did you manage that? I hate watching it on TV, let alone having to be here." The thought of Breanna's life in the city crossed her mind. The woman's job and apartment were both here. Reilly had left that part behind her. *How would this work if she wanted to stay here?*

"It was work. I just did what they asked of me while having a warm office to hide in between tasks." The shrug made Reilly feel a bit better about the situation. Maybe Breanna wasn't as attached to the city as she thought.

"Any kisses for the event?" Reilly blurted out. "I don't know why I asked that. You don't have to answer."

Breanna swerved down an avenue, still gripping Reilly's hand. "I'd worry about my history if I had all these events too. Call me silly, but I don't believe in any of that. It's like Valentine's Day. You should love the person all year, not just show up when people notice. The first kiss kicking off a new year is so cliche. So, no. No kisses at the stroke of midnight. Maybe if I found the right person to convince me all that stuff was worth it."

"I see . . ." Reilly trailed off as the desire to be that very person kissing Breanna at midnight washed over her.

Reilly looked skeptically at the door leading to Friedman's. The small diner-like restaurant attached to the Edison Hotel was not what she was expecting on their night out. This was more her speed, but a surprising choice from someone who probably ate in locations where the food cost more than an average person's weekly salary.

"I know this looks simplistic, but trust me, you'll love it. Kai and I came here often since we worked nearby. When we opened our own place, I could only get back here on weekends. The crowds are hell, but it's a diamond in the rough. I promise."

"And if I don't like it?" Her stomach was already in knots at being on a surprise date with Breanna. Adding food to the mix could make it worse.

"I'll take you to whatever fancy place you want with more forks on the table than is really necessary." The lack of judgement in Breanna's words struck a chord within Reilly. It eased the rumbling nerves that threatened to overwhelm her.

Reilly smirked but knew those fancy places were never her speed anyway. As the host led them to a small table by the front windows, Reilly followed Breanna, staring at their joined hands. The woman hadn't let go since they hit street level, and she found the connection comforting. Normally, she'd prefer a booth, but the tight space made her feel uncomfortable. Thankfully, the large windows made her feel like she could breathe.

"The salmon is excellent, but if you want a burger, they have that too," Breanna said, scanning the menu as her right index finger tapped it.

Reilly didn't reply. She just nodded and glanced down. Her eyes immediately fell upon a meal she hadn't had in years. In one way, it broke her heart, but in another, it opened the door to making fresh memories. The server took their orders. Breanna requested a salmon concoction Reilly had never heard of. When it was her turn, she gravitated to the meal Helen refused to allow her to order—a bacon, lettuce, avocado sandwich on sourdough. In her mind, it was another step in reclaiming herself.

The scaffolding outside the window was newer. The bright white legs and LED lights looked cleaner than the old silver poles, blue plywood, and metal sheets. "Perception is everything."

"True. But sometimes the cynic sees what they want to see and not the intention." Breanna sipped her water and took one of Reilly's hands in her own. "Take all the barricades and metal poles in Times Square. They did it to protect pedestrians from violent acts. But those same structures lead you to an area of gathering where families can sit, have some ice cream, and just enjoy the beauty of the city."

"Maybe, but I also see costume characters who sometimes push boundaries. People who photo bomb and when asked to leave you alone, then they yell at you for not wanting them included. Or if they did get in the picture, they get angry at you for taking a photo of them without permission. It's a catch-22."

"Kai once told me the sun must burn for it to eventually extinguish. We have to feel the warmth for us to see the light . . . and to appreciate it all once it's gone."

"How do you manage to sustain that view on things when the entertainment industry is so"—Reilly struggled to find the right words—"dark? Unrelenting? Unforgiving? I'm not sure if I'm using the proper phraseology."

"It's okay. The industry can be all of those things, but it's also beautiful, hopeful, and a lot of positive adjectives as well. I sometimes struggle to have that view of the world. Life is hard, messy, and dreary. Some days I want to stay in bed and watch the world spin by like an old record. But I love my friends, my job . . . And the world seems brighter when you're near me."

Reilly wrung her fingers and bit the inside of her cheek. "You're serious?"

Before Breanna could reply, their server swung the piled high plates onto the table. Reilly wanted to take back her question. Her date tucked into her food and avoided eye contact.

"I'm sorry. I didn't mean to sound so dismissive. You've taken me to a restaurant you love and given me a glimpse behind the wall of mystery that is Breanna Blaine. I shouldn't have blurted out such an idiotic question."

"It's—"

A pitch-perfect voice cut Breanna off. Reilly spun around in her chair to see her server, with a microphone in hand, belting out a Broadway showtune.

"They sing?" The jubilation in Reilly's voice was clear. She clapped and sang along, hitting some notes but missing most. Breanna just sat back, nibbling on her sweet potato fries, as Reilly enjoyed every moment. The unfettered expression and infectious energy pulled the neighboring table into singing with her.

As the song came to a close, the server bowed, and Reilly slipped them some money. She ignored Breanna's gaze as she went back to her meal. Dinner took longer than planned, with Reilly singing in between swallows of food. It amazed her that Breanna sat back, allowing her to enjoy these moments. She found the support endearing and extremely attractive. Instead, Reilly felt the walls around her heart crack as Breanna let her be herself.

"Where to now?" Reilly inquired. Her stomach was full, and her heart was content. *What else could Breanna possibly do to top this?* The thought barely made it to her brain before the marquee for the musical *Chicago* came into view. A massive image of her favorite singer and actress adorned the wall. "You didn't," Reilly cried out in excitement as they stood at the end of the line.

"I wanted to take you someplace nice, and your mom mentioned your love of the city. She also brought up the bad date you had with. . . some overly kinky woman. I mentioned some shows and when she saw Serena just took over the role of Roxy for a limited time, I was told to get those tickets. Apparently, you've been a fan for years."

"Not in a creeper kind of way, but in an *Oh wow, she can sing* sort of way. I thought about coming, but tickets sold out for her entire run before I could work up the courage. How did you manage it?"

"For that, you can thank Kai."

"Breanna . . ." Reilly couldn't help the sultry need laced in her voice. Breanna was making her warm with every touch and smile. "If you're trying to woo me with all this, take credit for some of it."

"I will for dinner and the surprise later."

"You better." Reilly pressed her lips to Breanna's cheek before security yelled at her to move.

"I'm glad you approve."

"I do. Not to bring up the past, but I appreciate you asking what I might be interested in and allowing me to indulge during dinner. Helen would have shushed me at the restaurant. Appearances being what they are, she would have been embarrassed by my singing."

"Quinn was the same way. It's a good thing we're together and not bogged down by our exes anymore."

Reilly slipped her hand into Breanna's elbow. "Lead the way, madam. Oh, and if you want to whisper sweet nothings, I'm all for it, but make sure the positions are plausible."

She felt the muscles in Breanna's arm tense as she led her up the stairs and into the theater. Reilly couldn't help morphing her date into her next book. It was a perfect blend of romance and fun. The anticipation of the after musical activity brought a shiver up her spine. She smiled to herself at the thought of trying those impossible positions.

***

Reilly cheered as Serena walked on stage for the first time. Breanna couldn't tell you much about the show, just how often her date smiled throughout it. The intermission came and went. Reilly spent those few moments raving about the entire experience.

Breanna enjoyed the theater, but it wasn't her favorite thing. Yet, watching Reilly take it in, she felt like that child seeing Times Square for the first time. There was something about Reilly's energy that washed over her. Goose bumps grew on her skin as the other woman held her hand. The show faded into the background as she drowned in the person sitting next to her.

It was only when the crowd launched to its feet that Breanna was aware of time. Nerves crept up as her surprise was forthcoming. As the crowd dispersed, Breanna kept silent, quietly leading Reilly out of the building and back to the street. Reilly spoke the entire way, recounting all the quirky moments of Serena on stage. Comments about the orchestra, the minimalistic sets, and even the actors' slightest movements wafted toward her but garnered no reply. She was too nervous to say a word, afraid of ruining the last part of their date, but also revealing Breanna didn't know what the woman was talking about.

"What did you think about it?" Reilly pried.

"I hate to say it, but I think the movie is more my cup of tea." Breanna reached for something she could talk about.

"I've never seen it."

"Well, then, sounds like another reason to spend time together," Breanna said, keeping Reilly's attention on her words rather than where she was leading the other woman.

"You need a reason?" Reilly pulled Breanna to her. "Thank you for this."

The kiss was soft at first, testing the boundaries for such a public display. But it was enough. Breanna pressed into Reilly and laid claim to her mouth. A few moments later, Reilly's bruised lips begged for more, but they were on a timetable.

"I'd love to show the world how addicted I am to kissing you, but we need to go."

"Right. The car . . . traffic . . ." Breanna could barely make out what Reilly was saying.

Breanna held onto Reilly's hand as she led her date through a black-painted door and into a dimly lit hallway. She felt the other woman's grip tighten when they entered an elegant lobby with one elevator to the right.

"Breanna Blaine, party of two."

The security guard pressed a button. The elevator doors dinged their arrival, and Breanna chuckled at how tightly Reilly held onto her. Her date didn't move the entire ride. When the doors opened, jazz music hit their ears, and Breanna could feel the tension leave Reilly's body.

"Where are we?"

"Jazz Nights."

"That club is invite only." Reilly's gaze shifted around the entire place, while Breanna kept her moving toward the hostess. "Bre, I don't think I'm dressed for this. I'm not—"

"You look beautiful. As for the invitation part, I called in a favor from a friend. I wanted us to have a drink and talk. I thought it'd be too loud someplace else."

Reilly whispered all the big names in attendance as Breanna kept her hand on her date's back, leading her through the throngs of tables. The hostess led them to a C-shaped booth secluded in the back, by her request. Breanna slipped in first and led Reilly to sit down with her back to the entrance. She ordered a glass of white wine for herself and a red for Reilly. Thanks to Wendy's help, this evening was progressing nicely. Breanna could only hope the next step wouldn't be too much.

"This night has been perfect." There was a hint of guilt in Reilly's voice that Breanna couldn't place.

"Is it too much? We can go. I just need to text someone, and we'll be on our way."

"It is a bit much, but not in the way you're thinking. I can't offer you this kind of evening. Date nights on the couch, burned toast, I'm your girl. But this?" Reilly trailed off.

"I can't do this often either, trust me. Things just fell into place with such ease, I had to take advantage of it all." Breanna brought Reilly's hand to her lips before a voice behind them made Reilly's eyes widen.

"Damn, Bre, you still got it!" Breanna's friend slid into the booth across from Reilly just like they planned. Her friend held out her hand for Reilly to take, and Breanna laughed out loud at Reilly's shock. "Serena, pleasure to meet you." Reilly said nothing as she accepted the handshake. "I think I broke your girlfriend."

"No, I'm sorry. Breanna never mentioned knowing you, let alone you'd be showing up to drinks."

"Bre was always good at keeping secrets." The server placed a glass of red wine in front of Serena. Breanna marveled at her friend and the ease at which she interacted with people "Thank you." She raised her glass and indulged in a long pull of her drink. "Oh, thank heavens. You don't know how good this tastes after the week I've had, but I'm here to meet the woman Bre won't shut up about!"

"S, I don't . . . it's not like that." Breanna stuttered. Having Serena spill her inner secrets was not part of the surprise. If Reilly was put off by the revelation, she didn't show it. In fact, Breanna could swear she saw a reflection of adoration and desire in her date's eyes.

"Not like what? One minute I'm getting frantic messages about job references and the next about some tall woman with eyes deeper than the ocean."

"Wow. Comparing me to undiscovered areas on the planet. Cool." Breanna wanted to slip under the table and disappear. Reilly's smirk added to Serena's good-natured ribbing. "I mean, if you like that sort of thing."

"Really? Should I tell my friend all about your clown porn fan fiction?" Breanna tried to remain stoic, but she couldn't finish her comment without laughing. Especially when Reilly dropped her head to the table in mock indignation.

"I do not write clown porn fan fiction! I don't even know where you got that from." Reilly lifted her head and squeezed Breanna's knee, which sent a bolt of desire up her leg.

"You tell her about the lemon zesting aliens?" Serena's comment broke Breanna's spell. Her friend was laughing so hard, her wine glass shook in her hand.

"It was an awful movie! Can we please not go there." Breanna tried to defend herself.

"Reilly, your girl over here drags me to some indie film festival. This was before either of us were far along in our careers. She and Kai lived across the hall in that horrible apartment building. Anyway, this one begs me to see this film since it had a lesbian couple as the main characters. One minute they're talking, the next minute aliens show up shaped like lemons." Breanna watched her friend devolve into a fit of giggles as she gasped to breathe. "And better yet . . . they zest them to death!" Serena pounded the table, drawing the attention of a few prying eyes.

"It wasn't that bad." Breanna tried to fight her laughter but failed. "It was that bad, so bad."

"It gets worse." Serena caught her breath a bit. "Besides the fact that they had graphic sex on a pile of dead alien lemon zest, one alien survives. Once the couple finishes enjoying one another, the alien stabs one woman in the heart with the handle of the zester. And the best part"—her giggles rose once again—"is they kidnap the surviving lesbian, bring her to their ship, and get a toaster oven as a reward for her capture." Serena and Reilly laughed hysterically as Breanna sipped on her wine, trying to hide behind the small glass.

"I thought it was a satirical piece about the nonsensical status of the media regarding the queer community, but nope." Breanna shook her head. Her old self would have left when the jokes got to her, but she found she enjoyed seeing the two women getting along. Even if it was at her expense.

"What happened to the filmmakers?" Reilly sputtered out.

"They won the major prize that year and continue to make indie films. More power to them." Breanna held up her glass and finished it.

"Anyway, I've heard a lot about you, Reilly. But I'd like to hear about you from the source. Hopefully, you don't have hidden aliens or zesters in your closet." Breanna laughed at Serena's change in conversation. It might seem abrupt, but

Serena wasn't one to beat around the bush. She was protective, and Breanna knew it was because they were family.

"No. Gosh, no. My closet's filled with boots, jeans, and flannels. Beyond that, not much to tell really. I'm sort of in a holding pattern, taking care of my family."

"She an editor." Breanna held her glass up and waved her hand around the table, indicating another round for everyone. "Not that I've seen any of your work."

"Nondisclosure agreements will do that." Reilly squeezed Breanna's hand on the table. If she didn't know any better, Breanna would swear she saw fear flash in Reilly's eyes. "You said you lived across from Kai and Bre?"

"Yup. Those two allowed me to crash more dinners than I could ever repay them for. Promoted every open mic night, film festival . . . I could always count on them to be there."

"Family," Breanna said, as if that one word explained their entire friendship.

"And you can thank me for her cooking skills. Kai and I suffered through so many burned meals, but she learned. Speaking of which, when are you making those maple glazed ribs again? They were to die for." Serena moaned into her wine.

"Serena is being kind. I love to follow recipes I've found online. I do love to cook, but I stick to what is written or what I know. No deviations. As for the ribs, you're the one with the busy schedule. Maybe after all this settles down, we can set a date." The server delivered the next round of drinks, and Breanna took that as a sign to switch the topic. "S, Reilly here is a big fan, and I wanted her to meet you in person. And as a side note, it was weird seeing you in fishnets onstage."

"Girl, you've seen me naked in my apartment and pantyhose bothered you? Okay, that didn't sound good, but let me explain. Kai had a habit of taking long showers. I lived alone in a closet of a studio and so I shared my hot water. Bre here would run in to take a five-minute shower that didn't freeze her nips off. Sometimes I'd just be getting out. She'd even steal my clothes." Serena turned her attention to Breanna once again. "Are you ever planning on returning my lucky sweatshirt?"

"Like you need it anymore. S is also forgetting the part that she is not modest at all. She'd walk around nude in her apartment all day if she could."

"It's more comfortable, especially in the summer heat."

"Now that is one thing, but we lived in a bug-infested building." Breanna shivered at the memory.

"Touché. I must admit my girlfriend hates I do that, though. Tells me the paparazzi are always somewhere looking for that million-dollar image. I must remind her about fences or which floor of the hotel we're on. It's adorable."

Breanna's watch beeped, reminding her of the late hour. She found her eyes closing every now and again at the bar. The surprise was a rousing success. Serena and Reilly hitting it off was the one thing she was concerned about. While her friend was a massive success, she'd been burned many times in the past. Because of that, Serena was protective of her personal space and her chosen family. Breanna and Kai often invited her to various events, but she'd politely decline, stating her security concerns.

"I hate to break up the love fest, but if we don't leave soon, I won't be able to drive home."

"Grab a room," Serena said offhandedly. Breanna shifted as she suddenly felt very awake. "Or not. Everyone, slide over."

Breanna wrapped her arms around them both when they were close enough. Serena lifted her cell phone and snapped a photo. Breanna immediately knew the image would be all over her friend's social media profiles in a matter of seconds. Serena loved to share photos of her meeting new people, but she also knew Breanna could use the exposure. One photo with a famous actor was worth more than Breanna's public relations firm could drum up with a release. Breanna slipped into her jacket and helped Reilly into hers.

"We should do this again," Serena said, pulling Breanna into a tight hug. "It's been too long, and I don't like it. Next time, let's bring Kai and my girl. Y'all need to vet her before things get too serious."

"Isn't she staying with you? I'd consider that a step toward serious," Breanna mumbled. "Before I forget, Kai said to tell your agent to submit your contractual demands before the end of the week. That'll give us enough time to get it off to the casting team. I don't think there will be any issues. If you truly want to do the film, that is."

"Sure. But if you get Kline on board, I call dibs on the lead. Work is work, but I'd love to stretch my acting muscle with that series."

Reilly twitched, and Breanna pulled her close. "You okay, Rei?"

"Umm, yes. Just thinking that queer hearts all over the world would love to see you in the lead role." Breanna could sense something was wrong, but she was too tired to press.

Serena pulled Reilly into a tight embrace. Breanna stumbled forward since she was still holding on to her date's hand. "Breanna's special. Please don't hurt her, okay?" Serena said. She pulled back, but the message was clear. "Just so you know, I didn't tag you in that photo. The press will know who you are in an hour if the internet has its way. Your clown porn fan fic should get thousands of downloads a minute."

"Not you too!" Reilly held her head in her hands, but the shift in her tone was not lost on Breanna. Another hint that something was off, but her brain was too foggy to connect the dots. *Maybe Reilly didn't want the photo shared.*

"Life's too short not to have a little fun." Serena hugged them both again before she flipped her jacket's hood up as she meandered out of the bar.

"You want me to drive?" Reilly's voice brought her back to the present.

"Nah, I'm good as long as we have music playing."

Breanna took hold of Reilly's hand and led her outside. The entire day had been a dream. She hoped she had replaced the bad memories that haunted Reilly. She couldn't undo all the negative things Helen had done to Reilly, but Breanna knew she wanted to replace them with happy moments.

***

The ride back to Reilly's was quiet, with soft music playing in the background. Breanna sang along to some tunes and, in several instances, with wrong lyrics. Their hands never left one another, and as the signs for home reflected in their headlights, Reilly's heart sank.

The house was dark, and Breanna turned off the headlights as she approached. "I'm still in awe you kept all that under wraps."

"I told you about all the help I had, but if you're referring to Serena, that was difficult." Breanna rolled her head to the side, placing a gentle kiss on Reilly's knuckles that caused her to shiver with need.

"Well, you did well. I'm horrible at keeping surprises a secret."

"I doubt it's that bad."

"I bought my brother tickets for some reunion concert back in the day. I literally bought them and called him once the confirmation came through."

"If you didn't, he might have bought them for himself," Breanna reasoned.

"Maybe? I don't know. I just remember being so excited I couldn't contain it." Reilly shrugged.

"Christmas must be very interesting in your family." Breanna's lips quirked into an inviting smile.

"It used to be." Reilly leaned back into the seat. She rested her head on her hand as she exhaled with the desire to be travel back in time to her childhood. "When we were kids, the holidays were everything. My parents didn't have a lot, so Mom planned for it all year. One year, she found the patterns for some name brand jeans and a jacket all the kids wore. She spent hours making us clothing so we felt like we fit in. When we got older, things changed." She didn't elaborate further. Her heart clenched with the memories. Thoughts of "the most wonderful time of the year" didn't bring her as much joy as it did for others.

"How so?"

"For one, I had to buy gifts for other people in my family. Please refer to point one. I cannot not keep a secret when it comes to a gift. Mostly, it was because gifts got more expensive, and we just didn't have the money. I tried to follow in Mom's footsteps and make things for people. I found out sewing was not my forte, as evidenced by all the Band-Aids on my fingers in the family photos." Reilly wiggled her fingers for emphasis.

"I could imagine that." Breanna shifted closer to Reilly as a yawn overtook her. "Before you ask, I'm okay. Continue, please. You rarely talk about you, and I'd like to indulge a bit."

"Let's just say making things doesn't go over well when people want something they've seen on television. My brother and I were raised differently, you know? Possessions were things to enjoy, but they didn't make you happy. They were a means to an end. But others in our family never felt that way. There I was in my twenties, struggling to pay bills and expected to buy a cousin some expensive gift. It was worse when Harrison and I started chipping in together to afford said gifts. People were upset and felt cheated. Kind of sullied my holiday spirit from then on."

The image of her uncle's disapproval, his finger waving as his anger dripped from every word, surfaced in her mind. He was a man of materialistic desires and wants. She hated him for how he treated her grandmother and mother, but in his mind, he was always the victim. Reilly knew he was alive somewhere. It was another reason her fear came forward, worried he'd crawl back into her life demanding help. If she didn't comply, he'd sell lies to the nearest tabloid and make himself out to be a loving uncle. She'd have to tell the world about his verbal and emotional abuse to everyone in her family. She didn't want to deal with that. No one in her family did.

"I'm sorry." She felt Breanna's hand rub up and down her arm.

"It's why the holidays are now just us. Harrison and Jenna's kids get the gifts, and Mom insists on getting us all something small. We all chip in and Get mom something nice, but it's never about the packages or the cost. It's just a simple reminder that someone cares about you."

"That sounds like a wonderful way to spend the holidays. Kai, Serena, and I used to sit in front of a TV screen of a yule log and have a small dinner. Now, it's a nice dinner and work."

"I have to ask. How did you keep your friendship with Serena a secret? You're not on her socials . . ."

"By design. In the beginning, we didn't want to influence each other's work successes or failures."

"What about the photo tonight?"

"She's working on a project or two for K.B. Studios, so it works in both our favors."

"I was in it." Reilly still wasn't sure how to handle that. She flashed back to her worry of her uncle seeing it and trying to reach out, and then the tabloids digging into her history and Helen selling her secret. But it was done, and there was nothing she could do to change it.

"Yes." Breanna yawned again. "Trust me, Serena's been trying to change our unwritten rule for a long time."

A comfortable silence fell between them. Reilly moved forward and brushed a strand of hair away from Breanna's face. Her breathing hitched at their proximity. They'd kissed before, something Reilly wanted to do more of, but privacy was limited.

"I'm losing my mind." The whispered words hung in the air as Reilly ran her thumb across Breanna's lips. "You're the most wonderful and terrifying thing I've ever come across." She moved closer, their quick breaths mingling.

"Maybe both of us need unraveling, to be vulnerable, to give this a proper try."

"You could undo everything and hate me for it all." Reilly's fear bubbled to the surface.

"I don't think it's possible, but if it was, I'd still be here, wanting to kiss you. Hoping to feel the heat burn from your body into mine." Breanna's hand brushed along Reilly's belt, barely touching the skin exposed above it. "To hear you gasp with pleasure."

"You're not playing fair." Reilly tilted her head and ghosted her lips across Breanna's neck. "I like a level playing field." She grazed her teeth against Breanna's hot skin, eliciting a sound so intoxicating Reilly needed to hear it again.

"Now who's not playing fair?"

Words fell away as their lips met in a frenzied passion. Reilly moved closer, but the center console dug into her side.

"Inside. Now." Reilly pushed the car door open with her back, desperate to keep the connection with Breanna.

The magnetic pull pressed Reilly into Breanna's smaller frame. She stumbled as her heel caught on a step, and she giggled into a kiss. Breanna's touch ignited an uncontrollable burn across her skin. She spun around as her hand dug into her pocket for the key. Breanna's lips pressed into her neck, forcing a sound out of her that Reilly never uttered before. It was guttural, filled with wanton desire and desperate need.

"You need help?" Breanna's hands slid around Reilly's waist, slipping into her jeans and pulling the keys free. "Here you go." The breathy sounds drove Reilly wild as she took them and fumbled with getting the key into the lock.

"You're not helping me," Reilly gasped.

Breanna spun her around and pressed her against the door. Her hand made a heated path down Reilly's arm to grasp the keys. Breanna's thigh pressed against Reilly's heat, forcing all rational thought from her mind. She leaned forward to kiss Breanna as the lock clicked open.

The lights came on inside. Breanna jumped away and slipped down a step before recapturing her balance to lean on the railing. The curtain near the window moved, and Wendy's smiling face appeared. Whatever heat Reilly felt a moment ago had now transformed into an ice block. Wendy waved to them as the chilly breeze cooled Reilly's skin.

"Sorry," Reilly eked out between breaths. "She has a way of . . . blocking fun."

"It's all right. I should head home." Breanna's words said one thing, but Reilly knew it was the last thing either of them wanted.

"You could stay." Reilly's thumb hooked into her belt, pulling it down to expose some skin.

"I'd love to, but now that I've seen your mom, I'll see her face—"

"Trust me, you'll forget in no time." Her thumb pulled her pants a little lower. Breanna's eyes followed her hand's path.

"Maybe, but the thought of her knowing what we're doing . . ." Breanna took the bait. Her body reacted to the temptation Reilly was giving her. "And to have to face her in the morning"—she leaned forward and kissed Reilly hard—"doesn't work for me. I'd rather enjoy you for the entire night."

"I know you're right, and I really want to go to your place right now and finish what we've started." Reilly stole a kiss before pulling the woman fully to her. "But Mom's inside probably waiting for a recap of our evening."

"Exactly." Breanna pressed her lips softly against Reilly's before backing away. "I ought to go before I change my mind." Reilly watched as her date walked backwards toward Kai's car. Breanna slipped more than once, but they never broke eye contact until Breanna got in the car and drove off.

Reilly stood by the door, her hand on the handle, watching the car drive away. She wasn't sure how their relationship would work—if the truth would destroy them or make them stronger—and she didn't care. Right now, all Reilly could think about was the warmth all over her body. The honeymoon phase of whatever they were doing was definitely in full swing.

Chapter Fourteen

Reilly stared at the email reply from K.B. Studios. For the past two weeks, Reilly had offered other opinions and options for Breanna's company to consider. Every reply was the same. Breanna would thank her for the information and turn the subject back to acquiring the Shadows Rise series.

The air left Reilly's lungs with an exasperated sigh. Even though the two women continued to see one another when Breanna's schedule permitted, it stalled at high school make out sessions. The guilt of deception needled the back of her mind whenever Breanna was out of sight. But Reilly knew her heart was becoming more entangled in this mess of webbing by the day. *There had to be a way out of this. Preferably one that doesn't break us.* She ignored the second part of her statement, unable to accept it was even a possibility.

Even as she called other authors whom she knew wanted their novels adapted to the screen, Breanna waved it off. Their agents called, and Breanna shifted the meetings to Kai. According to Jenna, Kai said they'd signed contracts with authors for the rights to several books. Since then, they had sent proposals to bring other production companies on board. Breanna let her business partner handle all the work while she remained steadfast in her commitment to acquire the rights to Kline's books. The company was moving in a positive direction. There was no need for her to hold on to Kline as the only option. Why couldn't Breanna let it go?

It was the unknown that triggered Reilly's fears. Breanna mentioned reading her books and the impact they had on her life, but why couldn't she just accept defeat and move on?

"You look stressed." Harrison stormed into her office. Reilly spun around in her chair confused at the sudden intrusion. She hadn't expected her brother to visit today. Her hand shook as she flipped off her monitor screen, hiding the email correspondence. Harrison seemed unfazed by her quick movement. His eyes darted across her office before focusing solely on her.

"This room feels so much smaller than I remember."

"Well, you're not a teenager anymore. Besides, you have a bedroom twice the size of this one. I think you did okay for yourself."

"True, but this house is quieter." His fingers grazed over her desk. "Everything just . . . changes."

"It's all relative. Why are you here? I thought we were meeting up at the park?" She had no desire to help him through a midlife crisis when she was struggling alone with hers.

"We were. Jenna's headed over there with the kids. I thought we could talk." He stopped in front of her window. His hands slipped into his pockets as his shoulders sagged under the weight of his thoughts.

"Everything okay?" Her tone was soft, but fear ran across her skin to her limbs. Her leg bounced, trying to release the energy.

"Yeah, family's all good." He didn't turn around, which caused Reilly to clench her fists as the negative connotations overwhelmed her senses. "They're worried about you."

Reilly's mind went into overdrive. He wanted to talk to her about Breanna, something she was not prepared to discuss. *How can I tell him what I did? He'd think horribly of me. Hell, I have no idea how to feel about it myself.* "I'm good. They're overthinking things."

"Rei, you never were a good liar. Why start now?"

"Harrison, I'm fine. I'll get through this." Even though she'd lose some of herself along the way, Reilly would survive. She couldn't visualize how things would go, but she always made it through. That's what chocolate and horror films were created for. It was her therapy.

"I know you will." Every time she looked at her older brother, all she could see was her dad. The man who promised to be there and do so many things but didn't. Harrison held the best parts of her father but none of the negative. He wasn't perfect, but he never abandoned her. He never left her behind, even after his marriage. She wasn't relegated to being just a relative; he kept her a sister. She mattered enough for him to be there. "How's the new book coming? You left the second one off with a cliffhanger. Not nice, little sis."

"Oh, come on, Harrison. It wasn't a massive cliffhanger. The answers are already in the book if you look close enough." He jumped to another topic she struggled to process. Reilly's fans mentioned the same thing in some of their reviews. Her brother knew how to knock her down a few pegs. She needed to finish the current rough draft and get back to the third novel.

"I did, several times, in fact. I didn't find anything that answered all the questions I had. So nope, you wrote a cliffhanger."

"Agree to disagree, and I'm writing a romance novel if you can believe that." Her knuckles turned white as the words slipped out of her mouth. She hadn't wanted to share that information, but she babbled when she was in an uncomfortable situation.

"Wait, you're not even working on the next installment? Rei, that cliffhanger was big. So, unless you wrote yourself into a corner, please get back to writing the book. I'm begging you."

Reilly scoffed. Of course she knew how her series would end. She had the plot points sorted out, regardless of her lack of confidence in that same outline. "Maybe I just wanted a change from the dark storylines." She shook off the negative thoughts.

"Rei, you're one hell of a strong human being, but you see the darkness and it feeds you. Always has."

"It protects me." She wrapped her arms around herself for comfort. Her brother hadn't turned around to face her, so reading his intent was impossible.

"If one obsesses with the darkness, one might be swallowed by it." Reilly watched his body shrink in front of the window. He sounded helpless, almost defeated. It never failed to spin her into confusion. Harrison was her hero, strong and impervious to the negative. Yet, moments like this reminded her how human her brother was.

"Stop being all philosophical." The conversation needed to become less serious if she wanted to get through it.

"Not trying to be. You always carry so much on your plate when you don't have to. You're not alone here. I know it might feel that way, but you've got an army of people around you. We've got you." Her brother finally faced her, leaned on her desk, and gave his signature smirk. It left her questioning if he had something hidden up his sleeve.

"I know, but—"

"No, Reilly. One thing at a time. As for Breanna, the girls are meeting her today, so maybe it's time to come clean."

Her chest clenched. Was she ready for that step in their relationship? Could she even define it as one?

"You're all ganging up on me. It's not that easy." Reilly hoped her brother could read between the lines. How could she express it to him when she couldn't explain it to herself?

"Maybe, but at least I didn't leave Mom alone with my girlfriend and sister-in-law to spill all the most embarrassing baby Reilly stories."

The reason behind his smile was evident now. Breanna was with her family while she was here with Harrison.

"Oh God!"

***

The kids ran circles around Breanna's legs on the basketball court. She'd only agreed to entertain them so Kai and Wendy could set up the picnic table while Jenna cooked on the grill. She'd been hesitant about attending at first, especially after Reilly told her the day's significance. The tradition to come together as a family and enjoy life again started after Reilly's father died. Breanna felt like she was intruding, but Wendy and Jenna insisted Kai and she attend. You didn't say no to those two.

"Perfect timing. You can take over cooking!" Jenna's voice brought Breanna's attention to the siblings walking up the path. Breanna's breath left her as her body seemed to forget how to function.

Reilly was a vision in her normal attire, but her smile was more beautiful than anything else. There was a lightness in her step as she left her brother to join Breanna and the girls.

"How are they doing?"

"Too much energy for me." Breanna welcomed her with a kiss and tasted the sweetness of her favorite white wine. "Moscato? How did you know?"

"Kai may have helped. It's rather nice." Reilly took another sip of the chilled drink before handing the glass over. "Why don't you go sit down. I'll take over for a bit."

"You sure? I could—"

"I'm about to make them run all over the court. If you want to join and get all sweaty, that's fine with me."

"Nope, I'm good." Breanna sat down at the picnic table, keeping Reilly in full view.

Kai's threat of renting a U-Haul to move her in with Reilly jumped to the forefront of her mind. She'd laughed at first, but the idea didn't seem so ludicrous. The studio's productions were moving along, and most of her work could be completed remotely with travel to the city as needed.

She'd found an addicting warmth with this family. She enjoyed watching Reilly with the girls, reprimanding them when they cheated at whatever game they were playing. The idea of sitting with Wendy and watching horrible cooking shows felt more like a blessing than a curse. She tried to convince herself otherwise, but she found herself putting down roots in the small town.

"More wine?" Jenna broke Breanna out of her reverie as Reilly lifted Edie up to dunk the ball.

Breanna gulped the rest of the contents of her glass and held it out for Jenna to fill. The warm sensation between her legs had become a permanent fixture since the two women met. Regardless of her desire to press Reilly up against a wall and pleasure her until she lost her voice, Breanna had held back. She could tell the other woman was hesitant, dare she say afraid, to take the next step. They hadn't talked about it, but they'd fall into bed and snuggle like otters, never letting each other go throughout their slumber. Self-pleasure had helped Breanna release some of the dirty thoughts, but as time went on, it was becoming more difficult.

"You okay there, Bre? Your face is all red," Kai teased.

"Yeah, I'm good." Breanna took several gulps of her newly filled glass and spun around on the bench. She needed to keep her attention on the others at the table. If she kept looking at Reilly, she wouldn't make it through the day.

"I wish Reilly would play again. She's a natural," Wendy said as she tossed Breanna a piece of chocolate.

"She should play in a softball league. I told her about Sandra's queer league needing a catcher." Jenna's comment formed a different image in Breanna's mind. Specifically, the idea of Reilly squatting behind home plate showing off her figure.

"And I keep telling you she creeps me out. The woman's eyes rarely ever leave my butt. Could you imagine if I was a catcher?" Breanna felt Reilly's breath on her neck before soft lips pressed against her forehead. A swirl of jealousy took hold within her. Whoever this Sandra was, Breanna didn't like her. "Your kids are gonna kill me for being late."

"They'll get over it," Jenna piped up, breaking the tension Breanna choked on. Jenna spun in her seat grabbing her children's attention. "Kids don't drag Aunt Reilly off. You girls need to sit down and eat some salad while Daddy gets the hot dogs off the grill."

Breanna heard Edie and Millie complain near the grill. "Our tummies hurt. We need hot dogs and potato chips." Breanna silently thanked the girls for changing the subject.

"I'm on it. Mommy will give you some chips, but you have to sit at the table," Harrison said. Breanna watched him push the food on the grill, mumbling something begging it to cook faster. This type of family experience was new to her. She couldn't stop a smile forming at the interaction between father and his two daughters. "Hey, honey. Latest Kline book ending. Cliffhanger, or no?"

Breanna heard Harrison's question, and she waited for Jenna to answer. The woman moved about the table, dealing with the girls with her face scrunched up in thought like her children's when deciding which snacks they wanted.

"Not really. Maybe? I don't know. I'd have to read it again. The author tends to hide important stuff buried in tedious descriptions. Like who reads that when it's almost a full page long? What do you think, Breanna?"

Breanna choked on her water at the abrupt question. Reilly's warm hand rubbing her back did nothing to help her focus. "Umm . . ."

"It's okay if you go against me. My wife and I have a tendency not to agree on these things." Harrison's soft tone comforted her some.

"You read Kline's books? I thought they were more female driven." Breanna let the words hang, hoping he would clarify.

"They are, but I've got two girls, and I want to know what they could be interested in."

Breanna wasn't expecting the heartfelt, yet simple answer. "Well, I would say yes, there is a cliffhanger. Not as severe as the one from book one to two, but yeah, it's there. I agree with Jenna, though. I've learned that Kline hides hints in her descriptions and book covers. You just have to figure out which ones are real hints, and which are red herrings."

"Interesting. How many have you found in the covers?" Harrison stood taller and waved the spatula around. "I mean, if you spoke to the cover designers, what would you say to them?"

"I would ask how the hell they come up with something that really hits all the points of the story perfectly?"

"I'd say hard work and a lot of insight from the author." Harrison's mouth slammed shut after he spoke.

Breanna looked over at Kai, astonished. They were in the presence of someone with access to the elusive author. The silence at the table unnerved her.

"Yeah, she's rather particular about what she wants. But it's through the company and all, so not common knowledge." Harrison added quickly.

The shift of mood at the table didn't go unnoticed. Breanna wanted to press Harrison further, but she looked over to Kai to help.

"Do you have any advice to get her to get on board with adapting the books to films?" Her partner's question filled the void.

"Truthfully, no. From what I gathered, Kline's a private person and doesn't talk about things like that. Just do me a favor. Don't let anyone know I said anything. It puts my job at risk." Harrison's hands shook as he placed two plates of food in front of the girls.

"Of course." Breanna stopped the conversation. Beyond the fact that Harrison looked terrified about spilling the information, she didn't want the family barbecue to turn into a business meeting.

"Online fans have their own theories about Kline." Reilly voiced while she helped Harrison bring the rest of the food over to the table. "They say the author's ex took advantage of her and the name she made for herself. Can't blame her for being gun-shy."

Breanna's heart broke for the author. She'd had similar relationships, and the last thing she wanted to do was add to the woman's pain. "I didn't know that."

An odd silence fell over the family as they ate. Breanna watched the others pick at their food on their plates. She hadn't started the conversation, but her inquiries had changed the course of it. The dour mood was solely her fault.

"Are you coming with us to mini-golf after? I'm sure the girls would love it." Thankful for Wendy breaking the silence, Breanna turned to Reilly. She hoped the other woman would give her an indication on how she should answer, but she was focused on her food. "Breanna?" Wendy pressed.

"I'd love to."

"Sure, maybe we can grab a drink later." Reilly smirked, drawing Breanna in even more. Breanna smiled in response, but she felt a pain settling in her chest. She knew something was off.

Chapter Fifteen

To say Reilly was bad at miniature golf would be an understatement. She leaned on the rented putter as Breanna made quick work on the angles on the first par three. Breanna scored a birdie, while Reilly struggled to finish every hole within six shots.

I should have insisted on a batting cage date.

"I have to ask. Is golf just not your sport, or are you letting me win?" Breanna questioned as Reilly missed another shot and almost fell into the small creek nearby.

"This place is a vortex that sucks all my athleticism away. I know what I've got to do, but my execution is no better than a toddler eating spaghetti for the first time. When Harrison needs a pick me up, he drags me here for a round. We play without a par limit until the attendants beg us to leave. Then it's a bunch of drinks to wash away my embarrassment. I don't think I've ever made a par three on any of the eighteen holes. Here or . . . well, any mini-golf course period."

Reilly walked over to the cloth square to take her first shot on the moving log hole. She'd played it with the kids before and always hit the swinging obstacle. Breanna's encouraging smile melted her heart. The woman gave her the feeling this swing would have a different result. Her warmth lifted her up in a way Helen never did. A simple look, and Reilly felt the world fade away.

Air filled her lungs as the red rubber putter pushed the matching-colored ball up the ramp at the proper angle. She watched as the log moved toward her ball and blocked it from the easier route. It bounced down the side, off the wall and into a tunnel around the back. The outcome all but guaranteed a par three if she could tap it in. Knowing her ability though, Reilly expected at least a par five. The best she'd ever scored, but still worse than most people on the course.

"I swear this place is evil. Wait until we go to a batting cage!"

Breanna's arms slipped around Reilly's waist, pulling her in close. "I'd like to see you in the cage. I bet it's sexy as hell."

"Right. You'd be the first to think that." Her date held her putter out in front of Reilly and took the shot for a birdie.

"I'm sure there are plenty of softball players who enjoyed watching you play. Sandra for one."

Reilly swore she heard the undertones of jealousy. "Maybe, but she doesn't have my attention." She tapped her ball off an angled corner and thanked the heavens it made it down the ramp near the hole. "Let me correct myself. My ex-boyfriend didn't think I was sexy when I played softball. We used to play on a co-ed team with his buddies. They would tease him relentlessly. *'Your girl is stronger than you.' 'Your girl's more of a man than we are.'* Normal crap they threw around to all of the women on the team. I ignored it, but he wanted me to quit. I refused because it was silly. But the guys didn't take it lightly. One day I showed up for a scheduled game, but the team wasn't welcoming. They were warming up with a baseball and informed me that I had a seat on the bleachers. They were so threatened by the women on their team, they dropped out of the league and joined a new all male baseball one. Didn't matter that we were in first place or that their girlfriends wanted to play. Nope, they decided, and it was done."

"Wow, talk about being a weak bunch of fools."

"Yeah, well, worst part was my brother was there with my sister-in-law. He begged me to let it go, but I was raised to stand up. Never to hit first, but always hit last, you know? Besides, I was livid. The bleachers were filled with my former female teammates. My ex expected me to be a dutiful partner and join them. My boyfriend had the audacity to tell me baseball was a man's sport, to just enjoy watching it and not embarrass myself. So, I dropped my bag, walked up to the plate and took batting practice. After I launched a few over the fence, I packed up my things, broke up with him in front of everyone and reminded him that softball was a woman's sport. Not everyone was cut out for its difficulty." She couldn't hide her acidic tone from the scarred-over wound.

"Their loss. I can't understand the need to prove your worth by belittling others."

"From what I know, his friends never let him live it down. I met Helen not long after and never looked back." But she did, constantly. The only two serious relationships she'd ever had, broke her apart in different ways. She hated feeling small. Hell, Reilly hated how much power they still had over her.

"Never looked back, huh?" Breanna lined up at the next hole and swung the club perfectly. The ball bounced off the corner, up the ramp, through the small spinning opening, and into the hole in the back.

"How the hell . . .?" Reilly stared in disbelief. "Yeah, that isn't going to happen here. Those damn spinning gators make this at least a par twenty for me."

"I have faith in you." That same encouraging smile released the butterflies within her.

"You know, Helen never liked it when we came here. I think I embarrassed her." The negative thoughts spilled out before she could stop them. "I'm sorry. I don't mean to put a damper on a nice time."

"I get it. For the record, your exes are entitled to their opinions, but they're both wrong. Personally, I'm enjoying watching you play. Especially the way you stick out your tongue when you're concentrating. It's adorable."

Reilly watched Breanna approach. Her heart rate sped up as Breanna's hands covered hers around the putter handle. "She never helped you get it just right?" The whispered words and Breanna's firm grip allowed Reilly to give up control of her swing. Her eyes widened as the ball followed the same path as Breanna's for a hole in one. "See? You just need a little help." Warm lips pressed against her skin. "I'll say it again. I love spending time with you. In the end, it's their loss."

"You're killing me." Reilly forced herself to recover as Breanna moved to the next hole. "Looking back, Helen missed a lot of opportunities in our relationship. Do you really want to have the ex-girlfriend conversation? I know I started it but consider this your opportunity to shut it down."

"It's part of your history. If you want to share, I'll listen." Breanna's sincerity added to her already burgeoning feelings. Having someone want to know her on a personal and romantic level was new territory.

"What about your closet? Any other exes I should know about?" Reilly didn't want to keep talking about her past when the woman in front of her was a delightful mystery.

"I don't have much of a list, really. Quinn moved in when Kai and I just opened the business. Everything seemed great until I came home one night and she was gone. No note, no forwarding address, nothing. Considering everything she owned was gone in a few hours, I knew she had help. That part hurt more than anything. The lack of communication, you know? She didn't respect me enough to tell me she wanted out. That leaves an indelible mark, you know?"

Breanna missed the shot as she spoke. Her smile was gone when she played around the main obstacle.

"I do." Reilly's hand found its way to the other woman's back. She rubbed small, comforting circles.

"As my career grew, I became attractive for what I could offer others. So, I created rules of engagement. No sex wherever I'm staying, no morning after, and discussions of family are completely off-limits. Basically, a friendly relationship with a physical component."

Reilly took a moment to process what Breanna had shared with her. They'd both been hurt by people they cared deeply about. But she wondered if Breanna's set of rules applied to her.

"Should I take it as a good thing you've already broken them for me?" Reilly couldn't face a negative response, so she focused on her swing. Somehow, her nerves induced the best unassisted putt she'd ever hit.

"Yeah, I was just trying to be nice." Breanna's light tone lifted the concern that gripped Reilly's chest.

They continued through the course keeping the conversation light. It was a welcome shift from the heavier topics before, allowing Reilly to sift through her emotions with every bad swing. Her score grew to a ridiculously high number, but Breanna never gave her crap about it. In fact, the other woman offered suggestions and allowed the impatient family behind them to pass.

When they arrived at the last hole, Reilly was somewhat relieved. While their conversation had been effortless, her competitive nature screamed in agony after every shot. She'd warned Breanna about the torturous eighteenth hole, but hearing her date laugh over the idiocy of the design brought a smile out of the depths of her massive defeat.

"Okay, first you need pace to go up the ramp, but not so much that you hit one of the chomping gators and bounce back down or off the course. Out of the three of those snapping things, only one has the right entrance for a hole in one. The other two lead to different sections in the back. Harrison and I figured it out one year, but we were kids, and I'm too old to remember it now. It's evil."

Breanna took her position and whacked the ball up the hill just in time for a gator to knock it back down. She tried three more times with the same result. After five strokes beaten back by the evil green chompers, Breanna dropped her putter. "I understand your hesitance to play this game now. This hole doesn't just take the ball back, it's a gateway to hell."

Breanna pushed out her lower lip as she pouted. Her date, the woman that oozed confidence and strength, looked adorable in her faux anger. Reilly couldn't help laughing, especially since Breanna breezed through the entire course to this point.

"When we were little, I'd be behind by more than twenty points. But after this, I'd only lose by single digits. Drove my brother crazy." She'd been so competitive she'd tried to learn the timing on this hole more than any other one. Sure, Reilly always lost the match, but she prided herself on not being blown out.

"I thought you hated the final hole." Breanna's finally sunk her blue golf ball down the return after fifteen tries.

"Oh, I do. I always mess it up, but Harrison was so much worse. He could never time it right. I remember it took him a full ten tries just to get it up the ramp properly. Being my big brother, he might have done it on purpose. Being the competitive person I am, I just play hole eighteen better than most." She closed her eyes, stuck her tongue out, and swung blindly.

"How the hell . . .?"

Reilly opened her eyes and saw the ball roll perfectly down onto the lower green, down the hole to oblivion. "That's never happened before. Maybe I should close my eyes more often." She took Breanna's hand in her own and kissed it. "Want that drink after? They have a small bar and finger food inside."

"I have wine at my place." Breanna stepped closer, creating a warmth Reilly craved.

"And a roommate."

"Who agreed to camp out with Jenna and the girls in their backyard. It's too cold for me, but Kai mentioned s'mores and not wanting to be around when I got back."

All thought slipped out of Reilly's mind as she moved out of her date's grasp. She moved in a flurry, dropping off the equipment and grabbing Breanna's hand before leading her back to the car.

Chapter Sixteen

Reilly usually loved to drive and take in the beauty of nature around her. Right now, she needed the people in front of her to drive faster. Breanna sat in the passenger seat, facing the window as her hand slithered up Reilly's leg. It was tantalizingly slow, and every slight movement made her already fiery core tingle more.

"You keep doing what you're doing, I'm going to crash."

"You're a safe driver. You won't. Plus, I'm not doing anything." Breanna smirked as her hand moved tantalizingly higher. Reilly's body tensed as the woman's fingers blazed a slow path on her skin.

"Fine. How about I pull over right here and devour you in the back seat?"

Breanna looked over her shoulder and leaned close enough that Reilly could feel the heat of her breath.

"Back seat's bigger than what I'm used to. If you want to pull over, that is."

Breanna's sultry tone did nothing to calm her down. As the rental house came into view, Reilly focused on getting to the house in one piece. Once the car was safely in the driveway, she fumbled with the seat belt before rushing around the car to greet Breanna. The passenger door barely clicked closed before Reilly had the other woman pressed up against it.

She leaned forward, close enough to swallow Breanna's exhale. The way her hands migrated along the sides of the pinned woman's body bordered on indecent.

"Let's go inside before the neighbors call the police."

"You were the one who mentioned the back seat." Reilly struggled to see beyond her desire. She'd written deep attraction like this in her books but experiencing it on a cellular level like this was new territory.

A gentle push caused Reilly to lean back. She allowed Breanna to take control and lead them into the house.

Once Breanna locked the door behind her, Reilly's insecurities overrode the warmth pulsing through her veins. She released the other woman's hand and swung her arms around the living area, trying to purge her system of the nervous energy.

Breanna was in front of her, the scent of her shampoo filling Reilly's senses.

"We don't have to—"

"Don't." The whisper flowed out of her mouth with ease. Reilly didn't want to hear the reasons they should hit the pause button. She was tired of waiting, being patient, and ignoring what she really wanted. And right now, all she needed was right in front of her.

Reilly swore she heard Breanna gasp for air as she dropped to her knees on the floor. She teased soft kisses over the woman's legs while her fingers untied her hiking boots. She smiled into Breanna's pants as the woman above her shook, trying to maintain control. She slipped her own shoes off and tossed them to the side. The thrill of being in control allowed her to tease her lover further with soft kisses as she rose to her full height.

Breanna's arms reached for her, but Reilly leaned back away from the embrace. She slipped her hands under Breanna's shirt, eliciting goose bumps on the exposed skin. Sliding upward, Reilly removed the shirt and pressed her lips against the crook of Breanna's neck.

The sounds coming out of Breanna's mouth encouraged her to take it a step further. Her hands gripped the metal belt buckle with a slight tug.

"Want me to stop now?" Reilly husked against Breanna's ear.

"God, no."

Reilly couldn't remember the English language ever sounding so sexy. "Bedroom," she mouthed between kisses.

Breanna led Reilly through the house, the two of them only breaking apart to remove clothing on their way.

Landing on the mattress, they tumbled into a tangle of limbs, their underwear the only barrier between them. In a swift motion, Reilly flipped Breanna onto her back and pressed their breasts together. Her nipples hardened as she met Breanna's intense gaze. The nerves that haunted her early were forgotten as pleasure built like waves against the sand.

With trembling fingers, Reilly eased Breanna's panties down her legs to the floor. Reilly used her mouth to explore every inch of her lover's skin as she moved to her heated center. With one swipe of her tongue, Breanna bucked as she moaned and begged for more.

Reilly toyed with the swollen nub, sucking gently before grazing her teeth against it. Breanna writhed beneath her as she slipped one finger inside her warmth. When she added another one, Breanna's hand found purchase in her hair as her hips bucked out of rhythm.

She continued her assault as moans grew loud enough to alert the neighbors. Reilly held onto Breanna's left hip with her free hand as a scream of pleasure filled the air. Breanna's legs squeezed tightly around her as the woman rolled along the waves of bliss. A smile formed on Reilly's lips as she lapped up the sweet flavor of her lover. Each swipe of her tongue elicited a moan and jerk of Breanna's hips as she came down from the precipice.

Two hands pulled at her as she worked her way back up Breanna's body with soft kisses. When their lips met, Breanna licked Reilly's lips clean as her hand pulled at her red silk underwear.

"Take these off." Breanna panted.

Reilly stood next to the bed. Her thumb pulled at the waist band of her panties as she made a show of dropping them to the floor. Breanna's lust fueled gaze forced a shiver up Reilly's spine. She kneeled on the bed and met the woman in a fierce kiss. Her back hit the sheets as Breanna took control. Warm heat surrounded her hardened nipple causing such pleasurable sensations she was thrust to the cliff faster than she'd ever experienced before.

Reilly's back arched as Breanna thrust two fingers deep inside her. She gasped at the sudden intrusion before moaning as lips pressed into her neck. When Breanna was close enough, Reilly kissed her fiercely and let herself fall into oblivion. Her body shook with pleasure as her nails dug into Breanna's back. Her kisses were sloppy as she rocked her hips in time with her lovers' movements.

All too soon, her body stilled as her breaths remained shallow. Breanna slipped her fingers free and seductively licked them one at a time.

"You'll be the death of me," Reilly whispered.

"At least you'll go with a smile on your face." Breanna kissed her softly as their breathing returned to normal.

"You think you're funny."

"No, just happy."

Breanna snuggled against Reilly's flushed body as her fingers ran up and down the other woman's spine. When she was broken beyond repair, she never thought she'd be in this position again. Yet here she was, relishing in the calm, post-coital bliss. This was what people read about in romance novels.

"Me too. I . . ." Reilly's voice trailed off.

"What?"

"I was about to go sappy on you. Not going to do it." Reilly laughed at herself.

"Really? No earth-shattering and eye-opening experience that showed you how good sex could be?"

Breanna's cocky expression forced a giggle out of her. "Oh no, that happened, but I wasn't going to say it. You've had me so worked up for days. I'm surprised I lasted as long as I did."

"But I never touched you."

"Breanna, you have no idea how beautiful you are. From the moment I saw you, I wanted to be close to you, get to know you and maybe worship at your sexual alter." She kissed the top of Breanna's head.

"Is that why you almost ran me over? You were so enthralled by my body that you short-circuited?"

"Well, no, I mean. . . I was more concerned about denting my car at that point. But in the coffee shop. I can't lie, the way your jeans hugged your body was just sinful. That caught my attention, but then you talked to me, and I was just a clueless baby gay with no idea what to say." Reilly didn't mind the vulnerability of the moment. "If I could do it over, I'd do it differently. I'd approach you and probably stumble through an introduction."

"I think you said plenty. And trust me, it took a lot for me to come over to you. I asked your aunt to bring the coffee over instead, but she said you wouldn't bite unless asked."

"Wait, Aunt Amy?" That tidbit caused Reilly's cheeks to flush. Leave it to her aunt to make comments laced with innuendos.

"Yeah, she was on her way to help you clean up. I figured she could bring it to you, but she declined. Said I should talk to you myself. Seeing no other option, I grabbed the drinks and tried not to trip."

"You're one of the most confident women I know."

"And the weakest when it comes to my personal life. I don't let many people in, Rei, but there was something about you that drew me in." Breanna's hand trailed down to Reilly's small patch of trimmed hair. "And now I'm hooked."

The compliments spurred something deep inside Reilly as she pulled Breanna into a slow, passionate kiss. She felt Breanna's tongue dance around hers as their hands fought to lay claim to any area of exposed skin. Breanna's thigh pressed hard into Reilly's center, causing her to lose control of the situation. Before she could respond, Breanna took their hands and pressed them above her head as their slick coated each other's legs.

She moved in tandem with Breanna, her body begging for more pressure. As if the other woman read her mind, she pressed down and moaned into their kiss. It didn't take long for Reilly's body to shake in pleasure. Her lover followed close behind, as their juices soaked the sheets beneath them.

Reilly shouldn't have been surprised by the speed of their second orgasm, but she was. Breanna brought it out of her with such ease. The woman's body was the missing part of her life's harmony and Reilly never wanted to let go.

Breanna rested her forehead against Reilly's, stealing soft kisses here and there. The smell of sex hung in the air as they tried to come back to normal. Reilly didn't want reality to seep in. She wanted to stay here in Breanna's arms for eternity. Or at least until she needed to use the bathroom.

"That was unexpected," Breanna whispered, breaking the silence.

"Do you always talk this much after sex?"

"It's a weird need to fill the silence. Sorry."

Reilly kissed her again. "You don't have to. Not with me." Reilly meant it, and so much more. Her heart pounded in her chest as the thought of love and completeness came to mind. This was everything she ever wanted. She just had to hold on to it.

"Can I tell you a secret?" Breanna hid her face in the crook of Reilly's neck as she spoke.

"Mm-hmm."

"I never stay the night or let them stay if we're at my place." The whispered insecurity took Reilly off guard.

"Do you want me to go?" Her heart sank as she made the offer.

"No, no. I'm not . . . My brain is thoroughly satiated and not making sense." A soft kiss pushed the negative thoughts from Reilly's mind. "It's always been sex. Catch and release. This isn't that. It . . . it feels deeper than that."

"Glad to know the feeling is mutual." The normal red flags Reilly had held onto during these last few years didn't rear their ugly head. Instead, Reilly enjoyed the moment without concern for what tomorrow brought. Right now, at this very second, she was content.

Breanna's stomach gurgled. "Forgive me for sounding old, but I need a snack. I've got cookies if you'd like some."

Reilly nodded, and Breanna moved off the bed, shaking her sexy figure as she left the room. Reilly's body was a raging inferno as small sweat droplets coated her skin. The evening had only begun, but she knew she'd need a nap tomorrow. Sleep was not her priority tonight. It was mapping out every inch of Breanna's body.

Chapter Seventeen

The shrill of her cell phone in the living room pulled Breanna from sleep. Reilly snuggled into her side, the warmth of her skin radiating through Breanna's body. The only person who would dare call this early was Kai. Knowing the current situation of the business, she didn't want to risk delaying a timely conversation. She rolled Reilly onto her back and kissed her forehead before sliding out of the sheets. The crisp morning air forced Breanna to shiver as she dug through her bag for sweats. With one quick glance at Reilly's sleeping form, Breanna slipped out of the room.

The beep of a voicemail hit her ears before her eyes could focus on anything but coffee. She and Reilly had thrown their clothes off as they stumbled to the bedroom, but she knew her jacket was somewhere near the door. She set up the coffee machine to brew a new pot, found her phone among the discarded clothing, and saw several missed calls from her business partner. The fluffy, warm feeling from being with Reilly settled into a chilling, fearful one.

The phone rang once before Kai picked up.

"First, I'm okay. Second, where have you been?"

"I just woke up. What's going on?" The beep of the machine allowed Breanna to pour herself a cup of coffee. The freshly brewed caffeine helped keep the increased worry at bay.

"It's almost ten in the morning." The receiver sounded muffled as Kai mumbled to someone on the other end. "Sorry. I'd love to hear all about your evening, but we've got business to discuss. You know all those proposals I sent out to other companies? Well, we got a hit. But before they sign on, they want to meet with both of us. So, hop on a train and get to the city."

"Are you kidding me?!" She bounced around as her coffee sloshed about in the mug, threatening to spill over the side. "That's amazing news. Anything else I need to be aware of?"

"I went out on a limb and had our lawyer draw up a contract for Kline. I know we didn't discuss it, but she's emailed us these crazy requests. It was time for her to put up or shut up. I've sent a copy to you."

"Kai—"

"No, Bre. Look, this was your baby, and I want to help make this happen. We can't keep playing the email game. It's time to put the final offer out there and see what happens."

Whether she wanted to admit it or not, Kai was right. She'd personally spent hours formulating emails to Kline bordering on begging her to sign. Normally the author would decline and either start renegotiating or change the subject entirely.

"I trust you and don't need to read it. But if her past actions are anything to go by, it'll get kicked back to us with some random reason. If there is a signature, I'd worry the apocalypse is coming or hell froze over. I agree, it's time to force her hand." She really wasn't, but she had no choice. It was business, and the company needed to move forward or move on.

"We've got a call with Michaela in the morning. I know it's Sunday, but she wants updates on our current slate of projects and Kline. I told her we could meet on Monday, but she's on location for the week."

"Yeah, here's hoping she doesn't pull the plug after I come clean about everything." The sip of coffee moved down her throat like lead.

"She won't be thrilled, but she's a businesswoman. I didn't want to take the call without you. If anyone can convince them to stay on board with another project, it's you."

Kai was trying to ease Breanna's guilt of her lie by omission. She could have called Michaela back and come clean a while ago. Instead, she ran around the back end, hoping to fix the issue with a signature on the dotted line.

"Doesn't this all seem too easy? It wasn't long ago we were scraping the bottom of the emergency drawer, praying for a project to keep us afloat. Now, we're inundated with agent pitches for adaptations to die for."

She swore she could hear Kai suck in a deep breath. Breanna imagined her business partner rolling their eyes in response.

"Bre, you make that sound like a bad thing. Just focus on the important positives here. We've got the rights to novels people want to see adapted to screen. We're working on funding. It means the doors stay open, the lights stay on, and we can keep our staff."

"You're right. This business is feast or famine, so let's eat." She cringed at her corny comment.

Thankfully it was only Kai on the line. They were used to her horrible one liners. "Yeah, just don't. I'm sending the contract to that new email you gave me for Kline. It's out of our hands after that." Breanna was sure she heard Kai repeat her poor "*Let's eat*" comment to someone else before breaking out into a fit of giggles as she disconnected the call.

Breanna shook her head as she took a long pull from her coffee mug. Things were looking up. Her business was on solid ground, and the woman she desired was sleeping in her bed. Her heart felt full for the first time in forever.

With a smile on her face, she opened her notes application and created a list of points to discuss for her meeting tomorrow. She hadn't been in a physical meeting with Michaela in a long time. Normally, a representative would come from the company to meet with her and Kai. She needed to focus and ensure she was organized and prepared.

A phone beeped, breaking Breanna from her thoughts. She scanned her notifications as the offending item beeped again. It was Reilly's phone somewhere buried under their trail of desire. She dug through and found it as the phone beeped and illuminated with another notification. Right there, below a message from Jenna, was an email from K.B. Studios. The title made her blood run cold.

Contract Attached for Perusal

Breanna didn't know Reilly's pin, nor would she violate her privacy that way. Yet, Breanna wanted to know if it was the Kline contract Kai had drafted and why she had received it.

"Where'd you go?" Reilly's voice was seductive in its lower, laden with sleep, tone.

Breanna placed the phone face down on the counter. Confusion and simmering rage pumped through her with every beat of her heart. She'd been candid with Reilly this entire time, but why would Kline's personal email be attached to her phone? A lump formed in her throat as the pieces of the bigger picture fell into place. It seemed so obvious now she berated herself for missing it. Reilly was Kline.

The moments with Reilly's family, Harrison stepping all over himself to correct his words, it all made sense now. They had to know. Why did Amy share Reilly's number? Why would Wendy be so kind and want her daughter to spend more time with Breanna? Was it all a joke to them? As more questions flew to the forefront of her mind, the less control she had over her emotions.

Reilly stood at the edge of the counter, wrapped in the flat sheet. Breanna's body should be raging with desire, instead she was thankful for the escape work meetings provided. "Kai called. I've got to head into the city for some important meetings."

"Or you could call in?" Reilly let the sheet slip down, exposing her breasts. Her nipples hardened from the chill in the air.

Breanna wished she could just ignore everything and indulge in the physical pleasures being offered to her. "I would, but this can't be done remotely." She reached out and lifted the bedding to cover the other woman.

"What's going on?"

"Your phone kept beeping, so I grabbed it for you. Not sure if anything was important. Figured I'd bring it to the bedroom, but since you're here. . ." She hoped Reilly wouldn't pick up on the shift in her behavior as she held out the phone.

Reilly took her device and Breanna watched as she unlocked it. She waited for a reaction to the email from K.B. Studios, but Reilly didn't show anything. If it was any other moment, Breanna would assume Reilly was fine and nothing serious was in her way. But Breanna knew better and the lack of a response bothered her more than she cared to admit.

"Hmm . . . Nothing I can't put off for some sexy time."

Breanna felt Reilly's arms wrap around her body as she pressed soft kisses against her neck. She knew what she saw on Reilly's phone, but she was torn.

The woman dismissed the email as something that didn't need to be handled immediately. The rational side of her brain reminded her that Reilly mentioned knowing Kline. Maybe the other woman forwarded the email along to her.

"But there would have been a forwarding prefix." The words tumbled out of her mouth before she could stop them.

Reilly stepped back and looked up at her quizzically. "Forwarding? What's going on, babe? Are you okay?"

"I'm sorry, just distracted with everything I need to get done. With all these new deals, and we just sent Kline a contract . . ."

Reilly broke eye contact. A glimmer of hope danced among Breanna's fear-induced anger. If she was involved, maybe there was a hint of regret buried somewhere. But she wasn't ready to face whatever the conversation would lead to. Not when she needed a clear head to work.

"I think I get it." Reilly leaned against the counter, looking up an Breanna. Her eyes were gray, cold, as if locking all emotions away in a trunk. "Will you come back tonight or . . ." The words hung in the air, unanswered. Breanna looked away, unable to face the intense scrutiny of Reilly's gaze. "Right. Are you coming back at all?"

"Hey." She kissed the knuckles of Reilly's right hand. "I'll be back as soon as I can." Breanna meant every word even though they sounded hollow. The last thing she wanted to do was hurt the woman who gripped her heart. But she couldn't deny her own pain and confusion.

Reilly nodded before pressing her lips against Breanna's. It was a simple one, that increased the sorrow gripping her chest. Reilly broke the kiss, hung her head and went back to the bedroom. The connection wasn't full of passion, it was one of acceptance. Of what, Breanna wasn't sure. In that moment, she couldn't see a clear future forward. If you'd asked her yesterday, the path was brightly lit with arrows pointing the way. Now, dark clouds and fog blocked everything.

She needed to know why Reilly had access to those emails. Breanna wanted clarity to either prove what the bigger picture told her, or that she was overreacting and there was a rational explanation for it. But before she could begin to figure that out, her job demanded she ace this meeting. Breanna couldn't let Kai or their longtime partner Michaela down. For now, her heart had to take a back seat.

***

Reilly read through all her notifications after Breanna left for work. She'd scanned them when Breanna handed her the phone, and part of her worried the other woman noticed them too. To distract herself, she chose to work on her novel until midafternoon. She might have finished the entire thing if Wendy hadn't knocked on the door, disrupting her.

"You need to eat." Reilly's stomach growled at the thought of food. She glanced at the time on her computer screen. Most of the day and two meals had passed her by as she ingested copious amounts of coffee and chocolate. Her phone vibrated on the desk before she could grab a bite. A message from Breanna brought a smile to her face.

Sorry, won't make it back tonight. Works a mess, and we're trying to clear out the rental house. Call later? Miss you.

Her face fell and she swallowed down the insecurity threatening to choke her. Sure, this was the honeymoon period, with a desire to be around one another all the time. But this morning seemed different. Reilly couldn't stop thinking the sudden change after being intimate was a sign. Her skin pricked with fear at the thought that maybe Breanna was ditching her like Helen.

Or maybe she was just projecting the past onto it because she was afraid of losing something good.

You can always stay with me when you visit. You're my favorite bonus blanket for warmth. Miss you too. Call me when you can.

She placed her phone down. This was why she was horrible at relationships. Reilly was used to being in control of situations. She didn't allow the negative reviews of her books to dictate her characters' sexuality or the path of the story. Yet here she was at the mercy of the unknown. She pushed the food around her plate.

"What's got you worked up?" Her mother rubbed her back, soothing her somewhat.

"Nothing much. Just stuck on this one section in the first draft. I'd like to finish it up while Breanna's buried at work." She took a bite and struggled to enjoy it. "Apparently, she and Kai have a mess to sort out, and they're clearing out the rental," she mumbled through a mouth full of food.

"Ahh." Her mother shifted to lean against the desk in front of her. "And after you came home late this morning . . ." Wendy trailed off.

"Mom, I'm not discussing this with you."

"I'm not asking you to. But if last night was a move in a specific direction and today she's cleaning out the rental, it makes me think your heart is hurting. Having lived through the previous times you came home like this, forgive me for being worried about you."

Tears pricked the corner of Reilly's eyes. "It was everything I hoped it would be and more."

"And then she's suddenly busy with work." Her mother added in understanding.

Reilly's head bobbed in affirmation. "But there's more." She loaded the email from K.B. Studios on her computer monitor. "They sent me a contract proposal this morning. I had a slim hope my demands and the other projects I sent their way would deter them. Well, I was wrong. I don't know how to answer this, and to make matters worse, I'm not sure if Breanna saw the email notification on my phone."

Her voice broke.

"Oh, honey, I can see how much this is ripping you apart. But as devil's advocate, what did you expect? You knew this was going to come to a head sooner rather than later."

Reilly hated it when her mother was rational. Right now, she wanted someone to commiserate in her pain and allow her to wallow. Wendy only used the devil's advocate card when Reilly needed someone to cut through the noise and smack reality into clarity.

"Maybe, but I didn't expect it this soon. I hoped to have more time . . . formulate an exit strategy or something."

"Reilly, your two worlds colliding didn't just happen overnight. It's been weeks." There was that truth bomb again.

"I don't want to talk about it." Reilly's stomach swirled with discomfort. "I don't even know if she's coming back anytime soon."

"Don't go down that road unless she leads you there. Sure, they've left the rental, but you said they had a ton of things on their plate with work. Maybe they couldn't be this far away from the office anymore." Wendy's hands squeezed Reilly's shoulders. "They've left the house, not the state."

"But what if she figured out I'm just a good time and a contract?" The soft, weak wisps of her voice sounded almost childlike and innocent.

"Reilly, you know I love you and will support you in whatever you do." Wendy brushed away the tears that slid down Reilly's face. "Maybe I'm partially to blame for your inability to move on from the betrayal of your ex. Lord knows I struggle with it myself and have never been a good role model in letting things go. But I'm begging you to learn from my mistakes. Don't let the pain of the past destroy the possibility of a beautiful future. Has she given you any reason to believe she's abandoning you?"

Reilly tilted her head to the side in thought. "I guess not."

"See? To top it off, that woman has spent more time with your family than Helen ever did, and you were engaged to that woman. Your brother's family adores her. It seems to be a mutual feeling. So, please, stop thinking of the worst-case scenarios and focus on what you factually know. She's working. Nothing more. Nothing less."

"And if she saw the notification? Or worse yet, what if she knew I'm Kline and that's why she's spending time with me?"

"If she knows, she knows. Theres nothing you can do about that. Maybe consider having a conversation about it to figure out the truth."

That latter thought was the thing that terrified Reilly most. Confrontation was something she avoided like Brussel sprouts, which was always.

"Mom, I can't—"

"Reilly, I gave birth to you and watched you grow up to become the beautiful woman before me. You put your life on the back burner to take care of your father in the end. Then you followed Helen to the city and all her . . . endeavors." Wendy's eye roll forced Reilly to smile. "And then you came back to take care of me. You sat with me in the hospital, saw things a daughter shouldn't see . . ."

"I don't want to relive the image of you in that chair with tubes coming out of your chest. I . . ." The voice of her mother's nurse screamed in her mind. *She's on bypass now. We'll call you when she's off it or if we need you.* Reilly shook her head to stop the terrifying images of her mother's surgery and subsequent recovery from continuing to surface. "I'd do it again, Mom. Always."

"I know, but I don't want you living here to hide from life outside the door."

Was she? "I'm not—"

"Yes, you are, and so am I. Watching you with Breanna . . . it made me feel good about living my life again. It's silly, but I needed to know my children were in a good place."

"Mom, you know the doc—"

"Told me to get healthy and live my life. I'm not getting any younger, Reilly. Your Aunt Amy and I want to see the country we live in. I want to travel with my best friend and drive into the unknown. I don't want to lie in bed reading books about someone else's life anymore. I don't want to just exist, sweetheart. I want to live."

"I get that, Mom. I do. But what happens if you're on the road and get sick? What if you get hurt? What if you send me an emergency text but I can't find you on the shared maps? Maybe now's not the right time for either of us."

"Or maybe we have to stop enabling each other to hide from life."

Reilly wanted to respond, but she couldn't. What could she even say? If she was being honest with herself, she had used her mother's illness as an excuse to avoid dealing with her own issues. It was easy. Seeing it clearly, it terrified her. Who was she when she didn't need to take care of someone?

"Mom, I just . . ."

"Right." Wendy stood, her shoulders slouched in defeat and turned away from Reilly. "Goodnight."

"You're my best friend, Mom. I can lose a lot of things in this world, but you . . . that'll break me."

Wendy didn't turn around. The strong woman she'd always known her mother to be, appeared broken as if Reilly had beaten hope out of her.

"Reilly, you're going to lose me one day. You can't outrun that, no matter how much you want to."

Without saying another word, her mother was gone. The toll of the conversation obliterated Reilly's hunger as she pushed the food aside. She tried to write, but the words failed her. Grabbing her jacket, Reilly was determined to clear her mind. She hoped the trail along the lake would help. Being alone always allowed her to process her thoughts. If her mind was receptive . . . well, that was another story.

Chapter Eighteen

"Please tell me you went home last night." Breanna felt herself smile like a cartoon character with big eyes at the sight of fresh coffee from her favorite place. "How's Max doing? He happy you're home?"

"He threw up in my favorite boots for being away too long. Besides, he probably wants you to save him from the lack of treats when he's with me. I appreciate you looking out for him." Lack of sleep clung to her voice like glue. The warm coffee slid down her throat, eliciting a moan from her lips. "Oh man, sometimes I think a good cup of coffee is better than sex."

"Look, Max and I get one another." Kai smirked. She knew those two were kindred spirits. "Second, if you think that, you're not doing it right. Third, did you get any sleep?"

Breanna scanned her desk. She'd gone home for a few hours but ended up working anyway. She showered, changed into something comfortable, and came back to the office. At one point, she lay down on the couch and closed her eyes. Maybe she got an additional hour or two, if that.

"A bit." She couldn't meet Kai's gaze as guilt weighed heavily on her shoulders. "Why didn't you tell me we were so behind on the paperwork? We've gone from famine to feast, and I left you to handle it alone. That wasn't right from a business perspective, let alone a best friend one. I'm sorry for letting my personal— For not being around."

"Bre, you needed a break. Reilly makes you happy. Why wouldn't I do everything in my power to ensure you got as much time with her as possible? Besides, your head was so focused on Kline and Reilly, it was just better this way. We're a team. When I faltered in the past, you carried the weight. It was my turn."

But Breanna knew there was more to it than that. She'd failed to notice how badly her friend struggled with responsibilities while she was indulging in her personal life. Kai kept a lot from her to ensure the company moved forward at great expense to themselves.

"Kai, Serena called me and told me the truth."

Kai bounced from leg to leg, their hands twisting in front of them. "I love S, but she's . . ." They stopped, probably because Breanna's expression left no room for fabrication. "What did she tell you?"

"We're family, so understand what I say is out of love and concern. You can't keep doing what you're doing."

Kai scoffed in response. "I mean . . ."

"Kai, stop. I've spoken to the payroll company. They're reissuing a check encompassing all the ones you never cashed. They'll do their best to help with taxes, but you'll need to pay a good chunk over."

"That's not—" Kai tried to shift the conversation once again.

"The company that owns your apartment building has agreed to let you pay a flat rate to clear all the back rent instead of court proceedings, but you've been evicted. Serena has movers emptying out your place and bringing everything over to mine. You'll have to share the spare bedroom with Max until we figure something else out."

"Bre—"

"No, Kai. We've been through the highest highs and the hammers of hell as a team. Before this, you've always kept me in the loop. I'm sorry I let things get out of hand. But not taking pay you're entitled to so our staff can cash their checks, it's noble but not right."

"That's rich, Breanna. You did the same thing."

Breanna knew she was pushing the buttons of Kai's insecurity. She reminded herself that if their positions were reversed, her business partner would do the same thing. Her stomach lurched as Kai continued to explain the reason behind their actions. Having integrity and compassion wasn't a bad thing, but allowing yourself to suffer so others could thrive. . . that was never smart.

"Kai, stop." She moved around her desk and physically held her partner still. "You're right. I did the same thing, but not to the detriment of my own well-being. I would cash the checks when and if I needed them. But I never put myself in danger. You once told me you can't help others if you don't take care of yourself. So, this is me taking care of my sibling and making up for my mistakes."

"I'm moving in with you?" Kai squirmed out of Breanna's grasp. "Like college?"

"Without me hearing you snore all night." It was obvious the conversation needed to lighten up now. "Okay?"

"Yeah, but I'm getting better food for Max. That crap you feed him is horrific. My baby deserves better."

"Understood."

Breanna shifted back into work mode. "Now, why are they increasing the budget for this film? I've gone through the numbers several times, and I can't find a valid reason for the request."

"I'll look into it and reach out to the producers. Giving them the benefit of the doubt, they could have forgotten something."

This was the side of business Breanna loved. The set-up, the design, and building the foundation for a project. If done well, she knew it would show in the finished film. But there was one more thing she needed to address, and it was part of the job she hated.

"There's one more thing."

"What's up? Oh, wait, you want the weekend off to spend with Reilly?" Kai wiggled their eyebrows in a suggestive manner. "I'll make sure you're on all email communications, and if something gets out of hand, I'll call."

"I'd appreciate being on all those threads, but that's not it." She couldn't prevent her emotions from seeping into the words she spoke. Her eyes darted to the pages in front of her. Breanna needed to fixate on something other than Kai's pitiful looks she was sure their face would hold when she told them what happened.

"Bre—"

"Did you email Kline the contract?"

"Yeah, but what does that have to do with a weekend with Reilly?"

"I saw the email notification on her phone. I wasn't snooping deliberately. I heard the beep and just . . . I was afraid it was something important, and that's how I saw it." She babbled as she stared at the contract in her hands. The words meant nothing to her as they danced through her tear-filled eyes.

Kai's phone blared from their blazer pocket.

"Answer it." She cleared her throat before taking slow, deep breaths. She needed to calm herself to make sensible decisions regarding her situation.

"What'd you find?" Kai's voice made the small hairs on her arms stand at attention. They rarely used that deep, protective tone unless warranted. Breanna wasn't sure if she wanted to know.

Kai's sudden movement to their feet added to Breanna's worry. Her partner just listened with occasional murmurs of understanding. After a few moments, they flopped back down on the couch and disconnected the call.

"Kai, everything okay?"

"Remember those friends I had as a kid? The ones I try not to talk about?" Kai didn't look at her.

"Yeah. What about them?"

"One straightened his life out, works for a high-level security firm. Anyway, he was who I called to find Kline. And he found her."

Kai's eyes were full of the pity Breanna tried to avoid. The notification was one thing, but factual proof made her want to vomit.

"Reilly." Her weak whisper sounded like a strangled sob.

The knife dug into her chest, cutting off oxygen to the rest of her soul. Reilly was dragging her along like a fool. Reilly, the woman who stole her heart, had toyed with her while she was trying to salvage her livelihood.

"Send me everything." Breanna's voice didn't waver. It was cold, empty, and determined. She turned her attention back to the papers in front of her, ending the conversation.

Breanna barely noticed Kai walk out of the office on another phone call. She was too busy sorting through her experiences with Reilly to see if there were obvious signs of deceit. Where did she go wrong?

Can I salvage any of this, or is it all one big lie?

Her inner voice spoke up, reminding her of the rules she set to protect her heart. And yet here she was, taken for a ride like a pathetic fool. Her phone buzzed with a message from Reilly. It sickened her. She put her phone on silent and buried herself in paperwork. Her business might be cutthroat at times, but it was always consistent. And she needed that more than ever right now.

***

Reilly took the scenic route to Jenna's house to buy herself some time to deal with the nervous energy crackling under her skin. When her sister-in-law called, she insisted Reilly get to her house immediately. There was no explanation, but she told her the family was fine. That sent a shiver down Reilly's spine. The only other person who could instill that kind of fear in her bones was her mother.

So, she took her time before walking into the fire without an extinguisher. Her parents taught her that problems never went away, no matter how far you run. In the back of her mind, the fleeting image of driving past Jenna's house and off into the sunset was inviting. But her sister-in-law would find her. That woman would hunt her down and make her face whatever wrath was headed Reilly's way.

But I could delay it as much as possible, right?

Reilly's mind sorted through all the different excuses she could use to explain her late arrival. She doubted any of them would hold up to Jenna's scrutiny. Instead, she just kept driving and avoiding the woman.

"Reilly? You better still be on this call." Lily's voice broke the bubble Reilly's mind created.

"I'm driving, but yes. Still here."

"What did Camila say?"

How was she going to answer that when she hadn't heard anything since she said hello. Reilly didn't mean to tune them out, but her fight or flight instincts took over her thoughts.

"That she should either move in with Vera or be the first of us to get married?" The sarcasm oozed off every word as she defended herself with a jab at her friend. The gasp on the line meant her comment had the desired effect. Then the guilt creeped in, and Reilly felt terrible.

"Reilly—" Vera was angry.

Reilly's mind shut down again. She had tuned out the minute they began breaking down all the ways she could have come clean and didn't. The way they dismantled her reasons and fears, leaving them like confetti on the ground. Reilly knew this. She felt it in her bones, but it didn't change the past. Now it felt like a pile on.

Her mother was giving her the silent treatment since their last conversation. Breanna hadn't called her yet today and all her texts went unanswered. She'd reached out to Kai with the same result. Reilly felt the walls closing in, and her response was to fight them all. No one understood. In that moment, Reilly didn't understand anything. It was all too much to process.

"I've heard this all before. Reilly is in the wrong. Reilly is an evil bitch who should have handled it sooner. I'm the one whose actions will hurt someone so badly they won't speak to me again. What else do you want me to say? I don't know how to fix any of it. It's done. I can't go back and reminding me of the past doesn't help. I love you all, I really do, but you're not listening either. I promised myself I wouldn't do this. I told myself repeatedly not to get involved with anyone. Then Breanna walked into my life, and I ignored everything I've ever been through. As if that wasn't bad enough, I fell in love with the one woman who could destroy what little of me there is left. So, please just stop. I can't handle anymore."

Her heart broke with the realization. She drove to the side of the road as her shallow breaths took over. Tears blinded her vision no matter how many times she wiped her eyes. This was not what Reilly wanted nor expected to happen. She'd built Fort Knox around her heart after her previous breakup to allow the scars to heal. *And prevent more damage.* She could have walked away from Breanna had her emotions not gotten involved.

Her sobs filled the car, but no sound came through her phone speaker. Her friend's silence was unnerving.

"I know. I screwed it all up and let myself fall in love with her. She's the reason I find joy in writing again . . . hell, in anything. When she talks about turning a film to life, that excitement . . . it's infectious. I've buried so much of my own life lifting others up and helping them find happiness, but I never allow that for myself. So, yes, I was being selfish in hiding the truth. Yes, it was wrong. But I need my friends' support, not a reminder of my failure. Please."

Reilly didn't wait for a reply from her friends. She simply left the Zoom call and allowed her body to crumble. She wiped her face, but the tears wouldn't stop. The winding road to Jenna's house felt like her life. With every step forward, the uncertainty of what lay beyond the turn and the fear of crashing made her cower. Her cell rang, and Vera's image popped on her screen, but she dismissed it. When the ringing stopped, a text message popped up.

Please answer. I come in peace.

When her phone shrilled again, she pressed the green accept button. If Vera pushed her in a direction she couldn't handle, she'd hang up again. But she didn't say anything, as it would give away how truly broken she was.

"I know you're there. I also know you don't want to talk. I respect that. No judgment on this call, okay? We shouldn't have done that, but seeing you happy . . . Rei, it means the world to us."

Vera's calming tone wrapped around Reilly like a soothing hug. Her shallow breaths became deeper as she sniffed, wiped her tears, and stared straight ahead.

"The last woman I loved destroyed me, Vera." Her whisper was so soft she wasn't sure the phone even picked it up.

"I know—"

"No, none of you know the full story. Jenna's the only one who does, and that's because of too much wine. Helen made me feel so insignificant all the time. I never dressed appropriately enough. Anything I wore was always to impress other men and disrespect her. You know I don't own anything too sexy because I don't like the attention. When we went out, she'd order for me, so I didn't overindulge. Don't get me started on her demands to have a clean home and dinner on the table when she walked in the door. In the beginning, I thought that was my job, you know? Take care of the house for her while she worked to support my career. But she was never home at the same time every night. She'd never call, and when my career took off, things stayed the same. I worked all day for my company and still had to do whatever she requested." Her whisper broke as her body shook. She clapped her hand over her mouth, preventing any sound from exiting.

"Rei, Helen wasn't a good person."

"You know why this series is so hard to write? Because Helen had a plan for it all. She loved the benefits and handed me outlines for promotions, marketing, movies . . . all of it. Just to keep the money rolling in. Even if I felt the story should end in, say, book five, Helen would tell me I had to keep writing. When we got engaged, Mom insisted I get a prenup. I was so under Helen's thrall that I planned to ignore her concerns and sign whatever Helen wanted me to. Hell, my ex knew I'd do anything to make her happy, so she had lawyers draw up all these documents about my career. I almost gave away everything I worked for because one woman said she loved me. How pathetic is that?"

"That's not pathetic. That someone being controlled. I think you need to work through this, Rei." Reilly heard Vera sigh on the other end of the phone. "We all have things that hold us back. I bought Camila an engagement ring a year ago. I'm too terrified to ask her."

Reilly's chest felt lighter after her information dump. She still blamed herself for so much of her past but appreciated the change of topic. Misery did love company after all.

"But you two love each other. Don't be afraid of her answer. Everyone knows she'll say yes."

Loud banging on the other end pulled Vera away from the call. The door slammed as muffled cursing came through the line.

"You okay, Vera?" Reilly never liked how the men on the site treated her friend. But Vera always dismissed it as if it was nothing to be concerned about.

"My dad and uncle ran this business when I was a kid. They didn't have a son, so they expected me to pick up the mantle and run it one day. No asking, just telling me. My father would grill me about tools, blueprints, and guidelines. Other kids were reading Shakespeare, while I was reading labor contracts and safety manuals. I became an architect, but he still reminds me that I'm a woman . . . and a son would have held more respect."

"He's full of it." The venom dripped from Reilly's tone as all the turmoil within her spun into rage.

"Not the point. My dad . . . he was a drinker. He was always rough with me, but I never thought he would hurt his family. When times were tough, I fell asleep to the sound of my mom crying as he ranted at her. When I was in high school, I came out to my mom. She begged me not to tell him, but to find a college away from home so I could explore who I was. I graduated with top honors, and he didn't even acknowledge it. My mom told me to walk away from the family business and never look back. I knew leaving meant she'd be alone with my father. I wasn't willing to do that to the woman who protected me my entire life. The outside world was terrifying and new. At home, he was the villain I understood well. He was the man women flocked to for his kindness and pleasure during numerous affairs. Yet, his family begged for the same compassion that he deemed us unworthy of. Hell, when he found out I was gay, he offered me one of his side pieces for my birthday. Who does that?"

"V—" Her friend's father sounded as vindictive and vile as her ex-fiancé.

Vera's breathing was labored, and Reilly knew her friend was trying to keep her emotions in check at work. She was blessed with the solitude of her car to fall apart while her friend needed to maintain appearances.

"Rei, just let me finish. I started working for the family business not long after I finished school. Dad and my uncle thought they could control me from behind the scenes. Make the company look all progressive and whatnot, but they never endorsed anything I did for our clients. One day, we had a meeting on a new building that my uncle and I both submitted designs for, like we normally did. This time, the client loved my creations and wanted to move forward with me at the helm of their account. My dad and uncle tried to convince them otherwise, but the client wouldn't budge. They threatened to take their business elsewhere before my father caved to their demands. My uncle blew up, hit the bar, and got blasted. I was home with Mom when he broke down the front door in an alcohol-fueled rage. He screamed at me, smacked my mom, blaming her for me existing. Next thing I knew, we were on the ground, and his fists hit my face faster than I could block them. The entire time, my dad watched and held my mother from interfering further."

Reilly heard Vera take a deep breath. Words of love and acceptance were on the tip of her tongue, but she held back, waiting for her friend to finish.

"Everything was a bit hazy for the week I was in the hospital recovering. But I do remember hearing my mom talking to me. I guess seeing me hurt was the impetus for her to fight back. She got a restraining order and a lawyer and proceeded to divorce my father. She sued the company and won. Apparently, she'd come up with the idea for it in college and even created the business plan. He took it, got my uncle involved and forced her to keep quiet. The point is, mom and I are still standing. Together we've made the business more lucrative than anyone thought possible. But I still cower when my dad calls wanting help or money. I'm still broken, Rei. That ring sits in a drawer because I'm terrified I'll become him once it's on her finger. Therapy helped me make a ton of progress, but trauma doesn't go away. It becomes part of you, something to manage and process as you work through it. I'll propose, and when I do, I want my family around us. That means all of you. Hell, why don't we go to the slopes Lily raves about? Let Camila see snow for the first time. Maybe then . . ."

Neither woman spoke, and that was fine with Reilly. Logically, she knew everyone was dealing with something negative. It was just life. But hearing how low Vera had been, even though it all happened before they knew one another, lifted her spirits a bit. It made her solitary picture a bit wider. She wasn't alone in her trauma, just the version of it she experienced. If Vera could overcome her past and continue to heal, why couldn't Reilly?

"You're an amazing human being, V. I can't imagine what that was like for you growing up."

"Rei, I appreciate your words, but I'm not bringing all this up for sympathy and condolences. We're both in a bad place, and that's okay. We get knocked down. We get beat up. But we also get back up. We ask for help when we need it. And we accept love when it's given to us. And trust me, genuine love is worth fighting for. It's worth facing your fears, holding on to what makes your heart sore, and loving yourself enough to let that person in fully. If nothing else, forgive yourself for the past, Rei. Like you said, you can't change it."

The woman's words gave instant clarity to the madness of Reilly's negative thoughts.

"God, I was a fool, Vera. I can't ignore that I allowed her to . . . just all of it. I let it happen."

"Then don't. Think of it as a learning experience. You were young. Helen was your first real relationship where you were truly all in. We listened when you were so desperate to make her happy, no matter the cost. Maybe take a deep breath and figure out why that is and accept that Helen was never going to be happy with you. Even if you followed her every whim, you'd never be enough, Rei. That part falls at her feet alone. It was out of your control."

"That's hard to do, but I understand. Love you, Vera."

"Right back at you. I've got to get back to work, but if you need anything . . ."

"I'll text you."

"I'll still be sending you annoying memes checking in. Just a warning." Vera's laugh calmed Reilly's racing heart.

Reilly felt better. Pulling back onto the road, she knew she was walking into the devil's den. Jenna would give her an earful, and she planned to block it all out. Everyone would try to get their two cents in, but none could give her guidance to fix the situation from here on out. Knowing that Vera was there for her, regardless of what happened, gave her a stronger foundation. Reilly would handle this in her own time and in her own way. She'd made the mess, and now she had to navigate through it. Surviving the journey though . . . that was a different story.

Chapter Ninteen

Chapter Nineteen

As Reilly pulled up in the driveway, Kai's parked car greeted her like a stab to the chest. Her entire body involuntarily stiffened in response. Whatever awaited her behind the brown fiberglass front door was not ideal. Reilly knew this. But as she slipped the spare key into the lock, she prayed she was wrong. Soft voices in the kitchen talking over mugs of coffee shot jealousy with a twinge of betrayal through her being.

"Hey," Reilly stuttered as she fought to keep her voice even. "You said it was important. What's going on?"

Jenna turned away from her with an expression she couldn't read.

"I know you're Kline." Under any other circumstance, Kai's directness was something Reilly appreciated. But with their hard expression and a glare that could pulverize diamonds, she switched to a defensive position immediately.

"Let me guess. You're going to tell Breanna unless I do?" The snarky reply didn't have the desired effect.

"She already knows."

The words knocked the sarcastic tone back into her childhood. Reilly stumbled over to the couch. She fell into it, allowing the soft cushion to envelop her in what felt like a safe hug. Reilly tried to hold onto some of the supportive comments from the phone call but failed. The fear of losing Breanna was overwhelming all her senses. "Then what? You here to break up with me by proxy?"

After everything Breanna couldn't even face me. You did this. It's all your fault. The negative thoughts swirled as she tried to corral them.

"I promised to send Bre everything I knew about the situation." Reilly swore she saw a glimmer of sadness through Kai's unrelenting stare. The lack of an answer to her query allowed a spark of hope within her to ignite.

"She came here looking for more background on the why of it all. But I can only fill in so much, Reilly. It's not my story to tell. That's why I called you here."

"How did you find out?" It was the only thing Reilly could grasp onto. She swore she'd had enough barriers in place to prevent anyone from finding out who Kline was. She needed to know where she went wrong before filling in the rest of it.

"It shouldn't matter where—"

"Please." Her voice boomed above theirs. Jenna and Kai both swiveled in their chairs to face her, but their expressions gave Reilly no indication of their reaction. "Did you hire specialists? Hackers? Make illegal dark web data purchases? I need to know." She hated how pathetic her begging sounded.

Reilly felt the cold clamminess of her hands as her heart picked up speed.

"Whoever you have on your team, they're excellent," Kai said. "But life is online. No matter what you do to cover it up, there are always breadcrumbs. I had a friend of mine follow the money, and it eventually led to you."

One look at her sister-in-law, and Jenna knew what was happening. "Reilly, deep breaths."

Her frantic eyes met Jenna's as her sister-in-law kneeled in front of her. She looked worried, and Reilly tried to do as requested. The turmoil within her was raging like rapids, and nothing could stop it now. She managed to expand her lungs with great effort and grasp some air. Of all the people she expected to betray her, Jenna wasn't one of them.

"You sent us all those submissions. Why?" Kai's tone softened but the anger within Reilly kept bubbling with a pending eruption.

"I didn't send anything. I talked to fellow authors, and I suggested they submit their materials to your company for production." Once getting air became less of a struggle, Reilly glanced over at Kai. "Just because I wasn't ready to share Kline with you didn't mean I wanted you both to fail."

"And it alleviated some of the guilt you felt for lying."

Reilly couldn't deny the statement Kai dropped on her. "Yes, but I'm thankful it worked out."

"I don't agree with any of this but thank you for what you did. The new contracts are keeping the doors open for the foreseeable future." Kai walked into the living room. They lowered themselves into a chair and crossed their legs, looking more like they belonged in a spy movie villain scene than in Jenna's house. "That being said, you need to tell Breanna the truth. If you care about her at all, you will explain yourself fully. No omissions. She deserves to hear it directly from you."

"I always planned on it." The words felt foreign on her lips. The intention was always in place, but the execution was the problem. In some way, she expected this fallout, just not the opportunity to explain herself. She assumed Breanna would leave, and she'd shrink back into obscurity. In time, she'd accept again that she was unlovable and lock her heart away for good. It was the easier path to walk than admitting fault and being vulnerable.

"Good. I might have confirmed that you were Kline, but I haven't shared all the details my people dug up. So, you've got one day before I send it all to Breanna. I can't guarantee how she'll process all the information without context. Don't make me regret it."

The laughter erupted from Reilly like she was a madwoman. "As if an arbitrary deadline will make this any easier. You have no idea how hard this is for me. Why this is . . . You know what? It doesn't matter. Do what you have to do."

Her body fought every movement as she forced herself to stand. She needed to leave and process all of this without the prying eyes of the two people who had cornered her.

"And you," she directed her rage toward her sister-in-law. "I've never expected you to be the one to slam a knife in my back."

"Oh stop the childish crap, Rei. You're not the victim here." Jenna's rebuttal hit a nerve within her.

"Right, because Helen—"

"She's not here anymore, Reilly. You keep holding onto the past like it's your safety blanket. The woman treated you like crap and broke your heart, get over it. Live moved on, but you're still stuck wallowing in your own misery to notice."

The searing pain of the comments forced her to swallow a rebuttal. There was nothing she could add to the conversation. Instead, Reilly did what she was good at and fled the confrontation. Their voices called after her as she ran out of the house. In a few long strides, she hoped into the front seat of her car. Her heart hammered in her chest as Helen's berating voice reverberated in her head. Stabbing pain radiated through her body as her life's scars tore open by Jenna's words. She cowered in the front seat of her car as her tormented mind had only one agonizing thought.

I wish I had never met Breanna.

The wallowing side of her tossed the thought to the forefront, but she shoved it to the side. Reilly's heart knew that wasn't true. That was insecurity whining, and pain coming through. She'd use the drive to let the angst flee from her system before calling Breanna the minute she was home. After that, Reilly had to let it go. Like Vera mentioned earlier, some things were out of her control.

***

Reilly knew she needed to lock herself in her office with music and a weighted blanket. It's how she processed things when her apprehension ruled her thoughts. It was only midday, and at the rate things were going, she'd need wine later. She wasn't even sure that would help her through the tough conversation she faced.

Kai's deadline bounced in her head. How would Breanna respond? Did she feel enough for Reilly to forgive her? Reilly was aware of how her heart and body reacted to the other woman. While they never applied labels, Reilly considered their relationship to be an exclusive one. She fell deeper down the rabbit hole every day. All the while, her mind kept denying the inevitable.

Does she love me too? After all this? Broken me?

Her thoughts stopped short when she returned home and noticed the RV parked in front of the house for the first time since winter began. Normally Wendy stored it at the local garage for maintenance and minor tweaks if needed. Seeing it on the driveway before spring came around confused her. Her emotions were already raw. Reilly wasn't sure she could handle any more surprises.

The sound of laughter coming from the basement sounded inviting, but Reilly didn't feel like laughing right now. These were the kind of days Reilly was thankful to have the upstairs of the house to herself. It was easier to slink under the blankets with a glass of wine and some streaming service to make the time tick by faster. Her therapist said it wasn't healthy, but it worked for Reilly, and that's what mattered.

She kept her eyes closed as the door clicked closed behind her. Tears slipped down her face, but she wasn't even sure why they fell. Was it the thought of losing Breanna? Was she reaching the limits of what she could handle? Reilly knew it could be either of those reasons, and so much more in her current state.

Her eyes popped open when her office chair spun around. Her heart raced as she locked eyes with Breanna. The woman was hunched over, her eyes red and puffy, the contract Reilly printed the night before in her hands. The bright-pink Post-it notes with reasons not to sign stuck to the edges of the pages. Reilly's heart sank as reality hit hard. Breanna knew everything. The truth hung in the air like a contagion, waiting to see how the two bodies in the room would respond.

"I didn't expect to see you today." Reilly broke the silence with a dismissive statement.

"I needed to see you. Wendy let me in." Breanna's eyes darted everywhere but where Reilly stood. "I'm sorry for intruding. It's just . . . it smells like your shampoo in here. It's nice."

"Bre, I'm sorry." Reilly stifled a sob.

"You lied to me." Breanna's voice sounded so small. The pain etched on her face brought Reilly one step closer. Breanna stood up quickly, keeping the distance between them. "You were Kline all along. You emailed me with these ridiculous demands, putting me through all this stress, and for what? Why?"

Reilly wrung her hands together. A snarky reply was on the tip of her tongue, but she bit it back. "I thought they were so odd you would never agree to them."

"I was desperate! The company was failing. We would have given you anything if it closed the deal. You knew what this meant to me, Reilly. You were actively sabotaging it."

An excuse popped into Reilly's mind immediately, but it went no further than that. Kai had thanked her for bringing other opportunities to the company, but they knew it was for selfish reasons. Reilly knew it would help K.B. Studios immeasurably, but she also wanted it to take the heat off her and her books.

"I don't know what to say."

"I'm such an idiot. It all makes sense now." Breanna tossed the contract onto the desk.

"Breanna—"

"Your ramblings that I always found adorable. You were trying to figure out an answer to my questions, weren't you? Is that why you never really let me in? Were you ever honest with me? For the first time in years, I felt safe enough with someone to open up, and you just . . ."

"That's why I communicated through email as Kline. I wanted you to know me as Reilly Vail, not some author whose signature you desired. I needed you to see me, the real me. When we were together, my heart reached out for you in every way. I needed—"

"What about what I needed?" Breanna's harsh tone cut through Reilly's pleading. "You say you wanted me to know you, but how do I know what was real? How do I know this wasn't some game for you to get revenge on the industry that treated you horribly years ago?"

"No, it wasn't like that!"

"But it feels like it, Reilly. I've been spilling my guts about my life, breaking all my damn rules because . . ." Breanna looked lost, as if words failed to fully explain her emotions. "I let you in," she whimpered. "For the first time, I felt happy at work and at home. The thought of coming home to you . . . it was always on my mind. I was a damn cliche looking for a U-Haul. But none of it . . ."

Reilly watched the woman crumble, unable to finish her thoughts. *This is the moment to lay all your cards on the table.* Her lip quivered as she twisted her fingers together. She wanted to pull Breanna into her arms and let her feel the pounding of her heart. Reilly wanted to show the other woman how much she desired her physically, emotionally, and mentally.

"The feeling was mutual." Or she could spit out a line that sounded more pathetic than just saying ditto. Reilly dug her nails into her hands to stop herself from smacking herself for the horrible response.

"I fell in love with you. And now . . . Was that even the real Reilly Vail?"

Reilly had a reply before Breanna's words sunk in. Breanna fell in love with her. She sputtered, both excited and terrified. "I never lied about the real me around you. Everything was real, including how I feel about you."

"Words are what you're good at. I've read them. Now they feel like cheap excuses for betrayal." Breanna wiped her face as Reilly watched her walls click into place. "Don't worry about signing. I'm not sure this deal is something K.B. Studios should proceed with."

The words froze Reilly to the spot. Breanna walked past her, and Reilly mumbled incoherent nonsense as the woman left her. *Everyone leaves.* She was in the wrong and needed to accept the punishment.

But she was also a stubborn mule.

Reilly was outside in a few strides, finding Breanna in a rental car across the street.

"Bre, wait!"

Her voice pierced the air, but Breanna didn't acknowledge her. The woman pulled the car into the street and drove away as Reilly waved her hands like a wild woman. She was only three steps into the road when the vehicle turned the corner and out of view.

If she was writing this story, the main character would follow their love interest, and they'd make up in the rain. But this was reality, and Reilly knew the one good thing she had was over. Breanna was gone.

A clanking noise pulled her attention to the RV and her mom loading items into it. She ran her sleeve across her face to wipe the evidence of the breakup away.

"Mom? What's going on?"

Amy shoved a binder into Reilly's hands before her mother could answer.

"Here's all the information we've got at the moment. We've planned the trip, but it's all subject to change. Your mom says you can follow us on that map app you've got. We'll keep you in the loop no matter what."

"Trip? Wait, what?" She couldn't stop herself from moving toward her mother, her eyes pleading for an explanation.

"What your aunt is saying is we're heading south to hit Miami before going across the country to California. We might even duck into Mexico for a bit if we feel like it. I programmed the trip into the computer like you taught me. I had the RV checked, and everything is good to go." Her warm smile and excited eyes broke what little control Reilly had remaining.

"How long have you been planning this?" Her body trembled as she stepped into her mother's arms.

"Honey, we can't stand another book club. It's time for me to live a little too." Everything seemed hazy as her mother pulled out of the embrace and met her eyes. "Consider this my way of giving you and Breanna the privacy to discover what the future holds for you both."

There isn't one. She almost spoke the thought out loud. Her jaw clenched into a forced smile hiding the fear beneath. One brick at a time, Reilly began to shut herself down.

"We're old, not dead, Reilly!" Amy chirped as she opened the front door.

Bubba bounced down the steps and sat at her feet. Reilly bent over and rubbed behind her ears as she licked her face. But once she had enough, the pup jumped into the RV, dropping onto the couch.

Everyone's leaving me. Mortar slapped against the wall as another brick was placed. Reilly would be an impenetrable fortress when this was done.

"Breanna's upstairs—"

"She left for the city." Reilly needed to change the topic before her mother prodded further. There were other pressing questions in her mind, like if her mother was really prepared. "Have you called your doctors? Do you even have enough medication for the entire trip? Alarms set on your watch to remind you to take them?"

"Yes, Mom. I switched all my appointments to virtual ones with an understanding that I'll get bloodwork at a local diagnostic place. I've got this covered, Reilly." Her mother held her at arm's length, forcing Reilly's puffy eyes to dart around and avoid hers. "Now why would Breanna leave so soon? What happened?"

"What about Millie and Edie? They're going to miss you!" She pushed out of her mother's grasp, walked over to the RV, and looked inside. "Edie's birthday is coming up soon and—" Her eyes scanned every inch of the vehicle, looking for a flaw. Finding none, another brick settled into place. Her mother was leaving, whether Reilly wanted her to or not.

"I gave the girls a map of the country with some pushpins. I promised to call every night and tell them where I am. The girls are excited about the *Where in the Country Is Grandma* game."

"And Bubba?"

"You adopted her for me when I was recovering. You really think she'd stay home when I'm not there? We can't sleep apart; you know this. Now talk to me. What's going on with you and Breanna?" Her mother's warm dulcet tones wrapped around her like a security blanket.

Oh, how she wanted that warmth to melt through her defenses before they fully formed. All she had to do was tell Wendy what happened in her office and her mother might stay. But the explanation never materialized. Instead, the wall around her heart hardened as the final row of bricks and mortar finished locking her emotions down.

Mom deserves to live her dream. Reilly refused to be the reason her mom didn't get to enjoy her life. She allowed the mask of happiness to slip into place and hoped Wendy would believe her.

"She's just busy for the next few days with work. Nothing to worry about," she lied.

"You sure?"

Reilly didn't risk answering for fear of falling apart. Instead, she pulled her mother into a tight embrace as her aunt jumped into the RV and Bubba barked impatiently at them both.

"I'll call you when we get to the first stop. It's late, so we'll only be on the road for a bit. Just enough to get beyond the city. We'll be seeing your cousins on the way. I'll tell them you send your love."

Reilly nodded, too numb to reply. With one last kiss on Reilly's cheek, Wendy bounced into the van-sized RV and closed the doors. With a honk and a wave, the two women were off. Reilly watched the RV roll down the street and out of view. The silence fell upon her like feet of snow—soft, simple flakes that are beautiful to watch as they fall. Until they bury you alive inside, cutting you off from the world around you. The tightness in her chest felt like a heart attack, but Reilly knew better. She slammed the front door shut behind her before an anguished scream erupted from her lungs.

Chapter Twenty

Three weeks slipped by as the calendar flipped from day to day. Deadlines written in bright red Sharpie had come and gone. The Word document filled with Reilly's story of love and wonder was left untouched. The emptiness of the house continued its oppressive attack on her psyche.

She barely left her room, let alone the bed. Reilly was good at tuning out the world. If the doorbell rang, she'd check the camera to verify it was a package or the mailman. Reilly ignored all the video chat invitations, calls, and text messages. She couldn't bring herself to reply. Instead, Reilly had her social media team spin her absence as some deep dive into her work. The people that cared flooded her direct messages with concern.

Her level of disconnection wasn't healthy, but Reilly couldn't fight her way out of it. It took all of her energy to put on a brave face when her mother called regaling her with stories about her exciting trip. Wendy informed her daughter of changes to the route as they went. Those calls were the closest Reilly got to the world outside her door. When she was really low, she'd watch her mother's icon move around the map application. It made her feel closer to Wendy. She'd considered joining the two women on the road, but that meant getting out of bed and facing questions she wasn't ready to answer.

Around week two, Reilly found some press releases from K.B. Studios. It seemed like Breanna's company was out of the woods. That brought some joy to her wallowing heart. Breanna's success and happiness was all Reilly wanted. Even if she wasn't the reason for it.

During the third week, the reality of her life hit her like a baseball bat to the face. She struggled to understand why she continued to take care of others to the detriment to herself. But when she didn't have others to focus on, the noise in her own head was overwhelming.

She missed the tiny humans underfoot asking for a lift to reach the cookie jar on the counter. Her friends were reaching out, but their social media posts indicated they were doing well. Aunt Amy's coffee shop was running smoothly, according to her aunt, and Bubba seemed to be thrilled about her new home on the road. Everyone was living life without her. And Reilly realized she didn't know how to be with herself.

Reilly had felt this way only one other time in her life, when her mother was still healing from major surgery. Instead of facing her feelings, she grabbed onto her mother's care like a lifeline to avoid focusing on herself. Avoidance was easy, but now she felt her inner demons fighting for attention.

Normally Reilly leaned on manual labor to help her process her emotions, but that required energy she didn't have. When she managed to get out of bed, she stared at the blank computer screen, the romance novel taunting her.

"What would you do?" Reilly asked her characters. "If you screwed up so badly that it felt impossible to fix, what would you do?"

Silence gripped her heart.

Desperate, she opened her social media accounts and logged in. Her eyes scanned old comments she was tagged on. Some made her heart sink further.

This is unadulterated homosexual porn. There's no warning.

The book referenced was one of her originals, with a lesbian lead character who didn't even kiss a girl until the end of the story.

This author can't write without shoving the queer agenda down your throat. You can't normalize sins with science fiction themes and decent writing. Well, at least her later books have good grammar. The older ones are trash.

The negative comments leapt off the screen, slicing her flesh to shreds. Her eyes were glued to the words, reaffirming her emotions.

Reading a story that makes me feel seen. @MEKline, if you ever see this, thank you.

Reilly reread the post again. With a tentative hand, she hit the return arrow and replied with a heart emoji. She didn't trust herself to say anything more than that, and she hoped it was enough for now. She found the next positive comment and replied to it the same way. One after another, she went back a few months and, after reading them all, replied with various emojis. Maybe her readers would assume it was code for something more. The marketing ploy ignited in a section of her mind that had lay dormant during her isolation.

"We can't write for everyone, but we always write for someone," she whispered to herself and the breeze coming in the window.

Her heart felt lighter in her chest after a few hours of reading all the notifications. Her dread of negative posts and reviews was valid, but she never expected the positive side. The way people connected to each character, fan art bringing her world to life, and the messages on all the platforms with personal reflections all lifted her higher.

She grabbed her phone and dialed the one person she knew would answer.

"Hey, Rei. What can I do for you?" Ellen's cheerful voice came through above the murmur of music in the background.

"It's Friday, so you're heading out of the city, yes?"

"I am, but I'm also rather creeped out that you know that."

"You told me you love going home to your parents' house to clear your nasal passages from the exhaust." She tried to imitate Ellen's soft, motherly tone but failed.

"I said that?"

"When we met. You were nervous, but that doesn't matter. I know it's the weekend, but I need help with something."

"As long as it doesn't involve me heading back to a stuffy boardroom, I'm in."

"I'll email you specific details and text you an address. Can you be there in the morning?"

"You got it." Ellen sounded a bit suspicious, but Reilly was being rather vague.

Reilly was about to toss her phone on the table when her eyes fell on Breanna's smiling face. The image was attached to the long thread of messages Reilly had read often since the breakup. Her fingers flew across the keyboard. She paused, wondering if the message would land the way she desired. Her thumb hit the backspace, and she watched the characters disappear one by one.

What could she say right now that wouldn't sound pointless? Was she sorry? Of course she was, but did she feel fully responsible for everything? She struggled with that. Reilly was seeing things clearly for the first time, and she needed to stop putting all the blame onto herself. It wasn't healthy or right. She was only accountable for her actions, no one else's.

She no longer had Helen in control of her every move. Her family no longer needed her at their beckon call. The ache of fear forced her to wrap her arms around her midsection. There was no one to distract or save her from facing the demons she'd avoided for so long. Her own words from one of her characters from Shadows Rise flew to the front of her mind: *You can run from life, or you can live it. It's yours to enjoy or waste.* Even her inner self knew it was time to grow up.

Her mother's icon bounced along an interstate in the state of Nevada. Wendy would probably tell Reilly to think before sending her marketing idea to Ellen. But her mother wasn't here, so Reilly sent the email before she chickened out. Ellen would refine the plan to work well, but she'd also hold Reilly to the commitment if she was truly on board with it. There was no backing out now.

"Time to start living, Reilly," she whispered to herself. It was time to follow Wendy's lead. Reilly felt the sudden urge to stop hiding. It was time for M. E. Kline to see the light.

***

Breanna stared at the pile of documents on her desk. She'd joked with Kai about it at first, but it kept growing as the days went by. As her schedule became busier than normal, those same documents added to the annoyance of her day. Breanna found closing her door and shutting out the rest of the office afforded her some quiet from the madness. But that only lasted for a little while.

Everything seemed to need her approval or signature. From simple agreements with personnel to press releases, she needed to verify it all. The tediousness of everything slowly ate away at what little control she had left. Breanna worked through the evenings at home with Kai and taking care of Max.

"Do you have . . ." Kai's voice trailed off as Breanna's stare met theirs at the doorway.

"Do I have what?"

"Okay, this isn't good." Breanna ignored the comment as she played a video a producer sent her way. The lead actor in the project was throwing a tantrum, destroying craft services while screaming expletives. "You think we can keep them in line, or do we need to consider reshoots inflating our budget?"

"I already spoke to his agent, hired more security, and he's been warned." Kai leaned down on the desk. "We can only hope it's enough."

"If you handled it, why was it sent to my inbox for approval?"

"I should have told you, but you haven't been receptive lately. Seriously, Bre, you can't avoid this forever. You barely sleep. I doubt you'd eat if I didn't put food right in front of you. You can't hide out in your office all day. It's not healthy."

"We're insanely busy, but I make sure to attend all the necessary meetings."

"True, but let's discuss how our staff walks on eggshells around you right now. That's if they have the courage to talk to you at all. Most people bypass you entirely and come to my office."

"That's on them, Kai." Breanna deflected how hard the statement hit her. Her employees avoiding her was not the culture she wanted to foster in the workplace. But she wasn't herself at all. "We've dreamed of this level of success, and now we're overwhelmed. I'm stressed like never before, and maybe I'm short with people, but it's not intentional. On top of that, neither of us has done a set visit to any of our productions. We have ten million things to handle, and an on-set issue hitting social media is not something we can afford. If we'd been there, maybe it wouldn't have gotten this far. Preventative, not reactionary, remember?"

"Yeah, but that doesn't mean you have to carry the entire load here." Kai grabbed the documents. "For your information, I've been to several sets, hiding in the background to confirm and handle any issues that were brought to our attention. Specifically, we had to remove a crew member for lewd and sexist comments to one of our leads. You'd know this if you checked our private Slack channels. Employees are only being vague with *you*, Bre."

"That's ridiculous. They—" She struggled with the new information.

"Dammit, Breanna, you're my best friend and my family, but will you listen to yourself? No one wants you on set right now. And everyone's afraid of you. That's why I'm the only one who comes in here. I can handle it, but our team doesn't deserve to be on the end of your anger. So, either you tell me what's going on in your head or go home until you figure it out."

Breanna dropped her pen and sipped the alcohol sitting on her desk. "I don't mean to be so short with everyone. I'm overwhelmed and . . ." Breanna took another sip for courage. "I see her everywhere, Kai. To top it off, her agent called telling us to expect a signed contract soon. No further negotiations, no more arguments. Just a call from someone I've never met about an impending signature we haven't seen on a contract we really can't afford. The woman doesn't contact me for weeks but has her people call me. Why? Why not tell me herself? If she really cared, she'd do that. Right?"

"Have you reached out to her? Told her we smoothed everything over with our partners and they understood we wouldn't be moving forward with her project?"

"No. I mean I guess I left it open for interpretation."

"And you're upset she intends to sign the contract that we both agreed would be the last offer even if it put a strain on the budget or not reaching out to you first? I don't get it, Bre. I'm not saying what she did was right, but you could reach out to Reilly if you wanted to."

Breanna's phone buzzed with a notification. The image and subsequent description left her cold. She held the device up for Kai to read the post.

Q&A with M. E. Kline. Will the elusive author reveal themselves to the world? Stay tuned for more information.

"Wow." Kai's confusion matched her own. "Why would she do this now?"

"To taunt me? Maybe to break my heart even more? Show our partners the level of my ineptitude?"

"Bre, serious question. Would you have kept in touch with Reilly if you didn't know she was Kline? She lied, true, but she had her reasons. Did you give her a chance to explain?"

"What kind of question is that? Are you taking her side now?"

"Hey, stop that crap. You know damn well I've always had your back. Part of loving someone that much means telling them the truth, even when they don't want to hear it." Breanna scoffed and turned her attention to the window behind her desk. "You told me Reilly couldn't keep her eyes off of you in the coffee shop. I know you and your idiotic rules. That girl would have enjoyed the evening and been dropped before morning came. Connection or no, you would have cut her off to protect yourself."

Breanna's shoulder sagged with Kai's words. There was a truth in them she didn't want to face. It was true that Reilly was an attractive woman and drew her attention almost immediately. The stares and nerves just fed into Breanna's strengths. But the woman left her at the coffee shop, alone.

"It started out that way, but there was something about her I couldn't put my finger on. She was different, and I couldn't get enough of her." Her chest ached as the memory of Reilly's warm embrace surrounded her.

"What was your plan for the evening? Coffee, sex, and farewells?"

"I don't know what I expected. Kai, I told you this before. I don't see the need to rehash it."

"You're going to."

"I don't know, all right? I wanted to ravish her and let off some steam. Nothing more. But then I spent time with her, got to know her and let her in. I was honest about our situation. She mentioned Kline and—" Breanna stopped cold.

"And you used her for a connection," Kai finished the unspoken truth. "Reilly still has a lot to apologize for, but you're not innocent in all this. Take the rest of the day to process that, and I'll see you tonight at the launch party. Understand?"

Breanna had no desire to go home or to attend the event this evening. Reilly's betrayal brought back all the pain from Quinn she buried long ago. Kai and Serena helped put her back together again. How could she repair the damage that ran so deep when she didn't want to let go of the woman causing it?

Chapter Twenty-One

Chapter Twenty-One

By the time Reilly finished setting things up with Ellen, she felt the need to get fresh air. It's how she found herself at the park, sitting on a swing by herself. The moon was high in the sky, illuminating the areas the new streetlights didn't touch. The soft breeze chilled her skin as it brushed her hair off her shoulders. She did a few kicks on the swing and leaned back, watching the ground come closer before sitting upright again.

"Haven't done that since we were kids." Harrison slipped onto the swing next to her, but she didn't stop her motion.

"What are you doing here?"

"You've been ignoring our calls. I stopped by the house before I passed here."

She didn't reply. The wind whipping her hair around as she swung gave her a sense of flying. For the first time in weeks, a smile crossed her face as Harrison caught up to her. She pushed harder to soar higher than her brother. She heard their blended laughter as the metal hinges squeaked with the motion.

It brought her back to reality. Even in places where memories flood your soul with levity, life pushes you forward to face whatever's beyond your desire. Her sneakers scraped along the wood chips to slow her speed to a stop.

No matter how far you fly, you have to come back down to Earth.

"God, I miss this. Just being . . ."

"Kids?"

"Yeah, that innocence." Harrison leaned back, staring at the night sky. "Remember how we'd climb on the roof to look up at the stars? We'd make up names and stories for every constellation."

"You tried to push me off the roof a lot."

"You always stole my blanket. Why didn't you bring your own?"

"I didn't want it to get dirty. Mom would notice."

"Rei, she knew what we were doing. Why do you think there was always warm hot cocoa in a thermos for us?"

"I thought you did that."

"Nah, Mom would make it, and then Dad would hang out his window to make sure we were okay."

"Well, crap, I thought they were just oblivious. It's nice to know they weren't crazy. They were just . . ." Words failed her.

"Ours? We wouldn't trade them for anything though, would we?" Reilly felt her brother's gaze upon her as she answered affirmatively. "I owe you an apology. When Dad got sick, I didn't know how to handle it. I saw you taking care of everyone and I just . . . bailed."

"You were taking care of tiny humans. It's all good." She twisted the swing's chains and lifted her feet to spin around. It gave her discomfort a physical form she could handle.

"Maybe, but I also felt like I wasn't needed. When he died, I blamed you. You made all these decisions without my input. They just left it all to you and . . . well, you never asked my opinion on any of it. You just handled it."

"Of course I handled it." She stopped her swing to stare at her brother in disbelief. "Harrison, once you got married, they asked me to be their medical proxy. They didn't want you to worry about it. When the kids came around, they were even more firm in their decision. You had responsibilities . . ." She stopped before her jealousy turned into a full-fledged attack on her brother for things he had no control over.

"Maybe, but then Mom got sick, and you took the lead again. You listened to me, but defended her choices, overruled me. Rei, I was angry and scared."

"So was I, but you didn't back me up either. She wasn't incapacitated, Harrison. You wanted control to feel better, but neither one of us had it. So yeah, I was just as terrified as you were."

He nodded at her. In the moonlight, her brother looked like the hero her younger self held onto for survival. But the shadows crept under his eyes, revealing how time had worn him down when she wasn't paying attention.

"Just when things seemed to be back on track with our family, Helen left. You didn't falter. I watched you fall apart piece by piece, but you just kept going. So Mom and I didn't push or ask if you were okay. We . . . I wasn't the brother who should have protected his little sister. You handled all the stress of Mom's medical care at home while fueling this amazing career and dealing with the breakup. It just proved you didn't need anyone. You were a force to be reckoned with, Reilly. And I didn't think you'd need me now either."

"I'll always need you, Harrison. You're my brother." Reilly stared at the depth of space and felt the negatives from her life wash away into the vastness of it all. "It's just different now that we're older. I can't lean on you for every little thing."

"This isn't something small, Reilly. This is your heart." She felt his hand wipe away a stray tear. "I liked Breanna. The kids did too."

Reilly smiled. She loved how the kids took to Breanna with ease. The moments they had together felt seamless. Taking Helen around her family had felt like dumping a bucket of ice water on people in below zero temperature.

"God, my butt hurts. How did we swing on these things for so long?" His laughter brought a slight chuckle from the depths of her chest. "You know we never liked Helen. All of us knew she wasn't good for you, but you seemed so happy. We didn't want to ruin that. If I'd known what was happening . . . if you'd have talked to me . . ."

"And said what? Hindsight's twenty-twenty, Harrison. When I was in the middle of it all, I never knew how to verbalize any of it. Same with Breanna. It felt so right, like she was my North Star, and I never thought about how I was screwing it all up." Her words of acceptance were laced with hope.

The future's what we make of it.

Headlights illuminated them as several cars passed by. Reilly took the moment to collect her thoughts. Harrison was right, she didn't reach out when she needed a shoulder to cry on. He was trying now.

"I'm afraid." Her voice was so soft she wasn't sure Harrison could hear her.

"Of what?"

"I don't know. Nothing. Everything. Both? I've never been able to move forward without analyzing something to death. Everything I've done was to prove someone wrong. I practiced every sport you played, just so I could beat you. Hell,

I learned all about marketing just to show Helen I could do it." Reilly paused and swallowed back the fear of being vulnerable. "I wanted dad to acknowledge my accomplishments without pushing them aside because his son did something similar or because other people had it worse and I should be thankful. And it's stupid because none of it matters now."

"But it does, Rei. You literally base your value on what you can give to everyone around you. How many times have we called while you're writing, and you drop everything to help? If I did that, I'd be out of a job. But I just assumed you were home and that meant you were available."

"You needed me," Reilly deflected.

"It was easier to call you than to figure it out on my own. My point is, Rei, since you could walk, you've helped everyone else around you. When Grandpa died, you barely cried. You just walked around making sure everyone else could mourn. Dad's funeral was the same way. You lost your fiancée because she was a vile person, but also because you put us before your relationship. Mom left to go travel and live her life. When are you going to do the same?"

She knew he was right. Reilly had said as much to herself, but hearing her brother agree with her inner monologue gave it validity. Her first book was a testament to his words. She'd get a few chapters written one week and not go back to it for another two or three because a friend or family member needed her assistance.

The minute Breanna told her how deeply the company was in trouble, Reilly had to help. Instead of being a comfort to the other woman, she'd offered to assist the producer with her goal. It was a fatal flaw in her plan to stay hidden and not sell the rights to her books. When Reilly realized her error, she reached out to others who were excited at the prospect of a film adaptation. Sure, she was vague in her discussions with everyone, but she was to blame for being in the situation to begin with. Her desire to feel needed and the inability to say no or set boundaries always led to her screwing things up. The end result was her fault.

Harrison held out a business card. Reilly slowed her movements and looked over at the name on it.

"I don't like talking to my therapist about, well, anything, but it's been helping me a lot. I know you've got one, but if you haven't brought any of this up yet . .

. maybe you need a new one. This is the number to my guy's practice. Just give it some thought." Her brother stood and gave her a soft smile. "I better get back to the rugrats before they drive their mama mad. Maybe we can do this again."

"I'd like to tell the kids about Kline and what the initials stand for, if that's okay. I know it's not necessary, but I don't want anyone in the dark anymore."

"They'd love to see you."

Harrison left Reilly staring at the card. She slid it into her pocket and went back to swinging as hard as she could. Her legs pumped faster, propelling her higher. She leaned back and closed her eyes. The blood rushed to her head as the tears broke free from her eyes.

***

By the time Breanna walked into the event space, the party was in full swing. SeaCliff Studios members milled about the open bar and dance floor. Her heels clicked against the tile floor as she moved through the throngs of people. Her tailored suit hugged her curves in all the right ways, and the admiring glances confirmed it was the right choice. She found a seat at the bar and ordered an expensive whiskey. If the company was paying for all the drinks, she might as well splurge.

"Breanna!" Michaela Woods pulled her into an awkward embrace. "I wanted to let you know the partners have all agreed to extend our contract with K.B. Studios. We'll be sending over the signed deal on Monday. Thought I'd let you know ahead of time."

"That's wonderful. Glad to hear it." She was being sincere, even though her voice and demeanor didn't support it. Breanna had a desk full of things she needed to go back to rather than schmoozing with this crowd.

"Where did you find all these people willing to sign so quickly? And to have several picture deals on series? You swooped in and found some hidden gems. I have to admit the slate is so rich we're bound to have more successes than failures."

"If I told you my trade secrets, I'd have to kill you." Breanna smirked before tipping her drink back. The second drink burned less than the one before it, reminding Breanna she should slow down. Kai and Breanna used to enjoy these events, but now she just wanted alcohol to help her relax. She needed it to numb the ache that formed the minute she left Reilly in the rearview mirror.

"You're too much." Michaela scanned the room and pointed to a man in a black suit with a plate full of mini hot dogs. "Oh lord, my husband's found the pigs in a blanket. Excuse me."

Breanna downed the rest of her drink as Michaela reprimanded her partner over his choice of foods. She'd been around the couple for years, and they couldn't be more different. Yet somehow it worked. In the past, it rekindled her hope in love. Now she just wanted to stick to her old rules. It was so much safer that way.

"You need a refill?" The bartender rubbed a rag across the bar top, her cleavage on full display. "Unless you're good?"

Breanna looked down at her empty glass and questioned if she should indulge in more. The alcohol-induced brain fog was settling in as her inhibitions fell away. "I could always use a bit more."

"They made specialty shots for the event if you'd like to try one?" The test tubes along the back row made Breanna laugh. "Not a fan?"

"No, it just reminds me of my old clubbing days."

The bartender grabbed two vials and leaned over, displaying her assets again as she handed Breanna the drink. "Bottoms up." The concoction of bottom shelf acid melted its way down her throat.

"Oh, man, that's horrible." Breanna cringed.

"I didn't mix them, promise." She coughed as she filled Breanna's glass.

Breanna downed half of it before her body stopped twitching. "Glad to hear it. Means I don't have to worry about battery acid in my drinks for the rest of the night."

"I got you. Name's Tina." The bartender held out her hand. Breanna hesitated but followed in kind.

"Breanna." Her flirtatious smile was too easy to display. It should have excited her, as it usually led to sex. Instead, she felt dirty.

"It's a pleasure to meet you, Breanna. Why are you holding up my bar and ignoring the other beautiful people in the building?"

"Ahh, yes. Well, that one"—Breanna pointed to Kai—"is my business partner. Most of these people know me and just want to schmooze to get something.

Besides, once I put in the required amount of time, I'll slip out to spend the evening watching my cat destroy everything on my coffee table." She swirled the liquid around as Tina filled it to the rim without prompting. The more she drank, the more Breanna realized the bar was helping her stand.

"Or you could keep me company." Tina's sultry tone left little to the imagination.

Breanna's mind screamed in pleasurable joy while her heart begged her to walk away. She thought she was ready to slip back into her old life, but the thought of Reilly reminded her she wasn't. She needed to leave but wasn't sure if her legs could hold her up anymore.

"I don't think I'll last the entire party if you keep filling my drinks this fast."

"Well, you look like you need to calm down from the stress. I assume you're in the entertainment world."

"Ha, yeah, you could say that." The whiskey slid down her throat without any discomfort. Her body swayed as she thought about the dinner Kai left on her desk. The same food that remained untouched. If Breanna trusted herself not to collapse, she'd grab some bread and water.

"So, maybe we slip out on my break to the back room. There's a great place to sit and . . . relax." The bartender's hand singed her skin as it crept over her forearm.

She might be drunk, but Breanna didn't want this. A few months ago, Tina would be screaming her name in the back room a few minutes after they met. But all she could see was Reilly. The way the woman smiled at her when they were playing miniature golf. The warmth just looked at Breanna and she was a gooey inside. She loved that she found Reilly, no matter how short their relationship was.

"When you know, you know." She hiccupped.

"Hmm?" Tina leaned into Breanna's space.

"I don't think that's a good idea." The slurred words barely registered with the bartender.

"If you're hung up on someone else, the best way to get over them—"

"Is to get under someone else, I know. But you don't just get over Reilly like that. She's too special." She hoped her honesty let the other woman know it wasn't her fault.

"If you change your mind, you know where to find me." She wasn't sure if the woman was accepting her refusal or sashaying down the bar to entice her further. Not that it mattered what Tina meant. Breanna only had one person on her mind.

She blinked several times to bring her cell phone screen into focus. Her fingers danced across the screen as she sent a message to her business partner. Then she tapped on Reilly's name in her messages list. Her eyes scanned the screen, the woman's apologies tearing at her chest as she read them. The words were heartfelt and honest. She wanted to reply.

"Think before you do that." Kai leaned on the bar next to her. "I know it's tempting, but you smell like a distillery, so I doubt anything you send right now will make sense to her. Trust the person who has no idea what you wrote in the text to me." Kai laughed as they held up their device with a emoji gibberish filled screen

"You're right, but I miss her, Kai." The slurred words dragged on longer than she desired.

"I know, Bre. Let's get you out of here."

Breanna felt herself lifted to a standing position and moved through the back door into the cool evening air. She wanted nothing more than to curl up in Reilly's arms and forget the past ever happened. But it wasn't possible. Kai was right. If she contacted Reilly, she'd make things worse. She always did.

Chapter Twenty-Two

Reilly hesitated at Harrison's front door. She hadn't spoken to Jenna since their confrontation weeks ago. Her self-imposed exile wasn't personal, but Reilly knew Jenna might take it that way. After her talk with Harrison at the park, she thought seeing everyone again would be easy.

Then why are you finding it so damn difficult to go inside?

Before she could war with herself further, the door swung open. Jenna stood, rigid in the entryway with an unreadable expression. She moved back allowing Reilly to step inside. The house looked and smelled the same. Maybe the girls had spread their toys out differently, but Reilly couldn't be sure.

Life moves on whether you participate or not, Reilly.

"Would you like some coffee, or does this visit require something stronger?" Jenna clicked the door shut.

"A coffee would be nice."

Reilly stood by the front door as Jenna slipped into the kitchen. Her fingers trembled as she wondered if she should make herself at home or wait for permission. Before Reilly could decide, Jenna re-entered the room. Her sister-in-law placed two mugs on the coffee table and sank into the plush couch.

"You're welcome to sit, unless you'd rather not."

The one line removed the barriers from Reilly's subconscious as her body moved to join Jenna on the couch. Her hands stilled around the warm mug as her right knee bounced to release the uncomfortable energy.

"Don't take this the wrong way, but I haven't heard from you for weeks."

"I was hoping you and the kids were free." Reilly spun the mug around in her hands. One side was embellished with a cartoon heart with the words *Best Daddy.*

The other side bore an image of the girls. The colors were faded after what she assumed were many dishwasher cycles. Another example of time passing her by.

"You've avoided my texts and calls this entire time. You bailed on me for our normal coffee dates, and now are hoping we're all free? What changed?"

Without a friendship as long as theirs, Reilly would have mistaken Jenna's words as pure rage instead of ones made out of worry.

"I needed to wallow a bit and figure my way out of it. It wasn't fair to anyone. I'm not perfect, Jenna. I royally screwed something up and felt the world collapse on me. I didn't handle it well, obviously."

"You think? Reilly, you've got to get up and face it head on. Burying yourself under blankets and ignoring the world doesn't help."

"That's you, not me. I need time to process, crawl back into my shell, and dwell on it. That's my coping mechanism. You've known me forever. You should know how I handle conflict."

"One would hope you grew out of it."

"Jenna, you're my best friend, but I'm not a child. You don't have to like what I do, but maybe you could give me some support here? I'm here trying to make it right."

Jenna flopped into the chair across from her with a heavy sigh. "If we're being honest, I owe you an apology too. We all encouraged you to get involved with Breanna, but I never thought you'd catch feelings."

"Maybe you all nudged me in that direction, but it was my decision." She sipped her coffee. Its warmth slid down her throat, allowing her a moment for the distractions in her head to slow. "You know, looking back on everything, I feel like such a fool. My fear of losing her was so overwhelming that I just . . . did nothing. And it all came out anyway, like all secrets do. The only thing I can do now is step out from the shadows and hope for the best." Her late-night online therapy session had helped her sort out the rest of her plans.

"Rei, your happiness is all that matters. As long as it brings you joy, I don't care if you rekindle things with Breanna or become the crazy dog lady. This is your path, honey and no matter what we'll always be here. And maybe I overstepped by bringing Kai into the equation, but every decision I made came from a place of love."

"First, being single forever sounds tempting, but I'm hoping not. Second, crazy dog lady? You saw how I was with Bubba. She'd give me those sad puppy eyes and I caved to whatever she wanted. Could you imagine me with more than one? And as for Kai, I didn't get it at the time, but I do now. Just promise you won't abandon me for them?" Her voice had shrunk to a whisper.

Jenna took Reilly's hand across the table and gave it a gentle squeeze. "I won't. Promise me you won't disappear when you make up with Breanna?"

"I promise, but I'm not sure if making up is a possibility right now." While she'd been working on bettering herself moving forward, Reilly understood the possibility of reconciliation remained a question mark.

"Alright, time for some tough love. Rei, you build these walls so high, so fast, the second life knocks you down. But guess what? Life doesn't care. People are going to stumble onto your path and maybe they add to your journey. But they might step on you to lift themselves up. Pain is inevitable. You can't hide under a rock and wait for it to pass. The only thing you'll lose is your precious time. No one else will care. So, quit bracing for the inevitable and learn how to ride it out. You've got this, Rei, even if you don't believe it yet. I do."

Reilly knew Jenna was right, but her father's voice minimizing her discomfort rang in her ears.

Others have it worse than you, Reilly. Be happy. Whatever it is can't be that bad.

Looking back on her life now, she knew that was where her problems started. How could she face negative situations when her father insisted they had no validity? So she just ignored it all and locked herself in her room.

"I want to talk to her, I need to, but I'm not sure how. Maybe an email or even snail mail? That's romantic, right? Sending a letter through the postal service? I'm so much better writing than talking."

"Sometimes it can be, but how would you interpret it coming from a best-selling author?"

"Right. So, in person it is." Reilly swallowed hard. "Have you heard from Kai? I have no right to ask, but have they talked about Breanna?"

"I have. Apparently, Kai moved into Breanna's place. They've bonded with Max, Breanna's cat and enjoy watching tv together. Beyond that, we agreed our friends are hopeless and planned to lock you both up in an escape room. That way, you'd be forced to communicate. Granted, we discussed that after we both ingested a lot of alcohol."

"You know they let you out if you don't make the time frame. Right?"

"Did I mention how drunk we were?"

"Still, might be interesting to add into a book someday."

The girls stormed into the house, screaming at the top of their lungs. They injected pure joy through her veins. She watched as they ran around, their laughter lifting the shadows she fought against.

"I know you wanted to talk to them, but they might be more receptive when they're not so amped up," Jenna mumbled before she ran to get the girls settled.

Reilly's relief was palpable. This felt right. Normal. She laughed at herself. For someone who loved writing angst-riddled drama, she preferred the simple family arguments over what's for dinner.

***

Three days later, Reilly stood on the platform, waiting for the next train into Manhattan. She'd wanted to run into the city after talking to Jenna, but her sister-in-law told her to take the time and find the right words. Reilly also had the live Q&A in the morning, so she needed to put a proper plan in motion.

She made calls to people she trusted with discretion. Several were confused and unhappy with her seventy-two-hour deadline, but she expressed her need and willingness to pay for the rushed timeline. In the end, their invoices didn't include any increases. When asked, she was told her loyalty to them was valued. It reinforced Reilly's confidence in her work ethic.

But there was one message she needed to send that she dreaded. With each passing second, her phone felt heavier as her thumb hovered over the send icon. The brakes of the train screeched as it slowed to a stop. Reilly took that moment to hit the button.

Reilly found a seat away from the crowd and pulled her bag onto her lap. The manila envelope stared back at her, taunting her like the devil with some dark chocolate. She knew what it meant, but there was no going back. Her therapist told her the only way forward was through. *Just ride the wave and don't drown,* she thought to herself.

Her phone buzzed.

Sure. Same place as always?

She sent off an affirmative reply with a time and shoved her phone into her bag.

"You look scared." The young boy across the aisle smiled at Reilly. "Trains are fun. Mommy says they used to use coal, but now they use power. So they are clean and safe."

"Tommy, let the nice lady be." His mother pulled the boy back in his seat.

"It's all right." Reilly turned her attention to the small boy. "I'm not afraid of trains, but the tunnels scare me. They're really dark."

"Do you know they go underwater? I want to drive a train when I'm big. Then I can be a scuba diver on a train when we go under the water."

"That sounds like an amazing job to have." Reilly found his innocence charming. It helped ease the stress in her mind and the roll of her stomach from sitting backwards.

"I can hold your hand in the tunnel. Right, Mommy?" Once she nodded, he slipped into the seat next to Reilly. "That way you're not scared."

Reilly took his hand. Tommy continued to tell her all about his dreams of scuba diving on the train. His creativity reminded Reilly of herself. She wondered if he'd be a writer in the future or if he would just tell the best stories to his kids. As the darkness approached, Tommy squeezed her hand. Reilly found the lights of Penn Station reflected the current situation. She was being helped through the dark into the proverbial light.

Gosh, this is some classic fairy-tale crap, all right. She laughed.

After saying farewell to her train mates, her feet moved as if on muscle memory. Her steps were swift and precise as she slithered through the slower pedestrian foot traffic. Since her date with Breanna, Reilly had looked upon the city differently. Now there was a fondness for the concrete jungle she had forgotten about. A connection to the smells, sounds, and feeling of the breeze hitting her skin. Everything about Manhattan had come back to life thanks to Breanna. She wouldn't move back, nor could she reasonably afford to, but the energy here invigorated her.

That same joy came with the pain of her past. She walked into the coffee shop, ordered a drink, and found a small table in the back. Reilly laughed at the thought of sitting in the dimly lit area of the cafe. Some would say she was defeating the purpose of dealing with her demons and coming into the light. She'd reply that she really hated being bumped into by people coming or going from the small area. Being in the back offered her some needed peace. She'd learned that about herself recently. When she had to handle something serious, she didn't want an audience.

"I grabbed your coffee. Hope you don't mind. They called your name, and you looked lost in thought." Helen stood there in a pinstriped three-piece suit that would have made Reilly drool back in the day. "Your message surprised me."

The woman sat down and leaned back in the wooden chair with such confidence that increased Reilly's anxiety. Her mind raced through everything she planned on saying or asking and found herself rationalizing all the problems in their previous relationship. She huffed as she considered just accepting the blame and leaving the meeting. Reilly knew her poker face was pathetic as Helen's lips curled up in a seductive smirk. The woman flipped her hair over her left shoulder as she crossed her legs and sipped her beverage. Reilly recognized the move easily since her ex used it on her before. Helen spoke from her position of power, complaining about the weather and craving a southern move.

Reilly's gaze bore into her ex-fiancé. The tingling of confusion inched its way forward. Helen's once alluring confidence now irritated her. The same woman who shone a spotlight exposing every shadow of Reilly's insecurity was nothing but a hallow mess. The once powerful vice grip that constricted her every move, was part of a crumbling façade. Helen's smirk was simply a mask to cover her own demons.

"I was hoping we could talk. We haven't done that since—"

"I left you. We could have, but you never answered your phone." The snarky reply smacked Reilly down a peg. Yet, unlike how she was in their relationship, this time she didn't cower.

"I'm sure you can imagine how difficult that was. One minute I had a ring on my finger, and the next it was gone, along with my fiancé." Her tone was low and laced with anger.

"It is what it is, Reilly. Regardless of how you felt, you should have answered your phone. I had your stuff at my place and business items we needed to handle."

Reilly scoffed at the suggestion. Whatever was still at Helen's place wasn't worth the effort and there was no business for them to discuss. No contracts were ever signed. She thanked her lucky stars Helen didn't insist on legal paperwork before she skipped out.

"Like you said, it is what it is. But that's not why I asked to meet you. At least not to discuss that part."

"I'm happy now, Reilly. If you're thinking about—"

"Trust me, I'm not." Reilly forced herself to drink her coffee. Helen was trying to twist the conversation and she used the moment to regain control. "I'm trying to understand some things, and part of it starts with our relationship. Especially regarding Kline."

"Kline," Helen ridiculed. "That always bugged me, you referring to your pen name as someone else. It was and still is you, Reilly. Why do you think I dragged you to all those parties?"

"Because you wanted to network?"

"Partially." Reilly couldn't prevent her eye roll at the blatant lie. "Okay, mostly. But I constantly accepted the invitation as Kline plus one. You were always on my arm as my date. An entire year of going to all those events, trying to get you to come forward, and you just cowered in the background. So afraid of your own shadow. The world loves what you created, and you want nothing to do with it."

"I never said that. You knew going to all those events wasn't me. But you . . . you loved the photos, the galas, all the power players who came to say hello."

"Yeah, and my career has flourished because of it. I've got a bigger place, a better retirement plan. I'm moving up, and you're sitting in a coffee shop wearing jeans and your lucky superhero jacket. You've got to grow up, Rei. Live in the real world outside of the pages you write and enjoy the perks you've earned."

"It was never about that for me." She never thought about popularity or advancing in her career. Her happiness was writing and spending all her free time with Helen. Now she hoped those spare moments would be shared with Breanna.

"And you lost me."

"You wanted to enjoy the life connected to my success. I told you so many times that fame and fortune never mattered to me, but you lapped it up. You pushed for more when I was burned out and needed someone to lean on. I wanted you to be happy with me, just me."

"I was." Helen uncrossed her legs and shifted closer to Reilly. "When we started working, we promised to be there for one another. You were a mess after the first book, and I never left your side. I paid the bills, I worked myself to the bone, and never once complained. I convinced you to keep writing. Supported you when developing this odd little idea, and it turned into a hit. You wrote something the world couldn't devour fast enough. They wanted to know the mind behind it, and it was your moment to stand up and help me advance my career . . . but you bailed. You backed away and made me the villain in your story."

The woman was a pro at digging little daggers into Reilly's chest with her words. The way she twisted it all let Reilly know she'd never accept responsibility for her part of their past. Reilly pondered that for a moment. All of those possessive hugs in public or on red carpets, fights over tickets to events and the demand of total control of her writing career weren't her imagination.

"I didn't make you the bad guy. I was terrified. The night before the holiday party, I begged you to let me stay home. My anxiety was all over the place, and I told you I was incapable of attending."

"That's always been your excuse. Did I force you to go? Yes, but you've always needed a shove in the right direction. How should I know when to press and when not to? That party changed my trajectory. God, do you really think I was cruel to you?"

"Not always." Guilt reared its ugly head again. Reilly had to admit that when thinking of their relationship, she never spoke of the happier memories. "We were so good in the beginning. But by the time Mom got sick . . ."

"You can't argue with me on that one. You packed a duffel bag and cried through an explanation. I didn't know what was going on, just that my fiancé had run out of the house in a panic. Harrison had to call me later with details about your mom's medical situation."

Reilly remembered that night very well. Not what the doctor said over the phone beyond heart attack and surgery. But the memory of Helen begging for an explanation came back to her. How they fought before she left, and how Reilly didn't care what her fiancée thought. She had a one-track mind and needed to get to her mom.

"You're right. That wasn't fair to you. I should have at least tried to explain whatever I could, not shut you out."

It was the first time she admitted that out loud. Though she was in the wrong, leaving to take care of her mom was her priority. She'd do it again in a heartbeat. Helen had watched her slowly lock up tighter than Alcatraz in its prime. Reilly pushed everyone away while she processed the possibility of life without her mother. She could recall every second after the nurse called and told her that Wendy was on the bypass machine during her heart surgery. It meant her mother was, for all intents and purposes, dead. Those moments ticked by slowly like they always do. Helen tried to keep Reilly busy, but it was impossible. She just held the phone and waited for the next call saying they had completed the procedure.

"You were there for me at the darkest moment in my life so far. I never thanked you properly for that." Reilly hated admitting it but stepping into the light meant accepting the truth.

Helen's face showed Reilly all she needed to know. Her words had been a surprise. "I'm sorry I cheated on you."

But sometimes coming clean wasn't necessary. Reilly's leg bounced, her jaw clenched. She channeled the strength of her lead character in Shadows Rise and found a way to keep her voice level. "You did what?"

"Wait, you didn't know?"

Reilly searched the woman's face for any sense of deception. She found none, so she remained quiet and let Helen continue. "Shit, I should have kept my mouth shut. But we were coming clean about things, you know? I thought it would be best to just put it all out there and not have it hanging over my head anymore. I'm an idiot." Reilly watched as Helen's cold, calculating façade slipped into place. This was the Helen she remembered and was afraid of. Reilly shook internally as she kept her expression neutral. "The woman I'm with now, we met at the last event we attended together. You were hiding at the VIP table. She was the bartender."

"How long?" The meeting didn't matter to Reilly. If she was being honest, neither did the duration, but she wanted to know for closure.

"A year, I think. It was so long ago."

"You can't remember when you started sleeping with another woman while still enjoying being with me as well? That seems far-fetched, even for you. I'm sure you celebrate anniversaries, so knowing the date shouldn't be that difficult."

"It isn't." Helen swallowed hard.

"Then what is it?"

"It'll just back up your claims that I'm the horrible one from our time together."

"Just say it." Reilly's voice betrayed her. There was a pain etched within the words that was unmistakable.

"I can't tell you specifically when it was during our relationship, because once I met her . . ." Helen paused.

Reilly could see Helen struggle over how to phrase the next dagger she was going to slam into her back. Tears threatened to fall, but Reilly wouldn't give Helen the satisfaction. This new Reilly would not allow someone else to destroy her for their amusement. She'd fall apart in private without a public display, without being put on every social media platform for the enjoyment of others.

Reilly sipped her coffee and waited as Helen squirmed. Her ex didn't want to tell the truth. But Reilly knew once the bartender and Helen slept together, their relationship no longer mattered. That's why Helen couldn't remember how long they were together. Reilly wracked her mind, trying to think of the last event she attended with Helen, but came up blank. There was only one important question she needed answered.

"It's not that you no longer meant anything to me. Just that she . . . we physically clicked in a way you and I never did."

The knife slowly twisted near Reilly's spine, forcing her to sit ramrod straight. "Before or after you proposed?"

Helen shifted uncomfortably. Her eyes darted to the door, then to a small table where a blonde woman sat staring at her tablet while sipping her beverage. Reilly questioned if that was her ex's new significant other. The glint of a diamond ring made her stomach turn.

"You brought it up, Helen. If you didn't wish for me to know, you shouldn't have said anything."

"Does it really matter now?"

"Well, we were coming clean about things, remember? Were you here for that part of the conversation or were you too busy staring at the woman by the door?"

Helen's demeanor changed instantly. The smirk fell from her face as her shoulders squared. "Fine. I asked you to marry me after meeting her. And before you ask, yes, it was because of who you are. I was struggling, and your name carried weight. I figured we'd get married and, down the line, divorce, and split everything. Instead, you stopped answering invitations and had your marketing team change the passwords and handle all requests. All because you were taking care of your mom and whoever else called begging for Reilly to save them. You put us on the back burner, and I couldn't do it anymore."

"You're right." Reilly shifted in her seat, rolling her shoulders to loosen the tension Helen helped put there. "I put our relationship to the side to take care of my family. I've already taken responsibility for it, and if you need to hear it again, I'm sorry. What I won't accept is you screwing another woman while planning to take advantage of that same generosity. My god, listen to yourself. You want to blame me for messing up your plans? You wanted to marry me for what? Money and power?"

"People have married for less." Helen's deadpanned delivery annoyed her. "Besides, you owed me after everything we'd been through."

"So you said earlier. Again, that doesn't excuse being a nefarious individual." Reilly turned to look at the woman by the door. Her piercing eyes challenged Reilly to confront her, something Helen must have told her she wouldn't do. "You probably gave her my ring, didn't you?"

"So? It was expensive."

That was the final straw for Reilly. There was no mistaking Helen's behavior as an aberration. This was a side Reilly hadn't been exposed to or ignored, blinded by love and lack of self-worth.

"I could never write you as the antagonist of my stories. They have heart and, albeit misguided, drive behind their actions. You . . ." Reilly stared at the woman she used to love. The images of fun moments, memories of laughter and pleasure flashed before her eyes as that part of her life died. "You are one-dimensional. Not worth the mental power it would take to flesh that character out. You're right, we would never work. I value substance, and you prefer material possessions."

"You're a real piece of work, you know that? You begged me to meet you here and now you're attacking my character?" Helen stood and fixed her suit. "May every book you ever write bomb like your first. You once told me I inspired you to write. Well, good luck finding that again."

Helen stormed over to the woman Reilly had noticed earlier. She leapt up, grabbed her coat, and followed Reilly's ex out the door. She sipped her cold coffee, digesting all the information laid out in the conversation.

It was clear Helen wasn't faithful for most of their relationship, but Reilly had gotten what she needed from the woman. Closure, regardless of how painful it was, still allowed her to move forward. So, she enjoyed her cold coffee and sent a message to Kai. While she waited for a response, Reilly's finger hovered over Helen's number. She deleted the contact information and opened her recent call list. There sat the now unknown digits Reilly memorized when they met. With two swipes of her thumb, the number was blocked.

After that was done, she sent a message to her lawyer. Since she was going public, she needed another layer of protection between her books and Helen's interference. Even with so much still unknown, Reilly's steps were lighter as she left the café. She was finally on the right path.

Chapter Twenty-Three

Reilly stood outside the skyscraper, her eyes focused upward to the heavens. There was so much riding on her ability to voice her emotions that she was currently second-guessing herself. Her conversation with Helen had given closure to some of the things Reilly feared. It also left her with more questions about herself moving forward.

She took a deep breath and centered herself before she entered the building. The high ceiling, open-air feel, and quiet made her question if she'd entered Narnia. However, the security guards next to metal turnstiles reminded her she was most certainly in the city, about to face her fears.

"Excuse me?" Reilly spoke to the security officer behind the desk. "I'm here to see Kai Vincent of K.B. Studios."

"ID please." He held out his hand, his sculpted muscles flexing against the seams of his shirt. The mesmerizing movement of his body reminded her of Breanna when they made love. Maybe she could add the ballet of seduction in the sex scene of her romance . . . that is if she could write it without blushing. "Ma'am, your identification?"

Embarrassed, Reilly handed over her driver's license as she mentally scolded herself. As the officer verified her details, Reilly's apprehension increased. Would Kai keep their word and let her in? Would they turn her away out of spite? The random thoughts kept piling up as her stomach clenched in response. Now she felt sick.

"Keep this with you during your visit. Tap the barcode to the scanner to get through. Take the left bank of elevators to the fifteenth floor." The officer handed her a visitor pass and her card back.

Reilly smiled and shoved everything into her bag after she passed the security turnstile. She just needed to get to the fifteenth floor, say her piece, and hope for the best. But as she pressed the elevator button, she found the urge to flee grow stronger.

The door opened, but she stood there frozen in place. The doors closed, and Reilly fought with herself.

You didn't come this far to back down now. One step at a time, Reilly.

She pressed the button again. When the car opened once more, she stepped inside and shook her hands to release the excess energy. As it lifted to her destination, she took several breaths and focused on her next steps when she reached the office floor.

Reilly exited to find Kai pacing back and forth in front of the receptionist's desk.

"Finally." She felt their eyes scanning over her anxious self. "Do you need some time to compose yourself? You can sit in my office—"

"No!" The word rushed out with her breath. Reilly stood, determined. "I need to do this."

"She's in the conference room, but—"

Kai waved down the hall, and Reilly moved with a determination she didn't think she possessed. She knew Kai was a few steps behind her, spouting off something, but it was muffled by the sound of her pounding heartbeat. There was only one door down this hallway. She took a deep breath and swung it open. Her breath hitched as she took in the sight of Breanna at the front of the darkened room. The tailored, dark-gray suit, high-heeled boots, and black-rimmed glasses. She'd never seen Breanna wear the spectacles before. The woman was stunning.

"I love you." The words fell from Reilly's lips. It wasn't how she planned to open her speech, but she was running on pure adrenaline now.

"Reilly?" Breanna's voice wobbled with confusion. "What are you doing here?"

"I've been waiting for you to contact me, but I understand why you didn't. So, I'm here." She paused as her eyes adjusted to the lighting as she noticed other figures in the room. One was none other than Serena.

Kai flipped the light switch on. Reilly now saw there were six people in the room with binders in front of them. Everyone remained still, focused solely on her. The pounding in her ears overwhelmed her senses.

Kai tried to cover up Reilly's intrusion. "I'm sorry. Ms. Vail needed to speak with you and—"

"I apologize for interrupting. I understand the implications of my actions, but Breanna did not know of . . ." She stumbled on finding the right words. Fingers twisted and fumbled together as her mouth ran dry. Warmth filled her cheeks, and her stomach lurched. "My name is Reilly Vail, and I write under the name M. E. Kline."

Breanna stood up to her full height, her arms folded across her chest, her expression unreadable. "Ms. Vail . . ."

"Breanna, let the woman speak. My team and I have no other pressing obligations before my show this evening," Serena said from the front of the room. "Please, continue."

"Thank you, Serena. I understand this might appear unprofessional. I'll say my piece and be out of your way."

Reilly's heartbeat pounded in her ears. With each step toward the front of the room, it dissolved into a blurry mess of muted colors. Breanna's eyes followed her, a glint of pain reflected in them as the woman kept her arms tight and jaw clenched. She thought jitters would make her words sound like a nursery school with instruments. Instead, she found what she wanted to say danced across her lips like a perfect melody.

"I know I've said it before, but I'm sorry. You might hear that statement again in the future, because I make mistakes. A lot of them. It's hard for me to face a problem head on, let alone accept the desire to work on it. I avoid promoting who I am because of my experiences with those who only wanted the fame and not the person behind it. The world seemed dark and devoured those who chose to walk along its roads. If was safer to hide.

"But then you came along with your film ideas and infectious positivity . . . everything I ever wanted in a partner, but you wanted Kline. It was about her stories, her mind . . . not me. I struggled to process that the smile that lit a spark within me, was also part of the darkness swallowing me whole. So I ignored it and hoped it would work itself out." Reilly stopped and wiped the stray tear from her right eye. "Crap, I'm horrible at this. If I could write you a letter, or a novella with the two of us as characters, it would explain everything so beautifully. Instead, I'm a bumbling fool trying to make a point with tangential strands of thought leading nowhere." She shrugged and let out a soft chuckle at her own expense.

"What's your point, Reilly?" Breanna accentuated each word. Reilly wished she could turn back the clock and start over. She so desperately wanted to remove the pain she saw in Breanna's eyes. "While Serena and her team might be patient with this outburst, we have deadlines. So, please, tell me what the point of this intrusion is?"

Reilly's hand flew to her chest as the bitter words hit their intended target. "I never wanted anyone to know who I was. Like I said, it was safer that way. But you . . . you made it hard to hide. I wanted to share every part of my life with you. From bad morning breath to evening cuddles in front of a campy horror film. For the first time in my life, things felt clear. I screwed that up. I was so afraid of losing that . . . well, I lost you anyway."

"Is that all?" Breanna was all business, and Reilly crumbled under the weight of her hard exterior.

"Maybe Ms. Vail should wait in your office so you can further this discussion in private?" Reilly appreciated Serena trying to stop her public destruction. "I think it would be prudent to say everything that needed to be said. Don't you agree, Breanna?"

Serena played with fire in a way Reilly toyed with words—masterfully. The room fell silent as Breanna stared Reilly down. "Sure. Kai, could you please lead Ms. Vail to my office? I'll be there as soon as the meeting has concluded."

Reilly's feet felt rooted to the ground as self-doubt coiled in her gut. Kai's hand on her shoulder offered a lifeline to escape her thoughts for a moment. After seeing this side of Breanna, Reilly wondered if she could salvage what they had. *All romance novels have a happy ending, right?* She couldn't answer that.

***

"Bre, what the hell was that?" Serena's words cut through Breanna's defenses.

"Nothing." Breanna flipped a page of her documents on the table. "I assume we can skip the presentation and get right to the contract."

"Usual clauses included? No nudity, percentages as requested, and all the other fun, random things I asked for?"

"Yes, we included a percentage of all future forms of media as well. As you can see on page—"

"Nope, I trust you." The actress flipped to the last page in front of Breanna. "This is where I sign, yes?" Breanna numbly nodded. She knew better than to argue with her friend when she was in her mother mode. The management team next to the woman expressed their concerns, but Breanna's fear was the aftermath of the signing. There was a lecture coming and she had no desire to listen to it. "Oh, calm down. Bre and I have been friends longer than y'all have worked for me. So just relax. You'll all get your cut, and frankly, I would have done this picture for base salary if not for your paychecks. So, can we just not have this little display of displeasure?"

"Well then, if our client agrees to your terms, then we're done here. We'll expect a copy of the signed document emailed by the end of business today." The male directly to her left muttered, slamming his briefcase shut. One by one, the management team packed up their things and meandered out of the door.

"What the hell are you doing, Bre?"

"I was trying to hold a professional meeting that didn't blur the lines of our friendship. I think I failed miserably there." She shifted piles around the table, collecting discarded papers left behind. Her left hand rubbed the center of her chest as she tried to calm her breathing. Reilly loved her. Of all the words she expected the woman to say, that wasn't on her Bingo card. Breanna prepared retorts to a myriad of excuses or apologies, but that declaration left her reeling.

"You're deflecting. That woman just stormed in here and said she loved you. What are you going to do about that?"

"You know." Breanna slammed her fists against the table. Of all the things they'd been through as friends, Serena was well aware of her history. Beyond the fact that trust was difficult for her, being lied to and played like a fool—that was a step too far for her to handle.

"You're an idiot." The actress stood, grabbed her jacket and slipped it on. Breanna immediately regretted her actions.

"I'm sorry. You don't deserve—"

"Stop. We're family and that means dealing with negative outbursts as much as the celebrations. But Bre, I saw the two of you together before all this drama. I don't know Reilly that well, but I know you. The way you looked at her was unmistakable. You're just as much in love with her as she is with you. Hide the truth from yourself all you want, but you can't lie to those who pick up the pieces when you walk away from something that makes you happy. Kai and I did that once, Bre. Forgive me if I don't want to do it again."

"Life isn't some romance novel or a film, Serena. She lied to me. She held me, crawled into my bed, made love to me, and did it while harboring a secret. How can I get past that?"

"What was her intent?"

"You've got to be kidding me. Does that really matter? This isn't a court of law, Serena. It's my life."

"From what I gather, she did it to protect herself from the producer who desperately needed her stories to keep their career going. She hid from the person who made it clear their intent was to seek someone who didn't want to be found and get them to sign the rights to their creative endeavors away. All to save themselves."

Breanna huffed as she took in Serena's words. She hadn't thought of herself being the aggressor. She had a business to save, people's livelihoods depended on her. That alone absolved her from guilt. Right?

"You don't get it, Serena. We needed something, anything, to work with. Otherwise, we wouldn't be having this conversation. Hell, we would be out on the street next month if things hadn't changed."

"I do get it Bre. You think I don't have employees to worry about? Every job I take increases media attention. My contract gets leaked and used as a reason crew and other cast members can't be paid fairly. If I take a pay cut to help the project, I'm hurting the equal pay movement. All of that noise messes with the paychecks of those working for me, from my assistant to my agent and managers." Serena grabbed her bag and stormed to the door. "Point is, Bre, you're ignoring your part in the problem. When I was terrified of dating again, my friend Bre told me love was worth the risk of a broken heart. If you don't love her, that's one thing. But if you do, you're throwing away the possibility of something real." Serena's words hung in the air long after her body left the room.

Breanna cleaned up for a meeting later in the day and to shake off the confusion. All she wanted to do was focus on the new projects alone in her office. With everything at K.B. Studios moving in the right direction, she needed to ensure it remained there. To do that, she needed to handle her biggest distraction. She could storm down the hall and end everything firmly before wallowing in a bottle of wine. At least she'd finally have closure so she could move on. Serena was right, she was an idiot. She allowed this entire situation to get out of hand. It was a wise decision, even if her heart begged her not to go through with it.

She took a deep breath to slow her racing thoughts. Ending everything was in the best interest of both parties. She just had to stick to the plan.

***

Reilly knew things hadn't gone well, but she was at a loss for how to correct them. She berated herself for being impulsive and not waiting for Kai to guide her. That's why Reilly called them in the first place. It was easier to have someone on the inside assist with her plan, but Reilly knew she blew it.

"You're making my head hurt," Kai muttered from the couch. "Will you stop pacing and sit down?"

"I shouldn't have walked in there. I should have waited for you." Reilly couldn't bring herself to stop moving as the impending dread gripped her chest.

"True, but there's nothing we can do about that now. Thankfully, Serena was in there, and she'll make sure things get on track. No harm, no foul. Just don't do it again."

"Of course there was damage done," Reilly continued, her mind rattling off all the negatives once again, overwhelming her senses and ignoring Kai's words. "Did you see how cold she was? I've never seen her like that."

Kai stood and grabbed Reilly's shoulders. "I need you to stop. First, you're giving me a headache. Second, you're once again not listening. Finally, sit down before I leave you in here to stew alone."

"I don't know what to do." Reilly felt the chill of the cold leather through her jeans.

"You do what you're best at—using words to express your emotions."

"I think you missed the part about hiding and speaking to people not being a strong suit of mine."

"Think of this as dictating a first rough draft. Just leave out the punctuation," Kai offered. "Look, Bre's been a mess since you two fell apart. She's always here in the office, ignoring her own well-being. I don't want that. So, if I'm being honest, I just want this to have a conclusion. If you work things out, fine. If you don't, it'll give you both closure."

"I just want her." Her voice cracked. She knew there was a possibility Breanna wouldn't accept her apology, but until she was faced with that outcome her heart refused to acknowledge it.

"Reilly, you had her. And as a rational adult, you know we don't always get what we want. You need to respect her wishes if she wants out. I also need you to understand that Bre is my family. If she wants to be left alone, this is the last time I'll be helping you."

"I wouldn't expect anything else. Just . . . whatever happens here, don't take it out on Jenna. Please. She values your friendship."

"And I hers. I give you my word on that."

"Could I ask you for one more favor?" Reilly pulled the manilla envelope out of her bag. "I need you to hold this for me. Open it with Breanna only after I've left. Regardless of the outcome, okay?"

"If it upsets—"

"It shouldn't. I need you to trust me on this one."

Breanna opened the door, cutting the conversation short. Kai took the envelope and walked out of the room before Breanna could say anything. Reilly watched her walk behind the desk, the wood furniture forming a literal and figurative barrier between them.

"I'm sorry," Reilly's voice cracked, the raw edges betraying a mix of regret and desperation "For interrupting your meeting . . . for everything."

"You're lucky it was Serena in that room. Someone else might not be so understanding." She noticed Breanna ignored the second half of her apology. The respite allowed her to center herself.

"I'm glad to hear it. She signed on, then?"

"Yes, a four-picture deal. First one will start shooting at the end of her Broadway commitment."

"Great, I'm sure the team and investors are thrilled by the development."

"It helps. I'm sure they won't be as thrilled with Serena's ability to choose the films she wants to do."

"It's good for business. A happy star leads to a better outcome in the long run. Plus, you're a good friend."

"You should work with a public relations company with your ability to spin things. I doubt others will see it that way. Not sure it matters since the films will bring in money and results always quiet the noise." Breanna leaned back in her chair, adding even more distance between them. "I think we need to stop the pleasantries and get to the heart of why you're here."

"Bre, can we please just . . . not like this? If we can't talk as people, locked away in your office, maybe there's nothing to talk about." Reilly's spirit reeled from the chilly conversation. Her mind bounced between accepting defeat and a desperate desire to fight against it.

"You lied to me."

"Yes. I did."

"And if I understand correctly, you say it's because you're afraid." Reilly nodded but said nothing. "As if that was a good enough reason to hide the truth."

"I know it was wrong. I didn't listen to wiser voices—"

"Who else knew?"

The question hung in the air. The answer would make Reilly look worse, but this was the point of no return.

"My family and the few friends I have. They knew you were hunting down Kline and recommended I come clean. I didn't feel comfortable enough to do that."

The admission hung in the air as Reilly studied the other woman. Breanna's once vibrant eyes dimmed into painful sorrow with the confession. Reilly watched as the woman's self-preservation clicked into place.

"You laid in my arms night after night and never once felt comfortable enough to tell me the truth? How can you say you love someone when you couldn't be honest about something that important?"

"Would you have listened? You walked into the coffee shop wanting the locals to turn me in. You went to the post office, for Pete's sake. And you weren't fully truthful with me either. Had I known you told your production partners you had the rights to my books before asking me, I never would have gotten involved."

"I didn't tell them I had the rights." Breanna spit out.

"Implied it. Is there a difference?" Reilly forced her rising frustration into her forming fists.

"Yes, there is. Maybe I should have talked to Michaela and cleared the air, but I needed those books to keep the company afloat. All you had to do was be honest with me."

"I was!" Reilly roared, the words exploding from her like a damn bursting. The sudden outburst forced her hands to cover her mouth. Tension sucked the air out of the room as she gasped for oxygen. Her mind was in overdrive, navigating what to say next and forcing her to slow everything down. She swallowed the lump in her throat before continuing, keeping her voice level. "I emailed you constantly, politely declining. Then you came into town, and I selfishly wanted more of you. So, yes, I lied to keep you around. Once I realized you wanted to know more about Kline, I emailed you privately so those discussions could continue. I wanted us to have time alone without thoughts of Kline hanging over it. I never wanted this to get as far as it did."

Breanna bolted from her chair to an upright position. The sudden movement startled Reilly, and she stumbled backwards. She watched as the woman turned and paced along the back wall of windows.

"I know what I did was wrong, Bre, but I still love you. We could start over, be honest, from both sides of the relationship. Be clear about what we want," Reilly pleaded.

"We weren't really in a relationship, were we? We never defined what we were doing. We just went with the flow. I never did that before—put my heart out there and just hope for the best. I never wanted the responsibility that came with work-life balance. My rules were in place for a reason. But you walked into my world and sank the boat I was sailing. Now, I'm barely keeping my head above water while I frantically put together a raft out of the pieces."

Reilly's steps faltered, her hesitation getting the better of her. Indecision weighed her down as she struggled with the painful admissions bathing her in fear. To continue the fight meant becoming more vulnerable than she already was. Walking away was easier.

Not this time. Her purposeful strides brought her next to the woman by the windows. "Let me rebuild it with you."

"I don't trust you."

"I'll spend every day trying to earn it back." Reilly whispered, her voice a fragile thread of hope. "Do you love me?"

"I do. More than I want to right now. You carved out a place in my soul and now it just echoes of loss." There was a slight tremor in Breanna's voice.

"Just have faith in that. We can get through this."

Reilly yelped in surprise as Breanna's lips met hers before a dam within her burst. The weight of their secrets washed away with the connection of their kiss. Her moan was filled with relief as she gave herself over to the warmth of Breanna's body against her.

Her hands tangled in Breanna's hair as the woman pressed her against the edge of the wooden desk. Heat flushed her skin as her hands released Breanna's mane, slinking down to the hem of her dress shirt. Her fingers roamed along the newly exposed flesh with a desire to go further.

"Breanna," Reilly whispered as they briefly parted.

Without replying, Breanna's lips were on her again, harder than before. The fire burning within her ran cold. This no longer felt like a kiss with the promise of a future. It felt like an end.

When Breanna broke their connection, she pecked her lips one more time before taking two steps back. Reilly reached for her, but the woman moved further away.

"I love you, but right now, it's not enough." Breanna's voice hitched as the door slammed shut on their relationship.

Reilly stood in front of her, hoping her unspoken plea to reconsider would be answered. But her now ex-girlfriend stood firm in her decision. Tears welled in Reilly's eyes, blurring the edges of the room. She squeezed them shut, refusing to allow their release. Not here. Not now. She gathered herself the best she could, moved toward the door and stopped.

"There are so many things I regret in my life." Reilly's voice shook. "But loving you will never be one of them."

Reilly slipped out of the office and past Kai, who leaned against the opposite wall. She nodded as she left for the elevator. Once inside, the beeps of passing floors were like hammers against her heart. The walls closed in, trapping her with regret and what-ifs. When she broke free of the building, the cold breeze gave a small comfort against her burning skin.

What were you thinking?

She knew it was a risk seeing Breanna at work. Kai had rearranged Breanna's schedule, ensuring Reilly would have time to talk to her. But Reilly had let her impatience give way and ruined the entire plan. Her guilt at interrupting the meeting and the bitter tone Breanna used was hard to swallow. But the heat she felt flowing through her veins had been cooled with Breanna's rejection.

Even though she loves me.

Those words made it even more difficult. Breanna loved her, but it wasn't enough. It wasn't enough for a second chance. For the possibility of redemption. Reilly stood to her full height and took several deep breaths. It wasn't the option she hoped for, but she promised Kai she'd respect it. In that moment, Reilly knew her future was exactly what Jenna joked about. Her future was at the house with as many dogs as she could handle. It was time to really accept what the universe had in store for her rather than fight an unstoppable force of fate.

The first step was attending the Q&A she set up with Ellen. Then she could go back to where she felt safest—home.

***

The click of the door broke Breanna from the zombie-like state. The unwelcomed sound signaled the appearance of her business partner. She fixed her shirt and grabbed the alcohol from its hiding spot. As the fluid poured into her glass, she replayed her entire relationship with Reilly. Where had everything gone so very wrong? She scoured her memory, but isolating the point it all went wrong eluded her.

It was destined to fail from the beginning, Breanna rationalized. She looked over at Kai, knowing they must have had a hand in Reilly showing up. That was a discussion for another day. In the end, she knew Kai only had her best interests at heart. No matter how misguided the execution of that plan.

"You want to talk?" Kai sat across from her and nodded to the bottle of alcohol.

"No." Breanna slid them a glass.

"Then listen."

"Not now. I don't know how much more I can take." She pulled out a larger tumbler and filled it to the brim.

"I get it, but this is important." Breanna knew something deeper was going on. "Want to fix yourself?"

Breanna ignored the comment and took another pull from her glass, steeling herself for whatever Kai had to say. Once they finished their speech, Breanna planned on heading home to down several glasses of wine in a hot bath. She didn't care that her shirt was currently untucked, or her hair was a mess.

Kai dropped a manilla envelope in front of her.

"What's this?"

"Reilly asked me to give it to you. Curiosity got the better of me, and I opened it out in the hallway."

Breanna slipped the pages out of the folder and scanned each one. Her eyes darted back and forth between the document and her business partner.

"This isn't what we sent over." Realization hit her like a gut punch.

"No. According to the note attached, she took the liberty of removing frivolous items from the original contract. She lowered her overall upfront fees and increased the percentage on the back end, but not by much. Everything increases on the sequels, but that's to be expected. If I'm being honest, overall, this is a much better deal for us than we initially offered. No strain on the budget going forward. This frees up a lot of capital for the crew, special effects. . ." Kai's voice trailed off and Breanna wondered what they were thinking.

"This is everything we wanted." Her voice was barely above a whisper. In one move, Reilly had given her a gift. Not just an agreement that benefited them both, but the trust to adapt her books properly.

"Do we sign it? We've got other projects, we don't need to do this."

The tears rolled freely down her face. She wanted to sign, but guilt weighed heavily on her shoulders. She dialed Serena and placed the call on speaker. Her thoughts and emotions were too tangled to make a rational decision without the help of the two she trusted most.

The office door swung open as Serena entered, the ringing phone in her hand. Breanna hung up as the actress flopped onto the couch. Normally, Serena's bubbly personality filled the room. Right now, the woman looked like a shell of herself, and Breanna knew she was the cause.

"I owe you both an apology. I've let all of this. . ." She took another sip of her liquid courage. "I've not been myself and you've both gotten the brunt of it. But it stops now. I handled everything so I can move on." A week ago, she'd hoped that meant Reilly by her side on a movie set. But she shut down any hope of that happening.

"Accepted." Serena's chipper voice warmed the chilled air around her. "You and Reilly made up?"

Breanna chose to ignore the question and move on to one of her own. "Did you mean what you said about Kline's stories? You'd want to be the lead?" Her voice wavered, trying to pivot the conversation to a safer topic.

Serena looked over at Kai, who simply shook their head in response. "Breanna, tell me what happened. Whatever it is, it can't be that bad."

"I need you to answer the question. Please." Breanna didn't want to delve into that emotional turmoil right now. She needed Serena to give her a definitive decision.

"Of course I would. I'd be an idiot to pass up a role like that. But it doesn't matter."

Breanna shifted her gaze back to Reilly's signature. It felt like divorce papers. Breanna replayed the scene over again in her mind, the guilt of her decision compressing her chest with each breath. Reilly was the air that kept her soaring and she'd unceremoniously cut her out of her life.

"Wait, you're telling me Reilly signed over the film rights?"

"The entire series, including the unpublished finale. She even included a deadline for publication of the last book to ensure the series would be released on schedule." Breanna was thankful Kai answered for her.

"Damn, that is one hell of a grand gesture."

"Really, S?" Breanna exhaled in disbelief. "Does anyone see my side in this?"

"I know you're a bit irritated at the moment, but yes, we see your side in this. We've had each other's backs since we stepped foot in this city, and I don't see that changing. What I think you need to realize is this woman just gave you a massive gift." The truth of Serena's words broke Breanna a little bit more.

"Normally, I'd argue your point, Bre." Kai picked up the contract and scanned it over again. "But I read it in the hall, and I still can't believe her concessions. She didn't even request to write the screenplays. Reilly's willing to take a back seat as a consultant on all of the films. This is her baby . . ."

"So we sign it, film it, and keep things professional." Breanna mumbled, the words tasting like ashes in her mouth. Her hand trembled as she searched the upper drawers of her desk for a pen.

Kai's hand grasped hers, stopping the frantic motion.

"Or we take a moment to think about this." The softness of their tone did nothing to calm the sudden onslaught of Breanna's thoughts.

"There's nothing to think about. Michaela wants the project, and the three films would be the highlight of Serena's contract with us. Everyone wins." She couldn't stop the slight tremble in her voice. This was everything she worked for, and she wasn't sure she wanted it anymore.

She felt Serena's arms wrap around her shivering body. "Not like this, Bre. Your happiness is worth more than these films. Grand gestures are romantic, but so is a simple apology."

"What if I can't . . ." Images of Reilly flooded her mind preventing her from finishing the thought. "I just need to work. Please." The whispered plea was all Breanna could muster through the loss threatening to overwhelm her. "Please."

She whispered again through her tears. "Just let me sign it and go back to what I know."

"Okay." Serena squeezed her one last time before letting her go. Breanna watched as her two friends hugged goodbye. "When you're ready, call my agent and set up a meeting. We've got a deal for overall films, but Kline's should have tons of merchandising with it. That wasn't discussed and needs to be ironed out beforehand. Deal?"

Breanna nodded, thankful for the change of topic.

"Kai, you keep me posted on how she's doing. I'll walk off the stage if necessary. Family first, okay?"

"I don't think that'll be necessary, but I'll call you later." Kai clicked the door shut and returned to the chair across from Breanna. She'd poured herself another drink and stared at the pen sitting in plain sight on her desk. She laughed at herself for not noticing it before.

"I'm hanging on by a thread, Kai." Her eyebrows bunched together as her lips trembled. She forced her shaky hands to grip the pen and hover over the signature line. One small move and she could go on with her life. Kai could handle all the correspondence with Reilly and Breanna could go back to the solace of paperwork.

"Maybe you should talk to her first."

"It's over, Kai. Trust me, I made that abundantly clear." Tears dripped onto the contract as her hand continued to waver.

"You love her."

Her signature was a jumbled mess of squiggles, far from the perfect penmanship she was proud of. But it was done. She flipped the document closed and slid it across the desk to Kai.

"I know. But it doesn't matter. I . . ." The words died on her tongue. What more could she say? Breanna knew she was the architect of her own suffering. Now she had to live with it.

Kai gripped the pages and slipped them back into the envelope. "I'll handle everything from here. But Bre, if you let that woman walk out of your life for good, you'll become everything you've always feared. A bitter and lonely person in a crowd of people."

Breanna didn't have the energy to reply. She swallowed her drink in one gulp as the door clicked shut signaling Kai's departure. She turned her attention back to the windows and the city below. The image of the masses milling about on the pavement usually brought her a sense of calm. This time, all Breanna saw was Reilly walking away from her.

Chapter Twenty-Four

Her frustration was all Reilly could think about. A month flew by as the words blazed onto the computer screen only for her to highlight it all and delete everything. Nothing on the page felt right. The story didn't flow, and her characters didn't listen to reason anymore. Reilly knew she was deep into a writing block but had no clue how to dig herself out of it this time.

As the days ticked by, Reilly hoped Breanna would send her a message. But as the days turned into weeks, she accepted that her grand gesture didn't change anything. Breanna's final words stabbed her again and again. *Love simply wasn't enough.* So, Reilly entertained her friends with normal conversations, her forced smiles hiding her pain. Her weekly online group meetings were back on. If anyone were to look at her life from the outside, all seemed normal.

Her mother, on the other hand, asked enough questions to break through the façade. After that, Reilly confessed everything and fell apart on the call. Her aunt and mother discussed coming home early to take care of her, but Reilly shut them down immediately. Wendy planned this trip for a long time, and Reilly needed to process her situation on her own.

Reilly's lawyer gave vague updates regarding the contract she left with Kai. All their inquiries were left unanswered. When she reached out to Kai personally, she was told the company was discussing it internally and nothing was confirmed at that time. Reilly didn't believe them. This was what Breanna's partners wanted. They wouldn't allow her to sit on the opportunity for too long. Of course, Reilly held out hope that if there was a conversation to be had, Breanna would call her. Her lawyers promised confirmation once a copy of the contract was safely back in their hands. So, Reilly continued to wait.

In the meantime, she formulated a plan to give her nieces the truth along with the last book in her series. At one point, she floated the idea of writing a different novel while she waited for her thoughts to clear. But her online meeting went crazy with objections and reminded her of the contractual agreement with K.B. Studios. In the end, they agreed to have silent working video calls. It would provide Reilly with much needed company and sounding boards, but still have the quiet she needed to work with.

But it wasn't helping that she'd write all morning, delete everything after lunch, log off of the chat, and go about maintaining the house. She'd attend her therapy sessions and work out, using weights to banish the negative energy in a positive way.

Today would be different, though. Jenna and Harrison invited her to a barbecue at their house. The girls were excited to see their aunt and practically begged Reilly to attend. She tried to refuse, but once the girls sent images of their professional pouts, she caved. Reilly reasoned the time with family might help her get back to writing. If nothing else, she wouldn't get a soggy salad from the pizza place again.

"Aunt Reilly!" Millie yelled as she wrapped little arms around her aunt's waist.

"Hey, munchkin. How are you?" Reilly lifted the girl into her arms and walked along the side of the house. "Where's your sister?"

"I'm fine. Edie is helping Daddy cook. She is his barbecue buddy."

"And what are you?"

"I eat the food, Aunt Reilly. You do too."

"That's right. What's Daddy making?"

"Steak, salmon, and hot dogs. Mom had me help with the salad, but I kept eating the cucumbers."

"She kicked you out of the kitchen?"

Reilly paused, lifted the lock on the gate, and pushed it open. It swung closed behind her as they entered the spacious backyard. Millie squirmed until her aunt placed her back on the ground.

"Look who I found!"

"How many times have I told you not to go out front without your father or me?" Jenna admonished her daughter.

"I heard Aunt Reilly's car, and Daddy put a string on the latch so I could reach it!" Millie argued.

"No. That was for your father and me to use from the other side."

"Well, that's silly. Then anyone could get in. You should take it down, Mommy."

Reilly snickered as she watched the two talk. Millie took after Jenna in so many ways. Her shrewd comments and quick wit at her age was impressive. There was always a comeback lodged in the girl's brain like a machine, just waiting for the right moment to come to the forefront. Reilly chuckled to herself as Millie squirmed away from her mother and ran off to play.

"That kid is going to be the death of me."

"I wonder if your mom has a voodoo doll of you somewhere. Imagine all the little torment she helps those girls cause."

"Don't get me started. She threatened me with kids of my own when I was in high school. I thought I'd get one, but both are a perfect blend of their parents' craziness. But they're healthy, so whatever. Now, how are you doing, and don't lie by saying fine."

"I'm taking it one day at a time. Trying to keep busy with the house, gardening, and such." Reilly surprised herself with the candid admission. Before therapy, she would have brushed off the concern with a shrug of her shoulders.

"Writing?"

Reilly shook her head and hoped that was enough to end the conversation. There was no way to express how she was stuck because finishing it meant the series was complete. Shadows Rise was the only remaining connection between Breanna and herself. Considering her agents only spoke with Kai, her mind refused to produce anything worth keeping. She just couldn't bring herself to finish it.

"You know we're here for you, no matter what."

"I know."

"I'm serious, Rei. I'm always here to listen." Reilly nodded in response, not trusting her voice.

Thankfully, her niece Edie slammed into her legs allowing Reilly to avoid more questions.

"You came!"

"Of course I did! Your pout was just too powerful to ignore."

Millie added to the pile attached to Reilly's limbs. "I told you it would work!"

Harrison's voice boomed over the music playing. "Kids, your aunt needs to walk, and dinner's almost ready. Come to the table."

The two girls dragged their aunt to the outdoor table. She let them lead her to the bench and sat between them. She was barely in her seat before the girls shifted closer to the point of sitting on her lap.

The conversation flowed easily from discussions about the girls' classrooms to their after-school activities. Reilly enjoyed the simplicity of it. That is until the girls excitement while holding their hot dogs ended up with ketchup on Reilly's jeans. Before she had a chance to clean it properly, a child's hand smushed it into the fabric.

"Millie, watch what you're doing!" Jenna barked across the table.

Reilly laughed and surprised herself. The calmness, the ability to joke with her family was so far from her mind mere hours ago, yet here she was, living again. She had barely touched her meal before the girls were off running, burning off their endless energy supply.

Jenna handed her some napkins, water, and a detergent pen. It was a simple gesture, but one that almost broke her walls down. She ducked her head and focused on the stain. The little action and Millie's wails of an apology brought up emotions she had worked to keep at bay. She excused herself to the bathroom, darting away before she lost control.

The door clicked behind her as her tears fell. She wet the napkin and dabbed at her jeans as she choked back tears. The strength she had a few moments ago swirled down the drain with the ketchup.

"You okay in there?" Jenna's voice came through the door.

Reilly tried to answer, but her voice failed. Her hands shook as she flopped down onto the closed toilet seat. She barely noticed Jenna slip inside the room and sit on the edge of the tub. Reilly felt Jenna's hand hold her own as she let it all out. The silent sobs tore through her violently as she gasped for breath.

They sat there for a few moments until Reilly's breath evened. The breaks in her carefully crafted facade slowly mended back to their previous position.

"Don't do that, Rei."

"I can't . . ." Her soft whisper barely registered with the other woman.

"Oh, honey, you have to."

"I did this to myself. I'll find a way to deal with it."

"Reilly Vail, you listen to me. You are not alone in this. I don't care who did what, or how this all came to be, I've got your back."

"How do I do this, Jenna? What's wrong with me?"

"Just take things one day at a time. One moment at a time if you need to. And there's nothing wrong with you, Rei. If Breanna and Helen can't see it, screw them. Those two little girls out there love the hell out of their aunt. Your brother, me . . . we love you. We love you as you are, flaws and all."

Reilly allowed the words to wash over her. Jenna was right, unlike her previous breakup, she had a support system in place. Accepting it was another step in her therapy, as was telling the girls the truth before someone else did. They might be small and unable to fully understand the meaning behind it, but Reilly needed to remove the secrets.

"I need to tell them."

"All right. Then let's get you cleaned up and outside. Harrison's reheating your food. Won't be as good, but you need to eat."

"Yes, Mom."

Reilly accepted Jenna's hug before she washed her face. The cold water felt like daggers on her flushed skin. She kept promising herself she'd move on, but still held herself back. That was something she needed to bring up in a therapy session soon.

Harrison placed her plate down on the table when the two women exited the house a few minutes later.

"I added some steak sauce so it wouldn't be a hockey puck."

Reilly kissed his cheek but said nothing as she sat down.

"Girls, Aunt Reilly needs to speak with you."

Reilly was nervous as the two girls raced over to the table. They both erupted with questions, speculating over what their aunt wanted to share. Millie swore up and down it was about the puppy she wanted. Edie insisted it was about ice cream.

"You know those books Mommy reads to you at night? The one's where the superheroes look like you?"

"Yes, we get a new one each Christmas. Mommy says the person who writes them sends them to us special." Edie leaned on Reilly's knee. "Did they bring us ice cream?"

"Sweetie, we have some in the freezer, but you have to wait."

Edie deflated against Reilly's leg. "Fine."

"Well, what would you think if I told you I was the author?"

"But your name is Aunt Reilly, not the one on the book." Millie scrunched up her face in confusion.

"I know. I write books under a different name, so no one knows it's me."

"Why?" Millie pressed.

"Well, I was scared that people reading the stories would make it about me and not what I wrote. But I also wanted my pen name to be something special. That's why I used the letters m, e, and k. M for Millie, E for Edie, and Kline was grandma's maiden name."

"That's our names." Edie stopped, confused. "We're famous, Millie!"

Reilly covered her ears as her niece screamed. The two girls bounced around the yard in excitement until Edie stopped short. Reilly watched as a large smile formed on her face before she rushed over to her aunt.

"Does that mean you can buy us ice cream?"

"Girls we already have . . . oh never mind. Come on." Harrison dragged the two girls inside to get dessert. The utter acceptance of her nieces released the last bit of worry she had about coming forward. Stepping out from the pen name's shadow was so freeing she felt like she was seeing the world clearly for the first time.

"I told you they'd love it. You used your mom's maiden name?"

"Yeah, wanted to honor her and Grandma."

"I didn't know that." Jenna took a long pull from her beer. "You should come to the show tomorrow night."

"You know I don't—"

"I know, but baby steps and all. I've had horrible luck for five years. Maybe this fresh start of yours includes sitting in the last row of my show? I swear this year its morphed into something amazing. Kai's help has been invaluable, and I just want to share it with you."

"Ah huh, or is it the fact that you need my truck to bring stuff to the theater?" Reilly threw out the joke to lighten the mood.

"That too but seeing the show would be good for you. Take back your life, Rei. Sit through the show. Sit in the back with Harrison. He'll make dumb dad jokes all night if it helps. Just think about it."

Harrison ran out of the house screaming. He held a tub of ice scream above his head as the little minions chased him. Reilly laughed at the scene. If this is all she had going forward, she was wealthier than most. She could learn to live with that.

"He's a dork." Jenna muttered next to her.

"He's yours." Her words held a hit of jealousy, but her sister-in-law didn't notice.

"Yes, he is. Rei, I really need help to transport things. If I promise to make you tiramisu cake for your birthday, would you be there?"

"Fine, but I don't know if I'll stay for the entire show. That's all I can offer right now."

"Deal."

Reilly took in the two girls playing with their father. She always wanted a family growing up, but not right away. She had grandiose ideas of traveling, writing books in other countries, and never worrying about finances. She was young and naïve. Now, the idea of home brought her comfort, with traveling occasionally to recharge her batteries. But she wouldn't change all the pain in her romantic life if it meant losing the scene playing out in front of her. Jenna was right, she had love here. It wouldn't fix her broken heart or the voices discounting her worth at every turn. But it was a start.

***

Reilly pulled into the school parking lot as a yawn overtook her. Her car was full of bins and various bags Jenna deemed necessary for the performances this weekend. The heated seats did little to loosen the tightness in her lower back from moving everything. The kids tried to help, but their little hands just got in the way.

Even with the pain radiating down her leg, for the first time, she felt content. She was good at this. Helping. While it distracted her from working on her deadlines or thinking of Breanna, Reilly was okay with it.

The morning started poorly when she had a video call with her mother. Reilly's concern raged like a wild animal when her mother slipped about missing several days of medication. Wendy laughed it off, saying it was only the evening dose occasionally when they were too tired to think. That led to a disagreement that left her mother offended.

After the call, Reilly put several alarms in her phone. When her mom switched time zones, she'd update them accordingly. Wendy wouldn't like it, but Reilly knew the only compromise was to send a text reminding her mom to take her medication. If her mother got infuriated, well, that would be par for the course.

The smack against her SUV's rear glass made her jump, banging her head against the ceiling. Another smack pulled her eyes to the side mirror. Jenna waved her arms around like her girls after too much sugar.

"I'm running out of time, Rei!"

"You're kidding, right?" Reilly unlocked the doors, and Jenna opened the tailgate. Her nieces were once again underfoot, hopping about like energy balls, wanting to help. She handed each one a light bag, and they scurried off.

"Did you feed them after midnight?" Reilly's brother muttered loud enough for his wife to hear.

"No, why would I do that?" Jenna tilted her head as her brain put the pieces together. "Harrison they're daughters not Gremlins."

"You sure? That energy screams gremlins." He called after Jenna's retreating form.

"We've got at least five or six trips." Reilly unloaded one bin, walked through the propped open double doors and started her trek up the four flights of stairs to the stage door. "This school needs to get an elevator in here."

"It's on the other side; won't help us." Harrison grunted behind her. There was some comfort in knowing they were both suffering.

"No matter how much changes around us, those damn stairs remain a torture device to my knees." She huffed up the final few steps, through the backstage entrance and onto the main stage.

"That's called getting old." Her brother stood next to her with a smirk plastered on his face. "Welcome to the club."

"If I wasn't carrying this—"

"Children, can we not damage the props for the performance?" Jenna yelled from the floor. "Put everything stage right unless it's marked for a specific location."

Reilly dutifully followed instructions. She repeated the trip over and over until her trunk was empty. It took a few hours, and her body protested. She swung her feet back and forth off the edge of the stage. Millie and Edie ran around the auditorium chairs, belting out made-up songs.

"Would you kill me if I said there was more I needed you to pick up?" Jenna flopped down next to Reilly, handing her a bottle of cold water.

"Are you serious?" Reilly cracked the seal, tipped her head back and gulped most of it. She sighed as the cool liquid chilled her overheated body.

"Unfortunately. Wendy kept some things in storage in the shed. I'd owe you one if you grabbed it."

"You already owe me a cake. Is it really that important?" Jenna hit her with the same puppy dog eyes her daughters used on Reilly to get their way. "See now you're not playing fair."

"It works on me too, just accept defeat and move on." Harrison called from stage right.

"Fine. Just give me a minute to breathe, okay?"

Jenna clapped excitedly and Reilly laughed at the childish antics.

"It looks like a bomb exploded in here." Kai walked out from behind the curtains. Their black ensemble was perfect for working stage crew. "Is anything separated yet?"

"We carried everything up here, but that's about it." Jenna replied as Kai pulled them into a hug.

Reilly's mind drifted away from the conversation, stuck on the sound of Kai's voice. She expected them to be around for the performance but was wholly unprepared for how raw her emotions still felt. The plastic water bottle slipped from her trembling hands, spilling water on the floor. The noise drew everyone's gaze and Reilly suddenly felt energized enough to run errands.

"Hey." Jenna looked at her with pitiful eyes. Reilly hated it.

"Is what you need labeled? I know Mom's got a ton of stuff in containers. So, if I don't have to dig through my entire childhood in one sitting, that would be great." Reilly kept her eyes on her sister-in-law, allowing the background to blur.

"I'm sorry. I should have told you Kai would be here earlier than showtime." Jenna kept her voice low, even though Reilly could hear Harrison talking to them out of earshot.

"You probably did. You know how I've been lately. Doesn't matter. The stuff in the garage?"

"Yeah, it's all marked. Should be easy to find."

"Great. I'll be back as soon as I can."

Jenna grabbed her arm, keeping her on the stage. "Take your time and do whatever you need to deal with this. If you need anything, we're a message away. As for the bins, just have them here by three in the afternoon, deal?"

She nodded but had no intention of wasting that much time. Reilly envisioned rushing home, grabbing whatever Jenna needed and dropping it off. The distraction of manual work was a better option than obsessing over the past.

Chapter Twenty-Five

Though she wanted to move quickly, Reilly drove the long way home. The breeze from the cracked windows cooled her skin while the heated seats warmed her sore muscles. The music blasting on the radio mixed with her bad vocals brought levity back to her day. Her normal twenty-five-minute drive was closer to forty-five when she finally turned down her street.

As her house came into focus, Reilly turned the volume down. A figure paced by the front stoop, hands moving about as if the individual was talking to themselves. As Reilly pulled closer, the world spun as her pulse quickened.

Breanna.

Reilly's breathing increased as she parked her car in the driveway. As she exited, she held Breanna's gaze, afraid the woman wasn't real. Reilly stood mere steps away from Breanna, unsure of what to do next.

"Rei, could we talk?" Breanna almost begged, her hands shoved deep into her jean's pockets.

"Why are you . . ." Reilly faltered. "Did you travel up here with Kai?" She tried to temper the excitement tingling within her. Just because the woman was standing in front of her didn't mean it was a social call. After all, her lawyers were still waiting for the signed agreement.

"It was that or take the train up here." Breanna shivered as her thin jacket failed to keep her warm against a cool breeze.

"So you were coming here regardless of the play. Why?"

"Yeah." Breanna stepped closer and the smell of strawberry shampoo assaulted Reilly's senses. "You hurt me and I retaliated badly. I thought . . . I mean . . . Dammit. Rei, there are so many things I want to say, to explain, but everything I come up with sounds like an excuse." Teeth chattered as another breeze burrowed through the trembling woman.

"Let's go inside and talk. It's cold and your thin jacket isn't enough." She slipped past Breanna and unlocked the door.

Reilly ushered her inside, the heavy door cutting off the frigid gusts. She hung her coat on the small bench and allowed Breanna to do the same. Fingers flipped the locks before she pressed her back into the wood. The harsh lighting cast shadows over Breanna as she rubbed her trembling hands together.

"The two of us haven't really explained ourselves well up to this point. I don't see the need to start now. So, just say whatever comes to mind. Don't worry about hurting me or messing things up, cause frankly it can't get much worse."

Breanna nodded even though Reilly could see the uncertainty in her eyes. "Sure. I can do that. Umm . . . You kept so much hidden from me. It sucked, Rei. My gut told me you were keeping something from me, but I didn't press it. I figured you'd talk to me when you were ready. Maybe I had an inkling you were Kline, but my brain didn't want it to be true. Cause then I'd have to switch to being all business and put more pressure on you than I already did. And that wasn't fair to you."

"Bre, the whole situation wasn't fair to either of us. You have no idea how much I wish I could change what happened." There was no rewind button, but her dreams showed her different pathways to fix it. Anything to assuage the guilt she couldn't seem to shake.

"I wouldn't." Breanna's hand grazed Reilly's arm. "Why we met doesn't matter. It wasn't ideal, but in the end, it's a crazy story for another day. Where we go from here matters, Reilly. The rest is just noise."

Reilly watched the other woman close the gap between them.

"Why hasn't my lawyer heard from you or Kai? Did you sign the contract?" Reilly tried to keep a level head as the other woman crept closer.

"We did. Serena's agreed to play the lead. I wasn't sure you'd talk to me if I sent an email." Breanna's fingers brushed her cheek leaving a fiery path in their wake. "I figured it was harder to avoid how I felt if I was standing right in front of you."

"Good job in signing Serena. I wrote the characters with her in mind." Reilly joked nervously as she placed her palm between Breanna's breasts. She stared, mesmerized, as it rose and fell with each breath. "My heart sings when you're near me. You didn't need to bring me anything. You'll always—"

"You had your grand gesture. It's my turn." Breanna laid her hand on top of Reilly's. "I've been miserable since you left my office. Even paperwork can't prevent my mind from wandering to the beauty of your eyes and the feeling of your kiss. I'm an empty shell of a human and even my cat's disowned me . . .

Reilly laughed at the idea of Max going to court to disown Breanna. Her mind was strange in its ability to conjure up creative images at inopportune times.

"At night, I miss the sound of you breathing and the thumping of your heartbeat in my ear. Rei, I'm a stubborn mule who's probably going to make a ton of mistakes in the future. But I want the chance to be the partner you deserve. To love you the way you deserve to be loved. You're more important than all of it. Say the word and the contracts go up in smoke. I don't care. None of that matters if I don't have you with me for the journey."

"Bre—" The woman was so close Reilly couldn't formulate a thought, let alone a full sentence.

"I love you, Reilly Vail. Please, say we can try again? Say you'll think about it. I don't mind. Just don't send me away."

"I . . ." She pulled the other woman to her in a fiery kiss. The warmth spread over her skin like the sun on a tropical beach. Her one hand buried itself in Breanna's hair while her other pulled at the woman's back bringing her impossibly closer.

Reilly broke the kiss as the other woman leaned in for more. Her thumb ran across swollen lips and in that moment the guilt slipped from its hold and slithered away.

"You're thinking too loud." Breanna nipped at her neck.

"I was thinking about how perfectly I fit in your arms."

"You always have."

Reilly kissed her softly. "I love you, Bre. Wherever life's journey leads, I just want to live it with you."

"Ditto." Breanna pecked her lips once more. "I know we can't change the past, but we can make new memories to replace the bad ones. With that in mind, would you be my date to the high school theater performance this evening?"

"What if I lose it and need to leave?"

"The minute you say so, we go. And before you ask, Jenna informed me it would bring bad luck on the show if we didn't sit in the last row."

"Yes." She said before she could overanalyze the reasons to reject the offer. "Was my lovely sister-in-law also responsible for you being here?"

"Her and Kai. The two of them are rather terrifying when they team up."

"We're in so much trouble."

Their laughter squashed Reilly's normal thoughts and insecurities. This was only the first step in their journey, but her heart knew it would be the trip of a lifetime.

***

They'd stayed home after Jenna admitted her errand was a ploy to get the two women alone. She tried to sound upset, but she couldn't fake it for long. The two conspirators laughed and made crude noises before Reilly hung up the phone. With several hours before the play, they snuggled up on the couch with hot cocoa. For Reilly, the afternoon was perfect.

But now, as she stood outside the high school with her feet glued to the pavement, Reilly thought it had turned into hell. Only a few hours ago, she thought this would be easy. Breanna would lead her to the seats and the new memories would overwrite the old ones. But it didn't. Trauma never gives up it's hold that easily. It prefers to remain in place, hidden in the shadows until you obliterate it with a flamethrower.

"Why don't we go back to the house. I'll let them know tonight didn't work out and we'll try again tomorrow. It's okay to take more time."

But it wasn't. Not to Reilly. For her to fully move on from Helen, she needed to do this. Without saying a word, she looped her arm in Breanna's and walked through the door. The lobby was empty as sounds from the opening number reached their ears. The They slipped into the last row, and Reilly focused on her breathing.

Breanna threaded their fingers together and gave a slight squeeze for comfort. Reilly knew intermission would be the biggest test. Once the lights came on, she could run away with the mass of people who went out to get a snack or smoke. But the warmth of Breanna's hand in hers just might keep her sane enough to make it through the entire evening.

Intermission came and went, and Reilly remained where she was. There were moments she'd turn her head to see Breanna just enjoying the moment. The missing puzzle piece clicked into place. This was how love should feel.

After the crowd cleared out, Reilly led Breanna backstage. Jenna and Kai's direction to clean up was drowned out by the frantic energy of the students celebrating. Reilly couldn't help but laugh at the two waving their arms trying to grab the kid's attention. She held back, arm still entwined with Breanna's, trying to avoid the whirlwind of chaos.

It didn't take long before her sister-in-law ran to her. Jenna skidded to a stop, took hold of Reilly's forearms and hung her head. Reilly was expecting some excitement for Breanna being her date or the show's first night being a success, not this unreadable stare to the floor.

"Tell me the truth. I can handle it. Was the show crap?"

"No. Truth be told, it was the best show yet. You two make a fantastic team."

Jenna jumped up, almost headbutting Reilly in the process. Her scream quieted the students for a moment before shaking their heads and resuming conversation.

"We do, don't we." Kai side hugged Jenna before the woman shrugged them off.

"Don't go replacing me just yet," Breanna joked.

"I wouldn't dream of it. I was just thinking the company could invest a little more in school theater programs. Maybe even the local companies where we honed our business skills." Kai looked invigorated, as if they found a new joy within the cutthroat business. It made Reilly happy to see the two of them enjoying the endeavor. Selfishly, she hoped Kai would help carry those bins up the stairs next time. Less flights for her would be a lovely bonus.

"They mean put on some horrible shows, screen iffy movies . . . But yeah, I think that's a great idea," Breanna countered with her signature sarcasm.

"Good, now make yourself useful and help me."

Reilly felt Breanna kiss her temple before scurrying away behind the black curtains. Her sister-in-law remained, staring at her like a villain in a horror film.

"Okay, creepy much." Jenna smacked her arm. "Fine, you were right. The plan you two concocted worked."

"Yay, but also, who cares? Did you have make-up sex? We gave you enough time, right? Isn't it amazing? Would be even better if we could skip the fighting part and just go to the sex section, but whatever."

"Oh no, we are not doing that! I do not need to think about you and Harrison."

"You have nieces," Jenna deadpanned.

"I choose ignorance." She pulled her sister-in-law into a tight embrace. "Thank you. I would have given up if you both didn't step in."

"I better get backstage before Kai puts things in the wrong place. You know how particular I am." Jenna smirked as she slipped away behind the curtains.

Reilly walked out onto the stage and scanned the empty theater. The words her mother said before leaving all made sense now. She had to find joy in living each day. Jenna's voice rose to match Kai's and Breanna's somewhere backstage. This was her life now. A mess of creative people arguing over their preferred method of storytelling. The ride was already worth the price of admission.

Besides, maybe she could write a play for this new theater Kai wanted to invest in.

Epilogue

Two years flew by before Reilly could blink. Only her friends knew they were the most stressful yet rewarding ones of her life. Outside of their little bubble, she was the consummate professional. Breanna and Kai insisted on a new, more balanced contract. She'd relented, but only after they'd explained her version gave up too much. If she ever wanted to produce her future books, companies might use the former contract against her in negotiations. Reilly wasn't concerned for herself, but when she investigated the effects such a low deal might have on other authors, she agreed.

She'd surprised Breanna with a first edition copy of the novel her girlfriend inspired her to write. Reilly remembered the private celebration they had when it hit number one on the romance charts. Her other release, the last installment of the Shadows Rise series, landed with mixed reviews. Some readers argued, saying it didn't have a true ending. Critics felt it was a somber, but rational, conclusion. If they only knew it was just the beginning of her world building, their response might have been different.

When any of her new books were released, Breanna made sure Reilly wasn't near a computer, and they turned her phone off. She'd planned an elaborate European vacation during the final Shadows Rise launch. Reilly threatened to check her social media feeds, but Breanna made a game of it. For every second she spent reading reviews, the same amount of time was used against her in bed. Namely, that Reilly couldn't touch her girlfriend or risk further punishment. Reilly called her bluff the first day, accumulating several minute's worth.

That evening was deliciously evil as Breanna teased her to the brink of climax giving new meaning to seven minutes in heaven. Reilly's hands squeezed the pillow above her head, begging the minutes to flick by faster than her girlfriend's tongue. Once the time ran out, Reilly had her revenge several times.

When it came to shooting the first film in the series, the script proved to be the most difficult. She wanted to show everything, but the restrictions of the medium made it impractical. The writers took her under their wing, and Reilly thought the result was as close to her novel as possible. On set, she hid in the background, just soaking up the experience. She understood why Kai said cast and crew become like families. Everyone protected one another.

Looking back on it all, her favorite moments were watching Breanna in her element. Her kindness and compassion were displayed every day in the way she took care of the issues that arose during filming. Breanna never gave the vibe that she was better or above anyone else working on the production. Both she and Kai covered breaks, helped with gear, and when a stalker became an issue for Serena, they hired more security at their own expense. It warmed Reilly's heart to see them put people above money or a project.

Word traveled quickly through the entertainment industry about K.B. Studios' new developments, including signing the rights to Kline's series. The press releases, awards from other films, and word of mouth increased the number of professionals reaching out to work with them. The influx was so immense, they expanded the department in charge of agent submissions.

The authors Reilly directed their way were thrilled with the success of their stories. A few re-signed new deals with the company for future endeavors. *Why sign with a large company where you're a number? With K.B. Studios, you're family.* That's what she heard during an author's online meetup she attended under a new pen name she was developing.

Reilly was sick in bed when Kai and Breanna won an award for one of their independent films. Breanna's speech left no doubt in Reilly's mind that the woman loved her. She wasn't mentioned by name because Breanna knew she was still concerned about her privacy. That was six months ago.

And now, she was sitting in a rented suite in the city, the hairstylist pulling her head in all directions for an updo. Breanna walked by in her tailored, navy-blue suit, her right-hand animatedly waving with each word. It was a trait Reilly found endearing.

"You look like you're going to vomit." Wendy smirked from across the table. "I didn't push back my trip to Alaska to clean up after you. That's Breanna's job now."

"Mom, we live together. We're not married."

"Well, hurry then! I'm not getting any younger. Plus, your Aunt Amy needs to know when it is. She's got to recover from her injury."

"Mom, she's recovering fine. Next time, I suggest you two not try to beat the young men at a bar riding the mechanical bull."

"Where's the fun in that? Besides, she lasted longer than all those loudmouth boys. We got free drinks the rest of the night!" Her mother laughed as she took a large gulp of her wine.

Reilly remembered the incident all too well. Wendy indulged in one too many Moscow Mules and could barely record stable video. Aunt Amy was whooping and hollering as the crowd cheered her on. When the alarm sounded, the woman was so excited she was bouncing around on the mats. One moment she was standing upright, the next she tripped and took some people with her. Her right leg had been in a cast ever since.

"The cast comes off in a few weeks. Then you two could jet off again . . . as long as you give me the information about the trip. Deal?" Wendy waved her off with one hand while tapping her tablet screen with the other.

Breanna came back into the room. Once again Reilly found herself staring. Even after all this time, being with Breanna made her stomach do somersaults.

"There's a ton of press already waiting."

"Oh." The happiness within her switched to dread. "Is there a back door?"

"There is, but I need to walk down the red carpet, and I'd really like you to be with me. If you don't feel comfortable, you and Wendy can slip through the back, and I'll handle it."

Breanna offering her an exit made her heart flutter a bit. It also solidified the decision she made on the spot. If her love was willing to let her out of it, she could muster the courage to face the flashing cameras. With Breanna by her side, she could face whatever they threw her way.

"It'll be fine. I'm sure they'll see Serena and not even care we're there."

Breanna kissed her hand as her phone rang again. "Sorry, I've got to take this. Be right back."

Reilly didn't have a moment to reply before Wendy dropped her tablet in her lap.

"Jenna wants to say hi."

"Is this what you're wearing tonight?" The stylist interjected.

"No, but don't worry. It's easy to get on over my hair."

She nodded and went back to pulling Reilly's nervous system out through her scalp.

"Rei, I am going to kill these kids!" Jenna screeched from the screen. "Kai's also driving me nuts. Why aren't they going to the premiere tonight? I'm sure they need to be there. Just say the word and I'll gladly put them on a train."

"Kai committed to helping you with the play before they set the date for the premiere. Trust me, Kai values their word over all this pomp and circumstance." Reilly winced as another strand of hair was lacquered to her head.

"That looks painful. Still not as bad as what I'm dealing with. Please help me."

"I don't know what you expect me to do from here."

"Have Bre call Kai and beg them to calm down. This isn't Broadway, it's high school theater." Jenna pouted on the screen, an image that brought Millie and Edie to the front of Reilly's thoughts.

"Hey, J, can I ask you something?"

"Shoot."

"You know Helen's been messaging me through social media since I blocked her phone number. She's making some outlandish claims and threatened to come forward when the film hits theaters." While Reilly's life had moved in a positive direction, Helen's hadn't. Her fiancée was apparently the sister of some high-level politician. The engagement was announced, and Reilly had the displeasure of her friends sending the links to the story online. She'd worked through things in therapy, but seeing Helen brag about her career and relationship was still a sore spot.

Of course, when you're engaged to someone in the public eye, you're under a different level of scrutiny. Other candidates looked for anything to bring their opponent down, and Helen was a treasure trove. It wasn't surprising when images of Helen in bed with another woman splashed all over the tabloids. It hit right after a major debate when her fiancée's sister mentioned moral values she lived by. Even worse, information leaked that the affair had been going on for months, and the woman was the wife of a known mobster.

Now Reilly's ex-girlfriend was digging up anything she could to clear her name. She claimed to own the rights to Kline's series and sold fabricated stories to whomever would pay. K.B. Studios' lawyers and PR team shut each accusation down before it gained traction. While Reilly listened to her marketing team and never mentioned her ex-girlfriend or the events they attended, she knew the desperate woman would do something to destroy her happiness. When the studio refused to be extorted any further, Helen played her trump card.

The messages began around the time the film's release date was announced. All of them were benign enough to seem innocuous, but the meaning was clear. Anyone who knew Helen would understand the point of the harassment.

"There's nothing you can do, Rei. She's a rat in a cage right now. You know the truth about the past. Sure, you did what you were told, but Helen was a controlling, evil human being."

"Yeah, but—"

"Oh, for heaven's sake just turn your phone off and ignore the woman. If we're lucky the cockroach will crawl into the bowels of hell and leave us be. Either that or we get a can of raid." Reilly laughed at her mother's antics. It was nice having her home for however long her aunt's recovery took.

"Or you could hire powerful attorneys and bury her under defamation lawsuits. At least that's what Kai said. That or just making her disappear. Either way, you're happy and she's not. Do you really want to waste time on her right now? You're getting ready for the film premiere of your book. That's huge. The girls were showing everyone the pictures of them on set. They said Aunt Reilly is famous and knows Serena."

"Your kids are too much." Being public about her alter ego was one thing, but she hadn't fully accepted the public attention. Serena was working with her on it, but Reilly doubted it was something she'd become accustomed to.

"Nah, you just have to show up with Serena to prove them right. And yes, that is a hint and a verbal request from the girls." Something crashed in the background of the feed. Jenna simply closed her eyes and counted to ten. "I'm going to go check that out, but I'm serious about the Serena thing. Their classes need some flair on 'bring a friend' to school day. Make it happen. Love you. Give my love to Bre and Mama. Jenna out!" She waved her hand in the air but didn't disappear. She repeated the action, but once again the call remained connected. "Well, crap. Goodbye." Jenna's face disappeared, leaving Reilly with her jumbled thoughts.

"Was that Jenna? Kai said she's driving them nuts." Breanna's presence gave Reilly instant clarity. No matter what was outside the door, she could handle it all with her girlfriend by her side.

"Rest assured the feeling is mutual."

"Figured. So, I just got off the phone with Michaela and her team. They're excited about the multi-picture deal if you're still interested."

"The entire deal hinges on my ability to publish seven to ten more books in the next five years." The offer from Michaela was a surprise, especially since her films hadn't shown their ability to succeed at the box office yet.

"Theoretically, but in truth the novels wouldn't be adapted that quickly. Plus, we still have the next two books in this current series. We're also considering splitting the last one into two parts—"

"No, absolutely not. I will not be that heathen who splits things up just for more profit. We've all seen what happens to the finished product. The first part is amazing, tells the story beautifully, and may or may not leave you at a proper breaking point. The second part, unless the book was filled with tons of information that didn't fit into part one, becomes nothing more than a drawn-out battle between the two sides of the story. I hate watching it, and I won't do that to fans of my work."

"Tell me how you really feel." Breanna's smile stopped Reilly's quick retort on the spot. "It was only a suggestion, but since you are adamantly against it, consider it off the table. But this deal is good. I should know. I hired the lawyers who wrote it."

"You're funny."

Reilly exhaled when the last strand of hair was glued into place.

"And you, Ms. Vail, are done. What do you think?"

Her hair was pulled high on her head against her scalp. Her mid-back length strands were separated into individual pieces and painstakingly sprayed, twisted, and held in place with bobby pins. After what seemed like twenty cans of hair glue, her bun was a majestic globe that you could see through. The final touch of glitter brought out her inner child that loved fantasies with strong princess characters. There was something to be said for professional hair and makeup. For the first time in her life, Reilly felt like a stunning beauty.

"Wow." Breanna's eyes sparkled with desire laced with love, and it brought a blush to Reilly's cheeks.

"I don't know how you turned my bird's nest into this, but you are amazing."

"Thank you very much." The stylist packed up her things and left.

"You going to tell me what you're wearing tonight?"

"Not on your life." Reilly glanced at her watch and noticed the late hour. "You better get going!"

"Michaela and the team can wait. I need to see—"

"Breanna Blaine, get your butt out the door and back to work. I'll make sure Reilly makes it on time. I'll text you when we're in the limo rolling in. You can meet us there." Reilly loved how her mother scolded Breanna as if she were her own child. Watching her girlfriend's eyes widen as if she was caught with her hand in the cookie jar was even funnier.

Breanna stood and fixed her suit shirt. "You sure this is okay to wear? I've never worn navy blue. Maybe I should go with the black one."

"Trust me, you look delectable." Reilly couldn't prevent her fingers from brushing along the sides of Breanna's suit.

"You two make me sick. Get out of here!"

With a soft kiss that left Reilly wanting more, Breanna slipped out of the room.

"Now, let's get you into that dress without messing up everything. I still don't know why you're wearing heels when Breanna's shorter than you."

"It's about feeling my best, Mom. If I'm throwing myself to the wolves, I want to feel like I've got something over them. Besides, Breanna's wearing the same height heels. Our shoes cancel each other out."

Reilly's mind flashed to Breanna in the suit, and her desire to remove it from the woman's frame came rushing back.

"I'm right here, so stop thinking those dirty thoughts."

"Never." Reilly smirked.

***

Breanna finished all the meetings and interviews Michaela required the production team to participate in. It was an easy compromise in the grand scheme of things. She wrung her hands a few times when her phone dinged with some breaking news. Helen had gone to the press about her and Reilly's history together. Her eyes scanned the accusations ranging from lying to event organizers about attending as Kline leading to loss of revenue when she didn't show, to stealing all Helen's ideas and making a profit without her. Even though the latter allegation had been squashed in the past, being attached to the new complaint that was backed with email evidence, gave it new life. If social media got hold of this, it could damage the film's ticket and digital sales. That could force them to put the sequels on the shelf and possibly have Michaela pull her offer. Her mind was swimming with worst-case scenarios, but she needed to talk to Kai and Jenna and get more information.

Breanna stayed on the phone as they relayed the main points, which were embellished and downright false. One specific thing that stood out to everyone was Helen's claim that Reilly would brag about her connection to M. E. Kline at all the events to raise her status within the communities. All of her egregious lies made Breanna want to lash out at the woman, but Helen calling Reilly's integrity into question pushed Breanna to the brink.

Even worse than the false claims, and the fact that they could be refuted with a little Google search, the topic started trending across social media. The premiere's red carpet was streaming live, and comments were pouring in, demanding the press grill Reilly for the truth. Breanna grabbed Michaela, intending to move Reilly to a different entrance, when her phone buzzed. Reilly's limo was next in line.

Breanna zipped in between people until Serena stopped her.

"Did you see it?"

"Of course, I did. I can't—"

"I got you." Without another word, Serena followed the distraught producer down the carpet.

"Where's your girlfriend?" Breanna tossed out as they rushed to the limos.

"Moving out." Breanna stopped short, her hand gripping Serena's. The woman shook her off. "Later, over a lot of chocolate and wine I will tell you everything. Not now."

Breanna made it to the curb with her phone at the ready as the limo rolled to a stop. An usher opened the door as her mind flew through ways to approach the topic. And then Reilly exited the car and her brain ceased to function.

Her blood-red heels connected to long legs, one of which was exposed by a thigh-high slit in a red strapless dress. Reilly stood at her full height, her red gloves holding a matching clutch as her mother exited the limo behind her.

"Hi, love."

Breanna stared, slack-jawed.

"Hey, sweetie. You look stunning." Serena leaned forward and kissed Reilly on her cheek. "But we have an issue, and since your girl's brain is freaking out over the sight of you in your dress, I'll fill you in. Helen went to the press about your past. Lying to organizers about who you were, getting free passes and not technically showing up. She posted emails backing up the accusations. To make matters worse, she claims you instigated everything, and reiterated Shadows Rise was based on her ideas. She cried on some post saying you stole them and cut her out of the profits."

Breanna watched the confidence drain out of her girlfriend. She stepped next to her, took her hand, and held her focus.

"Stay with me," Breanna whispered. "We're here together."

"We're all here. Bre, Wendy, and me, we're gonna walk the red carpet like the fabulous people we are. Let the paps take our pictures, and then let's go enjoy the movie." Serena added rubbing Reilly's shoulder.

"I thought you weren't supposed to stay through the whole thing." Reilly forced through shallow breaths.

"For you, we will," Serena answered. "We're family."

"Okay. I can handle this." Breanna wasn't sure she believed her girlfriend. After a few deep breaths, Reilly stood tall, pushed her shoulders back and looked ready to navigate through the media pool.

Breanna linked her arm with Reilly's. She nodded over to Michaela, who took her position on the other side of the author. They would head down the gauntlet first with Serena and Wendy behind them. She prayed the A-list actress would divert attention.

"We could just walk right down and wave as we go." Breanna offered another way around the prying questions from reporters and fans by the barricades.

"No. I can't let her have this. We did this, not her." A gentle squeeze on Breanna's arm left no room for debate.

"You did this, Rei. Without you, the story never would have existed." With a gentle kiss for luck, Breanna led them from marker to marker. They paused for various photos, but she never let go of Reilly's arm. "Just a few more and we're done."

Her date tensed with each flash of the camera, but she kept moving. Pride soared through Breanna's soul as she watched Reilly stand tall, fighting the desire to run.

"Why are you staring at me?"

Breanna pulled Reilly away from the flashes and down a narrower section of the walkway. It was slightly secluded before they went to the second half where the more popular news outlets were hiding.

"I'm staring because you're beautiful and I'm so proud of how you're handling this." Michaela tapped Breanna on the shoulder. "I'll go out first and try to head off some of the questions. You two follow when you're ready."

Nodding, Breanna turned her attention back to Reilly, who looked paler now than when she entered. "Hey, you're safe. I won't let anything happen out there. Promise."

"Let's get this over with."

Breanna took her hand and led Reilly into the fire.

"Reilly, over here!" The questions all blended together. Breanna attempted to place the voices with the faces, but with the flash of cameras, it was impossible. So, she just kept walking.

"Do you have anything to say to those people you lied to? What about those calling you a thief?"

Breanna felt Reilly's grip intensify to a painful level, but she kept them moving forward along the red carpet.

"Just ignore them. Focus on your breathing. We're almost done."

A nod toward security had them opening the door for Breanna to sweep Reilly inside for safety.

"What about the claims that your ex-girlfriend wrote Shadows Rise, and you stole them? How do you respond to her threats of legal action?" the final reporter yelled.

Breanna stumbled forward as Reilly stopped short. Her girlfriend's mouth hung open, her eyebrows contorted in confusion, as they stood there, unmoving. Breanna slid across the carpet, stopping in front of the taller man with a perfectly coifed hairdo and impeccable suit.

"We'll handle the frivolous and defamatory accusations after the premiere. Tonight, we're here to support the hard work of the entire cast and crew who worked so tirelessly to bring this film to screen."

Breanna hoped her words were enough to keep the questions at bay and get her girlfriend moving. But Reilly didn't budge. She took Breanna's hand in a vicelike grip and faced the reporter. The barricades creaked with the pressure of people against it as she was dragged closer to the melee. Breanna was worried. Walking Reilly down the carpet through this mess was one thing, but the woman was dragging her into the fray with no hint as to what she was planning.

"I might be many things in this world, but a fraud is not one of them. My ex-girlfriend, Helen Astin, has had a lot to say about our relationship, what we did, and how I was the ringleader. Well, she's right about one thing. I was in control of my words—my stories. I wove them together despite her constant nagging about my lack of income. Every bad review she shoved in my face, I committed to memory just to prove them and her wrong as I matured as a writer. If my past wishes to lay claim to my future now that I have success, let them try. Let me say under oath how I developed Shadows Rise from the ground up. How I struggled through a myriad of rewrites just to feel ready to release it into the world. Maybe I'll even regale them on how I still wish to make minor changes, even now. I could quote page numbers if they wanted. That's how well I know my creations."

"So, you admit you are M. E. Kline?" Breanna knew he was pushing for a scandalous clip he could use to go viral.

Reilly's sly smirk made Breanna swallow hard. The image of her girlfriend standing in her truth was as powerful as it was sexy and intoxicating.

"If you did your due diligence, you would know I am. I held a live Q&A over my social media channels eons ago. Ms. Astin's actions were simply a power play move. I am the author of the Shadows Rise series. As for Ms. Astin, she never worked an honest day in her life. She's thrived on the backs of others, using whatever underhanded tactic she's needed to push her career to the next level. I don't give any credence to the vitriol she spits out for attention. Neither should you." Reilly looked back at Breanna with a sincere smile and an exhale that seemed to relieve all the tension on her shoulders. Breanna kissed her knuckles and stood firmly by her side. "To those individuals whose events we attended under the pretense of Kline participating, if you look at the email correspondence, they never came from me. All emails were always from Ms. Astin. I sincerely apologize for not being strong enough to defy her and stop the deception. Beyond that, I leave you to ask these questions to Ms. Astin."

Reilly spun around and dragged Breanna away from the frenzy behind the barricades. Breanna struggled to keep up with Reilly's long strides, as the flashes continued. Once inside the theater, she bumped into her girlfriend's back. Breanna wrapped her arms around Reilly and kissed her neck softly.

"You are amazing."

"Thank you for not letting go."

"Always." Breanna breathed her in and allowed the warmth between them to calm her racing heart. "I'll get you situated and call the lawyer. Helen Astin went too far this time. Now she deals with the full wrath of your army."

"My army?"

"Yeah, the ones who will love you and will defend your honor." She turned Reilly around to face her. "We're also the people who will call you out on your crap, so don't get too comfortable."

"I wouldn't have it any other way, but don't make that call. Not tonight."

"Are you sure? I can be quick and back at my seat before the opening credits."

"It can wait until tomorrow. My response will get under her skin. So, let her stew in the mess she created for herself. Let social media split between those who believe me or hate me. Let them have it. Tonight, I just want to be with you. I want to see the creation that changed my life for the better."

"It's a story that resonates with millions of readers worldwide. I hope you see that."

"The series brought you into my life. No one will ever take that away from me. So, let's just let the world be and enjoy our little bubble for the moment."

She felt Reilly's soft lips press against her own. It was something she couldn't get enough of.

"You both coming, or do you need a room? I'm sure there's an office with a couch somewhere in here." Serena chuckled from the waiting area.

"You're one to talk. Your dressing room in between shows. Ring a bell?" Reilly teased back, causing Serena to turn a deep shade of red.

Breanna wanted to ask what they were talking about, but the lights flashed above. She led Reilly down the aisle and to the best seats in the theater. She made sure to scope things out and talk to the ushers to ensure Reilly had the best view. Breanna remembered the feeling of seeing Kai's and her first project on the big screen, and how it filled her with emotions she couldn't place. She wanted that for Reilly. Well, that and something more.

***

The lights dimmed, and Breanna shifted in her seat.

"If you keep fidgeting, you're going to make me nervous."

The film began with the opening credits, and Reilly had to admit the music surprised her, as it set the tone for the series perfectly. It suddenly dawned on her how far she'd come.

It felt like yesterday that she was terrified of being in her own skin, and here she was, spending the day with a beautiful woman and watching her characters come to life. She thought she would be prepared for it. After all, she had been on set often. But watching Serena move through the scenes at the beginning of the film gave her a chill. She wondered if others in the audience felt something similar.

Breanna pressed something into her hand, pulling her attention away from the screen. The small, folded piece of paper was clipped under a pen. Reilly turned her head to Breanna, whose attention was firmly on the film playing in front of her. Her leg bounced, signaling she was nervous about something, but whether it was the movie or the note, Reilly wasn't sure. She unfolded it carefully, trying to make as little noise as possible. Once open, Reilly saw the telltale script of her girlfriend's handwriting.

Do you want to make new memories with me tonight? Circle yes or no.

Reilly held in her laughter at the grade school ending of the note. The gasps of the audience forced her to look up and see what gripped them. It was the emotionally traumatic sequence that put the heroine on her journey through the series. She remembered Serena's concerns her performance might not be strong enough to pull it off. Reilly went through the dailies and assured the actress it was exactly how she envisioned it. Based on the audience's reaction, she was right.

When the full sequence shifted, Reilly turned her attention back to the note and circled yes. She folded the paper back up and slipped it under the clip. If she had to work to read the question, Breanna would have to work to get her answer. Reilly slid her hand with the note over Breanna's thigh and dropped it between her legs before turning her attention back to the film.

The woman next to her took a deep breath as she crinkled the paper open. Reilly noticed Breanna's knee had stopped bouncing, but she continued to fidget with something. She scribbled on the piece of paper and placed it face down on Reilly's lap.

When the ring hit her finger, Reilly's entire body tensed. Flashes of Helen removing her engagement ring rushed to the forefront of her mind. The absolute agony and rejection pounded in her chest, and she begged her heartbeat to slow down. When Breanna moved her hand, she flipped the note over for Reilly to read.

Reilly didn't. She was focused on the ring finger of her left hand and the diamond resting there. It was elegant, but not delicate. Breanna truly knew her and how she'd beat on her rings without knowing it. Wearing them while she did manual labor as well as on date night, Reilly would never take them off. Helen's cruel words echoed in her mind as the weight of the ring scorched her skin.

Reilly closed her eyes and forced those thoughts into the background. That person didn't have a hold on this relationship or this time. Her heart rate calmed, and she turned to read the note, knowing what the question would be.

Want to make movies together? Forever? Circle yes or no . . . and if it's no, it's okay. I love you anyway.

It was just like Breanna to make her laugh in the middle of a dark scene on the screen. She covered her mouth as quickly as possible, but several people turned her way, including Serena, who met her gaze and gave her a thumbs-up. If Serena only knew the tears threatening her makeup weren't because of her performance. Reilly didn't need to think about her answer; her heart knew it the moment she almost ran the other woman over. She circled yes and held the page for her fiancée to see.

Breanna pressed a kiss against her new ring before looking up at Reilly with an adoration she'd only read about. She would have watched the film with her head resting on her love's shoulder, but her hair might knock Breanna unconscious. So, as the movie played, she enjoyed their joined hands as a wonderful feeling swelled within her chest.

Breanna was never leaving. She chose to stay. She chose Reilly.

And that was all Reilly ever wanted.

THE END

About Kimberly

Thank you for reading my book.

I'm an indie author trying to put my thoughts on a page that not only entertains, but creates human connection. I write stories that interest me, ranging from crime to romance to dystopian and more. This is a one woman endeavor, so if you buy my book and sign up to my mailing list, you directly support and engage with me. There's no team hiding under my couch cushions, though there might be a coin or two.

Beyond my books, I'm blessed to co-host *Forever Fangirls* with my wife, Sheila. We react to and review movies, trailers, Broadway shows, and more. If you'd like to subscribe to the channel, you can click @ForeverFangirlsReviews.

If you'd like to stay in touch with me, you can visit my website KimberlyAmato.com. You'll find the social media accounts where I'm most active and a contact form to send me a message. While there, you can also sign up for my mailing list, or you can use the link below. I look forward to chatting with you!

https://www.kimberlyamato.com/newsletter

Also By Kimberly Amato

THE STEELE SERIES

Steele Intent (Book 1)

Melting Steele (Book 2)

Breaking Steele (Book 3)

Cold Steele (Book 4)

Steele Shield (Book 5)

Steele Influence (Book 6)

STANDALONES

Enemy

Find Her Keep Her

GRANNIES ON THE GO COZY NOVELLA SERIES

Murder at the Campground

www.ingramcontent.com/pod-product-compliance
Lightning Source LLC
LaVergne TN
LVHW090557110826
845146LV00001B/167

9798987371978